VINYLCUTS

EDITED
BY
CIN FERGUSON & BROOS CAMPBELL

SCARY DAIRY
PRESS

VINYL CUTS

Copyright © 2024 Scary Dairy Press LLC

Cover artwork by Lynne Hansen @ www.LynneHansenArt.com

Stories Copyright © 2024. Their individual authors. All rights reserved.

ISBN: 978-1-7320946-6-6

Scary Dairy Press LLC, Palmyra VA

DEDICATION

T
o everyone who understands the pain of loss, knowing it can take much longer than a year to pick up the pieces when your world falls apart.

To everyone who uses music to soothe their souls, and to patch their pain until they can finally start their stories once more.

To all those bright spirits who reached out and provided light to me when days were dark . . . this would not be a completed work without you.

My sincere thanks to you, dear friends.

GRATITUDE

BY CIN FERGUSON

On September 2, 2021, a motor vehicle killed my husband, Jim, while he was riding his bike. It was a lovely sunny day. He was on a straightaway, wearing all his safety gear. His helmet was on. His bright orange safety flag was in the air. Jim's death was sudden—at least, I hope it was. And me—I was propelled into a world of shock, grief, and depression. Only those who have lived such a thing can understand.

I swore I wasn't going to work on any more anthologies after Jim died. Ever. But in December 2021, EV Knight, K.L. Lord, and Chad Pritt approached me with this anthology idea. It was daunting—the idea of doing something like this so soon after Jim's death. But they were so jazzed to do a set of stories using music as inspiration for the tales that I couldn't say no. And it was a project that helped to pull me out of the dark, although I slipped back into the abyss from time to time.

So, I thank EV, K.L., and Chad, as well as Broos, our faithful editor. I thank all the dear authors in this anthology who worked as a team to help get this project off the ground and who patiently waited for me to get it together as I struggled along the way.

I also offer thanks to Lynne Hansen, who created rockin' artwork to wrap these tales. Her artwork is always a blessing.

Although it took over two years to get this manuscript ready to go, for me, it was just yesterday. It was just yesterday that my dear Jim left this earth. I give thanks to all those who understand that grief isn't over in a year or even two. Thank you to those who understand that people can't "move on" when you want them to. Grief is something deeply personal. It comes and goes, and it is unique to each individual.

And, finally, I give thanks to my dear departed Jim and to my two children—my family. Jim is on his journey, but knowing him, loving him, and sharing life and music with him are important in our world. My children, Kira and Sean, have encouraged me every step of the way. They help me keep writing, publishing, editing, and working with other writers — always backing me with the "You can do it!" attitude even when they are going through their own grief. And I love them for it. We share our music together, low notes and high, across decades and generations. The songs and their rhythms join us together and make us stronger. They help to heal us and preserve our memories. And I believe, somehow, they transcend space and time.

May these stories reach out to you with the elements of the tunes that inspired them. May they take you on tour and play the sets just a bit differently than what you've read or heard before. Enjoy!

FOREWORD

BY EV KNIGHT

I t seems strange to start the foreword of an anthology by asking you to consider
horror films, but I'd like to start there for a moment. Humor me, if you will.
Let's go way back to *Nosferatu: A Symphony of Horror*. This German silent film
from 1922 relied on its orchestral soundtrack to help amp up the terror, the suspense—the horror! In fact, the lost original score was rewritten a number of times
because it was necessary to create the atmosphere of the film. This reliance on
music to pluck at the emotions of a horror film's audience continued even as silent
films made way for "talkies." Imagine *Psycho*'s famous shower scene without those
screaming violins. Would Jason Vorhees's or Michael Myers's slow, methodical
approach be as adrenaline-inducing without the musical dread accompanying
them? *Jaws* has its "swim-up music," Freddy has a freaky children's song, and
Hitchcock has his *Music to Be Murdered By*.

Music, like fear, is universal. Except for those deaf from birth (and arguably,
even they can "feel" musical beats), we have all experienced both. We understand
how music relates to emotions and memories. There is an entire branch of psy-
chology devoted to music for this reason. It would only make sense to combine
music and fear to work symbiotically to elicit a response greater than the sum of its
parts. Think about the 2015 Robert Eggers film, *The Witch*. For me, it's a perfect

example of the content and the music working together to create something far stronger than either the script or the score alone.

Now let's talk about what you came here to discuss—stories. The horror "boom" for novelists began with Shirley Jackson and Robert Bloch. Their novels *The Haunting of Hill House* and *Psycho* set the stage for several contemporary classics and their authors—Ira Levin, William Peter Blatty, Stephen King, Anne Rice, Dean Koontz, and so many others. These terrifying tales set off a craze for the genre that continued until about 1990 when it lulled for some time (except, of course, for R.L. Stine's *Goosebumps* series) before again making a massive comeback in the twenty-first century.

Horror shared its growth spurt with a newly defined type of music: rock 'n' roll. Together, perhaps synergistically, they scared a conservative society filled with fears of Satan, murderous and/or sex-crazed teenagers, and the general dangers associated with the shake-up of the status quo. If your teenager read Stephen King and listened to rock music—you'd better get that child to church and burn their records and paperbacks.

Together, rock and horror fought their way past the bonfires of paperbacks and vinyl, the parental advisory stickers, the Satanic Panic, talk show hosts, and Tipper Gore to reach Final Genre status—bruised and bloodied but rocking on.

This anthology pays homage to the marriage of rock and horror. The authors you are about to read—some familiar and some new (like the track lists on your favorite albums)—captured favorite songs from the fifties through the eighties and played them to inspire unique tales of horror for your reading pleasure. Beware—you may never hear that tune the same way again. You're about to shift into a rock music story world and receive a new meaning to the word "earworm."

CONTENTS

VENGEANCE

YOUR TIME IS GONNA COME

Welcome to the first installment of *Vinyl Cuts,* where classic rock is still alive and well in the hearts and souls of many! We have a great set for you tonight, and it's a whopper. Nine tales of vengeance and horror. Are you an abusive misogynist? A serial killer on the loose? Messing with Mother Nature and her creatures? Let this set be a lesson, dear readers. Do someone dirty, and your time is gonna come!

D.O.A.

BY QUERUS ABUTTU

B lood pools around my head, its warmth dissipates into the open air. The sick iron smell smothers me, then fades, as the sticky fluid congeals against my cheek in the October chill.

What am I doing here? My body, almost prone on the ground, is privy to the view of a few gold and scarlet autumn leaves and patches of shredded brown grass—framing fresh trenches of upturned earth. A smattering of shoes race by. Torn wreckage. Oily black smoke. Orange flickers of fire and—bloody skin on a broken face—a face that looks familiar.

Voices shout. Sirens blare. I try to get up. My body fails. Instead, my left index finger trembles like it is laughing at me. The effort makes me gasp. Or try to gasp. My lungs gurgle. I'm not breathing. My brain screams.

Light blasts inside my head.

"I don't have time for this," I ranted at the nurse on the phone. "You'll just have to tell Sovina she's there for her own good. There's nothing I can do!"

Why did the nurse keep helping my wife with the fucking phone? Sovina's calls were more than a whining inconvenience. They were a blithering torment. I berated myself for answering the phone. I'd put the bitch in the hospital for a reason. Beating me up. Always nagging. Spending my money. Chain-smoking cigarettes. Talking to herself and answering back.

The Falcon 7X jumped like a Bronco, and I nearly dropped the phone.

"But Mr. Buckingham," the nurse pleaded, "this is urgent. We have to tell you—"

"Fuck! No, sorry, RN Rose, I wasn't talking to you. Just the turbulence up here—sure, sure, I know. I'll send more money—for cigarettes—art supplies—whatever she wants. Just—please, don't. Don't call for a while, okay? I know Sovina wants you to, but I don't have time. Next month, I can visit."

The plane lurched. My thumb accidentally hit the End Call button.

"Fuck!"

But it was good fortune, really. The call was over. Sovina was a regular pain in my ass. I'd married her right out of high school. She was gorgeous at the time. Golden blonde hair that curled around her ample breasts. Hazel eyes that seemed to turn whatever color she chose to wear, and legs that could have been sculpted by Michelangelo himself, if even he had the power to do them justice. She was lively and a damn talented artist. We traveled everywhere together during our years in college and after.

We were daredevils back then. We'd learned to skydive, fly biplanes, and scuba. Seven years later, she changed. Got moody—more than moody. Because of her, I changed too. Regardless, I couldn't put up with our marriage anymore.

Did you know that in the good old days, you could commit your wife to a mental institution and walk away? Not today. And so, Sovina threatened to take everything away from me. Threatened my stability, my fortune, my way of life. I mean, she became batshit crazy. The doc said *schizophrenia*. Said I could learn to help her with it. Medication and therapy. No, thank you.

Now, you need to understand—I mean, I *did* try. But multiple times, Sovina tried to stab me. She was utterly abusive. Everything I did, I did in self-defense. Everything I did to her, anyway.

This last time she was so violent, she nearly killed me. Beat me up with a twelve-inch statue of Hecate. It was almost comical—cute poly-resin thing but it had sharp edges—I think it was the dog's heads—and managed to take some chunks out of my cheek.

My years on the wrestling team served me well that day. I got her in a choke hold, she passed out, and I locked her in the hall closet. Couldn't think of what to do with her for a while. Then, I called the cops, let her out, and gave her a hammer as they pulled up so they could see her fly at me in a rage. Perfect timing.

They dragged Sovina away, screaming and cursing that she was going to kill me. The woman was an obese, filthy, and unkempt hag. The boys in blue looked at me with disdain. I read their thoughts. *Why can't that dude take up for himself?* They must have wondered why a man like me, a man with money—why didn't I hire a nurse or someone to help my wife make sure she took her medications and make sure she was okay?

I did, of course, hire several nurses. They are buried in the basement. Buried in what was once a dirt floor now covered with concrete. But they are not buried there because of Sovina.

I can't feel anything. At least I don't think I can. Someone is squatting beside me, and I get the sense of a pair of hands on my body.

"Randy, over here!"

I am still not breathing. Do I have a pulse? If I do, then why aren't they resuscitating me?

Help me!

Nothing emerges from my lips despite my efforts.

Another pair of shoes, red Converse, trot over with what must be a stretcher on wheels. I sense more than feel them lift my body. And now my perspective rises above everything. I see the man, who must be Randy—a red-haired, freckled youth in his twenties. And there's the first man to find me, whose name I do not know; he looks Latino, in his thirties maybe. They place a sheet over me and load me into an ambulance. I look out over the wreckage of my jet and see the parts of another plane scattered across the ground as well. I'm still confused and try to remember what happened.

My memories are jumbled together. A phone call—Sovina—turbulence—something . . .

The ambulance speeds away and the mind of me is roughly dragged along with it—like it has no choice—as if it is still magnetized to the body inside that mobile flashing box.

The flight attendant, Sarah—a pretty thing with dark eyes and black hair—said, "Buckle in tight, Mr. Buckingham. We are on decent. Jay says the weather is going to make the last few miles into Charleston rough going."

The plane shook. The entire fuselage dropped, and I reflexively gripped my seat as if it could save me in a true emergency. In my youth, I would have laughed off such a thing, but in my thirties, my heart galloped like I'd bet a million dollars at the Preakness.

My phone rang again. I looked. The call wouldn't pick up service well. Not in this weather. But accepting it might take my mind off this hellacious ride. I thumbed the Accept button.

"Carl Buckingham." I was very practiced at using my, '*you've really annoyed me beyond all comprehension*' voice.

"Mr. Buckingham," a nurse started, "this is RN Rose. I'm calling to tell you—"

"What? What is it this time? You've already asked for everything, haven't you? I told you I can't talk. I'm in a helluva storm up here."

"It's urgent, sir," RN Rose's voice escalated to a high pitch, "your wife—"

"What? What about my wife?" I was so irritated. This nursing staff never left me alone. They were incompetent in their ability to manage Sovina. Just like the ones in the basement at home. The plane shuddered, twisted, and dropped again. At least the call kept my mind busy.

"Your wife has escaped, Mr. Buckingham." RN Rose's voice was barely audible over the static. "She must have left early this morning. We can't find her anywhere!"

I thumbed the End Call button. I didn't want to know more. What did it matter? She'd left. If she was gone, they'd either find her or they wouldn't. Chances were, they wouldn't. Not until I landed, and then I would have to help them.

I glanced over and admired Sarah's legs, thinking about what I could do with them. Resting my head back, I turned and stared out the window at the rain bands streaming across the glass. There was a flash—bright white light and then maybe a green starboard light—the roar of engines—crashing—tearing metal—then wind and cold. So much cold.

I was finishing my evening meal in the dining room when RN Temsley appeared. The final bites of my extra-rare lamb were particularly delicious. The nurse had tucked Sovina in her room for the evening.

"Now, RN Temsley," I said, "you gave my wife all her medications, right? Even the ones for sleep?" I had to be sure. Sovina could not stumble in during any of my fun time tonight.

"Yes, sir. I gave the medications the physician ordered." RN Temsley's cheeks flushed a little. So, she hadn't done exactly as I had requested of her.

"And the ones for sleep?"

"She didn't want those, sir," the nurse said timidly. "She said they weren't her prescription, and she didn't want to sleep yet."

I stared at RN Temsley. Oh, dear Evelyn Temsley. A woman with legs so very long and shapely. I'd waited two weeks for those exquisite legs. This evening was planned carefully, just for her—for *them,* you see. I was careful not to allow my gaze to rest on her for too long. I didn't want to make her feel uncomfortable.

But those legs in the fishnet stockings—and the stiletto red heels—well, they were the perfect size. I knew it! The best my money could buy.

My breath was a bit too rapid now, and I took a moment to gather my composure. Of course, RN Temsley was being polite about my wife's response. Sovina had likely cursed at the dear, accused the nurse of trying to poison her with those pills—or said that I was trying to drug her and kill her.

But then, Sovina grew fond of the nurses, too, so in the worst-case scenario, she may have warned RN Temsley that she was in danger—that both of their lives were in danger. Problems, problems, but easy solutions.

"I see." I allowed brief disappointment to cross my face so that the expectation of the nurse doing her job and failing to do it was evident in my demeanor. I was immediately rewarded as RN Temsley's, Evelyn's, eyes widened, and she took on a genuine expression of concern. I allowed myself a second of fantasy, *her thighs against mine,* then repressed my growing excitement and turned away.

"I will do it, then." I ensured that the firm determination of the task filled my voice without imparting any depreciation of her. "Could you help Edgar with the kitchen? I know it's not your job, but since I need to do this . . ." I arched an eyebrow and walked away, not waiting for an answer.

"Of course, sir," she called out, and I was pleased.

That little bit of guilt would be enough to keep her there until I returned.

When I entered Sovina's room, the cigarette smoke was thicker than London fog.

"Sovina." I approached her bed.

The gargoyle of a woman was clothed in a gothic black gown. Her eyes were caked with mascara and black eyeliner. Since her schizophrenia diagnosis and the start of her medication, she'd ballooned from one hundred and ten pounds to two hundred and thirty, and her face was puffy and bloated. She was hideous. She'd dyed her once beautiful blonde hair a matte black.

Sovina made no reply. She only blew her Marlboro menthol smoke from between garish, red-stained lips and glared at me.

"You need to take your sleep medication, my love," I told her. "Either take it now, or I will help you. You *know* what that means."

"No! I won't. You want to kill me," she hissed.

"Now, now," I waggled my finger at her, "if I wanted to do that, you wouldn't be alive, would you? I need you to rest. It's important that you do."

I reached for the bottle of Ambien, each tablet 5 milligrams. They were mine, although I never used them. I shook out four pills and sat on Sovina's bed. "Only these four," I told her.

"Four?"

"Yes," I confirmed. "You'll sleep like the queens of Egypt and wake up feeling great. Promise, love. And I'll come check on you in the morning. We'll get you a bath and maybe a pedicure?"

"Pedicure?" Her face softened, then her eyes narrowed. "I haven't had a pedicure in forever."

"We'll do it," I promised. "I'll call Rena. You can get the black polish and a design on your toes. How about that?"

She almost went for it. Then her eyes sparked with fire.

"No! You're using me for something!" A sudden realization passed across her face. "It's RN Temsley, isn't it? Don't, Carl. I like her. She can't go. She can't!"

In the middle of her sobs, I moved quickly and pinned Sovina down. I crammed all four pills into her mouth, held her nose, pushed her water bottle into her mouth, and squeezed.

"Swallow," I ordered. "Swallow them now, Sovina."

She struggled and tried to spit and cough, but she was weak. Her body convulsed. Tears spilled so heavily from her eyes that they left black rivers down her cheeks and messed up my hands. I sighed and looked up at the ceiling. She did this every single time, but in the end, she always swallowed.

My gaze slid back down to hers and my eyes willed her, forced her with all their might—made her see that she had no choice. Finally, she swallowed. It was better this way. Better that she didn't really know what I did. She could guess, but at least she didn't *know.*

I got up and patted her head, ignoring her sobs. If I could feel sorry for her insanity, I might. But she was a disgusting bag of putrid, gelatinous flesh mixed with raging insanity, forever encasing what used to be a beautiful, intelligent woman. How could anyone forgive that? Feel sorry for *that*?

"We'll still do the pedicure tomorrow, okay? Don't worry, love."

I shut the lights off in her room, closed and locked her door, and gave her to the darkness.

Evelyn Temsley was still in the kitchen with Edgar. Edgar was my helper. Part handyman, part groundskeeper—he'd been with my family for over twenty years. He was good at everything, particularly family secrets.

They were feeding a young puppy some table scraps. The pup was only a few weeks old but obviously old enough for solid food. I looked at Edgar for an explanation as Evelyn pet the little squirmy thing and cooed over him.

RN Temsley spoke up before Edgar could. "Isn't she the sweetest? Edgar says it's a she. I found her outside crying. No mother around. And she has the prettiest white fur. I've wanted a puppy for so long. My neighbor will help look after her during the day. Her name is Elvera."

The pleasure on the woman's face was evident, but now the animal presented a problem. One I'd have to deal with.

Edgar held my gaze and spoke. "Sir, if you don't mind, and if Ms. Temsley doesn't mind, the veterinarian is supposed to come tomorrow morning for Mrs. Buckingham's cats. We could make sure . . ." he cleared his throat, ". . . *Elvera* gets her vaccinations. Distemper, parvovirus, Bordetella. She's old enough for those. Then Ms. Temsley can take the pup home tomorrow."

"A fine idea," I agreed, my eyes thoughtfully lighting on the nurse cuddling with her puppy. "It would be a shame to lose such a beautiful animal to a terrible, preventable disease."

Evelyn held the creature protectively in her arms but then smiled at Edgar.

"Oh, it will be so hard to wait to take her home, but of course, I want the best for her." She relinquished her hold on the creature and handed her to Edgar, who worked hard to look cheerful.

"I'll take good care of her, Miss. Truly, I will."

And I knew he would. That pup would grow up safe and sound, wanting for nothing. This was a life Edgar felt he had the power to save.

"Thank you, Edgar," I told him. "You can go now. I'll see you in the morning?"

"Yes, sir," Edgar nodded. His skin was leathery. Spotted from working outdoors for years. Edgar's eyes flicked over toward RN Temsley. He held the pup close to him and made for the front door, grabbing his jacket on the way out. "Goodnight, sir." His parting words disappeared along with him and the puppy as the door shut behind him.

"RN Temsley," I was quick to call out before she could follow him.

"Yes?" She looked over at me with those innocent lamb eyes as she reached for her jacket. I knew she wanted to tell Elvera goodbye, but I would never get the nurse back if she went out the door. I don't think Evelyn had been an RN for more than two years, the dear thing. I intended to tug on her compassionate heartstrings to help me with what I wanted to do next.

"Do you mind assisting me for a moment? I need help with my wife's clothing for tomorrow. So much of it needs washing, and I noticed she's gained so much weight—a side effect of her medication. I'm afraid many items don't fit her anymore. I think you have a good idea of what will no longer fit her. I don't want her to feel embarrassed, having clothes in her wardrobe that are too small to wear—you understand?"

The nurse's eyes softened as if they could possibly get any softer. They seemed to say, *Oh, what a sweet man to think of that for his wife . . .*

"Of course," she responded, immediately wanting to do what she could. "I would be happy to help. I can't stay too late, though. I need to be back early tomorrow, and I can't wait to see Elvera!"

I smiled with what I knew was a polite and kind smile. "Thank you, RN Temsley. You are too kind. May I get you some iced tea or lemonade? Or a glass of wine, perhaps?"

She relaxed a little. "Lemonade would be great. Edgar made fresh lemonade today. I can help you," she offered.

"No, no, you stay there. I'll only be a second. Do you like mint?"

She shook her head. "I never really liked mint much. Its flavor overpowers everything."

I smiled with what I hoped passed for understanding and went into the kitchen and made her a drink. Pulling a vial from my pocket, I slipped a mixture of liquified Ambien, morphine, Rohypnol, and vodka into her lemonade and mixed it well, then brought it out in a flash along with a regular lemonade for myself garnished with mint.

"Okay, here we go," I smiled and handed her the drink. "Let's head downstairs."

This new place seems very cold, though I can't feel it exactly. It is stark, bare, and stainless steel glistens everywhere. There are gurneys with bodies lined up side-by-side next to stainless steel tables, wide sinks against the walls, and scales hanging from the ceiling. How did I get here?

Ah, yes. I was on a plane. My whole life ahead of me. Major turbulence, and then boom! I'm on the ground, a bloody corpse. This must be the hospital morgue. I recalled the tethered ambulance ride.

Two women amble in. Physicians? No. Nurses. Yes, how I love the nurses. It would be so nice to see their legs, but they are wearing blue scrub shirts, matching pants, and long white jackets. Shame.

They stand over me. Nurse 1 pulls back the white sheet. Jesus, my body is a mangled wreck.

"This guy," says Nurse 1, "they're at his house right now. Fucking bastard. Hope he burns in hell for all eternity. Anonymous tip came in that he's a serial killer. Murdered thirteen nurses and buried each one in his basement. And get this. He cut off their legs. Had them preserved. Like a taxidermist does! There's a room in the house where he has them all on display. Some made into lamps, some standing up dressed in different stockings and shoes. Posed like mannikins. Apparently, he—did things with them. *Sexual* things."

Nurse 2 says, "No. That can't be true."

"Oh, it's true," confirms Nurse 1. "I know the death investigator on the case. But don't you dare tell anyone yet. Not public knowledge."

"Think his tiny dick made him do stuff like that?" Nurse 2 points and laughs. *How dare they talk about me that way? That is uncalled for. My manhood isn't*

. . .

They throw the sheet back over my body and go to the next gurney. Nurse 1 pulls the sheet away.

I suddenly realize why the broken face at the crash site looked so familiar—yes, broken—smashed in places—but the matted black hair, garish red lips, pudgy, fat face with ripped jowls that covered a once fine jawline—

"Here's the kicker," Nurse 1 chuckles. "This stiff here, she's his wife."

"In the same crash?" Nurse 2's eyes bulge in near disbelief.

Nurse 1 nods. "But—wait for it—" she pauses for dramatic effect, "—in a *different* plane! Investigators say she escaped from a mental hospital, got in one of the couple's other jets, then she plotted an intercept course and deliberately smashed into him."

Both nurses fall silent as they stare at Sovina.

If a spirit is capable of being in shock, then I am in shock.

I try to look around, but I can't see anything other than the morgue. If I am dead and my spirit, soul—whatever you call it, is here—Sovina's must be here too.

I can't see Sovina's spirit, but I suddenly hear her. She hasn't sounded so strong, so confident in years.

"Pretty good finish, wouldn't you say, Carl?"

A low throaty chuckle surrounds me—the kind of prankster laugh she used to make when we were young when she played fun tricks on me—back when we played them on each other.

"Sovina?"

"Dead on arrival and now till death do us part, right?" she taunts. "Well, we're officially parted, asshole. I'm not your wife anymore, Carl. Where do you think we go from here? I'm thinking the place for murderers isn't so nice."

How could she know? So far, there was no feeling here—nothing. It wasn't so bad.

"You're a murderer too, Sovina!" Who was she to play the holier than thou card? She'd murdered me, after all. And some innocent others. "My pilot. The flight attendant?" *And her beautiful legs. Those lovely legs.*

"I've paid my price, Carl. I paid for it long before I died. And if there's a price to pay now, then so be it."

Something grabs at the ephemeral thing that I am. It rips me away and envelopes me. I no longer see myself, no longer see Sovina's body or the morgue. Absolute darkness wraps around me.

An immense pressure pushes down on me—pushes hard in every direction on whatever I am. I scream with no scream—I drown with no water—I am smothered with no air, no lungs to breathe as if in a vacuum where something pushes, pushes, pushes me beyond all endurance—and a voice all around me and from deep inside me bellows:

"OPEN—SWALLOW—"

Querus Abuttu, or "Dr. Q.," writes strange dark tales, speculative fiction, and weird sci-fi. She loves foraging for wild foods, learning about edible landscaping, and trying to find 101 ways to thwart deer from eating her plants. You may find her in a local pub drinking craft beers and talking to random people. She is a lifetime member of the Horror Writers Association (HWA) and graduated from Seton Hill University (SHU) with a master of fine arts in writing popular fiction. Dr. Q. is also a retired military veteran and holds a master's degree in nursing and a Ph.D. in Public Health. Find her stories on her author page on Amazon: Querus Abuttu.

YOU HAVE TO BELIEVE

BY EV KNIGHT

I *nevitable.*

That word—that terrible, horrible word—echoed through Olivia's head in Dr. Khan's matter-of-fact voice. She refused to consider the second word of the diagnosis. It wasn't right—

This was her body, and therefore, her choice, and she chose to keep the pregnancy. But the whole "inevitable" part—like so many things in her life—meant it wasn't her choice. Hell, it didn't even feel like her body anymore. No body, no choice.

Dr. Khan knew. Olivia could see the pity and disgust in his eyes. But John was a cop, and this was a small town. No one dared question her oversized sunglasses and insistence that she tripped and fell again. Maybe not bringing a child into this mess was a good thing—yet Olivia still wanted this baby.

Please just let me have something, let me have the one thing—I'll protect her, I swear I will.

"You can't even protect yourself," she said, and as if her body needed to prove the point, her uterus cramped hard again, and a hot, viscous something slipped out of her.

"No, please, and no."

She squeezed her eyelids shut—just for a second, just long enough to get through the pain of passing a blood clot.

"Woof!"

She heard the dog—a loud, deep bark—before she felt the thump against the car. She opened her eyes and slammed on the brakes, but there was only time for a quick flash of black fur before the whole thing was over.

"Oh, God! Oh no!" Olivia shoved the shifter in park and threw open the door of the Suburban. She had to hop down rather than step out, and the abrupt thump of her feet on the ground garnered another gush of precious blood, but she couldn't think about the loss of both lives just then. She hit the dog—had to have.

There it was, lying, panting on the shoulder of the road. Panting was good, though; panting meant alive.

The crisp autumn air was still, but the surrounding woods provided shade cold enough that Olivia thought she could see steam rising from the dog's hot body. What was it even doing out here in the middle of nowhere? As far as she knew, the only house for miles on this road was hers and John's.

The dog was a huge beast of a thing. A Mastiff? Newfoundland maybe? Hell, maybe it was a black wolf—not a dog at all. No. It was a dog, for sure.

Olivia had dreamed of owning a dog since she was a child. Her father was allergic, though. When she married John, she'd hoped she could finally have her family—two kids and a dog. But having kids was proving to be impossible, and John was a firm "no" on the dog.

"I'm not picking shit up out of the yard constantly, and Lord knows I can't count on you to do it."

According to John, housewives were lazy and frankly lucky to have such wonderful husbands with good-paying jobs so they could sit around on their fat asses eating bonbons and watching daytime trash TV. Funny that at the same time, he had specific and severe expectations for cleanliness, balanced and often gourmet dinners paired with the appropriate microbrew IPAs, bills paid, and anything else he deemed appropriate for his trophy wife to do.

And trophy wife, she was expected to be at all times. Fully dressed and made up. But all that—all those expectations—yet somehow, he couldn't possibly imagine her managing another living creature. Wonder what he would say if she brought this one home. Just a stray, but she hit it, and she had to take care of it.

Yes, the dog was breathing, but he was not moving.

Olivia eased down into a squat; the dried, brittle leaves were still damp with the defrost of morning dew. John didn't like to wait to dole out punishments. It kept her out of the ERs in the midnight hours. He was kind enough to start first thing in the morning, so she could make a same-day office visit and spare them the impression that they were some red-neck couple on their tenth 911 call that month. She put her hand on the dog's flank, feeling her fingers sink into an ocean of warm, soft fur. She ran it up and down the dog's body, feeling nothing unusual or out of place.

"Hey pup, you okay?" She managed to get the full sentence out before a lightning bolt shot out of her vagina and grounded itself on the leaves between her feet.

The dog lifted its head, ears perked, and nose elevated in a sniffing position.

It was happening. Right there, on the side of the road, middle of the woods. She was losing the baby. Blood soaked through her panty-liner, oozed out the sides of her underwear, ran down the insides of her thighs, her calves, her ankles, staining the bottom of her skirt and coating the leaves in a much more vibrant red than autumn's changes could ever offer. The pain, though, the pain was far worse than the fear associated with the loss of that much blood. Her uterus was in a juicer,. It and her intestines were waiting in line. Everything inside her twisted and squeezed. She'd seen a dead frog squished on the driveway once. Its guts had been pushed out both its mouth and its backside. She knew what that frog's final moments had felt like.

The dog was up and pushing its muzzle into her neck as if the roles were reversed and Olivia had been run over. She couldn't hold herself up anymore. She grabbed the dog around the neck and let her head drop against its shoulder. Black fur turned into a black mist that turned into unconsciousness. Olivia welcomed it.

"Here, drink this, it will help." The voice was soft and kind. The woman it belonged to was a blur. Olivia rubbed her eyes and squinted. An older woman with long salt and pepper curls sat on the bed beside Olivia. She held a ceramic mug in her hand—its dark blue glaze with white speckles reminded her of the night sky.

"What is it?" Olivia asked, still taking in her surroundings and trying desperately to recall how she got there.

"Just a little herbal tisane I mixed up for you. It will help the cramps...and the swelling around your eye."

Olivia realized too late that she'd lost her sunglasses at some point. She touched her eye; the lightest brush of a finger elicited pain. "I must have hit it when I—have you seen a black dog? A big one? I think I hit a dog." She remembered. The dog, the car, and all the blood. "Where am I? Where is my car? What time is it? I have to get home!" If she missed dinner, if John came home and she wasn't there—well, the pain back on the road would seem like a paper cut compared to what he'd do.

"You're safe; your car is outside—I hope you don't mind I drove it here. You have plenty of time before your husband comes home, and the dog—Kira—is fine. She came and got me, and we brought you here."

Olivia sat up and winced. Her stomach ached, and her head swam. She was in a small cottage, two, maybe three rooms if it had a bathroom. Rustic but cozy. A fire roared in a stone fireplace across the room. Her bed was soft and piled with homemade quilts of various thicknesses. A braided rug supported two cushioned rocking chairs in front of the fire. One was accompanied by a small table, and the other a basket filled with twine, feathers, and bones. Bundles of dried and drying plants hung from the ceiling. The kitchen—which was really more of a décor transition, as it was just a third of the big open space—was more modern, with a fridge and stove and a round wooden table with three chairs.

"But where am I?"

"Xanadu. Well, you're in the back part of the shop, where Kira and I live. That door leads through a small storage room and into the shop itself." She pointed to a door in the far corner of the living room/bedroom combo they were in now.

"Xanadu? Like that old movie? It's a shop? I've never heard of it. What kind?"

"A shop of requirement, I suppose. We've been here for a long time. People don't seem to notice until they need us. And that's perfectly fine with us, isn't it, Kira?" The black dog who had saved her came padding up from behind the rocking chair.

"I'd love to see the shop. I always wanted to own a little shop. Sell crystals, learn to read Tarot cards, that sort of thing. But John thinks that stuff, well this stuff," Olivia lifted the mug, "is stupid and well, I can't work. He has a very busy, full-time job as a police officer. Someone has to keep the house and feed us and everything."

"Nothing is work if you love what you do. Now, really, I must insist that you drink your tea before it gets cold."

Olivia obeyed without hesitation. She should have hesitated. She didn't know the woman or how she'd really gotten there. Who knew what was in the tea? As she sipped and felt the warm, spicy fluid spread out within her like a weighted blanket, she realized she'd forgotten to ask the very important question. "Oh! Are all the ingredients safe in pregnancy?"

The older woman's entire posture changed. She slumped a little, her face bearing the countenance of pity. "Yes. It's safe."

Olivia's tears came suddenly, like a monsoon. She sobbed and held her belly as if that was all it took to hold on to the baby. "The doctor called it an *inevitable abortion.*" He said there was nothing that could be done to save it. She had no idea why she was sharing all of this with the woman whose name she didn't even know.

The old woman took Olivia's hand in hers. "Sometimes, inevitable is just another word for destiny. And destiny is when the universe steps in to help guide you. You have to believe."

"Believe in what?" Olivia sobbed. Was this woman implying that it was a good thing to lose the baby?

"Magic. The Universe. Destiny. Whatever you want to call it. There is a plan."

"Well, I sure wish the universe would find a kinder way of telling me."

"The Universe whispers to us every day. But then, sometimes, there is a rare alignment of the planets, and the message comes as a shout. ACT NOW! The time has come. It has to start now." The woman stood. "Drink your tea. I'm going to go put something together for you, then we'll get you home."

Olivia drank. The tea warmed her and gave her some strength back. By the time the woman returned, Olivia was standing. Kira at her side.

"Here." The woman handed her a muslin bag. "There is a candle in there. I want you to draw a bath, pour the herbs into the water, light the candle, and soak for at least thirty minutes. I want you to do this tonight before midnight, and then you must be asleep by midnight. Do you understand?"

"Yes, but what is this? Some kind of spell?"

"You could say that. Yes."

"For protection? For my baby?"

"If you do as I say, it will bring all your dreams alive."

"Thank you . . . uh, I never got your name."

"It's Clio."

"Thank you, Clio and Kira. My name is—"

"Olivia. Yes, I know. Now, you better go, get dinner ready for your husband. He will need to leave you alone tonight. You mustn't upset John. Not tonight."

There was time when Olivia got back home to roast a chicken and bake some potatoes to go with it. There was time, even, to clean herself up—noting that she'd had no further bleeding since Clio's tea at Xanadu. She'd become a wiz with cover-up too. John didn't like to be reminded of his punishments, and she needed him to be in the best of moods.

John was, in fact, in an excellent mood. He bounded into the house, all smiles. Olivia trusted this mood less than his violent ones.

"Hey! How ya feeling? Doc Kahn called me, told me about your visit, and said I need to make sure you quit overdoing it. I'm sorry, though, really. I know how much you wanted that baby. But I think I got something that might help you forget all about it. Close your eyes. I'll be right back."

He never stopped to give her a chance to speak. He knew how much *she* wanted the baby? Olivia didn't think he did. Because he clearly didn't give a shit. And whatever he had bought as an apology would never replace what he might have taken away from her.

She kept her eyes as closed as her mouth though, remembering Clio's words about not upsetting him. Instead, she practiced in her head expressions of surprise and delight at whatever it was this time. And then, she felt it. A warm, squirming mass of fluff, heavy in her arms.

"Okay, open your eyes!"

She did as she was told, and there it was—a puppy version of Kira!

"She's gonna be a big girl, I think," John laughed. "Anyway, I know you always wanted one, and now that you're not gonna have a baby to deal with, I figured, what's the harm in letting you have something else to raise? Now, what's for dinner? I'm starving."

He pushed past her and the puppy without another word. Olivia hadn't been able to close her jaw long enough to form a sentence, but now, there were plenty. She carried the puppy and followed behind him. He would go to the bathroom, change out of his work clothes, and wash his face and hands before coming to the table. At least that's what the old, predictable John would do.

"Honey?" she ventured. "Where did you get him?"

"It's a her. Weird little cabin shop off Pine Run Road. Weird ass new-agey name. Never really noticed it before, but I had to take a leak something fierce. I stopped, and while I was pissing, I saw a sign for free puppies. So, I checked it out. Figured if it was a bunch of those tiny rat-looking things, I'd tell her to shove 'em up her ass and have a good day. This was the only one she had left. I took one look at her paws and knew she'd be a brute. Just a mutt, though, so don't get too excited."

"She's perfect. Thank you." It was all she could think of to say. She had more or had thought she did until he mentioned Clio's cottage. But there were no puppies there this morning. Or maybe there were, and Olivia just hadn't seen them. Weird that Clio wouldn't have shown them to her. The whole thing was weird, though, wasn't it? The Like a dream.

After dinner, she took Hope outside to do her business and then snuggled her into a pile of towels near the tub. Hope went right off to sleep, and while John watched whatever mind-numbing shows he watched every night, Olivia had a bath by candlelight.

On Saturday mornings, John liked a full breakfast—eggs, pancakes, sausage, biscuits and gravy, and fresh squeezed orange juice. She'd put the first pancake on the griddle when the pain hit again. This one didn't ease up, and the blood that came out of her this time came out in clumps. By the time it passed and she could stand straight again, she'd burned the pancake and set off the smoke alarm.

John, who was "trying to get my fishing equipment together for fuck's sake," was not impressed with Olivia's mistake, and the beating he gave her reflected that. Hope did her best to intervene, and John would have none of it.

"Don't hurt her! Please, John. She's all I got."

"Well, she ain't staying." He opened the door and tossed her out. Olivia heard the gunshot but hoped it was a warning shot to scare Hope away and nothing more. As soon as she caught her breath, and as soon as John left to go fishing, she'd find her. But there was more anger in John, and since he couldn't take it out on the dog, he took it out on Olivia. The stomach kicks were bad; the last one, though, missed her stomach and broke her forearm and a couple of ribs.

"Clean yourself up. Sick of seeing your blood everywhere. And call Kahn on Monday. I want you on the pill."

If he said more, Olivia didn't hear it.

At some point, on the floor, in a pool of her own blood and lost pregnancy, Olivia was aware of Hope returning to lay beside her. She snuggled in tight against her aching and hollow belly. But when she opened her eyes sometime later, it was Clio and not Hope who sat beside her, holding her hand.

"How? How did you get in?" Olivia asked weakly.

"I've always been here, Olivia. I've always been in your mind." The woman touched Olivia's temple, making her point.

"No, I . . ." But maybe Clio was right; something felt so familiar about her. As if she had known her all her life. Or maybe it was just that Clio was the type of woman Olivia envied. One who could make a life on her own, be her own person, live for herself.

"Remember when I told you that you had to believe?"

Olivia nodded.

"Well, it's time. Destiny has arrived." Clio put John's service gun in Olivia's hand. She leaned close and whispered in Olivia's ear. "Don't let your aim ever stray."

"What are you saying?" Olivia managed to half-sit up, using her forearms to brace her upper body on the cold kitchen floor.

"I'm saying you can have a whole life. Follow your dreams, live a life like mine."

"I can't shoot him. I couldn't even if I wanted to. I'd miss, make some terrible mistake, and shoot Hope, or it would ricochet off something in the house and shoot me. I can't."

"You won't make a mistake. I'll be guiding you. Olivia, listen to me. There is no other road to take. You have to believe."

"Where's Hope? I need her. I can't do this without her."

Just then, Hope barked—a deep, menacing, fear-inducing bark. Olivia turned toward the sound. Standing in the doorway was an enormous black dog, not a puppy. Bigger than Kira. But even so, Olivia knew it was Hope. Hope was with her. And she believed.

The gun felt unmanageably heavy in her hand. The blood loss and broken left arm left her with very little strength, but nothing was going to stand in the way. John would never take anything away from her again. She decided to sit in the kitchen chair, facing the door, her arm resting on the table. He would be home any minute. The adrenaline had numbed her pain at least, now if only she could steady the shakes.

John walked in, and his eyes skipped right over Olivia to the spot where she'd lain, bleeding away her most recent hopes and dreams. He'd never encountered the aftermath of his punishments before. She'd always cleaned up after he stormed out. Not this time. This time, he was going to face what he'd done, see the pregnancy that was once inside her, and he would be given exactly sixty seconds to mourn before she pulled the trigger.

"Inevitable," she croaked. John's head snapped to her. He saw the gun. His nostrils flared, his lips thinned to a white line, and he threw his tackle box on the floor.

"What the fuck do you think you're doing? Give me that gun."

"Sometimes inevitable is another word for destiny. I'll use a sentence as an example. It was inevitable that our marriage would end in someone's death. Said differently, it was destiny that our marriage ended in death."

"Olivia, you would never. Do you have any fucking idea the punishment for killing a cop? You think I'm bad? Wait til you have to sit in jail your whole damned life or until they execute you. Give it to me, and I'll go easy on you."

"You killed so many of my hopes, my dreams, and now my baby. You're the one that will be executed, John."

He was inching closer to her. He probably thought she didn't notice. But she did, and she'd allow it. The closer he was when she shot him, the less effect the shaking would have.

"Olivia, I'm going to count to three, and if you don't hand me that gun, you will be sorrier than you have ever been in your life." This he said through clenched teeth. He was wrong, though, and Olivia knew it. If she handed him the gun, she would be sorrier than she had ever been. There was no other road to take now. Nothing could stand in her way.

"Don't let your aim ever stray; I'll be guiding you." Clio's voice whispered in her ear, and she felt the woman's hand cover her own, help her raise her arm, and pull the trigger.

The gunshot was deafening in the small kitchen, but it hit him right in the throat. Blood sprayed in a gush like when you first turned on the garden hose. He stumbled forward toward her pool of blood, slid in it, and went down, hitting his head off the sink, which spun him around so he landed face up.

Olivia dropped the gun in disgust and froze. What had she done?

Hope in the form of a giant black beast of a dog tore into the house, splintering the door frame. She bit into John's neck with a wild savagery Olivia had only ever seen on nature documentaries.

When the dog finished, what had originally looked like a gunshot wound now appeared to be the result of a wild animal attack. An animal drawn to the house by the blood from Olivia's miscarriage.

Olivia broke her arm and some ribs in her attempt to get away, and John, coming home at the right time, bore the remainder of the animal's attack, instructing Olivia to shoot at it. Where the bullet went, no one would ever know.

The puppy, having been hiding in the bedroom, was uninjured, and the wolf that attacked Olivia and John was never found. At least that's what the police report said. Open and shut. Sometimes, the planets align so rarely.

The bell on Xanadu's front door rang. Olivia had just put the roast in the oven. She wiped her hands on her apron. Hope lifted her drowsy head from the braided rug in front of the fire.

"You gonna go check things out? Or are you getting too old for this?" she asked the dog.

Hope stretched and yawned and moseyed out to check on the new customer. Olivia watched the girl browse the shop, never taking off her oversized Hollywood sunglasses. It was July, but the girl wore long sleeves and rubbed her upper left arm as if cold . . . or bruised.

"You keep an eye on her, old girl," Olivia scratched the back of Hope's neck. "I'll go make some tea."

E.V. Knight writes horror and dark fiction. Her debut novel, *The Fourth Whore*, was published in 2020 by Raw Dog Screaming Press. EV's short stories can be found in *Siren's Call* magazine. A graduate of Seton Hill University, she received her MFA in Writing Popular Fiction in January 2019. She enjoys all things macabre, whether they be film, TV, podcast, novel, or short story. She lives in the cold northern woods of Michigan's Upper Peninsula with her family and their two hairless cats.

DEVIL IN DISGUISE

BY ALICIA HILTON

S ven Hagen wore the face of an ordinary man to hide his inner monster. In the Indianapolis hotel bar where he was conducting surveillance, he blended into the crowd of conventioneers, appearing to be a typical middle-aged man, the kind of boring guy you wouldn't remember seeing after gunshots were fired.

His eyes were grey, his hair was medium brown with grey at the temples, his face was clean-shaven, his lips were neither plump nor thin, there was no cleft or scar on his chin, and a plastic surgeon had set his nose after it was busted during a scuffle with client #19.

Sven thought it was more respectful to call the people that he killed clients instead of targets or hits. After all, killing was just business, never personal. Like other successful professionals, he worked under a set of rules—rules that had kept him alive for nearly forty-two years.

Sven unbuttoned his shirt cuffs and rolled up the sleeves to his elbows. Sweating was his only tell that he was up to no good, a physiological process he hadn't learned to control, despite practicing meditation.

It was fortunate that few people were as adept at studying character as Sven. Manipulation was part of the job, but he didn't consider himself evil. How could any man be truly evil when his depravity was balanced with compassion?

Every year, he donated ten percent of his income to charity, supporting home-less shelters and animal rescues. And he was an organ donor, too. Someday, when he kicked the bucket, his organs would be harvested—corneas, heart, kidneys, even his bones if they could be useful. It was only right that a man whose business was taking life was willing to go under the knife to help others.

Most of his killings could be rationalized as a service to mankind. Nearly all the men and women that he shot, garroted, or stabbed deserved to be obliterated from the planet. The debacle with the explosives was an aberration—a horrific mistake that he faced whenever he dreamed. Sven was cold and calculated when working a job, but he did have a conscience.

Sven also was a man of ordinary desires. He didn't wear fashionable clothes or frequent golf resorts or dine at expensive restaurants. He lived in a small house in Chicago, in a neighborhood of working-class folks who didn't poke into other people's business. And the women that he dated were usually like the sedans that he drove—not flashy, but comfortable rides that got him from point A to point B with minimal fuss, and without attracting unwanted attention—a damn good reason to ignore the gorgeous woman who'd just walked into the bar.

A group of conventioneers who were sitting at a long table by the jukebox rubbernecked, staring at the tall, voluptuous brunette when she strode past them. She wasn't wearing a coat, though the snow was coming down hard outside, and her crimson sweater was cut so low, Sven could see the edge of her lacy white bra. With each step, her hips swayed, moving in time with the music that was being pumped out of the ceiling speakers, Queen's "Another One Bites the Dust." The jukebox was just a decoration, part of the bar's retro '50s décor.

There were empty barstools at the other end of the bar, where a female bar-tender was fixing flaming drinks for a couple—a man in his late forties, the woman young enough to be his daughter and wearing caked-on rouge and eye shadow that was so heavy, it looked like it had been applied by a mortician.

The brunette paused near the couple as the music changed from Queen to Elvis Presley singing "(You're the) Devil in Disguise." Her head swiveled like she was looking for someone, but it was just as likely that she was eavesdropping on the couple's conversation.

A man sitting at the bar near the brunette shouted, "Can I buy you a drink?"

The brunette didn't speak loud enough for Sven to hear her answer, but she started walking again at a slower pace, heading towards the restrooms. It was hard for Sven not to stare when the sway of her hips was so hypnotic. Damn, her jeans were tight.

He turned away and glanced at the table where client #45 was sitting. There were two pitchers of beer on the table, both nearly empty.

Sven felt a tap on his shoulder.

The brunette said, "Is this seat taken?"

"No, go ahead." Sven gestured for her to sit.

Red lips a shade darker than her sweater parted in a smile. "Buy me a drink?" She pulled the stool closer to him.

Her perfume smelled expensive, and her sweater looked like cashmere.

She seemed like the kind of woman who had enough money to buy her own drinks—in her thirties, confident, sexy in a classy way. The diamond ring on her wedding-ring finger had a center stone that was at least a carat. The ring on her right hand had a sapphire that was even bigger. Probably worked in the gaming industry, like the thousands of other dealers, pit bosses, and casino owners that were currently visiting Indianapolis for a trade show happening at the convention center.

Don't fool around with married women was rule #15 on his list of self-imposed guidelines, but he said, "What can I get you?"

"I'll have what you're having."

Sven waved to a bartender who was pouring a martini for an old guy who looked like he'd already had one too many. "Gin and tonic for the lady," Sven said. He took another sip of his own drink, tonic water with no booze. *Stay sober when you're working*, rule #6.

She said, "You come here often?"

It was such a corny line, Sven smiled. He said, "Just passing through," which was true, though he planned to spend another night in Indianapolis before driving back to Chicago—in a different hotel, of course. Only a jackass would stick around a crime scene.

"I'm Valerie," she said.

"I'm Michael. Good to meet you."

Always use an assumed name while working, rule #1.

He preferred to focus on his objective without distractions, but if he'd turned down her request for a drink, she might've made a scene, which would've screwed up his plans for the evening—taking out a blackjack dealer who'd borrowed money from a loan shark and welched on the debt.

Valerie started fiddling with her hair. It was wavy and flowed halfway down her back, so shiny that she could've been in a shampoo commercial, but Sven was focusing more attention on the group of conventioneers who were sitting at the table closest to the hostess stand.

In his peripheral vision, he watched them stand up and start walking towards the lobby. The blackjack dealer passed a fake tree that had red Christmas lights. The rosy glow gave his face a ruddy tint that made his bruises look more prominent. He was limping from a beating he'd gotten the previous weekend. One of the loan shark's thugs had roughed him up after he refused to pay the debt. Sven wasn't there when it happened. He was a specialist—no tune-ups, only final solutions, and his kills were always quick. *No torture*, rule #4.

The bartender put a frosty glass in front of Valerie, and Sven handed him fifteen bucks. "Keep the change," Sven said.

"Thanks for the drink," Valerie said.

Sven stood up. "Have a nice night."

Valerie said, "You have to leave now?" She put her hand on his shoulder—more of a pat than a caress, but the invitation in her eyes was obvious.

"Early meeting tomorrow. Nice talking with you."

As he was putting on his leather jacket, he felt a sharp pain in his lower back. Sven jerked around.

Valerie had already pulled her hand away and was reaching for her drink, but Sven saw a needle sticking out from the underside of her sapphire ring.

He grabbed her wrist. "What'd you give me?"

"What're you talking about?" She smiled innocently, but her eyes told another story. The irises were changing color—from deep brown to swirling crimson. Holy shit!

Sven felt a sudden wave of nausea. His vision blurred.

A man's voice said, "Buddy, you okay?"

Sven felt a strong hand grip his shoulder. Everything went black.

The moonlit landscape was desolate yet strangely beautiful—frozen tundra that looked like it belonged on a Christmas card, or in a nightmare.

Sven knew he wasn't dreaming because his teeth chattered, but he had no memory of how he'd ended up lying in the snow.

His stomach clenched. He rolled over onto his side and puked.

His belly compressed again, and more bloody vomit shot through his teeth. What had the bitch given him?

When his gut was empty, Sven stood up and brushed snow off his clothes. "Get ahold of yourself," he muttered.

His temples throbbed worse than the last time he got kicked in the head, and he was so dizzy, his vision was blurry.

Sven took a deep breath, shut his eyes, and opened them again.

After a few minutes, the dizziness dissipated, but his head hurt like hell, and his hands were so cold that he couldn't feel his fingertips.

He blew on his palms to warm the chilled flesh, then stuffed his hands in his pockets and stared at his surroundings.

The snow-covered field couldn't be near Indianapolis. There were no buildings within sight, no roads or fences, no sound of cars driving in the distance, just the wind, and it was blowing fiercely.

A blanket of icy flakes had obliterated his abductors' footprints, but at least the snow had stopped falling while he was unconscious.

The moon was nearly full. Stars also lit the night sky, scattered together in clusters. Having always lived in cities, Sven had never learned enough about astronomy to use the stars to find his bearings.

A howl drew his attention to a cliff about 100 yards away. The silhouette perched on top looked too large to be a wolf, but what else could it be? Sven's heart beat faster, so loud that he heard the *whooshing* echoing in his ears.

Another silhouette joined the wolf, a great horned beast that walked on two feet and looked like it was at least six feet tall.

Sven shut his eyes and opened them again, but the horned figure didn't disappear. The knockout drug must still be in his bloodstream, making him hallucinate.

The wolf howled again, and the horned beast roared. The unholy sound made Sven scream.

Across the snowdrifts, he fled. Panic made him pump his legs faster, but after running about sixty yards, he got a cramp in his side and slowed to a jog.

Gusts of wind made tears trickle from his eyes. They froze on his cheeks. With each exhalation, his lungs rattled. It felt like lead weights were strapped to his feet.

The howls got closer.

Sven climbed up a hill, weaving between evergreens and boulders. Underneath the blanket of snow, rocks jabbed his feet. He'd worn boots, but the soles weren't thick. At least the cluster of pines perched on the cliff provided shelter from the frigid wind.

Finally, Sven reached the top of the hill. Smoke rose from a valley in the distance. He saw a farmhouse with lights in the windows and felt a spark of optimism.

Behind him, branches clattered. Convinced that he was about to be gutted, he jerked around, but nothing attacked him except the wind. Distracted, Sven slipped on a patch of ice.

As he plunged down the slope, a low-hanging branch from an evergreen slashed his cheek.

Thud, he landed in a twisted heap. Searing pain radiated from his face, and his shoulder was sore, too. When he touched his cheek, he felt a wet gash as wide as a second mouth.

For a moment, he considered giving up, collapsing in the snow, and letting the cold seep into his bones, but memories pricked his conscience. A sob tore from his throat. He struggled to his feet.

The wind carried a musky scent. Sven heard a flapping sound, like a flock of birds approaching. He looked up at the cliff that he'd fallen from and saw a tableau so horrific that it couldn't be real, but he heard their howls and gnashing teeth.

The largest creature had Valerie's face, but curved horns like a mountain goat, and leathery wings that must've been ten feet wide. The rest of her body was covered in shaggy fur. Her fingers were tipped with long talons.

More than a dozen winged wolf creatures flew around the horned monster, howling and yipping. The breeze from their flapping wings made the trees that were growing on the cliff shake.

Terrified, Sven tried to run, but he couldn't move his body, as if he'd been turned to stone. Urine trickled down his legs. He hadn't pissed himself since he was four.

Steam puffed from the demon's nostrils. She licked her lips and said, "It's time to pay for your sins. My wolves feast on the flesh of unrepentant souls." Red light shot from the horned creature's eyes, so bright it nearly blinded Sven.

The slavering beasts were almost upon him when he felt energy vibrating through his body. Lurching forward, he hobbled away from the cliff. A second later, he was sprinting, running faster than he'd ever run before.

No human should be capable of moving so quickly, but bounding like a gazelle, Sven raced over snowdrifts, heading towards the farmhouse he'd seen from the hilltop.

He didn't dare to look behind him, but he knew the winged wolves were in pursuit. The sound of their howls grew louder, as if hundreds, not dozens, were chasing him.

Sven leapt over the fence that surrounded the farmhouse. The hem of his jacket caught on one of the wooden posts and tore, but he kept sprinting towards the porch. Amber light streamed from the windows.

"Help!" he shouted.

No one answered.

Paws scurried behind him.

Sven grasped the doorknob. The metal was so hot he jerked his hand away, but the door swung open, pulled by an invisible force.

Sven ran into the farmhouse, slammed the door shut, and locked it.

The foyer was empty—no furniture or people, but the air stank of smoke and burned meat, like a roast that'd been cooking for too long.

"Hello," he said. No one answered.

Sven rushed into the first room. There was a little boy sitting on the chair closest to the fireplace. Except it wasn't a chair, it was a car seat. *No kids*, rule #2.

Sven had access to Semtex, but he never used plastic explosives unless he wanted to take down an entire building. The car bomb was a relatively simple device, attached to the underside of the Jaguar sedan with a strong magnet.

Client #44 did not have a chauffeur, so the risk of collateral damage should've been minimal. There was less traffic late at night when the client left the restaurant and club that he owned, but he usually had muscle with him, or a mistress.

In the mornings, the client always took the same route when he left the Lincoln Park brownstone that he shared with his wife and kids, driving south on Broadway, and a left turn onto Fullerton, heading east towards Lake Shore Drive.

Sven wiped sweat from his forehead. He'd already watched a frigging parade of traffic pass the spot where he'd parked—two school buses, dozens of cars, three delivery trucks, a guy riding a moped that buzzed like a giant mosquito.

Finally, Sven saw the client's Jaguar approaching. The vehicle sped up as it got near the intersection.

Sven pressed the button on the remote that triggered the detonator. A split-second later, he saw a face in profile, sitting in a booster seat behind the driver. A little boy, client #44's youngest child.

"No," Sven shouted. But it was too late.

The explosion lifted the vehicle off the ground. Flames shot into the air as the gas tank ignited, spraying broken glass and twisted metal.

Sven stared at the boy sitting beside the fireplace. "I'm sorry," Sven sobbed. "I didn't mean to hurt you!"

The child's expression was blank as if his face was a mask that was carved from wax.

Sven knelt and began to pray, begging for forgiveness.

Wallowing in shame, he didn't notice the demon sneaking up behind him until she grabbed his neck and forced him to stand.

Talons dug into his flesh. The monster with Valerie's face snarled, "Look at what you've done."

In an instant, the farmhouse vanished, and Sven was transported to the inside of the Jaguar, sitting in the driver's seat. Guns N' Roses' "Welcome to the Jungle" played on the radio.

Sven stomped on the brakes, but the sedan accelerated instead of stopping. He glanced over his shoulder and saw the demon sitting next to the boy.

The boy lifted one of his hands to his face, opened his mouth, and began sucking on his thumb.

Valerie was in human form, except horns sprouted from her hair. Her lips peeled back in a mockery of a smile.

"Don't hurt him!" Sven said.

Valerie said, "Hurt him? Your wish is my command."

She snapped her fingers, and the Jaguar was enveloped in flames.

Sven's skin blistered and charred. The heat was so intense that even his bones cracked, but he was still conscious. He heard demon wolves howling and Valerie laughing. He'd never felt such excruciating pain.

The torture seemed to go on for hours until the radio got louder and the flames extinguished.

Sven's bones were covered in healthy flesh.

The boy pulled his thumb out of his mouth and said, "Daddy, I'm hungry."
The traffic light turned green, and the ordeal started again.

In a subterranean lair lit by torches, Lucifer lounged on a violet velvet sofa beside Valerie, his legs draped over her naked thighs. Except for the horns on her head and the talons on the tips of her fingers, Valerie was back in human form.

While she polished her talons with a file, the Dark Lord chewed flesh from a femur. Not Sven's. The leg bone belonged to a demon who had rebelled. The poor sap would soon be reconstituted to suffer more abuse.

Valerie suspected that her comrade was being punished as a warning to her. Lucifer was fond of psychological games.

When all the meat was gnawed from the bone, Lucifer tossed it on the stone floor.

Two of Valerie's winged wolves pounced on the femur. The other winged beasts growled with jealousy as the alpha wolves savored their treat. One of the smaller wolves lunged at his elder sister.

Valerie snapped her fingers.

The wolves quit fighting. Amongst demons, there was a respected hierarchy, and they knew she did not tolerate insubordination.

Lucifer purred like a cat and pulled her closer. He said, "Your escapades whet my appetite. Who's next on the naughty list?"

She flexed her talons. "You want to spoil the surprise? Anticipation enhances your pleasure."

"You are my favorite lieutenant." Lucifer cupped her breast and fondled the nipple.

She swatted his hand. "I'm tired of punishing mortals. It's time for me to retire."

Lucifer's pupils dilated. "You'll give me a child?"

"Never. I wouldn't wish my fate on a son or daughter. Promote another demon."

Lucifer hissed. His eyes flashed, the irises changing color from coal black to swirling scarlet.

It was a silent night compared to peak shopping time at the bustling Kringle Market, and unseasonably warm for a late December in Manhattan, a balmy forty-eight degrees Fahrenheit when Valerie strolled into Union Square.

A gentle breeze stirred the festive display of holiday lights and ornament-covered evergreens. A group of carolers were on the corner. Their voices were out of tune, but Valerie grinned. Holiday kitsch always made her smile.

She wore a jaunty fedora hat, mirrored aviator sunglasses, and a leather overcoat. A rather theatrical costume, but that was the point. Bystanders would remember what she was wearing, not the woman underneath the disguise.

Valerie paused by the hot cider stand and surveyed the crowd.

A teenage girl brushed up against an elderly man, picking his pocket.

Valerie didn't intercede to stop the thief. She understood what it was like to be a poor kid trying to survive on the streets. Stealing a few bucks was a paltry crime. Besides, from the fine wool fabric of the man's designer suit and his fancy cordovan loafers, he likely had plenty of cash stashed in banks. Losing the wallet was hardly a hardship.

Two men who appeared to be in their twenties loitered near the trash can. They bumped fists and parted. The guy wearing the dark denim jacket and jeans walked towards the subway entrance, and the stockier man with the leather jacket and torn jeans headed across the street towards a coffee shop.

The rest of the crowd looked like typical New Yorkers, grazing on sweets, shopping, oblivious to danger.

There was no sign of her quarry, but the market was one of his favorite hunting grounds. Since the night was pleasant, Valerie bought a cup of cider and a snickerdoodle cookie and listened to the carolers.

Nineteen minutes later, she spotted her target talking to a little girl wearing a green stocking cap like an elf. Not his daughter, but if she wasn't rescued, the girl would be his plaything soon.

Valerie opened her overcoat. The rifle hanging from a sling attached to her shoulder unfolded and unleashed an energy beam that vaporized the pedophile's face.

Swiveling, she directed another blast at his body.

The little girl screeched when the pedophile's flesh and bones dissolved in a liquid squelch.

Bystanders stampeded. The vibrations from their footsteps made the viscous puddle tremble and ooze across the asphalt.

Valerie heard another yell—not the girl; a woman was screaming.

The little girl cried, "Mommy!" as the woman enveloped her in a hug.

The sentimental display made Valerie's eyes fill with tears.

She held her weapon down at her side. She was about to make a quick exit, but a man working at the donut booth shouted and pointed at her. He yanked a basket of sizzling dough from a fryer and flung it.

The droplets of hot oil stung when they hit her skin, but the aviator shades shielded most of her face.

Instead of liquefying him like the pedophile, she directed the beam of light so only the hem of his coat caught fire.

The baker collapsed and rolled on the ground, snuffing the flames.

Emerging from the cloud of smoke, Valerie scanned the crowd. Two uniformed police officers approached from Seventeenth Street.

A gust of wind blew the fedora off her head, revealing a pair of gleaming horns growing from her hair.

Unholy night. Lightning cracked, streaking across the sky.

Whoot, whoot, whoot. A helicopter from the local news station circled above Union Square, blowing dust into Detective Andino's eyes. Three hours and fifty-two minutes until Christmas, and the searchlights were blindingly bright.

Other detectives and evidence techs swarmed around the Kringle Market, tagging and photographing abandoned shopping bags, purses, briefcases, and backpacks. But Dennis Andino and his partner, Jessica Sarno, had landed the biggest prize, the liquefied corpse. Since it had started to rain, they and two patrol officers were setting up a tent to protect the evidence.

Dennis had just secured the fabric on his side of the tent to a support pole when two black SUVs and a van screeched to a stop at the intersection.

Jessica said, "Feds are here."

Dennis watched a tall woman exit the van. She locked eyes with him. The left side of her mouth curved up in a barely perceptible smile.

Two other agents opened the back of the van and pulled out a cart.

Valerie walked away from the van towards the tent.

Dennis wiped rainwater from his face. Even when she was dressed in a raid jacket and cargo pants, Valerie looked hot.

Jessica said, "Put your tongue back in your mouth."

"Huh?" Dennis looked at his partner.

Jessica said, "You're drooling." She elbowed him in the side and whispered, "Everyone's going to know you're hooking up."

"We're not screwing. She's a friend."

"Yeah, right." Jessica snorted.

When Valerie joined them, Dennis said, "How're you gonna process that?" He pointed at the sludge.

Valerie said, "Shovel and shop vac."

Jessica said, "You're a sick puppy."

Valerie shrugged. "Don't I know it."

Three days later, Valerie was stalking another sinner.

Two minutes and forty-five seconds after leaving the FBI office at 26 Federal Plaza in the Tribeca neighborhood in Manhattan, she arrived at a tenement building on Jerome Avenue in the Bronx. Like other demons and the more fortunate angels who had not fallen from grace, she had the ability to bend time and space.

Her quarry's apartment was located on the fifth floor next to the fire escape. The door was locked, but the bolt slid back the instant she touched the doorknob. Telekinesis was more efficient than a lock pick.

The studio apartment stank of bleach. None of the lights were on, but streetlights streamed through the windows.

A body was sprawled across the bed. The man's face was pressed against his pillow, but she didn't need to check to see that he was breathing. She'd never heard such loud snores.

As she walked towards the bed, her horns grew. Appearing with her wings would've been a more impressive display, but the apartment was too cluttered to accommodate the magnificent appendages.

There was a rack of weightlifting equipment within her reach, but she didn't use one of the dumbbells as a bludgeon. Lucifer had demanded that she slay the cretin the same way that he'd killed his wife.

The murderer woke with a start as she shoved one of his own dirty socks in his mouth and tied another around his head, making a gag.

Grabbing him by the ankles, she dragged him off the bed.

The muscular lout thrashed. He kicked hard with his right leg, and she lost her grip on his ankle.

He thrashed again, slamming his foot into her arm.

Pain made her hiss. If she'd been mortal, her arm would've broken.

She grabbed his ankle again and squeezed it tighter. His struggles made her gut clench with revulsion. His wife had flailed while he'd slaughtered her.

Demons were loathed and feared for being evil, but humanity seemed to have an endless capacity for depravity.

Her prey whimpered.

"Mercy? You want mercy? Where was your mercy when your wife begged for her life?"

His face turned redder as he wept.

The brute's terror fueled her rage. She kicked his groin, and he quit resisting.

She dragged her prey into the bathroom and heaved him into the old cast-iron tub. He landed with a thunk.

The hacksaw that he'd tossed into the Harlem River materialized beside his hand.

"Cut," she said.

His fingers trembled when he grasped the weapon.

Of course, he didn't complete the butchery himself. No human was capable of sawing through his own neck.

Valerie left the dismembered corpse in the tub. In a few days, neighbors would notice the smell.

She pitied the police officers that would process the crime scene, but at least the Bronx wasn't part of Dennis Andino's beat.

She'd grown fond of the detective. He really put his heart into his job. Unfortunately, grieving about victims was giving him an ulcer.

Working in law enforcement was a stressful occupation, but at least you had the freedom to quit your job if you were a cop or an FBI agent.

Valerie had been an FBI agent for a decade, but she'd been Lucifer's lieutenant for four hundred and thirty-two years.

Sex with Dennis helped to relieve some of her stress, but physical contact did not provide true intimacy. She could never share her darkest secrets and unburden her soul to a mortal.

Her other lover, Lucifer, had lost the capacity to feel compassion and was a ruthless taskmaster.

Lucifer was a formidable foe, but his ego would be his downfall.

After she'd cleaned herself up, Valerie retracted her horns and left the apartment.

It was time for a woman to rule the Underworld.

Alicia Hilton is an author, editor, arbitrator, professor, and former FBI Special Agent. She believes in angels and demons, magic, and monsters. Her work has appeared in *Back 2 OmniPark, Breakwater Review, Creepy Podcast, Daily Science Fiction, Eastern Iowa Review, Litro, Mslexia, Neon, Not One of Us, Space & Time, Stoneboat Literary Journal, Unnerving, Vastarien, Year's Best Hardcore Horror Volumes 4, 5 & 6*, and elsewhere. She is a member of the Horror Writers Association, the Science Fiction and Fantasy Poetry Association, and the Science Fiction and Fantasy Writers Association. Her website is https://aliciahilton.com. Follow her on Twitter @aliciahilton01 and Bluesky @aliciahilton.bsky.social.

LEE HO FUK'S SATURDAY NIGHT SPECIAL

BY DONNA J. W. MUNRO

I remembered when Master made me. I was a faithful red dog to my master, father of many, and fought by his side in the battles against other masters. Then I'd only had a few thoughts. Please the master, eat the food, love my mate, and sleep in the warmth of my master's home. For those, I'd have fought the demons of hells undiscovered. For a kind look and a pat on the head from master's hard hand, I'd have ripped out any throat.

Walking along the slick cobbles of SoHo's Chinatown, the moments of old joy slid through my thoughts like the foggy fingers of night that flirted with my well-shod feet, dampened my tailored Versace suit, and clung to my red fur, speckled now with the silver of age.

I patrolled for my master's great, great—too many greats to remember—grandson, the famous Lee Ho Fuk, restauranteur and the world's most loved producer of westernized Chinese food.

My master was also a magician, just like all his grandfathers before.

Lee Ho Fuk, who'd never swung a sword. Lee Ho Fuk, lord of an underground slaving and drug empire with tendrils that stretched and grew like kudzu across the western world.

I was Lee Gami, his enforcer.

Patrol done, I lit a smoke and leaned against the brick wall of the alley next to Lee Ho Fuk's London restaurant. I sighed and let the smoke curl out of my lungs. Walking on two legs, wearing suits, brushing my wild red hair back and slicking it with grease was Lee Ho Fuk's requirement. Those days, running on all fours, wind and muscle and howls, lived only in memories and dreams now.

"Lee Gami," the chef barked out the back door of the restaurant. "Lee Gami, he wants you."

I nodded, crushed my smoke under my square-toed shoe, and made my way deeper into the alley. I didn't enter through the kitchen. Master's office and the restaurant had separate entrances so that the customers wouldn't have to see the monsters who came and went at Lee Ho Fuk's behest.

Up the dark stairs and past the guard beasts that once were invaders the Master captured one thousand years before. I growled at the dead-eyed Mongolian giants I'd once fought with. My master's descendants still kept them servants in the endless hell of serving the great Cantonese magicians.

At least they'd been enemies when they'd been consigned to eternal servitude. I'd been a loyal friend to his Master.

At the top of the narrow dark stair, I knocked on a black door carved with images and protective pictographs that had roots in the magic of the first emperor's court. Qin Shi Huang Di had given those words from the gods to the first Lee Ho Fuk as reward for his service of killing all Confucian scholars in fiery pits. Now, this Lee Ho Fuk used them to protect his drugs and his weapons.

"Come, Lee Gami."

I swept the door open with a clawed hand. I cast my eyes down and moved in front of the massive ebony desk decorated with inset gold and carved jade dragons for luck. I took a knee at a respectful distance, hating my master as I'd hated the first when he'd made me into a monster.

Even as the master sat, shuffling through the papers on his desk and speaking to one of his simpering human dealers of the poison Lee Ho Fuk brought into this new world, I felt the presence of myself, bundled in a shroud and locked away with Lee Ho Fuk's most prized possessions, behind a thick metal door with human locks and magical wards to protect them.

My head.

Remembering made me shake with a rage that this borrowed body couldn't contain.

I pressed it down into my gut, knowing that the master wanted that rage, that hatred for a job. He never called me up here if he didn't want me to rage.

"The old witch on Firth is threatening the trade, Lee Gami. She deserves your anger."

I ground my teeth, feeling the spells that kept my anger simmering fall away. I'd boil over and out of this skin.

"What is her name?"

"Mei Mo Lu," Master said.

Mei Mo Lu of the Chinatown Council. A warrior in a woman's armor, Gucci power suits, and Louis Vuitton heels. Slick black hair and flashing eyes. Powerful and wise—her age not hidden by makeup and surgeries.

"She has stirred up the council. They are 'cleaning up' Chinatown." Lee Ho Fuk smiled. "I'd like you to give her the Saturday Night Special."

I nodded and rose while my legs shook and my stomach filled with sick bile. There was nothing worse that Lee Ho Fuk could ask of me. Nothing more cruel.

As I walked along the filthy gray sidewalks where shopkeepers swept the stoops of their stores clean, only to have the trash spilling from bins blow in like a curse. I smiled at them,, and and they saw me with fear blooming in their eyes. Without exception, the old ones always held the broom like a staff and backed into their shops to slam the door.

Their hate fed mine, though I didn't blame them.

I was something that couldn't be stopped.

On Firth Street, I stood in front of Mei Mo Lu's traditional medicine practice, watching the lights as they flickered out for the night. She lived above the shop in an apartment as long as the block. Mei Mo Lu wasn't some poor street witch; that was clear. She came out of her shop with one of her assistants, speaking in lovely old Cantonese about the medicinal tea that the assistant could brew for her *mamm mamm's* arthritis. The young woman bowed deeply, once and twice, then turned and hurried away as Mei Mo Lu unlocked the door that led up to her apartment.

I watched her enter and turn to lock the door behind her. For a moment, she paused, looking directly at me even though I'd hidden in deep shadow.

A witch's eyes weren't fooled by mist and darkness.

She turned and climbed the stairs, and I crept across to her building. I abandoned my clothes in the alley because rage didn't honor designer clothes. The
magic wards she'd pressed into the bricks burned against my fingertips, belly, and
toes and somehow made the rage inside my gut feel justified.

I found a window open and climbed in.

The room inside didn't look like the modern reproductions of the old Cantonese court or the Forbidden City's gates like the rest of Chinatown featured.
Mei Mo Lu's apartment wasn't Chinese at all. The warm dark wood and paper
walls of a *minka* house belied a different origin.

"Come in, Lee Gami," the witch woman said.

"I am sent . . ."

"I know why that Chinese demon sent you. He uses you to destroy his enemies," she said. She'd changed from the modern wear into the traditional kimono
and paint of a geisha. She sat on the ground, knees folded primly beneath her, but
the fire in her eyes matched the one in my belly. "We are just painted tiles to him,
my friend."

I nodded, padding over to her on my elongated feet. The rage pushed my teeth
to points and the hairs of my birth to bristling through the skin of my curse.

"Sit with me, Lee Gami," she said. "I know what you are."

For a moment, the swirling heat building inside me dissipated completely. So
completely that I could remember . . .

"Your master had traveled to Japan as an envoy for Qin Shi Huang Di. He
learned about our magics. Stole our wisdom."

I felt the truth in her words, like a warm breeze from the orchards of home.

I remembered Master taking me from the court, a prize guard dog. Akita Inu,
the great dog. A specimen he might breed with the Chinese bitches. And I served
with blood and devotion for my life, fourteen years of love.

"He made you Inugami. The only one in China, and now the only one in the
world." Her beautiful eyes, full of dark fire, found me, and I knew she understood
my loneliness.

Master had buried me in the ground when I went lame in my hips. Only my
head peeked out of the dirt. He had the family put dishes of steaming meat
just out of my reach. The smells drove me mad with hunger. I barked, snapped,
screamed—but Master just came to me with words. Words I only remembered
distantly, from when I was a pup in Japan.

I saw my mate watching me starve, watching me wasted in the ground with only my head showing. They locked her away because she scratched at the stones they'd encircled my head with.

When the weakness came, Master's sword took off my head so I couldn't die and escape.

The last thing I heard was my mate's mourning howl.

"Then he took your head and wrapped it in silk. Buried you at the crossing roads and let the feet of many travelers torture your rest," she said. "Anger is what you are made of, Lee Gami."

"Don't call me that!"

She tipped some tea that smelled like a hayfield into a dish for me to drink. More dog than man, I lapped at the warm, sweet water, and it filled all my spaces.

"Give your hate to me, my love," she said. "Make me finally like you."

I looked into her eyes again. So deep I felt myself fall in. She'd been my mate, brought from the isle. Akita Inu. My match.

"How?" I sputtered around the tea. In my gut, the hate sat like a stone.

But she just smiled. "Love. I lived for finding you again. A witch found me and gave me these legs. She gave me magic. She'd been the wife of a Confucian scholar killed by our master, and she gave me the promise of revenge for us and her."

She crawled over to me and took me into her arms, laying her painted red lips on my long snout. I knew her then. My beautiful curly-tailed, brindle girl. My Wu.

And whispered it to her. "Wu, my love," and all the hate flowed out of my mouth into her.

Without my hate, I am weak. Human. I fell there next to her, unable to do anything but watch.

My spirit lay inside her gut. The hate that our Master made. My power and my curse tore through her, shooting light from every opening, every pore. The dog I knew, my lovely mate, clawed her way out of the husk she'd traded to the witch for her long life. Shredded and tattered, the skin fell, and she was like me. Half human, half dog, but the curse she blew into the bowl of tea to swirl in a circle until it dissolved there.

She took me into her arms and pressed me against herself, not knowing if she should hug me or lick my face.Wu's, In the end, we did both.

I climbed the steps behind Lee Ho Fuk's restaurant. The newspaper headlines screamed about the old Chinese woman found dead in the alley behind the restaurant. There were police and questions that I knew Lee Ho Fuk didn't want to answer. But it had been what he asked for. The Saturday Night Special.

Wu and I spent the week together. Securing her place. Creating her new identity. Gathering evidence and handing it to the police.

Lee Ho Fuk didn't know what had hit him.

I glanced back at Wu climbing the stairs behind me, licking the Mongolian zombie's bits from her muzzle with fetching flicks of her pink tongue.

We were going to make sure he knew what hit him.

Then we'd bury my head next to Wu's where no magician would ever use it again.

I knocked softly.

"Come."

"Let's bury him up to his neck," Wu whispered, a smile in her quiet growl.

I shook my head and licked my lips. "I'm too hungry for that."

And then we stepped in, ready for a new kind of Saturday Night Special.

Donna J. W. Munro teaches high schoolers the slippery truths of government and history at her day job. Her students are her greatest inspiration. She lives with five cats, a fur-covered husband, and an encyclopedia son. Her daughter is off saving the world. Writing is Donna's painful passion. Her pieces are published in *Corvid Queen, Enter the Apocalypse* (2017), *Beautiful Lies, Painful Truths II* (2018), *It Calls from the Forest* (2020), *Borderlands Vol. 7* (2020), *Pseudopod 752* (2021), and many more. Check out her novel, *Revelation: Poppet Cycle Book 1,* and her website for a complete list of works at https://www.donnajwmunro.com/.

THE CRYSTAL SHIP

BY GARRETT ROWLAN

The former independent movie producer and director Robert Sheridan reconsidered too late his death by drowning. He sucked in a lungful of breath, however, just before he hit the Pacific Ocean, at night and miles from the Southern California coast. He held his breath as he went under, as if, despite his resolution to die, he wanted to live as long as possible.

I don't want them to operate. Those had been his words, left in an envelope inside the boat's cabin, and the words mocked him now as he slipped under the water, the diving belt around his waist.

"I don't want them to operate," he had told Iris, his wife, weeks earlier. "I'm telling you now because when they find I've done it, they'll ask questions. You tell them I was depressed over my medical condition, which is the truth."

With a quiver of lips enlarged by collagen injections, Iris touched his spotted paw. "Robert," she said, "Cancer isn't a death sentence, not anymore. People survive. People have lived for years. These surgeons operate every day."

Robert Sheridan shook his head. "It's more than that. I'm eighty-two in a few months. The body is breaking down. I saw what happened to my father and to my friends. That's not for this cookie. If I'm a burden, if I can't walk, can't make love—not for me. Shuffling around like some old bastard, talking to myself, that's not living. And a lingering death, wheelchair, respirator, the yawning nurse, and at last buried in the obit page, that ain't dying. At least, that's not the way Robert Sheridan was meant to die."

He walked to the bay window and looked out over someone else's Hollywood. In a deep focus of memory, he recalled the premieres of his films in the '70s. Their titles said it all: *It Came from Below*, *Underwater Monster*, and *Beach Party Horrors*. Iris, barely twenty then, had a role in the last as a bikini-wearing teenager.

Eddie had been there too, listening to Robert's decision and nodding. Eddie was a friend and former actor and now gofer. And as Robert struggled with releasing the weight belt, he saw in a flash of airless insight how Eddie somehow reminded him of Boyd Griffith, the man Robert had killed years ago. Something was the same. Boyd was a promising actor—though Hollywood promises often came to naught—who died after he, Robert, and a shady fishing operator named Cannon were hit by something, or maybe the hull cracked by itself, as the boat was hardly shipshape. It happened when they were a few miles from shore. The water was choppy. Robert and Griffith had clung to a piece of wood that couldn't hold two.

It was an event that blemished what were otherwise good years, the years before *Jaws* hit it big, created a blockbuster mentality replete with accountants, and killed off Robert's low-budget style of filmmaking. He went into directing TV shows and made profitable investments in the Reagan years. Years later, younger audiences snickered through his retrospective. Robert smiled, knowing the joke was on him. But when his death would be announced, he would have the last laugh. He would be remembered.

"And let's not forget the heart," Robert said at the time of his decision. "The old ticker is not in great shape, either."

"There's medication for that," Eddie said. He was Robert's factotum and now the owner of a dry cleaning establishment in the Valley, an investment that Robert had helped finance and Eddie was repaying in a variety of ways, errands and help around the bathroom and a bent ear, one sometimes bit by Robert's japes and insults: Eddie's baldness, his childlessness (though Robert's relation to his own daughter was nil), his dependence on Robert, both today and when Eddie was a struggling actor.

Now Robert struggled too, trying to free himself from the weight belt, and he hardly had time for hallucinations, but there it was. Robert was maybe twenty or thirty feet below the surface when he saw the boat. It floated up from below, maybe a hundred yards away, something made of light and music, booming through the acoustic pillowing of water with the distant pounding of a tune

Robert couldn't identify but he thought of an old Doors' song, "The Crystal Ship," and it *was* a crystal ship, all glowing and gemlike, as it rose from the depths and headed for the ocean's surface. He stared at it, convinced that it was a message that he was meant to live.

It was then Robert finally tore away the weight belt and let it drift below, breaking his downward drift. The crystal ship went upward. As he struggled, he lost sight of the crystal ship but saw, in a blurred montage of inner images, his New York beginnings, the huge movie theaters, and then coming to LA and making movies.

He saw too a sailing boat capsizing and how he and Boyd Griffith clung to a wooden slab. Sometime toward morning, Griffith slipped off the plank. Robert held his hand and then decided it was just easier all around to let him go. Griffith reached up and Robert pushed his hand away. Griffith sank. The day dawned and, hours later, Robert alone was rescued by the three men on the boat.

He fought the bursting feeling in his lungs as he went upward. He fought too a grinding sensation in his limbs, the cold water, and most of all the vast black death under him. He thought of how Griffith had reached up, but it was the price of survival. It was just that, nothing personal. He liked Griffith, but he liked Griffith's wife more.

The memory burned, as did his lungs, ready to explode from the effort of holding in his breath. At last, he stuck his head above water. He breathed deeply, feeling that he was sucking in the stars at night. He saw the faint lights of his cabin cruiser with the suicide note inside. He didn't see the crystal ship, but that didn't matter right now. As he began to swim, he'd only gone a few sidestrokes when he felt something touch his feet. It wasn't painful, but the flaccid touch, like fingers of seaweed, that caressed the ankle sent a bolt of fear through him and made him redouble his efforts to reach the boat. Again, as his legs flailed, he felt the hand. This time it squeezed a toe. With a whimper of fear, he made a desperate grab for the fantail and found it and clung to it weakly, as he did to that plank twenty years ago. He managed to lift himself onto the fantail and collapse.

He heard something surface nearby and thought he heard breathing, or was it only the lapping of the water against the side of the boat?

He peered into the darkness and thought he saw a face faintly, that of Boyd Griffith, his features rotted by seawater to something pale with warts of milky white. His teeth were sharp when he smiled.

Robert crawled from the fantail to the inside of the boat and sat. He was cold and shivering and scared out of his mind, but he was alive. He had never felt so grateful to have something solid under him. The last he could remember was when the rescue boat came, an hour after he'd let go of Boyd Griffith. He'd sobbed in relief when they hauled him on board.

"What happened?" they had asked, and Robert had told it the way he'd rehearsed it over and over in his thoughts. Recalling that incident, and its aftermath, Robert understood the secret of his Hollywood success. In the end, he had the force of someone who believed his own bullshit. He'd told Boyd's widow, the same Iris, the same heroic tale—"I just couldn't keep him from sinking"—and a year later, he married her, a woman twenty-five years younger.

Now he heard another splash in the water. He peered over the side and again saw nothing, but he was taking no chances. He started the boat and spun it a hundred yards away from whatever had been pursuing him. He stopped and let the boat idle and remembered the crystal ship, but he didn't see it.

He found the envelope with the suicide note, and he tore it up and threw it overboard. It was then he became aware of a terrible thirst, and he drank water from a carafe below. He dried himself and put on a robe. His chest didn't feel right.

When he came back on board, he saw the crystal ship. He smiled in delight, maybe his truest smile in several years. It was maybe one hundred yards away. Its lighting was bright and colorful, the greens and blues and yellows and reds forming the hull and cabin and mast. And it seemed to be coming closer.

As it did, he saw its lights had a sullied radiance, as if shining through plastic, and then he saw it *was* plastic, that the crystal ship was made of discarded and glowing plastic, and as it came still closer, he saw it was filled with faces without eyes, or mouths, or even skin itself in some cases. He hadn't time or inclination to notice this because the boat was coming closer and closer and faster as it did, and he gave the idling engine gas and floored it, and glanced back to see the ship coming closer and growing larger. He sped away, looking over his shoulder, seeing the ship looming, floating as much as sailing but never overtaking him with its decks full of grim and grinning faces.

It went on for miles like that until he finally looked back and saw he wasn't pursued. What was that about? He had no answer as he piloted his cabin cruiser back to shore, tied up, put on a sweater and jeans, and walked weakly to his car. He was going to call Iris and tell her he hadn't gone through with it, but he recalled he left his phone on the boat with a last message for her, a message of love, before he jumped.

But he was halfway ready to get out and walk back down the dock when he saw the crystal ship again. He didn't see it clearly, but he saw those plastic lights moving on the water beyond the docked boats that he didn't see clearly, and he heard the sound of revelry, but he detected a hostile air, the shouting voices of a lynch mob, and so he started the car and drove away.

He worked his way onto the 405 and went north. As he did, he glanced to his left and saw a face passing in darkness, a face and a grin that might have belonged to Boyd Griffith, whose image hadn't troubled Robert for years but now flared in his mind like an irritated nerve.

Finally, with no more ghouls passing at 80 mph or crossing at the light and looking through Robert's windshield, he drove up the crosshatched streets in the Hollywood Hills and came to his house. He turned off the engine and sat and wept, the fear and anxiety and exhaustion breaking something in him, maybe the cancer making a new push for dominance over his body. He stepped out of his car. As he stood, wiping away the last of his tears with a handkerchief, a helicopter roared just overhead, its flashing lights seemingly timed to the rhythm of Eddie's heart and lungs. Another kind of crystal ship, he thought, but it wasn't chasing him. The police were chasing someone else. There was always someone to chase in LA.

At last, he felt his legs could support him. He passed a car. Was it Eddie's car? It was hard to tell in the dark, the streetlight being a half-block below. The hood was still warm.

He walked up the side of the house toward a faint light from the bedroom window. He heard music, a languid tune of floating chords. But who was listening to it? He moved up the driveway, and through a back window, he saw Iris in Eddie's arms.

They were fucking on the adjustable bed, their torsos lifted almost horizontally. Iris's knees and ankles formed wings around Eddie's sides. The man's head had a full head of hair, unlike Eddie's, which Robert had mocked many times before, buying outrageous wigs on Eddie's birthday.

No, this head was different. Its face wasn't Eddie's and wasn't human.

Robert recoiled from the mouth that formed a grin like a face that was sinking below the water, but it wasn't really sinking now: floating to the surface with those grinning teeth that looked to be made of discarded plastic, looking ready to bite.

Robert opened his mouth to scream when his heart felt like it was being crushed in the jaws of a vice, and he stumbled down the side path a few steps and collapsed. His heart roared red in his chest. Another helicopter floated overhead. It was bright and full of music, a celestial sound that seemed to draw him up to it.

Garret Rowlan is a retired teacher and lives in Los Angeles. He's published about seventy stories, a novel, and a novella. His website is garrettrowlan.com.

FOREVER COOL

BY TROY SEATE

S mall-town — 1961

"Be cool, Dickie-boy," his father told him. "Love 'em all before one of 'em traps your ass. With your handsome puss, you could charm the panties off a nun. You'll have the pigeons eating out of your hand and digging inside your drawers."

He'd taken the advice to heart once he realized what his good looks and a little bullshit could accomplish.

Dickie Lee Dugan cruises past a wooded area where teenagers park to love it up. A smirk contorts his face. It is where he lost his cherry, the same day he got his wheels. He'd played it cool with an older girl, and she opened the door to the hot-blooded world of beaver-hunting. It was *very* cool.

He considers most of the kids around town to be wackadoodles who don't know shit from Shinola. He doesn't form lengthy attachments. He usually takes a girl to the drive-in movie featuring some lame picture about atomic monsters trying to conquer the world by way of one skimpily-clad bad actress at a time. After showing his willingness to spend a few bucks, it's on to the woods, where he coaxes his damsel into the back seat. The girls usually want to talk, a diatribe of words mashed into an unending paste, when all he wants is to take care of business.

He reminisces about these conquests, thighs pushed up to chests, blouses and bras bunched about girls' necks, their eyes wide with joy or fear. Sometimes it is hard to tell the difference. He always finishes with a satisfying piss outside while the girl in the backseat scrambles back into her underwear.

Love? Maybe someday, but all that seems important now is scoring with chicks.

Dickie Lee became the Don Juan of Linden High by the end of his senior year. There was plenty of fruit ripe for picking, and he'd laid wood to as many as possible. A lot of them said "yes" right off. And, with the help of a little corn liquor and lots of schmoozing, most of the ones who said "no" didn't really mean it in the long run.

Small towns love their gossip as much as their preserves they put up in glass jars. The year before, one of Dickie Lee's conquests had abruptly left town, disappearing like a puff of smoke. That usually meant a girl was knocked up and had gone to stay with a distant relative to have her kid. Her disappearance played as well as when Lula Mae McDubb hooked up with a traveling bible salesman and hauled ass out of town, headed for the Promised Land. *Hallelujah!*

If true about the girl Dickie had porked, he wondered if he might be a father. But Lisa had been pretty easy. Hell, she had spread her legs in the backyard while her parents were in her living room watching Lawrence Welk and Myron Floren play "Lady of Spain" on dueling accordions, Dickie Lee's version of Dante's eighth circle of hell.

In the end, the backyard sex-fest had turned from pleasure to pain. In Lisa's haste to cover their actions, she tried to help zip up Dickie's fly before he was ready and caught a section of his pecker in the unforgiving teeth of his zipper. *Ow-ee-wow-wow!*

The remembrance turns a triumphant grin to a frown, but Lisa and his back-yard bang is ancient history. "New worlds to conquer," he says as he steers his souped-up '55 Chevy through the quiet streets of Linden, a town with only one soda fountain in the drug store. So that leaves the burger joint as the prime social hangout.

Buster's is nothing to scream about. Even if it's a piss-poor excuse for tail-chasing, small-town drive-in restaurants had become monuments to sex and rock 'n' roll, and it was the best place in Linden to hang out on a hot summer's night if you were on the prowl. Once in a while, kids from the junior college up in Rayburn drove through town and stopped for a burger. Those chicks were some of the hottest the sun had ever shone upon. Girlish sweaters stretched tightly over bubble breasts, and smooth brown legs dangling from shorts could sure rev Dickie Lee's engine, damn near make him cream his jeans. He might just go up to Rayburn and enroll next year. Boning one of these twitter-pated coeds would take maximum effort, but surely some would let him yodel up the canyon—another one of his dad's expressions.

Something to contemplate at another time. Tonight, he is restless and lonely and horny. He parks under Buster's neon lights replete with fluttering moths. Roy Orbison's "Pretty Woman" is playing over the drive-in's speakers. He could use a pretty woman tonight or even one not so pretty, if she is built for comfort.

He surveys the parking spaces. A hot rod, an old DeSoto, and a couple of beat-to-shit pickups nuzzle against Buster's like pigs attached to their momma's teats.

Tina Reed lumbers toward Dickie's open window. "Hi, Dickie Lee," she says, with what he thinks to be fear of rejection lurking in her voice.

"Hey, Tina. How're they hangin', girl?"

"Wha . . ." Tina looks at Dickie Lee with artless curiosity and blushes.

He has known Tina all through school and was nice to her even though she was a moose. He'd even let her go down on him once. It had been worth the ten bucks she'd given him. No extra cost to be nice to the beasts as well as the beauties. He orders his favorite: a cheeseburger and a chocolate shake. Tina writes the order down and scurries away.

Dickie Lee's cobalt eyes look at her uniform stretched tightly across her moon-shaped bottom. "Any port in a storm," he mumbles to himself. When Tina returns with his order, he tells her he might swing back by Buster's at closing time.

"Sure, Dickie Lee, if you want to," she says suspiciously.

Dickie Lee grins. "Hey, just thought we could have a couple of laughs if I'm still out and about. No big deal."

Like the woman in the church choir from days gone by, Tina sports a huge pair of knockers, and it wouldn't take more than a little humming of some popular ballad to get the front of her uniform unbuttoned.

While a song wails over the speakers about the night having a thousand eyes, Dickie finishes chewing his slab of ground round, licking mustard from his fingers and sucking up the dregs of his shake. He wipes the burger grease from his hands and prepares to fire up the noisy pipes of his pride and joy just as a silver Corvette glides into the parking space next to him. From the corner of his eye, he sneaks a peek at the sweet ride's driver.

The words "holy shit" slide between Dickie's lips as he turns his head to get an eyeful. The female is dressed in a black sweater that matches her raven hair. The sweater's V-cut reveals a breathtaking view of one of the milky mammaries encased within.

Dickie Lee gapes unabashedly. She looks straight ahead as she cuts her lights and motor and then glances at her reflection in the rearview mirror, checking her lipstick. The lens of hindsight isn't always clear, but as he feels his way through a labyrinth of memories, he's sure it's not every day a morsel such as this passes through Bumbly-Fuck. Dickey Lee straightens his back to sit higher. He decides to order something else so he can gaze upon this mistress of the night a while longer.

That's it. That's who she reminds me of—Vampira, the horror-flick chick on late-night TV. He listens to what he believes is despair in the woman's voice as she orders french fries and a Coke. *She's from out of town. She's weary. How about the way her chest is heaving?* He watches her long fingers brush back her hair, fingers that could rock his cock till Dick Clark quits grinning. When she leans in his direction to get money from her purse, he is rewarded with an excellent come-to-Jesus cleavage shot.

Dickey Lee's chain rattles. His Levis begin to bulge as he plots a hasty strategy. *This is mayday. Make a move*, he thinks, *but stay cool. James Dean cool.*

"You want anything else—now, I mean?" Tina has reappeared at Dickie Lee's window wearing the expression of a mind reader.

"Yeah, Tina. How about a vanilla cone with a cherry on top, just for me."

Tina blushes again and plods back to the grease barn. The Vampira look-alike samples a french fry and finally looks in Dickie Lee's direction. Her oval face appears to be as white as her breast. Her eyelashes are sooty, and the lipstick so dark it's almost black. He seizes the moment and flashes a smile that most girls swoon over.

Vampira doesn't smile but doesn't look away, either.

"Do you know what goes wonderfully with french fries?" Dickie Lee calls to her.

"Pardon me?"

"Those french fries. Do you know what they go best with?"

"A shot of Jack Daniels?"

Dickie Lee racks his brain for a snappy reply but can't quite capture one. "I hadn't thought of that," he says miserably.

"Okay, what goes with these wonderful french fries?"

"Allow me to show you." Dickie Lee opens his car door and climbs out, careful not to upset the window tray. That wouldn't be cool at all. *C'mon, Tina. Where's the frigging ice cream?*

When Tina appears, Dickie Lee snatches the cone from her hand, gives her a couple of bucks, and tells her to take away his tray. He slowly, coolly, leans into the passenger side of the-woman-I'd-do-almost-anything-to-screw's Corvette. He holds the cone up like a trophy. "This is it, Dickie Lee's ice cream supreme. I'd like you to have it." He leans in further and holds it almost under her nose. "Please accept it for stopping in our humble little town."

"Well . . ."

"Be adventurous. You only live once."

She smiles. "All right then, whoever you are."

"Dickie Lee. But call me D.L."

"How about Dick?"

"Sure."

"Get in if you want. I might need some help licking this thing. It's dripping already."

Hot damn. Dickie Lee opens the passenger door and slides into the bucket seat, reminding himself to take his time. *Not too fast. Be cool.*

The mystery woman eats another french fry and then takes a long, tongue-twirling lick of ice cream. "Hmm, this *is* good. Is this cherry for me?"

"Of course. Sweets for the sweet."

"Well, Dick. This is pretty impressive. So, what makes you think I'm just passing through?"

"Are you kidding? If you lived here, I'd know it. May I ask your name?"

"You have a lick, and then I'll tell you."

Dickie Lee places his fingers over hers and pulls the cone toward his mouth, raising his eyebrows and wrinkling his forehead, trying to be provocative. "Somehow, it tastes sweeter than ever."

"My name is Sadie, and you can cut the come-on. The fact is, I *am* just passing through. My boyfriend and I split up, and I'm heading west for a new start, I guess you'd say."

Dickie Lee's forehead unwrinkles. "Sorry, Sadie. I didn't mean . . . I guess you're kind of on the outs with men right now."

"Sure, you meant to come on." Sadie gives his thigh a pat. "It's okay. And to tell the truth, I could use a little company right now."

Dickie Lee realizes he isn't the one in charge this time, but he is more than willing to roll with the flow and pray he's getting the vibes he thinks he is. "I would be honored to be in your company."

Sadie sets the cone on the window tray next to her fries. "You're a little young. Still in high school?"

"Just graduated, but I've been around."

"Oh, I'm sure you have with that kisser of yours." Sadie glances at Dickie Lee's crotch.

She's looking at my hard-on. Holy Jesus on wheels.

"What's your impression of me, Dick?"

"Well, it's for sure you're not a missionary on her way to save souls," he answers, thinking another attempt at wit is the way to play this hand.

"You might be surprised," the woman says a bit wickedly. "Tell you what. I'm staying at the motel on the east end of town. Why don't you park your car somewhere and come along with me?"

"Whatever you say. Sounds like a winner." He tries to conceal his excitement. *If only Pop could see me now.*

Since his mother left a year ago, his old man has gone out a few times and appears to still have what it takes with women. When Dickie Lee's mom split, she left a note on the kitchen table. It read:

Dear son,

I've got to get away, but I want you to know I'll always love you. You're too much like your father for me to fight for you. Please stay out of trouble.

Love, Mom

Dickie Lee figured it would take his dad some time to adjust to his mom's absence after reading the note. He was right. It did take the man some time to adjust: five minutes, maybe six.

"It was bound to happen sooner or later," said Daddy-o with a shrug. "Women are so fucking possessive. We'll get by, Dickie-boy, and who knows, she may come crawling back some day. Women need men more than the other way around."

She hadn't come back, and Dickie Lee didn't want to settle for one woman either, not when evenings brought opportunities like Sadie, Sadie, sexy lady.

"I'll park my car up the street," Dickie Lee says to his latest infatuation.

"Good. I'm feeling a little fragile right now. If you drink, maybe we could have a couple when we get back to my room."

"Hell yeah, I drink."

"So, what are we waiting for?"

She is what his old man would call Juicy Fruit, someone built slim but carrying a high and heavy rack. Pops spoke of this openly and often, which no doubt contributed to mom's exodus.

Dickie Lee drives out of Buster's with Sadie on his tail. Glancing back, he thinks he sees Tina through a pain of glass giving him the finger. That makes him grin, along with the idea of screwing the sweet living hell out of Sadie. His radio is blaring out "Party Doll" by Buddy Knox.

"You said it, Buddy," he says as he drives, his headlight beams leading the way, trying to picture Sadie's creamy white torso and thighs in the yellow glow of a bedside lamp.

Then a perverse thought crosses his one-tracked mind. *What if this is a ruse? What if Sadie, if that's her real name, is just tooling me around? What if she suddenly zooms around and leaves me in her dust, makes like a bee, and buzzes off, laughing at the hick kid who thought he was going to get some prime out-of-town beef?*

Dickie Lee wheels into a deserted parking lot and waits. He exhales with relief when Sadie pulls next to him. It's going to be okay. He's going to play tootsies with a real woman tonight. *God bless America.*

"Well, get in, cowboy," Sadie calls to Dickie Lee. One side of his lip curls up in a practiced affectation kind of like Elvis's, and he obeys.

The Corvette's engine hums with power as she pulls back onto the road. A strange odor intrigues him. It is sensual and earthy, unlike the cheap perfumes or skin lotion most chicks load up on. He steals a glance at her bosom resting loosely under the sweater and tries to picture the size and shade of the aureoles, knowing they must be as enticing as the chrome hubs on her hotter-than-sin 'Vette.

Sadie is as fresh as a new set of wheels, something besides the usual creeps and heaps that belly up to Buster's. She drives toward the motel. Dickie Lee has never been inside, but he knows some older guys who have nailed some poon there. The Patience and Prudence ditty "Tonight You Belong to Me" wafts through his mind. Tonight, he can become one of the "older guys."

Sadie puts her hand on Dickie Lee's thigh and squeezes. He looks at her long fingers, luminescent under the dashboard lights, each tipped with a red fingernail. He pictures them wrapped around his cock, but he reminds himself to calm down if he hopes to make it to the motel. He has to stay cool a while longer.

Suddenly, Sadie slows and pulls off the pavement. "I found a little side road earlier," she tells Dickie Lee. "I'm not quite ready for the room. Let's stop and have a drink underneath the stars."

Dickie Lee never had much use for constellations. He is more interested in the heavenly body sitting next to him. Still, he is not about to rock the boat. If this chick wants to do shots or run bare-ass naked through the trees, he's game. He'd made outdoor love with Lisa, but that was kid stuff compared to Sadie's allure. Sadie is stacked, succulent, grade-A prime.

They step out of her car, Sadie revealing more of his dad's Juicy Fruit preferences: a waist you could nearly fit one hand around and a rear chassis that would provoke envy from every chicky-poo it passed, pure fuck-bait. It seems like charm won't be necessary to get this vixen out of her skivvies. *The things I could do with that body... hope to do,* he muses. Sadie leans against the front grillwork, and Dickie Lee stands next to her. He casually slips his arm around her teensy waist.

She gazes at the twinkling sky. "The night has a thousand eyes, you know."

"Sure, just like the song." He turns the woman's face toward his. Her eyes hold the moonlight.

"Wait," she says. "Let's have a toast." She recovers a pint of Jack Daniel's Black Label from beneath the car seat and hands the bottle to Dickie Lee. "You first."

"What are we toasting?"

"How about dead relatives?"

Dickie Lee grins. *All the better to make it with you, my dear,* he gleefully thinks and takes a swallow. It burns going down. He isn't much of a drinker. *Get the woman drunk if need be, but too much booze means no control. You can lose your cool.*

He hands the bottle back to Sadie, waiting for her to take a swallow.

"Do you remember a girl named Lisa?"

Dickie Lee is surprised by the question but recovers quickly.

"Lisa? Yeah, I remember Lisa. She left town a while back."

Make a move, he thinks, *but stay cool.*

"That's true, and she's gratified you at least remember."

"Sure." He isn't about to inquire as to the two women's connection and divert the direction he hopes he and Sadie are headed. "So, what can I do to show you a good time?" The words slither from his mouth.

"Well, golly, Dickie Lee. I guess you can show me what you showed Lisa. I'm sure many a girl has looked dreamily into your eyes, and you've given them what you wanted them to have." The woman's eyes drift south.

She's looking at my crotch again. *Holy Jesus on wheels.*

"Open up your jacket."

He complies. The mystery lady puts her hand on Dickie Lee's shirt and presses her palm against his chest, feeling the accelerating rhythm of his heartbeat. He looks at her long white fingers.

"It's a night much like the one when you were with Lisa."

"I guess." He tries again to capture Sadie's chin between his thumb and forefinger and kiss her, not caring about names, especially those from the past.

"Pull down your pants, will you, Dick?"

"What? Out here?"

"Why not?" A pale tentacle of moonlight filters between treetops, splitting the woman's torso in half. A finger traces a line across his cheek. "Lisa said you were beautiful. I want to see."

Dickie Lee unzips and pulls his Levis and underwear below his knees.

"Oh, that *is* nice. Have you pleasured many sweet young things with this?"

"Some."

She looks into his expectant eyes. "Trick or treat, Dickie Lee?"

"This ain't Halloween, but I'll take a treat," he answers excitedly.

She steps back. "Let's see that hard-on you're so proud of. Wave it like a wizard's magic wand."

Dickie's penis rises quickly as if saluting dear old Hitler. He tries to picture the dark triangle of hair hiding behind a layer or two of clothing. How cool is an erection on demand? Cooler than rubbing a cold Coke bottle against his nuts. That's how cool.

"Since I've seen *you*, you should see *me*," Sadie says.

Dickie Lee watches as Sadie's fingers disappear beneath the roots of her black hair. Her hands pull the wig away to reveal an unspectacular tangle of short brown curls. A small smile, and not a particularly attractive one, carves her mouth. "Let's make one more toast," the woman says. "This time, let's toast to Lisa."

"You said I could see you now," Dickie Lee whines impatiently, starting to feel less cool and somewhat defenseless with his trousers around his ankles.

"Sorry, Dickie Lee, but I'm afraid it's a trick rather than a treat—and you want to hear the scary part?"

He doesn't want to hear the scary part.

The woman puts her hands on her forehead. She slowly peels the pancake makeup—a mask—off in one solid piece. Underneath are vaguely familiar features. "The worst trick of all. Payback," she says calmly, with just a hint of pleasure. "You're about to experience hell on earth."

Despite his effort to remain cool, he can't mask the panic in his voice. "What's this all about? I haven't done anything to you."

"That's where you're wrong, Dickie-boy. You did something very bad to me." The woman now speaks as if she is talking to a child. "You made love to me and made me pregnant."

He looks into eyes, which have turned pale blue, no longer dazzling or entrancing. "Lisa?" It *was* Lisa. The night in her backyard flashes across his mind like a lingering itch. The ballyhooed erection begins to fade, deflating like air let out of a balloon. The sudden rush of desire turning into fear for his safety makes his balls ache. "But . . . no . . . I . . . might . . ."

"No *might*, pretty boy. You had sex with me but didn't have the decency to use protection. You said it would be all right, that priming your pump wouldn't bring a gusher. The time has come to answer for your sin."

"I wasn't sinful. Just horny."

"You have quite a reputation, you know. A handsome kid like you should be more careful, more considerate of girls who trust you, that give themselves to you."

Sex with Sadie is a distant memory. Dickie Lee reaches down for his trousers, but some power pins him against the side of the Corvette. He is feeling woozy from the Jack.

Drugged.

"I will . . . be . . . careful."

"I don't think so. Not then, not now, not ever. Let me tell you a story." The corners of the woman's mouth curve down, transforming her countenance into something feral and frightening, spitting her words at Dickie Lee. "I went away to have my baby but I never had it. You have any idea what it's like to be an unwed mother in a traditional family like mine, a small town like this? Of course, you don't, you selfish shit. I knew what it would be like, so I killed myself rather than go through all the crap. It's all because of your little love gun and your uncaring soul. Not exactly a back-slapping story, huh? Although death took me, I am still in pain, you see. But not for much longer."

Dickie Lee is scared. Why can't he move? As if by magic, the Corvette's radio begins to play "Tonight You Belong to Me." If only another car would come by. But it wouldn't matter. The occupants would just see some teenager showing off his goods to a young woman. They would laugh and drive on, more than likely producing a one-finger salute or flashing the couple a moon. On the verge of tears, he can only hope this is some kind of cruel joke. Maybe Lisa has come back to town, and his dirtbag friends have put her up to yanking his chain. Maybe his dad wants a good laugh at his son's expense. Maybe . . .

Then Lisa's face begins to change. She is no longer the mousy little girl behind the makeup of a sexy siren. Her features are rotting away, running down into her dress.

"Like what you see, pretty boy? Don't you want to fondle my breasts, touch me all over, and push yourself inside me like before?"

"Help!" Dickie Lee tries to scream, but his muffled cry only blends with the childish voices of Patience and Prudence, voices that are changing from melodious to loud and threatening—the roar of a monster now sung by imps of Satan.

Sadie/Lisa removes her dress. Dickie Lee expects to see more rotting flesh and bloody bones, no sexy breasts for sure. But instead, he sees nothing. The form of this shapely creature no longer exists; only the hideous head and hands with those long, spindly fingers remain. They reach out from the dark and brush his cheek. His flesh goes cold with the touch of her hand. He cringes and prays for this nightmare of all nightmares to rattle him back into consciousness. *This has to be a hideous dream, has to be, and it's very un-cool.*

"Are you ready, my love? Are you ready for the rush of a lifetime?" Lisa croons.

"This joke's gone far enough. I've been drugged," Dickie Lee cries in one final attempt at macho, trying to regain some cool, even now.

The dripping skull looks at him and laughs. "It's a joke all right. The joke is on you. Too late to come to Jesus. But here is the scariest part."

What could be scarier?

"Those on the other side are waiting to administer punishment while you give some thought to my dead baby and my bleeding wrists."

"Don't hurt me," Dickie Lee pleads. "Jiminy Christmas, I just want to go home."

"Oh, you'll go home. Part of you, anyway."

He doesn't know he is crying until he feels the hot tears running down his cheeks. No more bravado. No more cool. "Please. I never meant—"

"Yes, you *did*, and I mean to do what I'm going to do. Enjoy what's left of your last evening chasing tail. Time to dance with the devil. You are destined to belong to me . . . to us."

From sexual anticipation to terror. This night had been quite a trip. Dickie Lee puts up his hands as if they can hold off the hell that has found him. His agonizing screams go unnoticed as the phantom's fingernails, holding splintered reflections of the silver moon, as long as knives now, slash. Her teeth rip and tear at his nerve endings.

When Dickie Lee's father opens his front door the following morning to fetch the newspaper, he almost steps on what resembles a shriveled bratwurst. A note underneath it reads:

Dear Mr. Dugan,
This is all that's left of your son.
I'm sure you'll want to mount it.

Troy Seate: After Troy read a few stories to his parents, they booted him out of the house. Undaunted, he continues to stand on the side of the literary highway and thumbs down whatever genre comes roaring by. His storytelling runs the gamut from *Horror Novel Review*'s Best Short Fiction to the *Chicken Soup for the Soul* series. His fiction incorporates fantasy, suspense, or humor featuring the quirkiest of characters.

ONLY WOMEN BLEED

BY PETINA STROHMER

I t was cold; it was dark, and his head hurt.

Really hurt.

He could feel something warm running down the side of his face but couldn't lift his hand to touch it.

"What the—" he tried, but his mouth was filled with a rough rag.

His legs wouldn't respond either, but as he tried to move, sharp stars stabbed his eyes, and he slid back into unconsciousness.

"Lew," the bartender called across the smoky room.

No reply.

"Lew," he tried again.

A big man in a beer-stained shirt put down his beer. As he turned towards the bar, the shirt buttons strained across his belly. "What?"

"Shelly's on the phone."

"I'm not here," Lew shouted back.

The other men at the table laughed.

"She says she can hear you," the bartender tried again, "and you're not answering your cell. She wants to know when you're coming home."

"None of her goddamn business," Lew replied to another round of sniggers from his drinking buddies.

"She says she just wants to know when to do supper." The bartender held out the phone. "Talk to her, Lew. I don't do domestics."

Lew didn't move. "I'll be home when I'm home. That's all she needs to know."

With a deep sigh, the bartender relayed the message and hung up the phone.

Lew rolled his eyes at his friends. "Nag, nag, nag," he sneered. "Don't they ever stop?" Most of the men grunted their agreement. "I mean, it's not like they don't know what they signed up for."

"Whad'ya mean?" Mike asked. Like Lew, his stature suggested many nights spent at the bar.

"W.I.F.E." Lew replied. "Washing. Ironing. Fucking. Etc."

Everybody at the table erupted into coarse laughter. Everybody except Chris. But the wimp was largely ignored, anyway. If he wasn't the sheriff's son, he wouldn't even have a seat here.

"Hey, Lew," Mike said when he'd caught his breath, "why do brides wear white?"

Lew shook his head.

"'Cause all household appliances come in that color!"

The filthy coughing that accompanied the latest round of laughter spoke of as many cigarettes as bottles of beer consumed over the years here. "Lew's Crew" even had their own table at Benny's Bar, the one directly beneath the faded Confederate flag.

The only other people who ever sat there were strangers, and they were soon warned off. The old wood was marked by a thousand beer rings, and the chairs creaked and groaned under the weight of the patrons. Tonight, one of their number was missing.

"Anyone seen Hal?" Lew asked.

"His missus probably wouldn't let ol' Henpecked Hal out to play tonight," Mike said, screwing his thumb into the palm of his other hand.

"Well, he's only got himself to blame," Lew concluded. "Give those women an inch . . ."

"See, this is what they're too stupid to understand," Bill weighed in. "We give our wives nice houses full of nice things and all they've gotta do is look after them and the husbands who provided them. They're not the ones hauling timber at the mill all day."

"Well, to be fair," Mike said, "neither are you, you lazy bastard!"

"It's my bad back—you know it is."

Bill's old excuse was met with the usual heckling.

"He has a point, though," Lew added. "I work all week, out in all weathers, so Shelly don't have to take a job. That woman wouldn't know hard work if it jumped up and bit her fat ass."

"You had eight kids." Narrowed eyes peered at Chris, a lone voice crying in this sea of chauvinism.

"Sissy Chrissy speaks!" Lew jeered at him. "I did have eight kids. All boys," he added proudly. "What's your point?"

"Well, they didn't bring themselves up, did they?"

"They're all grown now," Lew countered.

"And poor Shelly's worn out. All she wanted to know was when to make supper for you."

"Still waiting for your point, boy."

"You could just make her feel wanted, feel appreciated, once in a while." Chris didn't bother adding "loved" to that list.

"She'll feel the back of my hand again if she keeps pestering me like that," Lew sneered at him, and the rest nodded.

"All I'm saying—" Chris began but was interrupted by a loud belch from Lew. The men dissolved into laughter again and the conversation was closed.

The bar door opened, and all eyes turned to see Carol, the young barmaid with blond curls and pendulum hips, arriving for the late shift. Her entrance was accompanied by a chorus of wolf-whistles and lewd jokes. She walked past the men with a sassy smile.

"Now *that's* a real woman," Bill said appreciatively. "If my old nag looked like her, she'd get ridden a lot more often!"

"That's why you gotta keep a fresh filly on the side," Lew agreed, "for when the old mare lets herself go. I mean, if she starts to look more old witch than hot bitch, what does she think is gonna happen?"

"Too true," Bill agreed. "As if it's my fault that my old fella don't rise to the occasion nowadays. After all, the angle of the dangle depends on the heat of the meat."

"Well—" Chris began, but was immediately silenced by the ton of testosterone braying around the rest of the table.

The evening wore on in a fog of dirty jokes, empty bottles, and cigarette smoke until Lew finally hauled himself to his unsteady feet.

"Well, some of us have gotta get up for work in the morning." He sneered at Bill, who belched back at him. "And my supper's waiting for me," he continued, "if the wife knows what's good for her."

He leaned over Chris, drenching him in alcoholic fumes. "Now, you won't be saying anything to your father about me driving myself home, will you?"

"He don't stand up to his woman, let alone his pa," Mike laughed.

Chris just shook his head.

"Good boy. There has to be some advantage to having you as part of the crew, don't there?" He patted Chris' cheek with a hoary hand and staggered out of the door.

Damn, it was cold outside. Stumbling towards his truck, he was looking forward to going home now. The fire would be stoked and the food hot when he got there. At least, it had better be.

He fumbled in his pocket for the keys, but before he could find them, a sharp blow to the back of his head dropped him to the icy ground.

When Lew woke again, his face had cooled and dried, although he was now aware of a warm wetness in his pants.

Over the years, he had become immune to hangovers, but moved his head as if he cradled a rotten egg inside. Some infernal blacksmith seemed to be using his skull as an anvil, the raucous clangs ringing in time with his racing heart. As he tried to shuffle into a seated position, his stomach lurched.

"Careful," said a voice in the darkness, "if you vomit, you'll choke on the gag." It laughed. "And where's the fun in that?"

Lew was trying to place the speaker's voice. There were familiar tones to it, overlaid with a hardness he didn't recognize. However, he could barely tell which way was up at that precise moment in time.

Pressing his tongue against the fabric in his mouth, he tried to speak, but could only grunt.

"It's tied too tight to talk," the voice told him. "Although you should still be able to scream! Besides, I think we've heard enough from you. Now it's my turn to speak. First of all, let's get you up. We can't have you lazing about on the floor all day, can we?"

A chain was pulled through a belt at his waist, hauling him to his feet. He groaned with pain and fear.

"Oh, was that a bit of a rude awakening?" the voice asked. "Let me tell you, it gets worse from this point on. Much worse."

Something suddenly tightened around his neck. Between the garrot and the gag, he couldn't breathe. Ignoring the sickening throb in his skull, Lew thrashed his head from side to side, feeling some kind of sack over his face, the drawstrings now cutting into the fat of his throat. Just as he was on the edge of passing out, the pressure eased, leaving him dragging in ragged gasps of air.

"If you try to fight back, that's what will happen," said the voice. "Scary, isn't it?"

Lew could only nod weakly.

"Okay, let's start with the knife."

His wrists were bound in front of him. Somebody lifted his hands and spread his fingers. Lew trembled as he waited to find out what would happen next.

He didn't have to wait long.

A sharp blade sliced under one fingernail, separating it from the nail bed.

Lew's scream was no more than a muffled roar.

Once all the nails had been removed, the knife cut the skin around the fingers and peeled it back, inch by sticky inch, until the whole hand had been de-gloved.

Lew twisted and squirmed, writhing against the chains that held him until they cut into the rest of his body.

Eventually, he calmed.

Then they started on the other hand.

Once they were finished, the speaker laughed mirthlessly. "That's how it feels to work your fingers to the bone. And let's not forget the knees."

In a world of agony, Lew couldn't be sure, but it felt as if both his kneecaps were removed with a hammer and chisel. His legs buckled but the chained belt kept him upright. He fell forward, panting in pain.

"Oh, while you're there . . ."

A broad, heavy collar was slung around his neck, bowing him further.

"And that's what it feels like to carry the weight of the world on your beaten shoulders."

Lew was left hanging on the edge of consciousness, waiting and wondering what would happen next. He had no idea how long he hung there, as time had little meaning left. He could feel the blood running down from his hands and knees, dripping onto the stone floor.

Eventually, the voice spoke again. "Terrifying, isn't it? Wondering when it will start again."

Lew could only grunt.

"What about this?"

At first, he could hardly feel the new notes against the general cacophony of torment, but after a few minutes, he began to register their sharpness—and their heat. In themselves, the hot pokes were relatively mild, but as they increased in both frequency and intensity, his skin began to burn. Soon he was howling against the searing stabs.

"When you're insulted . . . and bullied . . . and belittled . . . over . . . and over . . . again," the voice said in time to the jabs, "in the end . . . it wears you . . . out. Every . . . harsh . . . sharp . . . word . . . stings . . ."

Lew wailed in anguish.

"Like that!"

And then it stopped.

Lew finally exhaled—and was punched in the stomach. Hard.

"To say nothing of the physical abuse," the voice added. "Hurt and humiliation. How do *you* like it?"

Before he had time to catch his breath, Lew felt his pants being hauled down over his mangled knees. Chilled metal touched his penis.

He froze.

The speaker laughed. "Oh, don't worry. That's about the only thing that doesn't need cutting down to size."

It was the first moment of relief Lew had felt since this whole ordeal started.

And the last.

The cold chain made his balls contract upon contact. There was a brief pause before it began to twist and tighten. Crunching and crushing, Lew felt like he was being turned inside out as the pressure grew. White hot sparks crackled up his spine and his jaws gaped in a silent scream.

"Of course, some folks would argue that men like you shouldn't be allowed to reproduce." Lew could barely hear the voice over the paroxysm of pain. "But if you do, you should at least know what childbirth feels like."

Another twist and his eyes bulged.

"Try *that* eight times over, big man."

Another twist.

"Of course, the only saving grace," the voice added as Lew's whole world went white, "is that it comes to an end. Eventually."

One last twist and Lew's severed balls dropped to the ground.

His body hung motionless, but his tormentor had not quite finished with him. The strings at his neck were loosened and the sack was removed. Through glazed eyes, Lew could just about make out a group of figures.

Female figures.

Bill's wife. Mike's wife. Hal's wife. Is *this* what had happened to him, too?

Shelly stepped forward and cupped her husband's chin in one hand. He gazed into eyes he no longer recognized. "Oh, poor boy," she cooed. "Three decades of torment condensed into a single hour. Still, we've got everybody else's husband to get through too. A woman's work is never done."

"Goodbye," she said simply, slicing the bloody blade cleanly across his throat, "and good riddance."

Even as Lew could feel the warm rush down his chest and everything else fade around him, he heard his wife whisper in his ear. "And you thought that only women bleed."

Petina Strohmer is a traditionally published novelist and successful short story writer. She lives in the magical Welsh mountains with a raggle-taggle assortment of rescued animals. For more information, go to www.petinastrohmer.com.

I PUT A SPELL ON YOU

BY S.M.C. WAMSTEKER

T he shrill ringtone beats the birds by about three hours.

His head still buried in the pillow, James presses the phone to his ear, unable to utter more than a croaky moan. "Right . . . on my way."

Can't those little bastards wait till the sun's up? It's 2 A.M., the worst time of the night to wake up. Around this unholy hour, his tall body reaches its ultimate state of rest—well, unless he's been out, but that's something he can hardly afford to do anymore. Life's too demanding for it. Too . . . tight.

Fighting back the sticky fingers of that lovely slumber, James places his feet on the woolly wall-to-wall and gets up. In order not to rouse his wife even more than the jarring ringtone has done already—a feat that's doomed to fail anyway, she being an impossibly light sleeper—he slides open the wooden door only just enough to squeeze through. It's old and creaks when the rollers travel over the weathered bottom track.

The moment his left foot lands on the preternaturally cool and weathered marble slabs, a chill travels up his long leg.

We really should replace these tiles, he thinks. *Or put in underfloor heating. Get a furnace. Anything to get this inexplicable coldness out.*

Shivering as he flicks on the sconce next to the mirror in that thick quiet of the night, he takes a moment to contemplate his tired face and bushy chestnut hair. *God, this part of my job is so hard.* But he's not a complainer. He knows that some cold water and a big thermos of black coffee will go a long way to make him as crisp as he is during his daytime OR shifts. And if all else fails, the gratis adrenaline high will certainly do the job.

The house is still and reposing, and when he gets into his Firebird, the road opens up to him like a languidly horny woman. Stepping on the gas, he enjoys the vibration of the 325 bhp engine. *This baby never sleeps.* His colleagues scorn him for buying this particular automobile while having an entire three-kid family to transport. "Here comes Jimmy in his pussy wagon," they say. *Jealous idiots.*

Yes, it was folly to get a car like this, but oh, what exquisite folly. Every time he drives it, it feels like the first time. Saturdays, he goes to buy the weekly groceries at an organic farmers' market on the other side of town simply to extend the necessary driving time.

Felty clouds, solid as a roof, have drawn a dark orange cover over the world. *Must be a full moon somewhere.* Off in the distance, a stealthy flicker of light outlines an individual cloud. Seven seconds later, like a badly edited sound effect, a soft but threatening rumble follows. *A summer storm. About time; it's like living in a damn Turkish bath.*

The hospital is a mere five-minute drive, and before his brutally interrupted dream-mind has the opportunity to slink to the recollection of that unsettling meeting he had a couple of weeks ago, something that only occurs at moments when he's awake at night, and nobody else seems to be, he deftly slips the car through the nearly deserted lot and swivels into a parking space by the emergency entrance.

Pete, one of the nurses, meets him in the hallway, clearly relieved by his arrival. "There you are."

Showtime.

James opens the personnel closet and snatches his white coat. "So. Give me the drill."

"Haitian."

James frowns. "A Haitian woman?" *What are the odds?*

"Right. Contractions, since yesterday, probably. Stalled dilation. Three centimeters."

As Pete reports, like gunfire, they march along the hospital's sterile corridors towards the delivery rooms. Having conveyed the specifics, expectantly, he looks at James, who seems distracted.

"James? So?"

"Sorry . . . did you give her any misoprostol yet?"

"Nah. Don't know about allergies, medical conditions. Speaks no English whatsoever. French, and a language we don't recognize."

"I see. Haitian Creole, probably."

"We are reluctant to give her any labor-inducing meds at this point. Preferred to wait for you."

"Who's on duty?"

"Marta, Josh, and Caroline."

"What? Don't tell me Marta's feeling squeamish. That's a first."

"Yeah, well, this is not your average patient. She walked into the ER with contractions. Never been here before. No papers. And there's something about her."

"All righty then. What room?"

"Three."

A high-pitched howl ricochets off the sickly green walls. James glances at Pete, who raises his eyebrows in an I-told-you-so response as they enter delivery room three.

Seeing the patient, James flinches, even though part of him, some creature roused in the depths of his stomach at hearing the woman's nationality, expected to find exactly this. Well, *her*.

No one notices his disquiet. The woman's face is drawn in a fierce snarl. Her nose, including its bridge, is wrinkled up, and her prominent canines frame the eerie howling sound her body ejects. Only her face is bestial; her body is that of a woman giving birth. Or rather, *in need of* giving birth.

But it's not her appearance that's most jarring. It's the recognition. Some weeks ago, in the hospital's cantina, she had demanded his help.

Minding his own business, escaping the ever-prying eyes of his colleagues after a gruesome OR morning, he habitually eats his lunch out in the public lunchroom.

He has never really fit in with the other surgeons, who wear the kudos the patients tend to shower upon them with a self-evident pride. James believes it should be a job like any other. And then there's his wife, Pamela. He has an exhaustive array of excuses why she never shows up at any of the dinners or get-togethers. Tired, not well, other commitments, one of the kids has a fever, no babysitter. The real reason is that, like a delicate greenhouse flower, or a lobster without its shell, she can't go out. The world is too intense for her. Whenever she does, she needs opiates to mellow the edges of reality. She can only handle the outside in soft focus, and more and more often, the same goes for their household, especially when they have guests.

"I don't want to see these specters, these . . . omens," she once told him. When he asked her what she meant, she had looked at him intently, as if to gauge his willingness to believe or understand. "You know, just all these *people.*" A forlornness replaced the intent in her gaze, and sometimes a single tear would spring from it.

James feels powerless. *It's as if she's lost in the middle of this maze of which I have no map.*

He can't recall exactly when her shield started to dissolve, but it must have been around the time their first child was born. A baby girl, who would later turn into Giselle, came into the world seven months after they had left Haiti.

Pamela had always been a tough kid, a tomboy, adventurous and outgoing, never afraid of anything. So inquisitive and curious, she always wanted to know everything. *Maybe she came to know too much,* is a thought that crossed his mind more than once.

Another piercing scream yanks him back to the now. For a moment, he's stunned with fascination at seeing the woman. *Man, she looks like one of those Egyptian hybrid creatures.*

Marta, a promising intern and a strapping Mexican woman, is trying to tie a tourniquet around the woman's bulging bicep. "Hi, Jim, thrilled you're here. Please solve this riddle."

James walks up to the bed. "Hi. How . . . I mean, *bonne noche, comment ça va?*"

The woman's jaws remain clenched, and her eyes squeezed shut.

"What riddle?"

"Well. This is the aftermath of a seizure. She's had several."

"Okay, so it's eclampsia."

"No, it can't be, because her blood pressure is low. Almost dangerously low."

"Wouldn't have guessed, the way she's acting. Did you check the fetus?"

"It's fine. Heartbeat normal. Not breeched. Ultrasound shows no abnormalities."

"No internal bleeding?"

"Well, we can't . . ."

As soon as James touches her swollen abdomen, the eyelids flick open, and the rest of Marta's answer is lost on him. The woman's face lapses into human sadness and the snarl vanishes, but the white-blue eyes rattle him. Again. Instinctively, James withdraws his hands.

She recognizes him, too. "*Messieur . . .*" is all she says. Tears well up in her eyes and travel down her umber cheeks as she shakes her head mournfully. "*Trop tard.*" *Too late.*

Marta is puzzled and looks at James. He swallows hard.

When James met her in the lunchroom, her deep-dark voice was much louder, jarring even. He recalls the urgency with which she had approached his table and started talking.

"*Messieur, j'ai cherché lontan. Gen on moun la,* " she had said, while pointing at her pregnant belly. "*Chose mauvais . . .*" *Something bad?* She placed her words like heavy rocks for him to read. But he felt illiterate and intimidated.

Almost everyone in the cantina watched them, and Tom, the security guard, was alert. He liked James and would make sure he got to enjoy his lunch in peace. He took the woman's arm to lead her away. In a flash, she turned and stared at Tom, her fiercely bright eyes unnatural, almost zombie-like, against her dark skin. Tom had backed off for an instant, recovered quickly, and was about to lurch towards her again.

"*Votre femme!*" she exclaimed.

James held up his hand. "It's okay, Tom."

His wife. Pamela. *What about her?* For some reason, the woman had been looking for him. In high school he had picked up some French, and thanks to their sojourn in Haiti, he was able to identify the other language. *Haitian Creole.*

James had been invited to educate the Haitian surgeons on the topic of hygiene in order to reduce the mortality and morbidity rate among women and neonates. Pamela, at that time a young and ambitious journalist, couldn't resist the opportunity to dive into the poverty-stricken society and write a first-hand account of the state of the country and its political conflict. Her essay, titled "Baron Saturday, Lord of Haiti and the Dead," had been picked up by *The New Yorker*. It painted a picture of the country's totalitarian leader, François Duvalier, nicknamed Papa Doc.

So, while James worked and taught at the Albert Schweitzer hospital, Pamela had gone off into the communes of Port-Au-Prince. That she had been a bit fazed when it was time to leave the island was only natural, James figured. She was fearless but not emotionless, and in 1970, the year before Duvalier died, Haiti was in severe turmoil. A few people—friends and beneficiaries of the leader—lived opulent lives in classy colonial homes, but most of the population was terribly poor. Papa Doc used the country's other religion, vodou, to sow fear and submission. He dressed like the master of the dead, Baron Samedi, the most important of the *loa*, the vodou spirits.

"*Trop tard!*" The woman's low growl yanks him back to the delivery room. "*Pour moi ...*"

Marta is next to him, her hand on his arm. "James? Are you okay? What is she saying?"

"I'm fine. I was just trying to figure out what could be the problem. You checked for internal bleeding?"

Josh, another intern, crashes the conversation and answers for Marta. "You betcha. We checked, and the placenta is not extremely low. I mean, sure, it's low-lying but not previa, not even partial. It doesn't cover the cervix or anything. Looks normal."

Oh, you'll fit right in, James thinks. He prefers Marta. *But she's too straightforward for hospital politics. And a woman,* he thinks sourly.

"Thanks, Josh," Marta says, her eyes shooting daggers. "Fact is, we're not quite sure."

James takes a deep breath. "All right, get Pete to administer the IV just in case. She's relaxed now. I'll look at the ultrasound to check for any hemorrhaging and then try to talk to her, see if I can find out more."

"How is your *Français?*" Josh asks, laying on a ridiculous accent.

James shrugs. "Rickety. Basics are there, though." He doesn't want to tell them he met the woman before, but he can't understand why. *Well, she asked me to help her and I didn't, that's why.*

She stood at his table in the lunchroom, delivering a waterfall of words, a mix of French and Creole, and he only understood part of it. She made clear her name was Candela and kept pointing at her belly, mentioning "*votre femme*" and "*malediction.*" A curse. Something about his wife seeing bad things after the baby was born. And he recognized the name Papa Doc.

Upon publication of her critical article, Pamela was declared an unwanted visitor and told to leave Haiti. *But how did this woman know that?* She said something about a vodou priestess, but Pamela had never mentioned seeing one. In her frustrated anger at his inertia, Candela grabbed his knife from things on the table, aiming the sharp blade at her own belly. "*Liberté! Pour moi, et votre femme!*" She merely seemed to gesture, not actually about to stab her abdomen, but Tom wrestled her arm on her back and the knife from her hand. All the people in the lunchroom looked at them with alarm. Tom removed her, and that was that. Or so it appeared.

He checks the ultrasound. It looks fine. *No abruption. Still properly attached to the uterine wall.* The baby's head is positioned perfectly for delivery, and because the placenta is low, it's like a pillow in front of its face. The baby's mouth against it, the hands tucked underneath its chin, opening and closing. *Nothing out of the ordinary.*

James puts on medical gloves. To determine the dilation, he performs a vaginal examination. The woman looks at him pleadingly. "*S'il vous plaît, doulè. Douleur.*"

"Yes, *c'est normal,*" he tries to reassure her. Still hardly dilated.

"*Bebe diabolique,*" the woman whispers.

"That's it. I'm going to break her water."

Marta looks surprised. "Really? Dilation has increased?"

"No."

"But why then?"

"I'm not sure. A hunch. Can you check her blood pressure again?"

Marta wraps the cuff around the woman's arm. "Joder. 86 over 48."

At her words, a thunderous lightning flash illuminates the delivery room and the exhausted face of the woman, darkening her already sunken eyes. For an instant, her face becomes a skull.

"We can't wait any longer," James says. "If breaking her water doesn't induce labor, we'll go for a C-section. OR on standby."

With the next contraction, Candela has another seizure. Her shaking body makes it hard for James to reach the cervix. But he manages to find the amniotic sac and rupture it. A river of blood washes out of the woman.

"Damn! I knew it. Get her to the OR. *Now.*"

Another lightning bolt splits the now purple sky with such thunderous conviction it seems to shake the hospital's foundations. *Editor got it right this time,* James can't help thinking.

Within thirty seconds, the bed has been rolled to the operating room, the woman's body still shuddering. Pete hasn't even secured the bed when the baby is flushed out, covered in a blanket of dark blood.

"Take the baby!" James orders Pete as he puts on his operating mask. Candela is bleeding heavily. "I don't like this. At all. Where the hell's that anesthesiologist?"

Marta cuts the umbilical cord, and Pete grabs the child. He rushes out, carrying the silent and bloody bundle to the nursery to check its vital signs.

Marta turns to James. "We should prepare for transfusion, Jim. This looks like PPH, too much blood loss."

"Determine the blood type. We might need surgery too. Right, I'm removing the placenta. The problem must be there. And we need oxytocin."

Candela's eyes are open and white, her eyeballs rolled back into her head. Her skin has attained a grayish veil, as if she's covered in a layer of ashes. The convulsions have stopped, and her body is limp. She seems unconscious but breathing. Shallow breaths.

Standing between her legs, James gently pulls the umbilical cord. *Come on, please, detach.*

"Blood type O neg. Of course," Marta calls out in exasperation.

"What else . . . " James sighs. The hardest blood type to receive.

A nurse rushes into the OR, carrying bags of hemoglobin and saline. She starts preparing for the transfusion.

"Oh . . ." James utters with relief.

"What is it?" Marta, who has just re-entered the OR, asks.

"It's detaching, coming out. Thank god, didn't think it would be this easy." With a slow but determined movement the placenta slides out of the woman's vulva and, with a wet thud, lands in the metal bowl Marta is holding.

"It looks intact, but . . ." He's never seen this before. The big sac of veins has small marks all over it, tiny wounds. As if it got caught in a thorny shrub. Or attacked by a small animal.

The door of the OR slams open. Pete appears perturbed.

"James! You need to take a look at the baby. It's not —well, I don't know what it is."

James frowns and turns to Marta. "Are you okay to supervise the transfusion? Only for a few minutes?"

"Yeah, sure."

James rushes after Pete to the nursery. He cringes the moment he lays eyes on the baby. The infant looks as if it's been put together by a toddler in an arts and crafts class. All over its body are diamond shaped patches of parchment-like skin, but most of it is missing, wet and shiny flesh showing where there should have been skin. *Like a badly wrapped mummy,* James can't help thinking. The eyes are bulging and red and pupilless.

He does recognize it. "Harlequin ichthyosis. Severe skin condition."

"What's wrong with the eyes?"

"Those aren't the eyes. It's called ectropion. Inverted lower eyelids covering the cornea. Underneath it are normal eyes, but I doubt if this baby will live longer than an hour."

"And check these out." Pete carefully unfurls one of the baby's hands. Pointed and slightly curved nails of at least half an inch appear at the end of the infant's fingers.

"My god. That explains the marks on the placenta."

"It won't cry."

James shakes his head. "No. It's not viable."

The baby strains its mouth open and emits a howl, but the hardness of the facial skin prevents the mouth from opening wide like that of a normal baby. The sound is eerie and too soft, faintly resembling the cry of a barn owl.

One of the nurses bangs open the door to the nursery. "James! We're losing her!"

Back in the OR, James finds Candela having another seizure. He rushes to the bed and takes her hand, claw-like in its grip. "Candela," James says under his breath, so no one hears.

The woman's entire body relaxes, and she opens her eyes. Her dark lips are trying to form words, but at first no sound comes out. With an ultimate exertion she manages to expel one last sentence. "*Oblije kraze bokal. Casser—le—pot . . .*" James feel frustrated. He doesn't understand. *Break the pot?*

Then she closes her eyes, and her body goes limp.

"She's gone," James says to no one in particular.

"Busy night?" Pamela lays her hands on James's shoulders as he's sipping a cup of coffee. It's 9 AM, and he just got back from the hospital in time to see their kids leave for school.

He never mentioned the meeting with the woman at the hospital to Pam, and after a quick deliberation, he decides not to mention it now. "Only one patient. But she died. Baby too."

"Oh, I'm sorry. That's horrible. What was wrong?"

"The kid had a rare skin disorder. You could say it had none—well, only hard pieces of it, pasted onto its flesh. It was pretty awful, looked like something out of a horror movie. The baby died either of dehydration or respiratory failure. It had no chance of survival." James recalls its hands while contemplating his own. "And it had long nails, almost like claws."

Pamela puts some fried eggs on the table in front of him. "Jeez, that's spooky. How does that happen?"

He shrugs. "Not sure. A genetic mutation, I guess."

"You look exhausted. Can't you get some sleep?"

James notices something different about Pamela. She's extraordinarily chipper, but perhaps it just appears that way because he is so dead tired. "No. My first appointments were canceled, but I need to go in for the rest. I'll be okay."

"It's madness how they work you. I mean, every other employer would give you the day off after a night shift. Why should hospitals be any different? Just because you might *not* be called in? God forbid you should sleep the entire night *and* have the day off."

James looks up at her. *What's with the spunk?* "A lecture is not what I need right now. It comes with the job. I knew exactly what I signed up for."

She looks annoyed but refrains from pursuing the subject. "You remember my friend Tatiana?" she asks.

"I think so. From college, right?"

"Yes. She's an editor for *People*. I'm going out with her this Friday."

"You're kidding."

"I know, it's been a while," she says with a crooked smile that looks like an apology. They never really talked about her fear of the outside world. "Dinner and drinks. I'll get you some toast." Pamela steps into the pantry to get bread, but suddenly stops. "Hey, were you in the study last night?"

"No, I splashed some water on my face and went straight to the hospital. Why?"

"That jar, that souvenir I brought back from Haiti, was on the floor. Broken, of course."

A shiver runs along James's spine. "That thing you bought at the souvenir shop?"

"It wasn't from a shop. I got it from a vodou priestess. That time I attended a ritual. I couldn't understand what she was saying, but she gave it to me as a gift."

"You never told me you went to a vodou ritual."

"Are you sure? I must've told you. It was in the article."

"Yeah, but I thought you just heard about it. Interviewed someone."

"You must've forgotten. Anyway, the floor was covered with glass, the little doll lying in the middle of it. Saw fingernails scattered around too, and some other blackish, non-identifiable muck. Smelled like hell. Must have been happily rotting all these years. I felt bad it broke, but knowing the stuff inside was putrefying made me very willing to chuck it."

James frowns as he finishes his breakfast. "Well, I'm dragging myself upstairs to take a shower, purge myself of this night. And then I'm off again to the old House of Invalids."

As he climbs the stairs, the window reveals bright blue skies. The atmosphere has been cleared. It has lost its stickiness, while retaining the summer's fever. But it's a dry heat now.

Inside the bathroom, he looks at his tired face in the mirror. "Hello again. How was your night? Loooong." He yawns and takes off his clothes and shoes. Turning on the faucet, he notices something's off. Different, rather. As he opens the shower curtain, his breath stops. In the corner of the shower cabin is a tiny pinkish doll, with diamond-shaped patches all over its body, and red eyes.

"Pamela!" Panic tinges his voice.

Pamela comes rushing up the stairs and into the bathroom. "What's wrong? Are you okay?" She follows his gaze to the doll and chuckles. "Oh, it scared you."

"I thought you tossed it."

"Well, I wanted to keep the doll. So I washed it. I know it's a bit creepy. But in a cute kinda way, right?" She winks and removes the doll. "I'll let you shower in peace."

Pam takes the doll downstairs. James exhales, but something still feels off. He feels feverish. After removing his left sock and setting the foot back down, he suddenly realizes what it is.

For the first time since they moved into this house, the bathroom floor has relinquished its chill.

S.M.C. Wamsteker is a Dutch writer and journalist, currently living on the Spanish island of Ibiza with her two daughters and a Savannah cat, looking to return to Los Angeles, which was her home for four years. She holds a master's degree in both English Literature and Journalism. Her first novel is a coming of age story, titled *La Diary or The Dark Side of the Sun*, and a second one is in the making.

Her short stories featured in several different literary magazines, among which Babel in the Netherlands, and The Stray Branch, The Santa Barbara Literary Journal and Last Girls Club in the United States. In December 2020, *Delirium Corridor*, an anthology of dark fiction inspired by Black Mirror was released by Borda Books, featuring *Offline*, one of her short stories. In her blog, she tries to make sense of the sudden passing of her husband: www.sachawamsteker.com

RABBIT HOLE

BY LARS WITTLOCK

T his wasn't real. Jesse's life wasn't real. And it hadn't been real for months.

She had read up on it. In science journals and medical magazines, in articles on WebMD and Wikipedia. She had read messy blog posts, riddled with spelling errors, in the still of night when sleep and calm eluded her. Disillusion, delusion, detachment—they were all signs of textbook horrors: dementia and Alzheimer's and stress-induced psychosis. The sort of panic-inducing afflictions that only served to keep her up and awake while the rest of the world lay sleeping. So, she kept on reading.

Jesse soon found herself browsing the dimly lit corners of the internet, housing those who had already taken the red pill and now spent their days spreading the gospel from *The Matrix*. They knew. This was all virtual reality. Highly advanced post-human technology, man. Every one of us was hooked up to an organ-harvesting apparatus in the distant future, fueling the everyday life of intelligent machines that had taken up residence in the crumbling remains of our civilization. The feeling of life not being real was a sure sign of the virtual-reality device failing—the device that upholds our illusion of living. The realization that nothing was as it seemed was due to syntax errors and software crashes.

Jesse kept reading. Someone in an online forum, once dedicated solely to unfortunate souls having been abducted by UFOs, theorized it being death. That the realization of one's existence being a mere thin, ragged veil, hiding some god-awful truth, was in fact the epilogue of life. A postmortem encore, caused by a rush of biochemicals and a firework of neural signals. Jesse was most likely, perhaps, and almost certainly already dead.

None of it really convinced her, however. Something was missing. A crucial symptom of hers was lacking in the lists of known indicators of mental illness. Something that was not accounted for in the diagnoses proclaimed by self-appointed, formerly abducted cyber doctors in moldy basements.

Why were there white rabbits everywhere?

This wasn't real. The rabbits weren't real. It had become a mantra of hers. Something her inner voice would utter to her inner self whenever the uncertainty sneaked up on the three of them, blurring the lines between dreaming and waking and being irretrievably lost to insanity.

Jesse knew when it had begun. Not really why, but surely when. It had been an ordinary day at first. She had been driving home from work, not particularly tired. Nor was she in a hurry. And she was sober, for all she knew. It was mid spring, sunny and warm, with summer waiting just around the corner. Roads were dry and traffic was calm. She had the radio on, but on low volume, barely audible over the droning of wheels on the tarmac. It was some old, psychedelic rock song, a persistent echo of the hippie days Jesse's mom insisted on reminiscing about.

The Friday drive home was sacred to her. It was tradition to swing by McDonalds to kick-start the weekend, ordering plain coffee and apple pie, which she enjoyed clumsily behind the wheel while leaving the city center. On Fridays, she took the scenic route home. The winding road through the serene countryside. She rolled down the windows, breathing the fresh air. It smelled like flowers.

She neared the looming woods, which seemed to turn greener and lusher each passing Friday. On the rolling hills, grass swayed between the tree trunks. There stood stalks, heavy with flower buds, anxiously waiting to burst. The sun shone through rustling leaves, sending heavenly rays dancing on the ground. She eased off the throttle when heading into what could have been the motif of landscape paintings, passing the deer-crossing sign. No deer crossed, as usual. Something else crossed the road, though. Jesse spotted it too late as it came into view from under a thorny bush. She slammed on the brakes, heard them squealing along to the female singer wailing in the feverish crescendo of the song. The thump was loud, and she felt it through the seat.

Jesse pulled over and got out. Not wanting to see whatever she had run over, she hurried along the car's side and knelt by the front bumper. Specks of blood ran warm through the spots and dents in the car's white coat of paint. Whatever she had run over was clearly wounded. Badly, by the looks of it. A sudden gust of wind blew a feeling of guilt up her back that latched itself to her spine. She begged for the whatever she had hit to have made its way back into the woods to die in peace. She glanced over the hood to the rear of the car. Saw something white lying on the opposite side of the road. She cursed when she saw it twitching. Nausea welled up in her when she saw white and fluffy fur. She felt her stomach turning when the fur grew increasingly red as the creature drew heavy, strained breaths.

Debris from a fallen tree was in the road. With grim determination, Jesse strode over and grasped a piece she thought might be the right size. She took in a deep breath.

The stick was heavy in her hand. A solid piece of oak. She weighed it as she crossed the road. Jesse had grown up with cats and dogs. Farm animals from A to Z and beyond. Rodents of all kinds. Hamsters, guinea pigs. And bunnies. She knew she had run over a rabbit the instant she saw the bloodstained white fur, the big but crooked hind legs, and the long ears. Perhaps someone's escaped pet, she thought as she stood over it, balancing the heavy stick in her hand. You don't get too many white ones in the wild.

The blood ran like a river delta between snowy hills in its white fur, trickling down into the cracks of the road. It lay on its right side, with the left eye staring up at her, hollow and not blinking. Jesse felt like crying. She once saw a cow being put down with a bolt gun and the sound of it had haunted her for many a late night after. The cow's frantic panting before the violent pop of the gun, the jerking movement before it went limp, it all crawled out from within the crevices of her brain where bad memories nested. Knocked on the barred door of her mind and made a non-peaceful entry. She hated to see animals suffering, second only to causing them harm in the first place.

The sun bathed in the solid black of the rabbit's eye. The creature blinked, its chest heaving irregularly, while its ears lay flat. Apple pie and coffee clawed its way up Jesse's throat when she grabbed the heavy stick with both hands. The rabbit blinked again. Once, twice.

"Sorry, little guy." Jesse hoisted the stick above her head.

"Yes, you certainly will be," the rabbit said, and everyone laughed coarsely.

Jesse awoke to the loud beeping of her microwave oven. She got most of her sleeping done between coming home from work and eating dinner nowadays. The canned laughter emanating from a faceless sitcom audience off camera filled her apartment. She had trouble sleeping without the sound of the TV. It mattered less what was on. She saw some lovable goof trying to score a one-night stand and getting turned down by the hot girl in the bar. He would certainly be going home alone tonight, the girl said. Cue laughing track number fifty-seven. Both of them bore the heads of white rabbits.

She got up from the sofa and grabbed the leftovers from yesterday's leftovers out of the microwave. Her dreams were vivid and dark, oftentimes ending with her standing over the soon-to-be roadkill with a stick in hand. In reality, she never did strike the dying rabbit. She couldn't do it. Instead, she had sat in the dirt next to it, waiting for it to die. When its chest had stopped heaving and its eyes had gone hazy and blank, she had buried it where she had been sitting. Laid sticks in a cross next to the makeshift grave. After that, she went home. And then there were white rabbits wherever she went.

As she zapped through the TV channels, she noticed that all the shows were corrupted by what she had decided was most likely the guilt never letting go of her spine. It was either that or the slow realization that she was going off the rails, heading for an everlasting mental purgatory. She watched a nature documentary. David Attenborough whispered softly about the relentlessness of life. About how the lion would tirelessly stalk and hunt the wounded gazelle across the tranquil African savanna until the gazelle simply gave up out of exhaustion. David Attenborough failed to mention that there was no lion or gazelle to be seen. Just white rabbits lolling about in the tall, sunburned grass, black eyes staring into the documentary crew's camera. Another couple of rabbits debated climate change on the next channel. The Southern Strangler, a foul-looking white rabbit with a scar over the left eye, was grinning in a mugshot when commercials came on. "An all-new episode of *Wicked Killers: Southern Terror*—Tuesday at 11," the tagline read.

Jesse turned the TV off. In the dark reflection of the screen, behind her, in the farthest murky corner of her apartment, which the streetlight outside failed to illuminate, stood the worst rabbit of them all. She bit her tongue, forcing the scream trying to escape from between her lips to stay inside. The rabbit, a sickly greyish white, man-sized bipedal lagomorph with liquid red eyes pouring out of its split skull, grinned at her as she squeaked. Two long, yellow, jagged teeth hung like broken tusks from its upper jaw, unexplainably glistening despite the dense darkness. Jesse was mostly used to her world succumbing to the infestation of rabbits. Six months had come and gone since the accident, but the one in the corner never failed to scare her. It dragged its legs over the floor where it stood; the claws scratching the wooden floor, breathing vehemently, chattering hideously and reeking of iron and dirt. She had bought a lamp especially for that particular section of her apartment, and she cursed herself for having forgotten to turn it on.

It was the first rabbit she had seen a couple of weeks after the accident. She had stood in the doorway, shutting off the living room lights on her way to the bedroom, when it had first appeared. As she flipped the switch, the light of the bulbs slowly waning as her eyes adjusted to the sudden dark. It had seemed to step out from the wall itself over in the far corner behind the sofa. Emerging from the shadows, silent and fluid, as smoke from a toxic fire. It had risen slowly, as if limbs and muscles were strained from cowering patiently inside the foundations of her home, feeding on her guilt and bad thoughts. Then it had just stood there, with its wide, abhorrent grin. When fear and instinct tore Jesse's mind free and she had turned on the lights again, it was gone.

For that reason, Jesse didn't bother to turn around and look. She didn't bother facing the thing whose terrifying reflection haunted the TV screen. The furry corner dweller of nightmares was never there when she went to check. Only its scent would linger, a stench of malice and evil. She went out on the balcony instead. Looked at the couple in the apartment across the street. They were pressed up against the window, fucking like rabbits. In every sense of the phrase.

Her work went to hell and beyond fast. Her sales numbers plummeted along with her mood. She lashed out at those precious potential customers over the phone. They weren't precious to her. They were sad and angry people, trapped in loveless marriages and dead-end jobs, counting the days until their next and final cardiac arrest. She told them, too, sometimes.

"What the hell kind of shitty salesman are you?" said Mr. Serling, a junior executive at some firm that might be in need of reliable communications and web solutions for medium-sized enterprises, over the crackle on the phone.

"The kind who doesn't really give a shit anymore," Jesse said.

"You should look for a new job, sweetheart," said Mr. Serling. "You're shit at sales."

"I blame the rabbits, Mr. Serling," Jesse sighed.

"You blame the what?" asked Mr. Serling.

"The rabbits, Rod. Not turtles. It's rabbits all the way down."

"Don't call me again. And it's Tommy, by the way. Not that you care."

"You're right, I don't."

"Are you stoned?"

"If only," Jesse said and hung up.

Cary stood up in her office cubicle, peered over the padded partition. She wasn't one of the rabbits. Not yet. She kind of looked like one, though. Long teeth, exposed gums, and a small, upwards-pointing nose. Cary was the boss's pet. Not that far from being an actual one, really.

"You're screwing it up for the rest of us, you know," she said sourly.

"Please, Cary," Jesse sighed, resting her head in trembling palms.

"Go home, J. Call in sick. Or go travel. Whatever, really. You're miserable here."

"I'm miserable everywhere, Cary."

"Why?"

"Because everywhere I go, they are there."

Jesse had tried talking about it to the few people around her who would feel obligated to listen. It wasn't easy trying to explain the excess of rabbits in her life. Mom and Dad urged her to seek help and offered to pay for any treatment the doctors deemed necessary—whatever she'd need, just as long as they didn't have to face their daughter's delusions themselves. She didn't have a lot of close friends, either. Nadine was abroad, finding herself and the meaning of it all in lukewarm mimosas on a beach. And Lola was head over heels in love with being a soon-to-be mom and had other things to worry about. Jesse had a couple of exes she still hung out with sometimes, but relations were already strained. If not for the tainted history of love and carnal sin, then for their new spouses and girlfriends not being all too happy about their significant others hanging out with an ex.

Cary was just a coworker. And not one that Jesse longed to share her twisted everyday life with. She wouldn't need to, either. Not today, anyway. It was 3 p.m.

and the sales manager made rounds on the floor, calling everyone to the meeting room.

It was a regular meeting. Charts with numbers that weren't high enough and goals that hadn't been reached. It was income and expenses and the constant threat of downsizing. The sales manager, a greasy, Ivy League–pretender and cocaine connoisseur called Eric, locked eyes with Jesse as he uttered the words "pending layoffs." She scoffed and drank her coffee. Looked at everyone seated around the table while Eric called for the employees to remember that they were in fact lucky to have a job. That they all could advance within the company. That the sky was the limit and well within reach for a select few, whom he didn't name. Cary apparently took it all to heart, straightening her back and blushing. Jesse looked at Cary. At all of them. Then she looked at Eric. Deep within, she was hoping for someone to ask Eric about the white rabbit hopping around on his shoulders. No one did, so she screamed loudly till the world went black and she fainted.

Two paramedics carried her out to the lunchroom and laid her on the worn sofa. Shone a light in her eye and measured her blood pressure. Asked Eric and Cary if she was a drug user.

"Maybe. Like, I really don't know, but probably, yeah," Jesse heard Cary say.

"Come on now, miss, try keeping your eyes open," said one paramedic, an older woman, well into her fifties.

Jesse opened her eyes. Nodded to the female paramedic. Answered questions about medical conditions and diabetes. No, not a diabetic. Was she sleeping well? Not really, no. Any history of epilepsy? Not that she knew of. Any medications? No, but she was open to suggestions.

Jesse kept nodding and answering, her eyes fixed on the ventilation grate in the ceiling. She stared at the furry ears sticking out from in between the slits of the metal grate. Stared at reddening eyes in which lay bathing a black orb, peering down at her from inside the ventilation shaft. Listened to the chattering sounds emerging from beyond the grey plaster, echoing in the metal tunnels running through the building.

"I think you will be all right," the female paramedic said, while her colleague sneaked a peek at his wristwatch, likely yearning to quit work for the evening. "Drink a lot. Water or a soda. And eat something."

She patted Jesse on the leg. Both paramedics got up, gathered their things, and took off down the hallway. The grotesque, man-like corner dweller followed them. It turned to her before disappearing along with them, pressing its paws to its lips. Trying to hush, but making only a long, drooling hiss.

It was late when Jesse left work. She got in her car feeling like she'd come to the abrupt end of a three-day bender. Her head aching, eyes straining to keep open, it felt strangely appropriate to take the scenic route home, to drive through the woods, to return to the scene of the crime and cruise along the ground zero of her crumbling reality. She realized it would be the first time she'd come that way since the accident, and she loathed the choice as she pulled off the highway. It just had to be done. Not even her decisions felt real anymore.

They don't even feel like my decisions, she thought, trying to ignore the faint sound of teeth clicking somewhere inside the car.

The headlights did their best to shed light in the gloom of late autumn. She drove slowly, passing under the last flickering streetlamp as she headed into the woods. The full moon reflected off the car's hood, causing her eyes to water. Jesse squinted, slowing to a snail's pace as she passed murky groves and hazy glades among leafless trees. She tried keeping her eyes straight ahead. In the periphery of her already blurred vision, she saw white figures arranged along the roadside. Like tin soldiers on a shelf in the room of a little boy. They seemed to wave at her as she passed, and she tried ignoring them.

Coming around the bend where she had run over the bunny that had sent her into a downward spiral of madness, she had to stop the car. Across the road stood a crowd of white rabbits, apathetic and dutifully holding hands. Or feet.

Jesse got out. The rabbit from her apartment's dark corner emerged from the crowd. She saw the stick of oak she had held in her hands half a year prior still lying on the ground. She thought of picking it up and beating the devilish being to death with it as it stopped in front of her, eyeing her from head to toe and back again. It tilted its head to one side, whereupon the surrounding rabbits did the same—as if they were hard-wired into one another, connected by some unholy force.

"What the fuck do you want?" she said.

The rabbit nodded, its subjects mimicking, as if contemplating whether to dignify her with an answer. And then it spoke.

"Many are the moonless nights we have waited for you, girl," it said in a sort of croaking voice, its accent and cadence reminiscent of something favored by radio presenters long past.

"Why?" Jesse asked defiantly, determined not to question the reality, or lack of it, standing before her.

"For it is you and you alone, girl, who caused us a great deal of hardship and sorrow," it answered.

"What is this? What do you want from me?" Jesse said.

"An eye for an eye, girl. Such is the order of nature and all things."

Jesse stared at the rabbit. His glaring eyes examined her. It began stomping its right leg, its nose wiggling as if trying to smell her. More white rabbits emerged from behind boles of trees, from behind bushes and boulders. They closed in around her, all stomping their feet in a heinous rhythm. The talking one nudged her forward with its front feet, down along a seemingly abandoned hiking trail, leading away from the road and into the woods and the night.

The procession of white rabbits hopped along behind Jesse as she walked the trail.

"For it is we who bring the young girl to thee. We who pass the final judgement. We who ask of thee to lay thy eye, all seeing, on this girl who to us has returned!"

The talking rabbit held mass behind her, the others chanting and chattering in its wake, as they emerged on the other side of the woods, passing into a desolate land of moonlit plains. Trudging through a rancid, marshy land, the temperature fell as they carried on. The air reeked with the excrement and the remains of animals putrefying in shallow puddles of brown water. In the distance, Jesse saw the outlines of a massive tree. The rabbits turned increasingly frantic with every step.

The trail ended in front of the tree, a withered oak with crooked, drooping branches. Dug out from under the trunk gaped a large, seemingly bottomless pit. From it seemed to emanate a distant rumble, a deep, resonant roar as if a wildfire raged deep underground. The talking one turned Jesse around and pushed her to her knees. Then it laid its muddy feet on her shoulders. The moon shone impossibly bright in the sky behind her captor, crowning the abomination with a cold, lifeless halo.

"You've wronged us, girl. Hurt us deeply," the rabbit said, and the others wailed as if in tremendous pain.

"How have I wronged you?" Jesse asked, adamant about not fearing what might come to be, as none of this could possibly be real.

"You took the life of one of us. And you prolonged its suffering. We all felt it. And we all cried as we lay dying by your hesitant hand."

"I'm sorry. I really am," Jesse tried.

"Sorrow is of little worth for quenching the thirst for penance," the rabbit said.

The light behind it grew brighter. Jesse could no longer make out the terrifying facial features of the one before her. She covered her eyes with her hand.

"We have been waiting for you, girl. Biding our time, patient but longing."

"Longing for what? What is this? Who are you?" she shouted, hoping that this new kind of nightmare would end the way all other nightmares did—with her awaking on the sofa back home.

"For you to make amends. This is your hell, girl," the rabbit said, and shook its head, almost as a sign of pity. "That which you sought to defer with a blasphemous cross by our grave."

"I don't understand," she said, straining in the rabbit's grip. This had to be a new sort of nightmare, a kind more vivid than she thought possible.

"Look upon it, girl. Look upon that which your wrongdoings have called down to us. That which gazingly awaits."

It stepped aside and the scorching moonlight shone on Jesse. She turned her head, closing her burning eyes. The hysterical trampling of the rabbits began anew. Wilder and madder than before. She opened her eyes, and the light turned into an otherworldly, dark glow. She squinted at the moon.

On the moon's once bone-white surface, an eye peered down at her. A pupil the color of obsidian, glossy and empty like the lightless voids of cosmos, watched her. In the iris of the moon's eye, cracked, bloody veins ran like roaring crimson rivers. It seemed to suck the air out of her lungs, draining her mind of all that was happy and good. The moon blinked. Once, twice.

"Many are the years since a girl of men has wronged our kind," the rabbit cried as the moon seemed to draw nearer, while the earth trembled from impossible numbers of stomping feet. The hills and plains around them were bathed in furry white, like the topside of cottony clouds as seen from an airplane.

"What is your name, girl?" the rabbit asked.

"Jesse," she stammered, not being able to recall the last time she felt this alive and now fearing for a life she hitherto had thought wasn't real.

"I've been with you long, girl. I've stood by your bedside, whispering your wrongdoings into your ear, watching you writhe and whimper in the terrors of night," it said.

"Am I dreaming now?" Jesse asked, hoping to wake up.

"Not all who behold white rabbits dream."

It ran its claws along her neck and Jesse felt the burn and the bloodletting as her skin snapped and tore.

"What the fuck do you want of me?!" she cried.

"For you to endure what pain you caused us. We want for your flesh and fears and fantasies to fertilize our earth from within."

"How? How do I do it?!" Jesse screamed.

"Sacrifice!"

The roaring from the pit grew louder. She realized the sound of crackling in the ground was more akin to the chattering of a leviathan rabbit, something with jaws and teeth the size of mountain ranges and deep-sea trenches.

"Have you been taken ill by our presence, girl?" the rabbit asked.

"I have," she sobbed.

"Do you wish it to end, girl?"

"I do," she said—and meant it.

"So it is that a rabbit must do what a girl would not. To end the suffering."

The other rabbits all cried out in unison, feral chants that rose up together and grew into ear-shattering shrieks. They all cried the same phrase, falling in and out of rhythm. The talking rabbit seemed to smile, a smile that was insidious yet strangely content. Then it turned around and kicked her in the chest with its hind legs. Her ribcage shattered from the impact. It felt like she was burning up from inside. And then she fell, limp like a slaughtered cow, into the pit underneath the crooked oak tree. Plunging headfirst into the unknown.

Tumbling along the pit's sides, bones cracking and breaking on protruding rocks, before her sight surrendered to the hits and blows, she glimpsed what lay in wait at the heart of the dark. She saw a maelstrom of jagged teeth, a maw the size of a primordial meteor crater. Eyes blazing like the orifice of raging volcanoes in the gut of the Earth. It bellowed like thunder, gnawing in anticipation of the gift of flesh sent from the land of the once free and the home of the now doomed. Jesse tried screaming, only for it to drown in the barely distinguishable chants of countless white rabbits from above:

"Feed the head! Feed the head! Feed the head!"

Lars Wittlock is a Swedish author, hopelessly in love with the horrific, the weird, and all things fantastic, fueled by the fascination of the macabre and fear of the unknown. Born and living in Sweden, he cut his teeth on tales and legends whispered throughout Scandinavian history. His works deal with the nature of reality and the unfortunate ones living through the strange corruption of it. He works as a subtitler and journalist and writes stories of the otherworldly because everyday life is a little too mundane without it. His works have been published in anthologies and podcasts.

SOULS FOR SALE

I Wanted Everything

W elcome back! Glad you're still with us for the second installment of *Vinyl Cuts*. Tonight's set may be shorter but is no less intense. Are you willing to pay the ultimate price for success? The next four tales may change your mind. The consequences of riffing on the dark side may be closer than they appear.

GOLD DUST WOMAN

BY K.L. LORD

F rankie blinked fiercely a few times to bring the bright figure into focus. The
   fae hovered in front of her, exuding an opalescent golden glow that dusted
the air around her as butterfly-like wings fanned lazily to keep her afloat. Frankie's
heart swelled and she gripped her guitar to keep from jumping up to hoot and
holler. It worked. *It worked.* There was a fae right in front of her.

"You came." Frankie's voice was low and breathless.

"Indeed. What a charming little setup. Someone's been a busy bee."

"I'm so glad you like it. What should I call you?"

"Whatever you like, my dear." The fae's voice was high and light, like the
tinkling of chimes.

"Goldie," Frankie blurted out. Her very own Gold Dust Woman, just like the
song she'd been singing.

The small fae threw her head back in laughter, bobbing up and down, showing
double rows of needle-like teeth. Frankie stifled a gasp. The hairs on the back of
her neck stood on end despite the warmth of the summer day.

"Sing me another song," Goldie bid her.

Frankie strummed the opening of "A Woman Left Lonely" without hesitation. This was what she'd been hoping for, and no way would she blow her shot now. The fae settled onto one of the toadstools inside the faerie circle and closed her eyes. When Frankie finished, she set the guitar on the grass next to her. Goldie had slid down onto her back at some point during the performance, and her bare, shimmering legs swung back and forth.

"What is *your* name, mortal?" A little grin broke out across Goldie's face, a scant hint of teeth showing.

"Oh, Goldie." Frankie let out an uncomfortable laugh. "I knew enough to work on this circle. Did you think I wouldn't know not to tell you my name?"

"Clever girl. But I had to try." Goldie winked at her, then rolled off the mushroom and sauntered over to the spread of treats. Placed at the base of the willow at the heart of the circle, a dollhouse bistro table, replete with a silver cup no bigger than a thimble. The cup was cast from a silver bracelet her grandmother had left her—a gift and a sacrifice.

"You can call me Janis." Heat surged to her cheeks. It felt a bit presumptuous, but this was just between her and Goldie.

Goldie did not respond. Instead, she ladled milk into the thimble and drank. Next, she tore off hunks of bread and dredged them in the honey, shoving the hunks between her pointed teeth. Once she'd eaten her fill, the fae picked up the bowl of wine and downed it in a single go. Frankie was shocked that the small creature could lift the bowl with such ease. She couldn't have weighed more than a single pound.

"I . . . I hope it's all to your liking."

Goldie wiped a glittering forearm across her wine-stained lips. "Mmmm. Quality. Though I will require one more thing from you. For today."

"You name it—" Frankie stopped herself from adding *anything for you*. That could have been a fatal mistake. She needed to be more careful. "I'll see if it is something I am willing and able to do."

Goldie chuckled. "Such a cautious petal." She took flight again and hovered before Frankie's face. "I require a bit of your blood."

The chill returned and Frankie schooled her face. She must not offend the creature now, not after she'd worked so hard. Despite her hard work over the last decade, she was approaching her twenty-seventh birthday with little to show for it. If her gran had not left her the house six years ago, she'd likely be couch surfing. She was the last of the Darling line, and she wanted to make them proud. Everyone told her how good she was, that she should be on stage opening for

Dylan, Simon, Fleetwood Mac. But year after year, she found herself trapped in the Chicago suburbs barely making ends meet.

She swallowed hard. "Yes. Of course. Should I... should I get a knife?"

"No need." Goldie flashed her teeth. "I'll take it for myself. Hold out your hand, my lovely."

Frankie hesitated, then held out her left hand, calloused fingers facing up. She'd need her cord hand this weekend if she was going to make rent, but the gesture illustrated trust. Goldie landed on her knee and took the proffered hand in her dainty, claw-tipped fingers. Fierce talons wrapped around Frankie's wrist, and it was all she could do to keep herself steady. She clenched her right fist to her belly. Goldie bent her head and opened her mouth wide. A sharp, burning pain radiated from the meaty part of her thumb, followed by a soft, lapping sensation as the fae drank from the wounds she'd inflicted. Blood dripped from the fleshy pad under Frankie's thumb, and she cringed at the sight. She shuddered, a chill settling over her as if this lovely summer day had turned late fall.

When she was finished, Goldie pulled her face away from Frankie's arm. Blood reddened her bottom lip and dripped down her chin in a crimson line. The sight sent shivers down Frankie's spine, and for the first time, she questioned her judgment. The small fae pulled a vial from seemingly thin air and held it up to Frankie's bleeding hand. Once she'd collected a few drops, she capped it, and it disappeared.

"That will be all, my delicious Janis."

"But—" She hadn't even brought up her request.

"You. Are. Dismissed."

Frankie slunk back into the house, not sure if she should be exhilarated or disappointed.

The next day, Frankie brought her guitar and sat in front of the toadstools. She played whatever came to her mind as she waited. Frankie's gold dust woman appeared after she'd run through a handful of her favorite songs. Her heart skipped a beat as the fae landed on a large toadstool, the same she'd sprawled out on yesterday. *Maybe today . . .*

"Today's offerings are lovely." Goldie's crystalline blue eyes flashed with something that sent a shiver down Frankie's spine.

Goldie hummed a little tune and skipped from the toadstool to the table. The inky black of her pupils overwhelmed her irises as she sank her fingers into the bread. She tore it apart more viciously than yesterday. Size be damned, this fae would rip her apart if she chose. Frankie's pulse quickened.

Goldie licked the last remnants of honey from her fingers and let out a groan of satisfaction. "Delectable."

"I'm glad you enjoyed it." Frankie fidgeted with her guitar.

"You desire to be a musician?"

"More than anything." Frankie gripped the neck of her guitar. "It's all I've ever wanted. It's who I am."

"Oh? And what makes you believe this?"

"My mother named me after her favorite singer. I can't remember not having a guitar in my hand. I only feel at home, at ease, when I'm on stage." The words rushed out of her. She wanted the fae to know she meant it. That she was serious.

"So, you were born to sing?"

"Yes." Frankie wanted to cry, but she held it in. "Please, what do you need from me?"

"My darling, I am so glad you asked. I require a tooth."

Frankie blinked at Goldie, wanting to believe she was joking. "A tooth...from who?"

"One of yours will suffice."

After a long pause, where Frankie searched the fae's face to see if she was joking, Goldie said, "Go ahead. I'll wait and enjoy some of this delicious wine."

Frankie got up and went inside. *Am I really going to do this?* It wasn't really a question, though. *I can't stop now. I've come too far to anger Goldie and ruin this. Okay. Okay. I can do this.* She pulled a tray of ice out of the freezer and took it to the bathroom. She located the gauze and some oral numbing rub from her last canker sore. *Pliers.* Suppressing a shudder, she dug around the hall closet until she located the needle-nose pliers and the slip-joint pliers, unsure which would work better. Back in the bathroom, she washed both pairs of pliers with hot, soapy water and then doused them with rubbing alcohol. Next, she soaked a piece of gauze with the numbing gel and shoved it between her right upper lip and gum in hopes of deadening the pain. She rubbed some more of the gel on the inside, behind her first bicuspid, and then held an ice cube to the spot.

Seconds ticked by, and Frankie wondered if Goldie was still waiting for her. Her belly tightened. *Now or never*. Frankie discarded the ice and gauze and contemplated the pliers. With a deep inhale, she picked up the needle-nosed pair and clamped it against the bicuspid. Immediately, the pliers slipped from her tooth, slamming into her lower lip. Blood welled from where the inside hit her lower tooth.

"Fuck."

She tried again with the slip-joint pair. Same outcome. Her lower lip throbbed, but all her teeth remained firmly in her head. Laughter bubbled up and escaped as a deranged giggle. Tossing the pliers into the sink, Frankie ran back to the toolbox. This time she grabbed the hammer and wood chisel—the tooth needed to be loose first. That was the problem. Looking in the mirror, she lined the chisel up with the bicuspid, pulling the flesh lip back as she did. The first hit was light. Practice, she told herself. Hit number two landed with enough force to cause her to cry out. She tried not to gag when the first drops of blood hit her tongue. Number three landed with force. Frankie dropped the hammer and cupped her face in her hands. Tears streamed down her face, and blood pooled in her hands, dripping onto her pale gray rug.

After a few deep breaths, Frankie stood up and examined the damage. Blood oozed from between several of her teeth. The bicuspid wiggled some, but not enough. More tears fell as she picked up the chisel and hammer one more time. Pain bloomed up her cheek and through her jaw with the fourth hit. This time, she collapsed to the floor with the discarded hammer. A sob wracked through her, and she vomited. *Almost done*. Determined, she got back to her feet and grabbed the slip-joint pliers. Without hesitating or giving herself time to doubt her actions, she secured the pliers and yanked. Roots ripped from her gum with a crunch that resonated internally. Now, the tooth dangled, still partially attached. Suppressing another sob, Frankie finished the job.

Frankie walked out of the house into the backyard, blood and drool running down her chin. In her hand, she clenched the precious tooth. She hadn't even bothered to put more gauze or ice in her mouth. At the faerie circle, she opened her hand.

Goldie clapped her hands and bounced up and down on her toadstool. "Very good, my dear." She plucked the proffered bicuspid—nearly as large as her own hand.

"That will be all."

"Wait. . ." The word was slurred with blood and pain.

Goldie's eyes changed again, just as they had earlier. The black wells pulled Frankie. Those were the eyes of a predator, but she *needed* her. A small sob escaped Frankie's lips, and she ran into the house, leaving her guitar behind.

That night, Frankie cried herself to sleep after downing two PM painkillers and half a bottle of wine, terrified she'd destroyed her relationship with the gold dust woman.

Frankie took the fresh loaf and her guitar out to the garden. She placed the basket of bread next to the table and smoothed the mulch until everything was perfect. With no more puttering to do, Frankie sat down and played her most soulful rendition of "Gold Dust Woman" yet, despite her sore mouth. It was a desperate prayer to the fae, filled with all her longing, sadness, and loneliness. When she finally opened her eyes, Goldie was dunking the warm bread into the honey with reckless abandon. Honey dripped from her gold-tinged arms and glittered with the dust from her wings.

"You came back." Frankie's voice shook.

"Of course I did, silly girl. Did you think I would abandon such fine hospital-ity?"

"Well, I don't know. You sent me away."

"I had to know you were serious."

"About what?"

"Why, me, of course."

"Oh, Goldie, I am beyond serious. I am so relieved that you're here." Frankie's words ran together in a breathless surge. "Will you help me?"

"That depends."

"On?"

"Your third day's offering."

"I've laid out all my offerings. I have nothing left to give."

The fae laughed, sharp teeth showing.

Frankie held her breath, not sure what else the gold dust woman could possibly want from her. More than a year of her life had gone into this project. It couldn't end with a flap of this little bitch's wings, no deal even mentioned, could it? She'd sacrificed a tooth, yanked from her own head. Nothing else could be that bad.

"Play a game with me."

Goldie went back to her favorite toadstool with a skip and a hop, a playful light in her eyes. The fae swung her dangling legs back and forth like a child and clapped her hands.

Frankie shrugged and nodded. Knowing she'd do whatever necessary to get her favor.

"What kind of game?"

"One of truths. I will ask you questions. If I can tell truth from lie, I win. If you can fool me, you win."

"What is it that we win?"

"You'll win your dream, dear Janis."

Frankie's heart sped up in her chest. Here was her chance. Tell the truth. Simple as that.

"What is your favorite color?"

"Lilac."

"Favorite song?"

"Blue."

Easy peasy. If this kept up, she'd be singing on a stage with a crowded audience in some stadium in no time.

"What is your deepest fear?"

"Oh." Frankie paused, racking her brain. Spiders, heights, not convincing this fae to make her into Janis, dying alone and unknown with nothing to show for her life... "Failure."

It came out sounding more like a question than a statement of fact.

"Is that so?"

"Yes." Her voice sounded only slightly surer.

Goldie flitted up in front of Frankie's face. "How fae of you to only tell a partial truth instead of an outright lie, but I know *failure* isn't the extent of your deepest fear. Is it, my dear?"

Frankie shook her head, refusing to meet the fae's gaze.

"Since you did not lie per se, I'll give you another chance."

"Anything!" Frankie clasped her hands over her mouth, knowing she'd have to comply with anything the fae wanted after that utterance.

"Gift me an organ of your own free will, and I will consider you the winner of this game."

"An . . . organ? Which organ? How do I even do that?" Frankie's voice rose to a pitch she didn't recognize.

"If you don't want to . . ."

"No," she shouted. "I'll do it. But I'll need your help. Come inside with me?"
Frankie stood, legs shaking and turned toward the house.

"Bring some knives and bandages. I'll wait."

Frankie darted inside and slammed the door behind her. How stupid she'd been, thinking any game with a fae would be easy to win. She'd been careless with her answers, lulled into security by the first few softball questions. Now, she was rummaging through the first aid drawer looking for supplies to stop the bleeding after she cut out one of her own organs. A hysterical bubble of laughter escaped a chilling sound in the silence of her home. In the end, she grabbed the entire drawer and took it with her, piling towels on top, and stopping in the kitchen to grab the X-Acto knife she kept for projects. It seemed the most scalpel-like object in the house. Her pulse throbbed in her temples and her hands shook as she went out the back door.

There was no time to think—no time to second guess herself. This one last thing, and her wish would be granted. She laid everything on the ground inside the faerie circle and said, "This is the last thing I have to do, right? And then you'll grant my wish?"

The little gold dust woman flitted up and stroked her cheek. "The wish will be yours when this is done."

Frankie unfolded one of the towels, spread it out, and knelt. Then, she set out the gauze and tape, as well as a few hand towels. Finally, she poured rubbing alcohol over her hands and dropped the entire X-Acto knife into the bottle. She had no idea how long it should be in there, so she went with the recommended hand-washing time—two rounds of the birthday song.

All the while, Goldie sat perched on her favorite toadstool, watching and waiting.

Once the preparations were finished, Frankie stripped down to her bra and underwear. Deciding the only choice was to gift the gold dust woman a kidney, he doused her side with the remaining alcohol and lay down.

"I'll give you a kidney," she croaked. "But I'm not quite sure where to cut. Can you do it?"

"The first cuts must be yours. Right there below your rib cage." The fae guided her as she adjusted the scalpel. "A little more to the side."

"Here?"

"Perfect." Goldie gave her another of those unsettlingly toothy grins.

Frankie scrunched her eyes closed and pressed the knife into her flesh. Sharp pain made her grunt, but she didn't stop until she had a three-inch slice in her side. Blood ran down onto the towel in rivulets, but this was only the outer layers of skin. Frankie went back to the beginning of the incision and started again, pressing as hard as she could bear. She gasped in pain, tears streaming down her face, blood running down her side.

"How much more?"

"One more time, and then I'll do the rest. You're doing so well, my little dear."

Frankie sobbed, squeezing her eyes shut until bright sparks exploded. No pain in her past came close to this, not even the extraction of her own tooth. *Why am I doing this to myself?* To be famous. No, more than that—to become a legend. This thought catalyzed her back into motion. With a loud scream, she slashed into her weeping side one more time with as much force as she could muster. She dropped the knife and lay back panting hard.

"I need your permission to finish."

"Yes. Take my kidney as a gift, my gold dust woman."

As much as she didn't want to, Frankie looked at Goldie as she settled onto the ground next to her. The fae wore a look of satisfaction and determination. Goldie rubbed her hands together and the claws at the tips of her fingers seemed to grow several inches. Those claws ripped into the soft tissue remaining between them and the kidney. If the knife had been a new level of pain, Frankie now thought she might actually die from the shock of those sharpened claws burrowing inside of her. Darkness edged at her vision and her hearing became muffled and distant. Someone was screaming and she wished they'd shut the hell up.

"And what, Billie Francis Darling, is your greatest desire?" The gold dust woman's angelic voice broke through the static.

"I want to be the next great folk singer." The words left her lips in a weak whisper. She was vaguely aware that something was wrong—she'd made a mistake. The carefully crafted plan had not gone the way she'd expected. Her little gold dust woman had already discovered her true name. *How?*

"Very well then." Goldie took to the air and flew around Frankie three times, dusting her all the while. The shimmering faery dust coated Frankie's skin and hair until she could not see or move at all. Panic gripped her as the dust permeated her lungs, and she could no longer breathe.

A humming overtook her. A sense of weightlessness.

Nothingness.

Frankie woke up in a room she didn't recognize. The walls were smooth stone decorated with rich tapestries. A shimmering gold canopy of ethereal fabric hung from the four-poster bed she found herself on. She swung her legs off the side of the bed, and a wave of dizziness overcame her. Nausea roiled through her, and she cupped her face in her hands. The side of her face ached where she had yanked out her tooth.

Goldie.

The events of the last three days flooded back to her. "Hello?"

"You're awake." Goldie's delighted voice rang out from another room.

Frankie stood up and noticed an open doorway. Inside, Goldie sat in a rocking chair by a fire. Somehow, she and Frankie were the same size, and Frankie couldn't help but wonder who had shifted. She settled onto a couch next to the fae and waited. Memories of the last three days pinballed through her mind, refusing to settle and allow her to make sense of everything.

"My name." Frankie finally latched onto a memory. "How did you know?"

Goldie smiled, showing her brutal teeth. "Blood. Bone. Flesh. Together, the pieces gave me your name."

There was nothing Frankie could say to that. She'd made a fatal mistake, thinking she could bargain with a faerie. Her gran would be so disappointed.

"Get your guitar, girl. It's almost dinner time."

Shackles made of thorny vines appeared around her wrists and ankles, allowing her enough range of motion to walk slowly and hold a guitar. She picked up the instrument and followed Goldie down a long, stone hallway. Along the way, other fae stepped out of doorways and joined them: a tall, spindly brownie, a shorter gnomish character; someone with a cap that dripped blood as he walked. All of them ignored her. At last, they stepped into a cavernous, candlelit chamber filled with tables. The aroma of cooking meat filled the air. Goldie led her to a stage off to one side.

Once in front of a collection of sticks and flowers that resembled a microphone, Goldie said, "Here for your entertainment, tonight and every night, the next great folk singer: Billie Francis Darling."

K.L. Lord is a queer American author of horror and dark fantasy. She loves to explore twisted themes and dark realities, often delving into the dark side of relationships. Growing up, she devoured novels by Anne Rice, Mary Shelley, Stephen King, and anyone else she could get her hands on. She is a lover of all things ink, collects books, gothic and macabre art, and tattoos. Find her work in publications by Ghost Orchid Press, Writers Resist, Propertius Press, Ink Stains, and Scary Dairy. When she's not working on her English Literature Ph.D., she's hanging out with her family watching horror movies and doing her own creepy crafting.

THE 27 CLUB

BY SCOTT A. JOHNSON

C old rain dripped down the back of Gib's shirt, runoff from a hole in the tin roof overhead. The clapboard shack across the street looked like nothing special, another shitty little bar that could get knocked down by a strong enough wind, but it had been there since he could remember. Hell, it had been there since before his daddy—or his granddaddy—could remember. It didn't even have a sign outside to state its name, but most folks around knew it as "The Crossroads."

"Don't say anything. You can answer questions, but don't ask anything."

Gib looked up at the man next to him. He looked different than in the rock and roll posters and the slick magazine covers. In photos, Shifty Smith smoldered with the arrogance of a musical god. But the man who stood beside him in the rain bore only the slightest resemblance to his "Shifty" stage persona. He was just Steve, and he looked scared.

Gib pulled his jacket up around his neck, hugged his guitar case close, and followed Steve into the downpour, across the street, and up to the door.

The doorman glared from behind dark glasses, arms crossed and a scowl on his face.

"He ain't old enough to come in."

"C'mon, man." Steve's nervous smile didn't come off easy. "The big man's coming tonight."

"Big man's here every night," said the doorman. "He just don't make an appearance unless there's something worth showing up for."

"He's worth it," said Shifty. "Trust me. The big man's going to want to see him."

"Bullshit," said the doorman. "You're just here to save your own ass."

"I know what I'm doing," said Gib. "I know the rules. You gotta let me play for him."

"That a fact? What's his name?"

"I don't know," said Gib. "But, if he's here, I gotta play for him. Please. It's important."

The doorman lowered his glasses and gave him a good once-over. Gib shivered under his gaze. He was sure he didn't look like much in grubby sneakers and jeans with holes in the knees. His jacket was two sizes too big, and the case hugged tight to his chest was worn and battered. But the doorman's mouth cracked into a smirk and he shook his head.

"G'on, then," he said. "Up on the stage with you. If you're sure that's what you want."

Gib didn't need a second invitation. He hurried through the door and took in the room. It wasn't at all what he'd pictured. From the outside, he figured the place would've been picnic tables and plastic chairs, an Igloo cooler for a bar, and maybe a wooden platform for a stage. Instead, the tables were dark wood atop iron posts. Chairs and booths encircled a small stage, upon which stood a single microphone stand and a stool. A guitar cable lay in the pool of light and trailed off into the darkness while a man in white shirtsleeves served behind the mirrored bar.

Shifty took the front-and-center table and pulled out the other chair, then he ordered two drinks from a waitress who didn't look much older than Gib.

"I'm not old enough to drink," said Gib.

"It's not for you," said Shifty.

"There's only two chairs. Where do I sit?"

"You don't. You're going to be up there." He pointed at the stool.

Smoke drifted up from the tables, stained the ceiling tiles with nicotine and tar. Not that anyone paid attention. The stage lights were too bright, and all eyes stayed glued to an older man on the stool with a beat-up acoustic guitar on his lap. His music was decent, but nothing special.

Anywhere else, the doorman would've been arrested, or at least fired, for letting a kid like Gib inside, much less on stage, even though he was accompanied by a famous musician. But he had to be there, had to try at least. Shifty had promised the man would be there, and he had to play. If the man heard him, he'd make Gib a legend.

Legal or not, Gib shrugged off his soaked jacket and hung it on a peg by the door. When the man on stage finished playing, the audience gave polite applause.

"G'on," said Shifty. "You're up."

Gib walked onto the stage and put the old case on the floor. He flipped the latches and lifted the lid. The guitar inside wasn't anything special. It wasn't even name brand. In fact, it was a homemade job that *almost* looked like one of the more famous guitars played by the greats. A real Telecaster was beyond Gib's budget. Hell, most of the time, a hot meal was beyond Gib's budget. But the guitar was more important than food. The jack buzzed as he picked up and inserted the cable, and the rattly tuning pegs looked impossible to keep in tune. Then Gib stared at the floor, away from the crowd, took a deep breath, licked his lips, and then ripped a thundering chord. The audience stopped their chatter for a moment in the aftermath.

"That's right," said a woman at the back of the room. "Kick that shit!"

"Give us a lick!" hollered a man from somewhere in the darkness.

Shifty's face broke into a wide grin, his eyes wide.

Gib took another deep breath, tried to calm the kick drum of his heartbeat, then closed his eyes and launched into a blistering solo. The big man, whoever he was, had to hear it. If he heard it, he would come. For all the noise in the bar, nothing mattered except the arpeggios, the shrieks and squeals of his homemade beauty, the metronome of his heartbeat, and the screaming from inside that what he was doing was dangerous. Wrong even. But he didn't care. All he cared about was that the stranger hear him and come like he'd come for so many before.

When he opened his eyes, the bar was empty except Shifty and a stranger at the table.

He wasn't at all what Gib envisioned. The way Shifty talked about him, Gib pictured an old man in a long coat, burning coals for eyes, and an ear-to-ear grin that showed pointed teeth. Most of the stories even had a bone-skinny dog that ran beside him. But the stranger at the table was something else. His pinstriped slacks seemed to blend with the shadows of the floor, broken only by the mirror shine of his shoes. He wore no coat but was clothed in a dark shirt with the sleeves rolled to the elbows. A loosened red tie hung from his unbuttoned collar. The façade of a tired working man who stopped for a drink fit him well.

"Been a while," he said. "What're you doing here?"

"This kid," said Shifty. "He's good. He wants to play for you."

"You wanted my attention," said the man with a sigh. "You've got it. What's on your mind, kid?"

Gib stood motionless for a moment. The weight of the guitar on his neck was all that kept him from running away or floating up above the stage.

"I ain't got all night," said the man. "Speak up."

"I want to be famous," mumbled Gib. "Like, Hendrix famous."

"How come?"

"I got nothing else." It was true. He didn't have a mother anymore because she'd died. His father disowned him over and over again over things like grades or the trouble that followed his curious nature. He had no future, and his present sucked. All that he had left was the past, and it was something he was eager to leave behind.

"You got that guitar there," said the man. "Lemme see that." He held out his hand and gestured. Shifty gave an over-encouraging nod.

Gib slowly took the strap from around his neck and handed it over. The man gave it an appraising look, then propped it on his knee and strummed it.

"You didn't pay money for this thing, did you?"

"No, sir," said Gib. "I built it myself." It was the easiest explanation, if a little simplistic. The body he'd built from a tabletop using tools he'd borrowed. The neck, he'd gotten off a broken instrument that he'd found in a dumpster. The pickups and hardware he'd stolen from several music shops, one piece at a time. When it was all said and done, the guitar was no beauty, but it was his. There wasn't another like it in the world, in looks or sound. It was, as the man said, the only thing that was truly his.

"Well, that shows passion and determination," said the man. He nodded toward Shifty. "Where'd you meet this paragon of virtue?"

"I snuck into a show," said Gib. "Managed to get backstage."

"I caught him pawing one of my guitars," said Shifty.

"And you're sure this is what you want? He explained how it works? How old are you, anyway?"

"Sixteen," said Gib. "That gives me eleven years."

"Oh," said the man with a grin. "You're one of *them*."

"I know 'em all," said Gib. "Morrison, Hendrix, Joplin, Cobain…"

His heroes. Every one of them, musical legends. Every one a member of the notorious twenty-seven club, visionaries who died at the age of twenty-seven of one cause or another but whose talent outlived them all.

"There were a lot more before them," said the man. "And there'll be a lot more after."

"You made a deal with Robert Johnson, didn't you?"

"Did I?"

Gib nodded.

"That's what you want?"

Gib nodded again.

The man closed his eyes as he played, lost in the music that flowed effortlessly from his fingers. When he'd finished, he opened his eyes and smiled.

"Okay, kid," he said. "Take it. But know this. Once you're in the game, it's hard to get out."

Gib reached out for his guitar. As his hand closed around the neck, heat shot through his arm, followed by the searing pain of razors through his palm. Everywhere his fingertips touched, the fretboard stabbed and sliced. As he lifted his fingers, the blood pooled, then soaked into the thirsty rosewood.

"Put it on," said the man. "It's gonna hurt, but nothing great is easy."

Gib followed the stranger's instruction. As the strap fell to his shoulder, it burned into his flesh and fused with it. The guitar body sprouted spines, barbs that bit into his abdomen and bonded the instrument to his body. He cried out at the pain, but the sound that erupted from his throat was less agony and more the wail that had marked blues singers since the early days.

"Now play, boy." The man grinned, and for a moment, his true nature was revealed. The teeth were too long, the mouth too wide, the eyes burned with thirst while his knuckles blanched with the effort of his grip on the table.

Gib strummed the guitar, and as he did, he was overcome with a drunken euphoria that only came with the best weed or cheap, stolen whiskey, but it was the music that gifted him with bliss. He hit a second chord, and a shiver started at his toes and didn't stop until it made its way out the tips of his hair.

"Keep your eyes open," said the man. "You've got to know what you're doing to yourself."

Gib opened his eyes. Just above him, a shimmery mist floated and rippled with the waves of sound. Every time Gib let loose a riff, the mist shivered and roiled.

Shifty sat in his chair. Even though he hadn't brought one in with him, a guitar was fused to his body as well. But it was swollen, engorged like a tick full of blood. It pulsed and wriggled. Shifty's arms were thin, wrinkled. The skin on his face was sallow, drawn. The guitar was sucking the life out of him.

"Sing," said the man.

Gib had thought about what he would sing for the man if he came. But in the moment, there was only one song that came to mind. He pulled a glass slide from his pocket and played a blues standard, an old story about a young man who fell to his knees and made a deal at a crossroads somewhere in Mississippi.

"Good choice," said the man. "Always liked that one."

In that moment, it became clear how the deal worked. Play the blues. Play with soul. It wasn't an expression.

The stranger tilted his head back and drew in a deep breath. The mist floated toward him and entered his body through his nostrils. He shivered as he lowered his head and giggled.

"He ain't even had a woman yet," said the man. Then he turned to Gib. "You taste so innocent. Of course, that'll change. You'll have women. Men too, if that's what floats your boat. But I got to taste you first. It's my privilege."

"I don't care about that," said Gib. He stopped playing but couldn't take his hands away from the guitar.

"What's it about, then?"

"You know what it's like to be a nothing?" Gib's voice was low, so much so he thought maybe the man wouldn't hear him. "Like, less than nothing? You know what it's like to be such an afterthought that your own pops don't care if you live or die?"

The man's smile drooped a little. "I know better than anyone," he said. "My father threw me out. All because I wanted him to be proud of me. Only he couldn't have a son that wanted to take over the family business."

"I don't care about the money," said Gib. "Or the women. Or the fame. Or any of that bullshit. I want to be *somebody*. I want to be able to look my pops in the eye and tell him that I made it, and I didn't need him to do it. Or better, I want him to come to me, just so I can walk away like I don't know him. See how he likes it."

"Anger," said the man. "Stronger than greed any day. I thought maybe I tasted it."

"So," said Gib. "What now?"

"You still in?"

Gib nodded.

"All right." The man pulled a roll of yellowed paper from behind his back and placed it on the table. "You know what has to come next."

The paper unrolled and was, for a moment, blank. Gib peeled his hand away from the strings and pickups. Chunks of finger meat clung to the strings, but he didn't care. The bones of his fingertips were better for signing, anyway. He placed a bloody hand on the page, then lifted it away. The red shifted, raced across the page until it formed words. A contract. *The* contract.

"You first," said the man.

Gib lifted a finger and took a good look at the bloody, exposed bone. Better than a ballpoint. He scrawled his name at the appropriate spot. The man's expression darkened, then he signed below Gib.

"So that's it," said Shifty. "Right? He's number ten. I get my soul back, right? I'm out of the deal?"

The man stifled a deep laugh in his chest, then shook his head.

"You promised," said Shifty. "If you lied . . ."

"Don't NEVER call me a liar!" roared the man, slamming his fists on the table and glaring at Shifty. "I said ten for one, and you'd be out of *our* deal."

"Okay," said Shifty. "So I'm out."

"You sold yourself to me of your own free will. But do you think there's a place in Heaven for someone like you who brings me kids?"

"But . . . but you said . . ."

"You have to read the fine print," said the man. "I live in the details, don't you know."

"You can't . . . I got out . . ."

"Please, allow me to introduce my associate, Mister Scratch."

From the corner of the room, the shadows congealed into a mass larger than any man Gib had ever seen. If the man at the table wasn't what Gib expected, the shadow man in the corner was made of nightmares. From the scars down the side of his face to his coal-black eyes, there was no mistaking who or what he was.

"This wasn't the deal," screamed Shifty. "I made good on my end!"

"This isn't our deal," said the man. "This is separate. Hell isn't just for stupid people. Bad people go there too."

"You evil son of a—"

"I punish evil," said the man. "I can't help it if I enjoy my job."

Mister Scratch stepped away from the wall, and the shadows came with him. He moved with the speed of darkness, flowed like ink in water. Before Shifty had time to scream, the shadows covered him like paint. A moment later he was gone.

"They'll find him about ten miles down the road," said the man. "Probably call it a drug overdose. It's after midnight, so he died on his twenty-seventh birthday, just like all the rest."

Gib stood in shock. Shifty Smith was gone.

"Welcome to the game, kid," said the man. "Now if you don't mind . . ."

"One question," said Gib.

"*Now*, you have questions?"

"I only just thought of it. Is there any way out?"

The man chuckled as he rolled up the contract and stood.

"Sure, kid," said the man. "Here's the game. You want to live past twenty-seven, you find me ten souls to take your place. Every one of them has to be the same age you are now. Every one of them has to want it so bad they wait until after signing to ask questions. And it's all or nothing. You get nine, you get nothing, and I'll probably get them anyway. But, um... Well, you saw what happened to your friend."

"So, no one's ever figured a way out?"

"Not yet," said the man, a hint of sadness in his voice. "But I keep hoping."

"So now what?"

"You get back up on that stage," said the man. "You play so hard your balls finally drop. Let me take care of the rest."

Gib did as he was told. The pain in his hands, in his shoulder, in his guts where the guitar was bound to him, chewed at his bones and spit out his soul. A small price to pay if the man kept his word.

But then, he always kept his word. The legends said so. Which meant he wasn't really the bad guy, was he?

"Back in three . . . two . . . one . . ."

The house spotlight hit him in the eyes and blinded him, but he didn't need to see. Everyone was back. The drunks in the back acted like nothing had happened. The only difference was that the table where the man had sat with them was empty. Two glasses marked his and Shifty's places, but nothing else.

Gib looked down at his guitar. His hands looked normal, as did the guitar. But when he tried to take his hand off the neck, it still hurt like the strings sliced open his fingers and drank his blood.

"You gonna play, or what?" The drunk woman in the back let go a cackle at her own heckling skill. Like he was just some dumb kid. Like he didn't matter.

Gib hit a power chord and let the filthy wave of sound wash over him and through the audience. Then, fully aware of what he was using to assault their senses, he let go with his soul.

"Pleased to meet you," he cried. He had eleven years to find an answer, to figure a way out. But he already knew the stranger's name.

Scott A. Johnson is the author of seventeen books, numerous short stories, and more than a hundred articles, all centered around the world of horror and dark fantasy. He teaches at Seton Hill University in the MFA in Writing Popular Fiction program, as well as at Emerson College in their Writing and Publishing Popular Fiction program.

Scott lives somewhere near Austin, Texas with a growing number of cats and dogs, and can often be found cruising the twisting back roads on his motorcycle. For more information, check out his website at http://www.creepylittlebastard .com.

ROCK & ROLL NEVER FORGETS

BY BEN MONROE

A large bus, nondescript with tinted windows and a plain maroon exterior, barreled along highway 40 in the middle of the night. Jack "Bullet" Dixon and the Reloads used to travel by private jet, but that was in their heyday when they played bigger arenas and more frequent dates. They'd slowed down now. Most of their fans had, too.

Jack was sitting in the rear of the tour bus, staring at the landscape as it raced by. He'd seen this same stretch of highway a hundred times, but if you put a gun to his head, he couldn't tell you where he was. There was home, and there was the road. And the road was a blur.

As he stared out the window, Billy Amos—the Reloads' manager of the past 15 years—slid into the seat across the small table from him. "Jack," he said, quietly, so as not to disturb the other members of the band sleeping nearby. "We gotta talk."

"Stow it," Jack grunted. "I know what you're going to say, and I'm not interested in hearing it."

Billy leaned forward, steepling his hands on the table in front of him. "You've sung these songs a thousand times. Hell, you wrote most of 'em, man. You shouldn't be stumbling over them."

Jack glared across the table. "I'm tired. Good night's sleep, something decent to eat—I'll be right as rain."

Billy leaned back in the seat, vinyl squeaking as he shifted. "You can't keep on like this, Jack. The fans're noticing. They're talking about you on blogs and social media . . ."

"Fans," Jack said, disdain dripping from his voice. "Most of 'em are deaf as a post. The ones that aren't are usually drunk on the watered-down beer they serve at the shitty venues we're stuck with."

Billy sighed. "Yeah," he said. "Maybe you need a rest. I could cancel Barstow. It'd be a hit in the wallet, but if you need a rest, say the word."

Jack turned back to the window. The horizon was a sea of cobalt blue blending to black, a spray of stars like ice chips in the sky overhead. He thought about the last few shows, his fingers stumbling over the frets of his Strat. His tongue frozen in his mouth as he stammered for a word, a forgotten phrase. How many times had he smiled widely at the audience, held his microphone out toward them and let the stadium take the next stanza because he couldn't remember the chorus to "Cool Water Baby" or "Lonesome Wanderer"?

He could call off the tour. Easy enough to feign illness or have Billy make something up. But that wouldn't just be a black eye for Jack. It'd put the rest of the band on hiatus, techs and stage managers out of work. Too many people were relying on him for a paycheck.

"No," he said, eyes still on the night. "I'm fine. We'll keep going as long as I can."

Billy stood up. "Suit yourself," he said. "But I'm telling you, man, you keep on like this, pretty soon you'll either be in the hospital or we'll be lucky to fill a rec center." He turned and walked to the front of the bus, taking a seat behind the driver and leaving Jack alone with his thoughts.

"He's not budging," Billy said. He sat on the edge of the motel's bed as he undid the buttons on his shirt. "We can keep it up for another couple of shows, but if something doesn't change, this is the end of the road."

A huffing, hissing noise escaped from under the bed where Billy had stowed his suitcase when they checked in earlier. It was a sound like dried sheets of paper shuffling in a deep abyss, wispy and hollow.

"I tried it in Jacksonville, yeah," Billy said.

The rustling again, papery and distant. It reminded him of growing up in Virginia, and the summers when the cicadas emerged from the ground. The perpetual rasping, tearing sound which suffused their brief emergence. The sound made his skin crawl.

Billy thought about the tour, the trouble with Jack's memory. "How far am I willing to go?" he asked the empty room. "I'm surprised you even have to ask."

Silence.

Then a knock at the door. Billy waited a moment, then rose and crossed the small motel room to open the door. Jack stood on the landing, graying hair blowing slightly in the chilly night air. He peeked over Billy's shoulder. "Hey, sorry, I thought I heard you talking to someone. Figured you were still up."

Billy looked back into the room, then turned back to Jack. "Oh, I was just calling the manager of the venue," he lied. "Wanted to make sure they had the motel info in case they needed it."

Jack nodded, then took a step back and leaned against the walkway railing. "I just wanted to apologize for blowing you off earlier," he said.

Billy nodded. "Come in, man. Don't stand out there in the cold. Not good for your voice."

Jack shook his head. "Nah, this won't take long," he said. "Look, truth is, I have been struggling lately. Maybe it's just getting old, maybe all the crap I pumped into my body when I was younger." He shrugged. "Probably a little of both."

"Sure, man," Billy said. "It happens."

"That's right. Shit happens," Jack said. "That's what they say, anyway." He crossed his arms against the cold. "So, we're booked up through Alcosta, right?"

"Right," Billy said. "Nothing after that, though I'm working on a few things."

Jack shook his head. "Let's just call it there," he said. "Don't call it a farewell tour yet, but maybe after the Alcosta shows, I need to take a break."

"You sure?" Billy asked. "I mean, whatever you want, of course. But that's still a week out. I can keep putting out feelers, and then cancel if you're not feeling up to it."

"No, I think Alcosta's it for now," Jack said. "After that, we can head down to LA and let the band go home for a while. They all need a break, anyway."

"Sure," Billy said. "If that's what you want."

"That's what I want," Jack said. "Maybe after a few months of resting up, we can talk about a new record or something. I've got a few new songs I've been messing around with."

Billy smiled and nodded. "Sure." But he knew what fans the Dixon and the Reloads still had weren't interested in any new songs. They wanted the old ones sung on constant repeat, like weaponized nostalgia. And sung well.

"That's all I wanted to say, man," Jack added. "And thanks for sticking with me. The last few years would've sucked without you pushing me along."

Billy forced a smile. "No problem, man. Now go get some rest. You still got a gig," he looked at his watch, noted it was past midnight. "Tonight, I guess."

Jack slapped him on the shoulder. "You too. See you later." He turned and walked back down the walkway. Billy watched after him until Jack disappeared into his own room.

"The hell?" Jack said as he got off the bus in front of the Barstow Drive-In. Jack stopped next to Ray Farber, the band's bassist, both staring at the marquee as Billy walked up to take a place next to them.

"What's wrong?" Billy asked. "I know it's not Caesar's Palace, but it's a decent venue."

Jack shook his head. "Not the venue, man. We've played here before and it's good enough. What the hell is *that*," he pointed at the marquee. Red letters glowed on the dingy white plastic background.

TWO NITES ONLY!
JACK DIXON & THE RELOADS!
WITH BLACK MAGIC MARKER!

Billy stared at the letters. "Is there a typo or something?"

Jack turned to him. "Who the hell are Black Magic Marker?" he asked.

"They sound like some suburban punk kids' garage band playing the local high school prom," Ray added.

Billy shrugged. "The venue manager selected the opening act from local talent."

"Guess when you're playing a drive-in in Barstow, the pickings are slim," Jack groused.

"Don't let it get to you, man," Ray said, his voice a thick Southern drawl. "Nobody's here to see them. They're just the warm-up while the audience is finding their seats."

Jack glared at the marquee. "Whatever," he said, hefted his guitar case off the ground, and stomped across the lot. Ray followed him.

They entered the asphalt slab of the drive-in's lot, and Billy was pleased to see that prep was going well. Stage crew had already set up the portable bleachers around the stage along with a couple hundred folding chairs for the "premium" tickets. Reminded him of his high school graduation.

As he was surveying the space, a large, extraordinarily sweaty man approached him. "Hey, you Billy Amos?" the man said, extending a hand.

Billy took it and shook it. "I am," he said. "You must be Clarkson? The theater manager?"

"The one and only!" Clarkson replied with a broad grin. "We're about done setting up the stage, and your boys can do a sound check in half an hour, if they want."

Billy nodded. "That'd be great." He turned to see Jack and the rest of the band standing near the concession stand. Jack looked pissed. "Where can they hang out in the meantime?" Billy asked.

"Oh, sure," Clarkson said. "There's a room next to my office. It's about as close to a green room as we've got. But it'll do."

"I think I remember that," Billy said. "We were here a few years ago."

Clarkson nodded. "Oh, yeah, for sure," he said. "I was the assistant manager back then. You probably dealt with Robbie."

"Robbie Mason, right," Billy said. "What happened to him? Retire?"

Clarkson shook his head. "Nah. Unless you call a head-on with a semi 'retirement'."

"Fuck," Billy said.

"No shit," Clarkson said. Then he clapped his hand on Billy's shoulder. "But let's get your boys settled in." He led Billy by the shoulder toward where the band had congregated around the concession stand.

Billy waved at Jack as he approached. "Clarkson here's going to get you all sorted out while I make sure everything's going as planned."

Jack turned to Clarkson. "Hey, who's this other band, Black Magic Marker? Never heard of them."

Clarkson nodded and swallowed nervously. "Oh, wow. Jack, Mr. Dixon. Big fan of yours, man. Big fan." He stuck out his hand but dropped it after an awkward few seconds when Jack didn't take it. "Ah, local boys. You'll love 'em," he said. "They've been playing bars and stuff, you know? Folks around here love 'em. Should be a big draw. They played the high school prom last year."

Jack glared at Billy. "Sounds great. Can't wait to meet them."

"Oh, I'm sure they're looking forward to meeting you and the Reloads, too." He stepped back and motioned them to follow.

Billy had other things to do.

For the next half hour, he supervised the seating setup, checked in with the sound and lighting crew, and just made sure everything was going okay. He also spent some time checking out the stage wings. It didn't take Billy long to find a spot where he could wait backstage and monitor the front row of the audience.

Front row were the most expensive seats in the concert, of course. And only the biggest fans of the band would pony up the cash for those. And what Billy thought Jack really needed right now was one of his biggest fans.

The concert started off well. Turned out Black Magic Marker was a Ramones cover band. And for a bunch of kids, they weren't half bad. They were, in fact, a bunch of kids. Billy was unsurprised to discover the reason someone had tapped them to play the high school prom last year was because they'd been in the graduating class and did the gig for free. He was, however, surprised to find out the front man of Black Magic Marker was Robbie Mason, Jr., the son of the drive-in's previous manager. Turned out Clarkson got them the gig because he sort of felt like he owed the family or something.

But they knew all the songs and played them well, and that was really all that mattered. And the Reloads' fans were of an age where they got a kick out of seeing teenagers covering songs of their youth. Even if most of them hadn't much liked the Ramones when they were kids themselves. They finished the set with "Sheena Is a Punk Rocker" and had the audience on their feet.

When the band exited the stage, Billy clapped Robbie Jr. on the back as he walked past and shouted, "Not bad at all kid!" Then handed him his business card. "Call me if you want to talk about your future."

Robbie smiled at him as sweat dripped down his lanky black hair. "Hell, yeah, man! I will!" He bounced off-stage, showing the card to his bandmates.

As the kids disappeared around a curtain, Billy dropped the smile from his face and took up his spot in the wings. He could see the center front row clearly from where he lurked. A middle-aged couple, tan and blond, sat dead center. The people sitting on their sides and behind them were about the same age. Same age as most of the band, too.

But about halfway between them and the edge of the far side was a younger man. Probably in his late twenties or early thirties. He was wearing a Reloads T-shirt, the cover of their *Sidewinder* album from '87. "Damn, shirt's probably older than he is," Billy muttered. The guy was talking to a woman sitting next to him, who was smiling and obviously excited. She wasn't wearing the band's merch like him, but she was clearly a fan.

The stage lights dimmed, and a hush washed over the audience. If there was one thing Jack "Bullet" Dixon could do, it was play up the theatrics. The crowd began to mutter and whisper. Then the lights flooded across the audience, circles of light spinning and spiraling in crazy patterns until they came together, coalescing on Jack standing dead center of the stage.

"How the hell are you, Barstow?!" he yelled. "Damn, it's good to be back!"

And the band blasted out the first chords of "Snake Venom Sting," and the crowd went wild.

While all this was going on, Billy noticed the kids from Black Magic Marker had surrounded him. But they weren't interested in him at all. Their attention was on the band. He didn't think he'd ever seen anyone so star-struck before.

"I can't believe we just opened for fucking Jack Dixon," one kid said.

While the Reloads belted out "Snake Venom Sting," and Black Magic Marker stood enraptured in the wings, Billy snuck around backstage to the other side, where he could get a better view of the guy and his girl down front.

For the next half hour, the band performed as well as they had recently. Billy cast his eyes between Jack Dixon and the young couple in the front row. Jack only missed the beat once or twice and mumble-yelled through a line or two.

But whoever the guy and his date in front were knew every song. It was loud enough (and Billy had earplugs in anyway) that he couldn't tell if the guy was actually singing, but he was mouthing along with all the songs. Knew every word, every beat, every note. And the girl was giving him a run for his money. The people around them looked over their way occasionally, but not like they were irritated. More like they were catching the young couple's infectious enthusiasm for the band. Wasn't long before the whole first few rows were singing along.

Which served Jack well. By the second half of the show, he was slowing down. He fumbled a few chord changes, and by the time they got to "Road-Weary Blues," he put the guitar down and focused on singing. But soon, even that was too much for him, and he was falling back to getting the audience amped up, holding out the mic and letting them sing while he rested, smiling along like he hadn't forgotten the chorus to a song he wrote a lifetime ago.

And the guy in front, the guy Billy had pegged as one of those "Number One Fan" types, he and his girl sang along, clapping their hands in sync. Hell, if the guy could sing, he could probably lead the band.

Billy thought about maybe pulling a Journey. Put Jack out to pasture and run some kind of social media contest to find a new singer and keep the rest of the band.

But then the papery whispering slithered around the back of his mind. He knew exactly what he needed to do to fix the problem. Billy felt a cold sweat break out along his spine, inch up the back of his neck, and crawl over his scalp. He knew what he had to do. If he wanted to keep the band together, anyway.

As the show wound down, Billy sent an usher to grab the guy and girl in the front row before they slipped out with the crowd. They were confused at first but ecstatic when they got to watch the encores from the wings.

"Jack wants to meet us?" the guy—Eddie, it turned out his name was—said, a look of complete bewilderment on his face. His girl was similarly excited.

Billy nodded. "That's what he said, yeah."

"That's amazing," Eddie said. "Any idea why?"

Billy checked his watch. Nearing 10:30, and the band should be leaving any minute now. "Just something he does sometimes," Billy replied. "He'll designate a couple of seats for a surprise meet and greet. Lucky for you two, I guess you happened to be sitting in them tonight."

The girl, Lisa, took Eddie's hand and squeezed. "So awesome!" she said. "Right baby?"

"Totally," Eddie replied. "Totally awesome." He looked around the stage. The band had finished up and left the stage a few minutes ago, and the audience was filtering out of the lot. "So, do we wait here, or...?"

Billy checked his watch again. "Jack should have been here by now," he said. "Look, you hang tight, and I'll go check on him. Give me five minutes, okay?"

They both nodded. "Yeah, sure man, can't wait."

Billy slipped away into the flurry of activity backstage. He jigged and swerved around stagehands and lighting techs until he'd positioned himself behind a stack of crates. Peeking around them, he confirmed he couldn't see, or be seen, by Eddie and Lisa. He flicked a match, lit up a cigarette, and took a deep drag. Smoke filled his lungs for a moment before he let it out with a long hiss.

"Hey, man, those things'll kill you," Jack said to his right.

Billy snapped around in surprise and looked at the fading rock star. He took another drag on his cigarette, then dropped it to the ground and crushed it out underfoot. "Yeah, guess they might at that," he replied.

Jack leaned against the stack of boxes. "How'd we do tonight? It felt pretty good to me," he said. "Couple of glitches, but okay, I guess."

"Could've been worse," Billy said.

Jack nodded. "Yeah. Could always be worse."

"Look, I'm going to wrap up a few things here. Why don't you and the guys head back to the motel. Get some rest. I'll catch up with you."

"You sure? You don't need a ride?" Jack asked.

"I'm fine," Billy said. "Just a few things to sort out with the staff and manager here, and then I'll grab an Uber or whatever."

"Suit yourself," Jack said. "Hey, Ray!" he called out, spotting Ray Farber nearby. "Round up the boys. Let's blow this taco stand."

Ray gave him a thumbs-up and wandered off to find the rest of the band.

Jack turned to walk away, then stopped and turned back to Billy. "Tomorrow'll be better, man," he said. "You'll see. We're really gonna rock the hell out of this place."

Billy forced a smile. "Sure, Jack. Barstow won't know what hit 'em." He watched Jack Dixon walk away, and then waited a few more minutes until he saw the tour bus leaving.

The papery hissing scratch sounded faintly in his inner ears. It was a message of intent, more than thought. He knew what it meant, what it *wanted,* even if it wasn't being vocalized in any language he understood. "Showtime," he muttered as the sounds abated.

Eddie and Lisa were right back where he left them. "Hey, there you are!" he said as he approached them. He saw they were looking around him, past him, as if to see if anyone more interesting than the band's manager might follow in his wake.

"Okay, so not a good news/bad news situation, but sort of oops news/good news kinda thing," he said.

They exchanged a confused look. "What do you mean?" Lisa said.

Billy smiled. "Sorry if that was a little dramatic," he said. "One pitfall of working in showbiz. We can be a bit theatrical sometimes."

Lisa laughed. Eddie did too, but his seemed forced.

"Just a miscommunication," Billy said. "The band took off before I found them. But!" he said, as he saw disappointment flow across both their faces. "But! I got him on his cell, and if you don't mind a quick detour, Jack and the band would still like to meet up with you before they crash out for the night. Just back at the motel, right down the highway. You can pop in, meet the guys, get some photos, whatever."

They exchanged another look. Lisa seemed concerned.

"Totally up to you," Billy said. "And I know it sounds weird, right? Just trying to make the best of my mess-up."

"I guess that'd be okay," Lisa said.

"Yeah, no worries," said Eddie. "That's fine. Totally fine."

"Brilliant," Billy said. "You know the Coppermill Hotel? Just off Highway 40? That's where we're staying. I'm in room 206. Come find me when you get there, and I'll round up the guys."

Billy Amos paced back and forth, alone in the motel room. The room was dark aside from a desk lamp in the corner, and the yellow glow of light filtering through the curtains from the lights in the parking lot. The papery rasping was deafeningly loud in his mind. Harrowing and insistent.

He reached into the nightstand next to the bed and pulled out a sheaf of paper. A handful of pages were stapled together in the corner. Printed photos of scanned pages of a book he'd only been able to glimpse briefly. The weird old man had shown him the book during a stopover for a show in Providence months ago. The old man with his collar up and the brim of his hat down, his eyes lost in shadows. All Billy really remembered of him was the pale skin of his hands and chin and his strangely wide, toothy smile.

The text was in old-style English. Sort of reminded him of reading Shakespeare back in college. Even though it was recognizably English, it had still taken Billy a long time to figure out what the words said. Now red pen marks marred the page where Billy had annotated and corrected the text and clarified the pronunciation. But if what the guy told him was true, this was the ticket. The magic beans that'd give him access to the treasure in the clouds. He'd read them out loud first in Jacksonville, and the papery voice had been his constant companion ever since.

He hadn't had the stomach to do what the voice asked of him then, but now he was desperate. Billy whispered the words again, reading them slowly and carefully. The voice became louder, more insistent. It was thunderous in his head. And then a knock on the door, and it went quiet.

He took a breath. "Come in!" he called out.

The door opened slowly, and he saw Lisa and Eddie standing on the walkway outside. "Come on in," he said. "I was going to find Jack, but come on in for a minute. Something really cool I want to show you both."

Eddie shrugged and entered, pulling Lisa along behind him. "Yeah, what's that, man?"

The door slammed shut behind them, and Lisa spun around.

Eddie hissed the ultimate word of the incantation, finishing the long passage and sealing the pact: "Whisper . . ."

Fingers of darkness stretched out from beneath the bed. Long and tenebrous, they reached forward. Then hands and arms followed. Soon vaguely human shapes slithered out from the crevasse, lunging forward on lean, long limbs, joints knobby and swollen. Threads of darkness floated off the things, as if made of smoke.

Lisa screamed loud and long while she scrabbled desperately for the doorknob. Eddie threw his hands up before his face as one thing rushed him, wrapping its thin, spider-like arms around his body twice before squeezing him tight.

Soon, the slithering darkness of the shadowy smoke-like creatures had engulfed the couple. They fell to the dingy hotel carpet, silent and still. The shadow things had lost any semblance of their vaguely humanoid shapes. The bodies of the young couple on the floor now looked cocooned in smoking shadow.

Billy watched all this with a feeling of growing horror. His guts roiled and his bowels turned to water as the smoky shapes constricted further, accompanied by the sounds of cracking bones and squelching meat. The sounds of human life being squeezed into pulp.

The shadowy cocoons grew smaller, shrinking in on themselves until they were each about the size of a large bowling ball. And then the shadows dissipated. They decayed into threads which crawled and slithered away, dispersed into the corners and shadows of the room until there was nothing left on the floor aside from two small blobs. Pulpy gray spheres shot through with deep red veins or striations.

Billy reached down and picked up the two globs. They were warm to his touch and pulsed slightly. The gooey spheres continued shrinking until they were like desiccated pellets of clay. And then they crumbled to a fine, powdery purple dust in his hand.

He walked to the bathroom, shaking. There were paper-covered glasses by the sink, and he removed the covering from one and scraped the dust into it. He poured tap water into the glass and stirred it with his finger. A faint smell of jasmine wafted from the glass.

"Billy?" he heard Jack's voice. He crossed the room, holding the glass with both hands so as not to spill it, and went to open the door.

"Hey, Billy," Jack said. "Can I come in for a minute? I wanted to talk about the rest of the tour."

"Yeah, absolutely. Funny you mention that," he said. "I've got a new... Guess you could call it a health supplement I wanted you to try." He handed the glass to Jack. "I think is going to really help you out a bunch."

"Yeah?" Jack said. "Well, hell, man. Bring it on."

COMEBACK, BABY!
BY KEVIN BISHOP

EXCLUSIVE TO THE ALCOSTA TIMES

WHEN ROCKERS HAVE BEEN AROUND AS LONG AS JACK "BULLET" DIXON AND THE RELOADS, YOU HAVE TO FIGURE THEY MIGHT SLOW DOWN A LITTLE. AND FROM REPORTS OF PREVIOUS ENGAGEMENTS ON THEIR RECENT TOUR, YOU'D THINK THE RELOADS WERE MORE LIKE THE RETREADS. THIS REPORTER HAD HEARD ABOUT PERFORMANCE PROBLEMS WITH THEIR LAST FEW SHOWS, EVEN THEIR FIRST SHOW HERE IN BARSTOW. SOME WERE SAYING THE BULLET'S FIRING BLANKS.

BUT FRIENDS, I HAVE TO SAY WHAT I SAW LAST NIGHT DURING THEIR SECOND SHOW WAS NOTHING SHORT OF A COMEBACK CONCERT. JACK "BULLET" DIXON DIDN'T MISS A BEAT AND SOUNDED AS GOOD AS HE EVER HAS. IF YOU'VE BEEN A FAN FOR YEARS OR JUST LISTENED TO THEIR MUSIC BECAUSE YOUR DAD WAS INTO IT, YOU OWE IT TO YOURSELF TO CATCH THEM WHEN THEY COME TO YOUR TOWN.

AND LUCKY YOU, THE TOUR THAT WAS RUMORED TO END IN ALCOSTA, CALIF., HAS BEEN EXTENDED! DETAILS STILL TO COME, BUT THEIR MANAGER, BILLY AMOS, CONFIRMED THAT THE BAND'S FEELING GREAT, AND

Dixon's looking for more venues to extend the tour for the next few months.

"He's in great shape and has never sounded better," Amos told this reporter after the show last night. "Bullet's on a new diet, eating healthy and taking some great supplements, and full of energy. He and the band are looking forward to keeping this up as long as folks'll put up with them!"

Which is all great news for hardcore and casual fans alike. Watch the band's website for new tour dates, band merch, and all that good stuff! Amos said they're even talking about releasing some new material, which this reporter is very interested in hearing.

In other news, Barstow PD is still asking for help to find Eddie and Lisa Botkin. The couple was last seen leaving the Barstow Drive-In after the Reloads first show two nights ago. They never made it home, and we encourage anyone with any leads on the missing couple to contact the Barstow PD.

Ben Monroe has spent most of his life in Northern California, where he lives in the East Bay Area with his wife and two children. He is the author of In the Belly of the Beast and Other Tales of Cthulhu Wars, The Seething, the graphic novel Planet Apocalypse, and short stories in several anthologies.

You can find more information about him and his work at www.benmonroe .com.

CHERRY BOY

BY T.M. MORGAN

Verse

The jukebox pumped the Everly Brothers, their two-part harmony saying to "dream, dream, dream, dream." An elderly man stood behind the long counter, a withered hand pressed to his back. Each red stool stood empty down the line.

The front door swung open, and a boy of twelve walked in with a grin, a warm summer breeze at his back. He hesitated on entering, then seemed to fall into a dreamy stupor as the soda shop came alive with its fruit and mocha smells.

"Hi, Mister Bryant."

"Good afternoon, Mister Timothy. And what can I do for you this fine afternoon?"

Bryant spoke in the high, arched tones of a cantankerous butler. He put his chin on his palms and leaned as low as possible so he and the boy could look eye-to-eye once young Timothy climbed onto the stool. Because he had asked what the boy wanted, Bryant's face stretched into a mocking look of anticipation.

"Why, a cherry malt, sir."

"Oh-ho-ho! Cherry, huh?"

Just as Bryant moved to begin the creation of the malt shake, the jukebox emitted a clunk when the Everly Brothers 45 ended and the next spun from its rack to the needle. The cream and sugar pop of The Robins exploded with their doo-wop single "Cherry Lips." Bryant snapped his fingers and shook his hips.

"Gee, Mister Bryant, you know how to dance?"

"Of course!" the shopkeeper said as he spun. "And The Robins! Every time I hear this song, it makes me happy."

"Why's that?" The boy's voice, so polite as to be sickening, grated on Bryant's nerves. "I would think a growing boy such as yourself would understand. Do you know the lyrics?" When Timothy shook his head, Bryant laughed. "Why, it's about kissing a girl, wanting to feel her pain. You know about that, right?"

The boy stared as if trying to work out a math problem. Bryant turned to the back counter: two scoops of vanilla from the freezer cabinet, a pour of cold milk from the next cabinet down, and then a heaping scoop of malt from the shelf. The mixer buzzed loudly once he placed the cup into place. As the thick shake churned, he dribbled cherry syrup from an unlabeled coffee can, with a fleeting glance over his shoulder to raise an eyebrow.

"Haha! And voila!"

The poured malt got a high spray of whipped cream and a maraschino cherry, and a straw. Bryant set the glass in front of Timothy.

"Ten cents, my fine sir."

Timothy snatched the glass and sucked down the malt, allowing a crest of whipped cream to sprout on his nose. The cherry fell to the counter, bits of quickly dying cream on its red skin. Only when the boy reached the bottom did he come up for air.

"Gee, Mister Bryant, you make the best cherry malts." The boy wiped his lips and nose with his forearm.

The shopkeeper tapped his finger on the counter. "Ten cents."

The boy looked at his hands sheepishly. "Gosh, Mister Bryant. I'm sorry. I promise I'll come back tomorrow with it."

"Young man," Bryant said, "you've promised me the same thing for—how many days now? I've been very kind to you, as I understand your situation. But it's been four months, and you've been in every afternoon with the same tale. I've kept tabs. You owe me over ten dollars. Do you understand? An entire ten dollars."

The boy nodded. "I do, sir. And I promise, swear on my mom's grave, I'll pay you in full tomorrow."

Bryant stood straight up. "Don't go swearing on things like that unless you mean it. You bring that money to me, or there will be consequences."

Timothy held up three fingers in a scout oath. "Tomorrow."

"Fine then. And you're forgetting something."

"What's that?"

They both followed the line that extended from Bryant's finger to the evacuated cherry which lay limply at the edge of the linoleum counter. Both laughed as Timothy plucked it between index finger and thumb, tilted his head back, and dropped it into his gullet, stem and all.

Chorus

Though it had been a hot summer, the next afternoon brought an odd arctic chill. Timothy kept his hands in his pockets and his jacket zipped to the neck. At the soda shop, he pushed open the door to find Mister Bryant in his usual spot and one customer with him, a girl Timothy's age. She struck him momentarily dumb. It wasn't just her red hair, of a crimson he'd never seen. She also wore a bright red dress, red socks up to her knees, and shiny red shoes like Dorothy on her way to Oz. She and Mister Bryant had been caught mid-laugh, only to each look up and eye Timothy.

"Hi-ho, Mister Timothy! Come to pay the piper?"

"Oh, gosh, Mister Bryant, your money. I swear, I asked my dad, and he walloped me good for running up a debt. He told me to come down here and offer to work it off."

The girl sucked loudly on her straw, eyes planted firmly on Timothy. Bryant grabbed the white towel that hung over his shoulder and slapped the counter in a mockery of cleaning.

"Young sir, you swore yesterday. Didn't I say there would be consequences? The holiday is almost here, and how am I supposed to buy gifts when my customers don't pay? I suspected this would happen."

"Holiday? I never—"

"The summer solstice," the girl said with a glint. Her voice had the ring of a precocious little girl, her pronunciation so precise as to be alarming. "You never heard of a holiday in June?"

Timothy was still decked out in his jacket and cap. As the girl watched and Bryant puttered around, slapping at the counter, he removed the garments, dropping them on a bench that sat beneath the front window and leaving himself in T-shirt and jeans.

"How did you know what I was going to say?"

"Seemed where you were headed with that," the girl said.

"Who are you, anyway?"

"I'm a fairy, silly. Isn't that right, Mister Bryant?"

Bryant turned with a devilish grin. "Why yes, that's right. Came in for a cherry malt, just like you. Always good to get a *paying* customer. Bills to pay, Mister Timothy."

"A fairy? You two are pranking me. I haven't seen you at school. You just move here?"

"I'm a fairy. Here for the holiday." An accent crept in. Though Timothy couldn't quite place it, the wives on *The Honeymooners* came to mind.

Timothy turned his gaze from her innocent face to Bryant's wide-eyed grinning. "Do you mean the Fourth of July?"

The old man and young girl burst into laughter. Now when Bryant slapped the counter, it was to emphasize a fit of hysteria. He kept trying to answer before sputtering into chuckles.

"Why, no!" he eventually spat out. "The solstice festivities, of course! But the true way, as they used to do it."

"Oh," said Timothy. "I don't know that one."

"Don't know? Why, it's fantastic," Bryant said, now leaning down so his head rested atop his hands. "You have a Christian holiday with a tree and decorations and presents, right? To celebrate the birth of your Lord?"

Timothy nodded. "*My* Lord? He's Lord to all of us."

Mister Bryan and the girl broke out into loud guffaws.

"Well, depending on how you look it," Bryant said. "Regardless, our festival has many of the same things, except ours came first. As it turns out, Gwen arrived just today in time for the celebration. She's a relative of mine, you might say, and comes every year. Gwen, meet Mister Timothy; and Timothy, meet Miss Gwen."

Timothy walked forward to take her hand but drew back immediately upon its touch. "Nice to meet you, Gwen. Your hands sure are cold. You should have gotten a hot cocoa rather than a cherry malt."

Mister Bryant turned himself fully around to laugh into his fist. Violent coughs shook his chest, so that from Timothy's perspective it looked like the old man was having a seizure.

Gwen snapped her fingers in Timothy's face so that he turned dumbstruck. "Don't mind him." She leaned far forward to whisper. "He's got the croup, you know."

Timothy also leaned forward, as the two of them were now keeping secrets. "Oh, that's terrible. Is he going to get better?"

She rolled her eyes, threw up her hands, and tossed her head. "Well . . . you know," she said and flashed her eyes toward Bryant.

With the old man hunched over, one hand on the counter and the other holding the towel pressed to his mouth, little specks of red bleeding through, Timothy stared at Gwen as he might a toy in a shop window. Her eyes wanted to draw him in, to fill the vast space behind them.

"You don't talk like any girl I know."

She scoffed. "You don't know the right kind of girls."

Wind howled against the shop's front pane, rattling the glass in its frame. Rain had rolled in, coming down so thick that Timothy couldn't see the five-and-dime across the street, a river of water overflowing the curb as it ran down Main Street to the storm drain. As he thought to turn and get his jacket and cap back on, Gwen laid her hand atop his leg.

"No, stay with us. You'll get all wet out there."

"But if I don't leave now, I might get stuck. The town's flooded before."

The old man bent to a knee, his coughing fit so debilitating only the crown of his head showed above the counter. His attempts to clear his throat sounded to Timothy like the growl of some beast, and for a moment he pictured the shopkeeper rising to reveal a face twisted in transformation. Then he blinked and wondered where such a thought came from.

"Are you all right, sir?"

"He'll be fine," Gwen said. "Hey, I have an idea. Why don't we show you how we celebrate?"

Timothy shrugged. "Sure, I guess."

Gwen finished her malt with a grand sucking sound; her eyes popped open and shut again as if to highlight something momentous. With the last of it gone, she reached her small hand inside and withdrew the maraschino cherry still covered with melted whipped cream. Like Timothy the day before, she arched back her head and let the whole cherry drop into her mouth.

Bridge

Bryant took to rearranging the several tables and chairs in the open part of the shop by pushing them so they lined the outer wall. Once the space stood cleared, he strolled into the supply room as Gwen watched, only to lurch back with a thin, darkly stained table, each end having a single pedestal upon which to stand. It took several tries to get it positioned in its precise location, and then he retrieved one last item: a black box he held like a baby.

The lid came open, and he extracted seven bronze candle holders and matching candles the color of fresh blood, which he placed in evenly spaced slots along the back edge of the table. He also produced a sprig of pine needles, a sliver of meat, and an egg along the table's front like three gems. A Zippo appeared from his pocket, his thumb flicked down, and each wick came to life.

"*Honorifico lapsis! Et videbunt matrem iterum!*"

"What's he saying?" Timothy said.

Gwen sighed. "It's Latin. This part of the ceremony honors the dead."

"What is that twig for?"

Bryant lifted it. "This is a sprig of Dutch spruce. Do you know its uses?"

Timothy shook his head. "It's just a twig, right?"

"Just a twig! Inserting one of these sharp spines into your eye can make you see beyond the veil!" Bryant plucked a single green needle from the sprig and held it up to the light. "Mister Timothy, have you ever seen beyond the veil?"

The boy shook his head vigorously.

Gwen leapt up. "Not him. It's my turn this time."

She walked in front of Bryant, who lifted her face with a finger to meet his as he lowered his puckered lips toward her, placed a kiss on the center of her forehead, and then slowly slid the needle into the moist, soft pulp of her left eye. At first, she showed no reaction. Bryant was bent downward, lips inches from Gwen's head, his right hand barely touching the half-inserted needle. Balls of light began to float across Timothy's vision, as if he had rubbed his eyes hard with his palms, and sweat gathered on his brow.

"Ah, fuck, that feels so good," Gwen finally said.

Bryant plucked the needle out, stood upright and, after taking a moment to suck the needle clean, placed it back on the table. Then he took up the sliver of meat, which was beginning to brown at the edges. He dangled it like a worm over Gwen's open mouth. The tip graced her lip and dipped within the cavern. Like a crocodile's bite, she snapped her jaw shut and severed the piece of flesh. As Bryant held the remnant in his fist, Gwen chewed with a great amount of force, exaggerated in how she spread her jaw as wide as possible without unsealing her lips.

She swallowed, and turned to Timothy with a look of ecstasy. "So good," she said.

"You're both acting really strange."

"Oh, Tim, don't be like that," she said. "The needle in my eye allowed me to see my dead family. Rituals. Do you understand?"

Timothy nodded, but stared through her. "What kind of meat is that?" he said as if in a dream.

Gwen laughed and opened her mouth wide to reveal a straggling lump on her tongue. "The flesh of my family. Like I said, it's a ritual. You drink the blood of Christ and eat of his flesh. You do not call them wine and wafer but the essence of Christ. We have the same."

"What's the egg for?"

She laughed again. "The resurrection, of course." Then she put her hands close to her chest and hopped around in front of him. "Like your Easter bunny."

Bryant, who had been leaning a hand on the table while Gwen gave her response, snapped to attention. He delicately lifted the egg, which had a slight brown tint. Timothy expected the shopkeeper to crack the egg open and pour its contents into Gwen's mouth. He instead reared back and viciously smashed it against his own forehead, allowing the yellow yolk and transparent albumen to flow down his face in left and right streams.

"*Illa surgit iterum!*"

Bryant's shout caused Timothy to back all the way to the front door, only realizing what he'd done when the glass touched his hands.

"What did he say?"

Gwen strode to the boy. She was taller than she had been before. Her breasts touched his nose, and they were engorged, ripe, shocking.

"The ritual asks for an act of love now. Would you like to kiss me, Tim? Taste the cherry on my lips?"

"Wha—I—go home—"

Bryant shouted. "You swore on your mother's grave that you would pay me, young sir! Come here, boy, and suffer your consequences."

With a dramatic flourish, the old man ate the remnant of meat, black mold spots and all, then sprang toward the boy, who stood entranced as Gwen's wet lips moved closer, closer . . .

Chorus

As the shopkeeper and Gwen gave chase, Timothy ran in circles until his lungs seemed about to explode. Bryant stopped and clutched his chest, moaning in pain. Gwen proved gracefully quick and eventually snagged Timothy's shirt, pulled him down, and straddled his chest.

"Got you now, you bad boy."

Her body had morphed again, now fully woman, her thighs pressed tightly, the crevice of her legs planted intimately to his belly. A shudder swept down his chest and into his groin. A disturbing excitement traveled in every blood molecule.

"Tie . . . him . . . up," wheezed Bryant, whose face contained so many red blotches he looked diseased.

Gwen lowered herself so her lips were so close that Timothy could see their moist lines. Her breath carried a hint of cherries. The smell was intoxicating. "Now," she said and pressed their mouths together, her tongue finding its way to his.

Bryant crawled toward them, withdrawing a jumble of twine from his pocket. Then they were both on Timothy, clasping his wrists together in front of him, and within seconds he was as snug as a fly caught in webbing. They dragged him under the ceremonial table. Bryant procured a curved knife from the supply room.

"What are you going to do?" Timothy cried.

Gwen, having kicked off her shoes during the chase, pushed the sole of one foot into his face and pressed down, making his mouth warp to the side.

"Why, wait for your mother to arrive, silly."

A sound like a balloon popping burst from the supply room, followed by wet, sloppy steps across the black-and-white linoleum floor. Timothy's head twisted so he could see the opening. His mother shuffled into view. She was mostly skeletal, with thick strands of ashen flesh strung from her bones. The body struggled to maintain its form: with each step the grotesqueries that were her muddy feet stuck to the tiles—*slurp* when yanked upward, and *splat* when planted. Her eyes were deep cavities where worms crawled. As Timothy's mother lurched her way diagonally across the room, Gwen stood to the side of the table while Bryant had moved to the counter and now leaned against it, his tall frame on the verge of collapse.

"Hurry," he called hoarsely, "I can't wait much longer. I need it now."

Timothy saw the edge of the curved blade poking over the table's edge. He lifted his leg and gently kicked the pedestal. No one noticed his efforts until the knife fell with a clatter next to him. Bryant turned but coughed so violently he fell to a knee. Timothy snatched the knife and sawed through the twine at his ankles. When Gwen finally noticed and bent down, his legs were free, and he ran, though his arms remained bound in front of him. He first scooted to the corner by the front window, but Gwen, now at an enormous height, head close to the ceiling, needed only to turn and take a few steps. That same height, though, made her clumsy, slow to grasp. Timothy went through her legs. He knocked the table over as Bryant tried to grasp at him from the floor and then sprinted past his mother. The stench of her rot made him retch.

There was no door in the supply room, only shelves and boxes. Gwen, crouching like Alice through a too-small door, squeezed through after him. Her smile was so wide as to be disorienting. *Nothing that large should smile*, Timothy thought in a panic. Next his mother was through, and then Bryant, who crawled on hands on knees.

"I need it!" he screamed.

Timothy swung the knife in an arc at them.

"Please, leave me alone. I want to go home. I swear I'll find a way to get the ten dollars, Mister Bryant. I swear on—you can buy whatever you need then, buy all your gifts. You're scaring me. Mom, is that you? You would never hurt me."

He began to cry wholesome, shuddering sobs. The trinity closed on him even as he swiped the knife with full force. It nicked Gwen, and a trickle of blood fell.

If only he could get past her, he thought; the others were too weak to hold him. With one last swipe, he dove through her legs.

Coda

The boy stood inside the door, taking in the amazing smells of the shop. Bryant worked at the counter with his back to him. When he turned, the boy nearly jumped in the air.

"Hi ho! Welcome! What's your name?"

"John Figgins, sir."

"What a handsome name! Please sit, Mister Jonathon. What can I get for you?"

"Gosh, I don't know. What do you have?"

The man bowed and opened his arms. "I have only the best ice cream, made by myself with dairy straight from our town's teats. But my very best is a malt. Have you ever had a splendidly made malt?"

John shook his head. "I only have a nickel. How much for just a scoop of ice cream?"

Bryant laughed. "No, no. Don't worry about that. If you want a delicious malt, you can owe me. Okay? Keep your nickel. I know you're good for it."

John beamed. "Really? Wow, that's swell. Yes, then, I'd love a malt."

"Might I suggest a cherry malt? It's the best I have."

John nodded eagerly. "Yes, sir, that sounds great."

Mister Bryant turned to the back counter, a wide smile on his face. He glanced over his shoulder as he worked, first scooping vanilla ice cream into the cup, then adding milk and malt. Finally, he reached for an unlabeled coffee can and dripped the syrupy red liquid. As the machine churned the malt together, he glanced again over his shoulder to show his bright teeth.

John startled when his malt appeared. A mound of thick whipped cream rested atop it, along with a bright red maraschino cherry. Mister Bryant bent down so they were at eye level.

On the jukebox, The Robins clanked into place and sang about needing those cherry lips, sweet as sugar cane.

T.M. Morgan lives with his wife and children in southern Maryland near the Chesapeake Bay, where he's resided most of his life, save for stints in Boston, San Diego, Denver, and NYC. He has work in *Vastarien*, *Pseudopod*, and *Lamplight*, as well as other anthologies. You can read more about him at thetmmorgan.wor dpress.com.

FAMILY IS HELL

ESPECIALLY FOR CHILDREN

H ere we are again for the third installment of *Vinyl Cuts,* where records bleed! If you think your family is hell, check out these seven stories just burning for your attention.

BLOOD TIES

BY RYAN BENSON

The frigid wind cut straight through Jeanette Tanner's jacket and burrowed into her bones. She pulled the hood tight over her rosy cheeks and braced herself for the intermittent ice patches marking the sidewalk. A newfound hatred of NYC winters left her counting down the remaining days at York College. Despite the foul weather, leaving Queens would have been unthinkable mere months ago.

Jeanette walked a path she had almost worn smooth over the years. Friends and family populated the houses she passed on her way home. Each house remained well maintained, and Jeanette could smell the warm crackling fireplaces. Only her house had changed—*darkened*.

To lighten her mood, Jeanette fiddled with her silver locket. The dying winter sun reflected off the cross decorating the jewelry's face. She flipped the locket over and read her parents' inscribed names, "Danny and Pam." Happier times.

Jeanette reached her house sooner than expected and would've passed it if a gruff voice hadn't roused her attention. She brushed raven hair from her neck and placed the locket back under her blouse. Out of sight, out of mind.

On the porch, her father, wearing his NYPD blues, shouted at a tall bald man in a black suit. "You've wasted my time! I showed you the book. Now get out of here."

The tall man reached into his jacket but noticed Jeanette and relaxed. "Very well, Danny."

"That's 'Sergeant Tanner' to you, James," said her father.

Jeanette wondered what the man hid in his jacket. As on edge as Danny had been, she half expected him to draw his gun. Did he fear the strange man or now lack any fear of death at all?

James shot Jeanette a twisted expression she could have taken as either a smile or a grimace. Sweat ran down her frozen back as she watched James stalk down the street. His lanky arms swung like pendulums, and his stride stretched three times what it should. The herky-jerky movement belonged in a malfunctioning filmstrip more than on the streets of Queens.

The slamming door refocused Jeanette's thoughts. Her father had disappeared back into the house, but at least he had gotten a little sun. For weeks, he only left the house at night. Maybe he would get some color back into his pallid face.

She missed her mother.

As Jeanette ambled up the walkway, she noticed the cracks in the concrete. Water filled the breaks before freezing and widening the gaps, over and over, until the fissures expanded, but such was life in a northern town. Now, however, Jeanette felt something unholy peering up and out of the depths.

The rusty squeak of metal chains in the side yard caught her attention. Wind moved the old swing set like decades-old ghosts reenacting her father pushing her as a child. *Higher, Daddy! Higher!* She exhaled and continued to the front door.

Inside, Jeanette found her father banging the kitchen cabinets, searching for God knows what.

"Where is it?" he muttered. He pulled out the utensil drawer, crashing its contents to the floor. He spun around and collided with his daughter. "Where's your grandmother's silverware?"

"In the dining room." Jeanette looked into his eyes—rabid and unrecognizable.

Danny rushed past her. That's how they lived, her father ignoring her or casting her unsettling looks. Sometimes morose. Sometimes ravenous.

"Who was that?"

"What?" he yelled from the other room.

"The man at the door. Did it have to do with Mom?"

"Mom? No. He said he had information about the book I got in Massachusetts." Danny returned, silver carving knife in hand. "But he just wanted to buy it."

Memories of their family trips to Boston flooded Jeanette's mind. Her mother always rooted for the Red Sox against her father's Yankees. Jeanette fought the emotion and returned her thoughts to the massive tome. It looked almost like a family bible, bound in leather, and covered with ornate golden flower flourishes. "Why'd he want the book?"

"Later, Jeanette. That old fool wasted my entire afternoon. I have to eat!"

Jeanette smiled. When had she last seen her father eat? Maybe his hunger and his trip outside pointed to things returning to normal. "I'll make hamburgers. How much did he offer to pay?"

"Screw him and screw you." Danny slammed the door behind him and descended the basement staircase. Within seconds, Alice Cooper blasted from the speakers in the cellar.

Jeanette closed her eyes tight, fighting tears. So much for family dinner. Jeanette and her parents had gathered around the table every night, laughing, recounting their day. She sifted through her memories, searching for even one instance of Danny raising his voice, but came up empty.

The door squeaked open a sliver. Danny had forgotten to lock it. He had sealed it for weeks and forbade her from entering, even for laundry. What lay beneath?

Jeanette pushed the door open. The raucous horns of "Welcome to My Nightmare" hid the creaking of her steps. She reached the bottom and tiptoed to a second door for the tool room. Alice sang loud, but her heart beat louder. She turned the knob, and the dank odor slammed into her like a phantom escaping out of the room and up the stairs. The cellar always smelled musty, but this unnatural stench stung her nose.

Shadows danced on the tool room walls as if terrified of the single hanging bulb's wan light. A gagged man lay on the workbench. Crimson rivulets coursed from his shackles down his chafed skin and dripped onto the table's surface. He noticed Jeanette and his dark eyes silently screamed, *Help*. Danny leaned over the bench, his lips near the man's jugular.

Jeannette screamed, her body outpacing her mind, before clamping a hand over her mouth.

"Jeanette?" At the sight of his daughter, Danny's jaw hung open. On the verge of tears, he cut the music.

"Dad, what're you doing?" Jeanette took a few steps into the room before pausing.

Danny stepped toward her. Jeanette retreated, knocking the carving knife off a stool. His lips peeled back, canines lengthening before her eyes. Jeanette grabbed the knife and pointed it at her father.

"Careful." Danny nodded towards the man. "I use that after feeding."

"Feeding? Are you crazy?"

"If I let them turn, the city will fill with vampires."

"Vampires?" She contorted her face in disgust.

"It's all right here." Danny picked up the enormous book from New England. "Let me read you something." He opened to a spot bookmarked with a ribbon.

Jeanette froze. The book no longer resembled a pious Christian text. Now bound in pustule-covered flesh, a twisted face replaced the golden flourishes.

"Oh, jeez." Jeanette's breathing quavered.

The book smiled before a snakelike tongue slithered out of its maw and licked its own eye. Incomprehensible lyrics from an ancient song flowed from Danny's lips. Jeanette swayed before her consciousness fell into blackness.

Dull light from the bulb greeted her when she next opened her eyes. Why had she blacked out? She was never the helpless maiden. As the tendrils of fog retreated from her mind, Jeanette realized she sat in a chair. Handcuffs held her in place as she fought to stand.

"I need you to calm down." Danny smiled. His canines had shortened but still jutted lower than his other teeth. "Please." He moved the sweat-matted black hair from her eyes to behind her ear.

"Why are you doing this?"

"Must I repeat myself?" Danny threw up his hands. "Every living thing needs to eat."

"Vampires aren't alive." Jeanette narrowed her eyes. "See. I pay attention."

Danny nodded. "You believe me?"

"I believe you think you're a vampire, and you did something to your teeth."

"You'll change your tune soon enough."

Jeanette struggled against the cuffs. "Did you drug me?"

"No, honey, we are both sober as priests on Sunday."

Jeanette's attention drifted from Danny to the boombox and then to the man on the table. Shallow breaths escaped the prisoner's chest as his eyes focused on the ceiling, and tears spilled down his temples. Music had blared from the basement for weeks. "How many—"A glint of light reflected from Danny's hip. The silver carving knife was tucked into his belt, hanging by the handle like a lazy samurai. Bile bubbled up to her throat, interrupting her questioning. She swallowed and forced the caustic spit back where it came. "How many people?"

"Don't worry. I'm a cop. Remember? I pick people no one will miss. Besides, their bodies turn to ashes once I pierce their hearts." Danny pulled the silver knife from his belt. He drove the blade into a wooden stool in a blur, leaving it standing like the sword in the stone. "They never feel a thing. I can hit their heart on the first try now. It has to be silver though or at least silver-plated, like our heirloom silverware. I've tried with carbon-chromium-whatever-steel, but no dice."

"What am I? Your emergency snack?"

"Never." He held her face and softened his voice. "I was waiting until you were ready to turn. Not like—" He caught himself.

"Like who?" Jeanette pulled back. "Did you do this to Mom? Did you kill her?"

"I turned Pam and gave us everlasting life together." Danny looked at the floor. "But your mother wasn't ready for immortality's sacrifices. Pam wouldn't feed. She stepped into the sun and killed herself."

"You're lying!"

Danny shook his head. "If only."

"But *you* were in the sun."

"Yes, because of the book's spells. It's why I visited Massachusetts."

"Spells? You promised to find Mom."

"The book can bring her back." Danny read from the tome. "'*What I was once, alive, I am still now. The contradictions of life and death are disavowed.*' We'll be a family again." He shook the book at her. "Forever."

Danny moved behind Jeanette. She held her breath until she felt the metal bindings fall away.

"I'm hungry." Danny rushed to the workbench and wiped blood off the man's wrists. He rubbed the liquid between his fingers and smeared it on his tongue. "Wait upstairs. Soon it'll be him or you." The prisoner's eyes widened again as he begged the only way he could. Cries escaped through the gag. For the first time, Jeanette could tell his young age. He might as well be one of her classmates.

"Go on." Danny nodded to the stairs.

Her father had protected her all her life. Nurtured what he deemed good and nipped what he deemed bad. Eternal life with her father would give her freedom, but it would always be conditional. The Grim Reaper would pass her by as long as she kept him fat with her own constant victims.

Jeanette pulled the silver cutlery from the stool. She had helped her mother polish it each Thanksgiving. As she tilted the knife in her hands, Jeanette saw her eyes reflected in the polished metal—the same brown as her mother. Her gaze drifted to her father, nearing his victim, then back to the reflection of her eyes.

Mother, help me.

Jeanette stabbed her father—the man who gave her life—in the back. She pulled out the knife and stood silent, like a child awaiting a reprimand. Danny turned and hissed. His full two-inch canines and pointed ears exposed the changes within the monster.

Rage at the months of emotional abuse bubbled up and exploded out of Jeanette. The knife cut undead flesh, driving Danny back, though each slash failed to draw blood. The absence of blood splatter kept her moving forward—no harm, no foul. Or so she convinced herself.

Danny's flailing arms hit the hanging light, sending it swinging and creating a strobe effect like at a haunted house. It all seemed like a game—a dream. *It's so silly.* She couldn't really be in a life-or-death battle with her father. Could she?

The momentary pause in Jeanette's attack allowed Danny to retreat a few paces from the knife's reach. Collected and no longer off-balance, he came forward. A distended grin revealed rows of ivory fangs. Huge unblinking eyes, bloodshot and bloodthirsty, glared at the petrified woman.

With inhuman speed, Danny's claw-like hand darted forward and encircled Jeanette's throat. Out of instinct, she swung the blade, but he caught her fist and crushed her digits against the knife handle.

Blackness seeped in around Jeanette's view as her father strangled her. With her nearly limp left hand, she reached into her shirt and pulled out the locket. Danny shrieked and released Jeanette at the sight of the cross. Dropping to his knees, Danny covered his face and crawled to the corner.

Jeanette approached the soulless husk. The silver locket dangled from one hand while the other clutched the knife tight. After closing her eyes to protect any remaining sanity, the little girl inside Jeanette screamed. She raised the weapon, and her arm fell not once, nor twice, but many times. Silver plunged into faux human meat, piercing skin, tissue, and ribs.

Memories of Danny pushing her on the swings returned, but this beast had taken her mother. Grasping the knife with both hands, she brought it over her head, opened her eyes, and drove the weapon downward, severing the demon's heart.

The human form resembling Danny ignited into smoldering ashes. Her father was now gone—though, in truth, the man she loved had died months ago.

Jeanette staggered to the bench and unlatched her father's last meal.

"Thanks." The man rubbed his raw skin and winced. "Saved by a brunette Buffy."

"Huh?" Jeanette's gaze fixed on the ashes.

"*Buffy the Vampire Slayer.* You look like Sarah Michelle Gellar." He stared at his trembling hands. "Sorry, I'm just a little shook. I'm walking down the street when I'm kidnapped by a cop—worse, a vampire cop." He locked eyes with Jeanette once more. "And all I can think about is that dumb TV show."

"Totally fine." Jeanette burst out laughing at the absurdity of what occurred. How could she explain her missing mother and father? Should she tell the police—her father's friends—the truth? Would this strange man (who had since started laughing himself) corroborate her story? Laughter continued a few seconds longer until her giggles dissolved into sobbing tears.

"Jeez." The man hugged Jeanette and smoothed her hair. "My name's Xavier. Xavier Glover."

Jeanette blinked tears away, hoping to awaken from this nightmare. She used her sleeves to rub her eyes dry, but she was still in the basement, and her parents were still dead. After a deep exhale, she buried her face in Xavier's shoulder and threw her hands around his neck.

Something felt odd about the wetness of his skin. It was slipperier than sweat. Thicker. Jeanette's face went ashen. She stared at her bloodied fingertips—and the two puncture marks on his neck.

Xavier touched the blood. "Oh, sh—"

Ryan Benson (he/him) resides outside of Atlanta, GA, with his wife and children. Ryan keeps busy writing short fiction stories and his first novel. *Night Terrors Vol. 1* (Scare Street), *On Spec Magazine, The Sirens Call Publications, Trembling with Fear* (Horror Tree), and *The Nights End* podcast have published his work.

You can find Ryan on Twitter @RyanWBenson and Instagram at ryanbensonauthor.

RUB-A-DUB

BY STEPHEN COGHLAN

It might have been an eternity, but to Robert "Dizzy" Deacon, the water was still as warm as when he had entered the bath. Normally, the water cooled down well before the heat had soaked into his old and decrepit joints and soothed his arthritic limbs. This time around, he had enjoyed the luxury, closed his eyes, and relished the soak without complaint.

At least, he tried to. Despite his best efforts, Robert could not ignore the tune that rang in his ears. He knew the songs from his youth, his jiving days, back when he used to slap the soles of his shoes on the dance floor while courting the lovely ladies who lined the walls in wait of a handsome and slick partner to join them in bouncing and twisting alongside the other dancers in eager abandon. Although he sometimes played such songs on his well-kept Kenmore stereo, as the radio no longer played the songs of yore, he doubted that he had left the music on. Even if he had, the small forty-fives he prided as his collection should have ended long ago.

"Sprish-sprash, Im'ma scrubbin' in the bath." He surrendered to the music, singing to himself, twisting the lyrics to fit his modern life. It was a game to him, a mockery and defiance of his status as a senior citizen.

"A rub-a-dub, just driftin' in the tub."

No, it wasn't just a game. It was a mental exercise to keep his brain sharp and his wit keen.

"Thinking my arthritis is all right."

He chuckled despite anticipating that his chest would ache from the effort. A little pain was good for the heart. It reminded him that he was alive, so when no red-hot agony stopped his mirth, he paused in surprise.

No, he hadn't added anything to the water to ease such pains. The basket of toiletries that Patricia had gifted him still sat on the counter, unopened and unused. Yes, there was going to be some guilt when she next passed by unless Robert had at least sampled some of the solutions, bars, and powders. Making a mental note, he tried to schedule what he was going to use when. He didn't want a repeat of last time, when he had locked himself within the washroom upon her arrival, faking some stomach issues while he emptied some bottles into the toilet.

He hated to lie to her. She was always looking after him, her "ol' Uncle Bobby," always offering natural and holistic cures to the man who had doted over her like she was his own. Patricia had been an infant, barely out of his sister's womb, when Uncle Bobby had been involved in the life-changing accident. Therefore, Patricia learned to walk by imitating Uncle Bobby while he learned to use his legs again. It was her request, as a toddler, to have a bottle so she could drink like Uncle Bobby, her eyes wide open and innocent, that had awoken him from his depression and alcohol dependence. It was Patricia who had encouraged Uncle Bobby to clean up his act, get his life back together, to stop wallowing in guilt. And so, Patricia had become Uncle Bobby's special little angel.

It was Uncle Bobby who had taken her to ballet, then baseball, and who had taught her to drive. It was frightening. He hadn't been behind the wheel since the accident, but her father was too busy to teach her, and her mother, bless her heart, was too busy with the other three kids to spend any time looking after the oldest. So Uncle Bobby had sucked up all his courage, plucked the keys from the countertop, and finally got back behind the wheel of the family station-wagon so he could teach sweet Patricia how to handle a stick-shift. It was Uncle Bobby who had walked Patricia down the aisle when she wed, and no one in the family had objected. He had earned the right to hand her off to her husband, but even her marriage never tore them far apart.

"Gosh darn, I'm a sentimental coot." He sighed to himself, wiping away the tear that rolled down one wrinkled cheek.

The music grew in volume, betraying that it wasn't just in his head, but definitely coming from down below as the bath water vibrated, forming ringlets made by the pressure of sound waves hammering the walls. Robert couldn't make out the lyrics or the tune anymore, but it still made an impression on his psyche. Curious and energized, he pulled himself out of the water with ease. Normally he was forced to rely on the shower-bar that Patricia's oldest son-in-law had installed for him, but this time there was no straining or grunting, and by the time he was standing on the mat beside the tub, his toes tingled and he shivered. Maybe he had used one of the gifted products after all, but a cursory glance confirmed that the caffeine-infused soap was still in its box, encased in cellophane. Shrugging, Robert wrapped a towel around his nakedness, tucked his feet into his favorite slippers, and hurried down the stairs.

The tune crescendoed as he approached the living room, but failed to drown out the laughter, merriment, and cheers of many people enjoying themselves. The forewarning stopped him from being shocked into stupidity at how crowded his living room was, but he was still surprised that so many people occupied the space.

While the tunes didn't stop, Robert no longer heard them. How, how could the room be so full? How could it be so packed with so many people he swore were no longer alive? There was Reggie, but hadn't he died from pancreatic cancer ten years ago? There was Miss Ellen, his high school English teacher, who had inspired Robert to attend literary college. Hadn't she died only a few years later from heart-related disease? There was "Dashing" Don, and Mr. Kekoa, and Mrs. Auski and—

And there was Glory. She was waiting, the way she often had. Her black, curly hair was pulled back into a single-knotted ponytail, and with her hair out of the way her deep brown eyes sparkled in the light from overhead. The glance she threw looked both mischievous and playful as her grin narrowed her already-high cheekbones. She swam through the crowded dance floor, shifting her hips with cat-like grace and sidestepping those who were too oblivious to notice her. The emerald green dress clung to her, barely creasing, and the water in her whiskey tumbler never spilled until she placed it on a passing tray that was wielded by a server that Bobby thought they knew but could not remember from where or when.

"Are you going to stand there all day," she said, "or are you going to take my hand and join me on the floor, sugar?"

Glory was charming when she needed to be, and sassy, due to surviving her upbringing. Hated by her father's people for being too dark and loathed by her mother's bloodline for being too light, Glory had grown up with a savvy head for politics. She had the ability to deflect insults into compliments, and to lash back when needed. Heaven help the object of her scorn, as her tongue stung worse than an open-handed slap or a closed right-hook.

Despite her beauty, it was not her stunning looks that had made a first impression on Robert. It had been her voice, and what a hell of an impression it was.

Robert had been out with a few friends from college that night, discussing the latest controversies of Vladimir Nabokov's recently published novel. They were seated in the corner of the local bar, where the wood floors leached the scent of stale booze despite being washed every night. Smoke wafted from the burning cigarettes that resided in overflowing ashtrays, filling the air with a haze akin to a mist on a Halloween evening. Karaoke wasn't a thing at the time, but there was a stage, and patrons were invited to head up with instruments, poems, or their own words.

With a voice made husky by the remnants of a cold, and aggravated by the hovering smoke, the siren-songstress began.

"Stars shining—"

And he was sucked back to the present as the woodwinds and brass took up the silence of Robert's shock. Ivory keys tickled his senses while Glory took his hand and pulled him onto the makeshift dance floor that the shag carpet had become.

Uncaring that only a towel garbed him, or that his feet were stuffed into slippers instead of proper dancing shoes, Robert let a smile crease his lips as he pulled Glory tightly against him. Her emerald, green dress was smooth against his naked chest. It was a finer material than she had ever been able to afford before. Even the prices at the pawnshops and thrift stores were too much when it came to such silk. Cinnamon and spice filled the space between them and he blinked back tears as he inhaled greedily. Unwilling to break down in front of his lover, he closed his eyes and focused instead on moving his lithe body with hers.

Dancing was just another form of making love for them. It had become their own joke, when they said they were going to hit the floor together. Both were gratifying, intimate, and a moment of sharing between them that was theirs and theirs alone.

"You can look now, lover," Glory chided him. "Let me see the ocean."

It was her code to see the blue in his eyes.

"And I see the earth," he whispered back, admiring the rich brown of hers.

They laughed together, moved in close, pressed their lips against each other's.

Reaching behind, he pressed his hand against the back of Glory's head to push her tighter to him, but he met no resistance past her hair, and his fingers slipped into a soft and jellied substance. Glory didn't seem to notice, and her husky moan brought urges Robert had not felt in a long time. Uncertain whether to react to the material squashing between his fingers or to Glory's firm yet yielding flesh against his own, or to keep some semblance of public decency despite only wearing a towel and his slippers, he instead played it as cool as he could and decided to savor the kiss as long as the moment allowed.

And then he forgot everything except the moment, and as she breathed he inhaled, and sweet chili and unmistakable cayenne rested on his tongue. It did not last, however, as, when she pulled away gently, the creases of Robert's knuckles met something unmistakably wrinkled and carrion.

It was just like the last night that he had been with her, the night he had rolled the car, when he had pulled his broken and battered body from the wreckage, had held Glory in his arms, and when he had lifted her head to his lips for one last kiss his fingers had vanished into her skull and the mangled remains of her brain.

Shocked back to reality, Robert broke the embrace and stared at the glistening liquids that coated his palm. Gone were the sweet scents and tastes of his lover, replaced with the odors of blood and leaking oils and evaporating gas.

He wanted to believe that nothing had happened, but when he looked up and around to ground himself, he stared into and through the gaping back of Bennie, one of his high school pals who Robert had lost contact with when Bennie had joined the military. Bennie hadn't noticed Robert's attention though, as he was jiving and swirling around with a woman Robert didn't recognize, but they were both laughing and having a grand old time.

There was another friend from high school, good ol' Howdy, so called because he resembled the puppet Howdy Doody. Both had red hair, freckles, and a grin that could cut their faces in half, but friend Howdy also wore his thick glasses, and was forced to push them back up his face after a particularly ambitions twirl which had also loosened the handkerchief around his neck and exposed the weird burns and bruising that the blue cloth had covered. Hadn't he been found in his parents' garage, having hanged himself after a breakup?

At the other end of the floor, Aadarsh laughed, and when he did an eye popped free from his skull and hung from his head, just like when he was apparently beaten to death by white supremacists early one morning. Unperturbed, Aadarsh caught the organ that swung in front of his face and pushed it back into the crushed socket, only for it to fall again a moment later.

Clutching his hand over his chest, Robert tried to steady his heart, but couldn't feel his most-vital organ beating through the numbness of his limbs.

"What is going on?" he asked, confused and desperate for an answer. His question was unguided and broad, pleading for anyone to help him make sense.

Viscera and offal mixed with serenity and stillness while the music continued to sing from the speakers and the floor spun and the ceiling shook and Robert collapsed to his hands and knees as his youthful body's chest ached and seized and he gasped for air and the panic threatened to overcome him.

Glory's hand closed over his shoulder, and for a moment, nothing was wrong.

"Sprish sprash," he gasped. "I was scrubbin' in the bath."

Shaking his head, he swallowed.

"Now I'm reeling with the feeling and the floor's moving and grooving, rockin' and a-rollin'."

"Dizzy, dear," Glory said. Her tone was the one she used when explaining something to him that he had never experienced before. "I was dead long before that song was released."

"I know," Robert sobbed. "So, how am I talking to you?"

With tender fingers, Glory turned his face until he was looking her in the eyes. Brushing her hair out of her face, Glory pulled her hair behind herself, tying it together with her usual expert motions, covering the gaping wound that Robert knew was there.

"Sprish sprash, you *were* scrubbin' in a bath." Glory spoke softly through her smile, her words somehow piercing the loud cacophony from the dance floor. Her fingers rested over Robert's chest, pressing where his heart normally beat.

"But you're also almost a centenarian," she continued, "and you climbed into the bath by yourself."

Robert blinked as he tried to put her riddle together, and then he answered, "I suppose I'm not climbing out, am I?" The tightness in his chest eased, and he sucked in a great lungful of air.

Patting her head, Glory grinned and undid her bun, exposing her now-intact and untorn scalp.

"No, Dizzy, but it's not your problem anymore."

The front door rattled as a key was pushed into the lock. There was only one other person who had a key to his house. Patricia was stopping by? Of course she was. She only lived two blocks away.

The rattling ceased, and the music stopped as the front door cracked open, and then it slowed and ceased to move.

The uninvited guests applauded as Glory pulled Robert to his feet, his body no longer burdened by creaking joints and arthritic agony. The hands of the grandfather clock were frozen mid-swing, and dust motes hung locked in place.

Blinking, Dizzy wondered how Patricia was going to react when she found his corpse in the tub.

"It's the end of the line," he said, hinting to everyone that he now knew what was going on.

Miss Ellen wrapped her arms around Robert's chest and gave him an affectionate squeeze. "And the start of something new."

And he was no longer naked, but instead dressed in his favorite waistcoat and suit, and his hat was perched playfully over his head, and his tie was tight, but not enough to restrict circulation.

A bright light grew into the wall where his stereo system stood. One by one, the guests walked into the illumination and vanished until only Glory was left holding his hand, their fingers interlocked.

"What if I refuse?" Dizzy asked.

Glory shook her head. "You won't be able to resist for long. It's okay to be scared, love, but sooner than later, you'll follow." Her smile never faded as she untwined her fingers from his. "Do you want one last look around?"

Taking a steadying breath, Dizzy held it and wondered how he really looked in the tub. Was his skin ashen and pallid? Was his face relaxed and serene? Would it be okay to run upstairs, grab a towel, and cover his nakedness before poor Patricia saw him?

Was he that desperate to know how he looked that he would dare walk away from the love of his life, even for a minute, ever again?

This time, he took her hand, and with a light step, a twirl, and a bow, he invited Glory to dance with him into his unknown. Laughing, she curtsied, and together they walked into the blinding light.

Stephen Coghlan is a multi-genre, multi-small-press-published author writing from Canada's national capital. When not lost in his literary lands, he can be found crawling around in ventilation, antagonizing his long-suffering wife with his macabre humor, or running every errand as he fakes being a responsible adult.

Although his genres are varied, from deep sci-fi to an alternative-Edwardian-period erotic-human/centaur-crop-opera, he is known for including found-family, positive LGBQTP+ rep, and diverse characters because his family is, and he wants to write something that those he loves will be proud of him for creating. His website can be found at http://scoghlan.com.

LEADER OF THE PACK

BY STEVEN STREETER

"T hanks for taking her at short notice." Betty sounded relieved.

Jeff did not even bother with the pretense of a smile. "I knew you'd call me tonight," he said evenly. "I made sure I had no plans."

"Don't you like spending time with our—*your*—daughter?"

Now he did smile. "Betty, you know I do. And you know I would love to spend more time with Ellie. But you make me jump through hoops just to see her when I am supposed to see her." He held his hands up defensively. "But I'm not here to pick a fight. I knew you'd be calling me, so I made sure I was ready. So how long would you like me to look after her?"

Betty gazed at the girl holding on to her father's hand as though happy to be going away from this place. "Three days?" she suggested.

Jeff stared at her for a moment. She had not even started to take the bait he had just dangled in front of her. No hint of an argument, no scowling, no anger, nothing. But maybe he should have expected it. After all, this was really the reason they had broken up five years before, and the divorce had only seemed to make her obsession worse. And with tonight being the twenty-fifth anniversary . . .

He looked at his thirteen-year-old daughter and she smiled at him, almost gratefully. They spent every second weekend and half of each school holidays together, so this was a bonus. Jeff decided to push it a little bit further. "How about I drop Ellie back on Sunday?" he suggested. "We'll make a weekend of it."

"That okay with you, honey?" Betty asked the teenager. Again, Jeff was stunned. There was not the slightest indication that she was going to fight him on anything tonight.

The smile spread from one side of the youngster's face to the other. "Yes, mum," she whispered. "Please."

"Okay then." Betty returned her gaze to Jeff. "She's all yours. I'll see you in five days." She kissed her daughter on the cheek, but the child winced at the contact. "See you then," she said, almost pushing them out of the door.

"What's wrong with mum this time?" the girl asked as they made their way to the car.

He smiled a little. "I tell you what, after we've had something to eat, I'll tell you all about it. This time of the year is, well, special to your mum, and tonight's an important anniversary. It's also why your mum and I aren't together anymore. So, I think it's time you knew the truth." He cast one last glance at the house he had shared with Ellie for so many years and shuddered. Twenty-five years, and yet to Betty it might as well have been yesterday . . .

The middle-aged woman fishing on the edge of the bridge looked around as a motorcycle engine revved again and again. She was wary; bike riders never came here.

She stared into the darkness curiously, and with some trepidation. This road had not been open to traffic for a long time, at least twenty years. It was one of the reasons why it was so popular with the local fishing community. While still wide enough to maybe take a car, the Causeway Bridge was now just a walking track across the river, looked after by the locals.

And in the past ten years—as long as she had been coming here to fish—she had never heard an engine like that one.

Loud and raucous, and deliberately so.

She peered through the night, feeling increasingly nervous.

And then there was a squealing of tyres and a cloud of putrid smoke as the red taillight flashed into life before it disappeared into the night. The sound faded slower than the light, lasting much longer than any visible signs of the vehicle.

She shuddered a little as a feeling of coldness ran through her bones.

She did not want to be here anymore.

She quickly reeled in the line and packed her gear into the plastic box, then ran all the way back to her house on the outskirts of the town.

Ellie scooped a mouthful of noodles out of the take-away container and dropped half of them onto her lap. Jeff laughed, and she quickly joined in.

"You mess," he snorted.

"Dad," she said with mock hurt, and they laughed again.

He passed her a napkin, and she carefully cleaned up the mess. "So, dad, what's up with mum?" the teenager asked.

He stared at the mess of chicken and vegetables in the box in front of him. "Have you ever met your grandfather, your mum's dad?"

"Mum said she doesn't have a dad," Ellie said. "She said he was dead, like your dad."

"She's still saying that, huh?" Jeff paused briefly and shook his head. "Well, he's not dead. He still lives in the same house your mum grew up in. I've only met him twice, the first time about a month after we got married. He actually tracked me down at work. He told me that there was another man who he was sure would come between your mum and me, and he was right."

"Another man?" Ellie's eyes were wide with anticipation. "Ooh, tell me more!"

"Now, now," Jeff chided gently. "The guy's been dead for twenty-five years."

"I don't understand."

"No, it's not easy. But your grandpa—George, his name is—told me all about it. Your mum blames her dad for a lot of what happened, and she says he's even the reason why Jimmy's dead." He ate some more food, then added quietly, "Your mum doesn't even know I've spoken to George." He sighed. "And, truth be told, I didn't even know about Jimmy until we'd been married for a year. That was the tenth anniversary of his death. She acted weird for about a week. We argued a lot, and then, one day, right out of the blue, she just started to act as though everything was normal. But I noticed a photograph on her desk that I hadn't seen before. I asked her about it, and she just said one word: 'Jimmy.' Over the years she told me a few things, but I had to work out a lot by myself. Then I found George again and asked him a few questions as well. And then you came along and . . ."

"She never wanted me," the teenager suddenly muttered.

Jeff touched her on the leg. "That's not fair, honey," he said soothingly. "She loves you. She just . . ."

"She just what?"

"She just wishes you had a different father, that's all."

"What?"

Jeff smiled and it was so sad Ellie felt a tear form in her own eye.

"His name was Jimmy," Jeff said.

George Morton flipped the channel on the television until he found a replay of the weekend's football game and settled into his chair with his second beer for the night. If his wife had still been alive she would have nagged at him for having two of them, but it was just him alone in this house now. Sure, his children, Daniel and Maryann, and their families made sure he was all right, but, really, he was all alone.

His eyes fell to the two family portraits on the mantle-piece—Daniel, his wife and their two children, Maryann, her husband and their four. Such good kids; such a good family.

The third picture, hidden at the back, caught his eye and the smile on his lips froze. He, his now-dead wife, and their three children, Daniel, Maryann, and Bettina. Bettina . . . Betty. Their middle child. The one who had disowned them all after . . .

His brow furrowed. He could almost hear the motorbike outside, revving its engine as that no-good Jimmy waited for Betty to go out and join him. He had been the leader of one of the local motorcycle gangs, and a nasty piece of work, if his police rap sheet was anything to go by. They had put up with it for three months. And then he had put his foot down and told her that Jimmy was no good for her. His wife had backed him up completely, and Betty had run outside into Jimmy's arms.

He had left without her. And then . . .

Why would he think about that now? It had been so long since he had even thought about how Betty was back then, let alone that idiot biker.

An engine roared somewhere in the night.

Was that it—the motorbike outside sparking those old memories? They never came into this suburb anymore. The residents here were older, beyond that sort of thing. He turned back to the television, trying to clear his mind.

The date ran across the bottom of the screen as a news headline about a storm approaching the area ran across it. He looked at it as his memory whirred into gear, and then his heart sank. He knew that date.

It was the date of the accident when Jimmy was no longer a problem for them. He thought about it for a few moments longer. Twenty-five years. It had to be.

The sound of the bike grew louder.

He pushed himself up from his chair and walked to the front window. He drew back the curtain a little and stared through the gap.

The bike was parked in front of his house. It was dark out there, and the rider was wearing black, but George recognised the shape of the bike. It was a shape that he had seen in only one other machine, modified by its owner.

But that was impossible. That bike had exploded in a fireball after crashing through the side barrier of the old Causeway Bridge.

So, what was this . . . ?

The headlight flashed on, and the front wheel turned. The engine gunned even louder, and then, in a cloud of rubber smoke and a screech of tyres, the motorbike roared across the front lawn of the house.

George's eyes widened in fear and he stumbled backwards, tripping over his chair and falling to his back as the front window exploded inwards in a shower of broken glass. The bike screeched to a halt on the front carpet.

The visor of the helmet snapped up and George could only whimper pathetically through his terror.

"No," he pleaded. "No . . ."

And the bike's engine once more roared into life.

"Wow! So, my grandpa told mum to stop seeing the biker guy!" Ellie was genuinely surprised.

"And apparently she went out and told him what her dad had said and he just drove off," Jeff went on. "Just like that, it was all over. Your mum never forgave her dad for making her do that."

They ate in silence for a few moments more, then: "I don't get why she didn't just sneak out and see him," Ellie said. "I mean, twenty-five years ago, that was the 1980s. I know they didn't have Facebook or anything like that back then, but surely she could have kept on seeing him in secret or something."

Jeff laughed a little. "Yeah, things were easier to keep secret before there were computers, that's for sure," Jeff sighed. "And you know, you're right. They could easily have kept on seeing each other, but . . ." He shrugged.

"But?" she urged.

Jeff looked at her, and she returned the gaze, but neither could say anything. For a long time they merely looked at one another before Jeff said quietly, "The night she told him what her dad had told her, there was an accident. A bad one. Jimmy didn't make it."

Betty stared at the photograph, the only one of Jimmy she had. Black and white, tattered at one corner, crinkled where her tears had fallen on it for too many nights, but it was him. Black leather jacket, modified motorbike, baseball cap on the back of his head, long greasy hair, and a pose that was pure James Dean. She smiled a little, but the memories of that night were still so fresh. It wasn't a quarter of a century, it was yesterday. She had tried to tell him how much she loved him, that it was all her father's fault, that they could still see one another if they were careful, but she didn't know if he had heard anything after, "My dad told me I'm not allowed to see you again." At least, that was when he had revved the engine and just roared off down the street on that unique bike of his.

She held the photo against her chest and started to dance around the room as the sounds of Duran Duran flowed from the stereo in the corner of the room. He pretended to hate that sort of music, but in one of their quiet moments together he had admitted to liking some of their songs.

That was all she had needed to hear.

And when she played this album, she was sure that sometimes she could hear the engine of that modified bike of his sounding in the distance as he led his gang through the streets of their town, maybe even coming to visit her.

She even imagined sometimes that she could hear the rumble-thump-thump as he idled outside her house, waiting for her to meet him in the night air, where he would take her away from her boring parents and siblings and into a world she could not have imagined existed.

The song stopped on the stereo and the arm lifted off the vinyl record.

The sound of the idling engine remained in the air.

And then it revved into life.

She froze.

But there was no denying the smile that crossed her face.

"He died? That is so sad."

Jeff stared at his daughter for a few moments before deciding that she was being serious.

"And she's held a candle for him ever since," he sighed. "When I decided there couldn't be three people in our marriage, she chose him over me. So, we broke up and that's where we are now." Jeff scooped some more food in his mouth, not because he was particularly hungry but just to stop himself from saying anything else.

Ellie stirred the chopsticks through her food. "Where did he die?" she asked.

Jeff shrugged. "Not sure," he muttered.

"You know," she insisted. "Where was it?"

He sighed. "Yeah, I know. I looked it up in the old newspapers at the library. He crashed off the old Causeway Bridge. Back then it was part of the River Road, but when they built the new bridge and diverted the road, that's when it became part of the national park—"

"Yeah, my school did an excursion there," she interrupted, then appeared thoughtful for a moment. "He crashed off that bridge? But wouldn't he have landed in the river?"

"Went so fast he slammed into the rocks on the opposite bank. Looking at the picture in the paper, it started a pretty big fire."

"Can we go have a look?" Ellie asked, her voice nervous.

"What, tomorrow? I guess so. It's a bit, well, unpleasant, though, isn't—"

"No, Dad. Tonight. Now."

Jeff's heart felt like it skipped a beat. "Look, I don't think so, dear," he sighed.

"I'll bet Mum'll be there," Ellie went on. "We can see what she does."

"I really don't think it'll be a good idea," Jeff insisted.

"Why not?"

He shrugged, and then decided to be completely honest with her. "It's the twenty-fifth anniversary of his death tonight. I would feel really uncomfortable going there."

"What? His ghost or something?"

"Just the thought of it." Jeff shook his head. "It doesn't feel right."

Ellie stared at him, smiling a little, and he groaned to himself. This was yet another argument with his daughter that he was not going to win.

Betty opened the front door.

She knew that bike.

It was unmistakable. Designed by Jimmy himself, as black as the night, it was now sitting in front of her house.

And he was on it. Black leather jacket, black helmet, black boots, blue jeans. Just as always. The sheer impossibility of the situation did not even enter her mind. It was him and he was here and that was all that mattered.

She closed the door quietly behind her as though still a teenager sneaking out of her parents' house and ran on tiptoes to the machine. Without even thinking, she swung her leg over it and grabbed the rider around the waist as tight as she could.

Even the smells were the same. The leather, the petrol, the oil, the grime, the deodorant he always wore. All just as she remembered.

She closed her eyes and let her mind travel back twenty-five years as the machine roared into vibrant life, and they sped off down the street, the wind in her hair, the feel of Jimmy in her arms.

It was all going to be all right.

Jeff pulled to halt in the car park at the end of the Causeway Bridge. A large sign detailed the history of the bridge, dating back over a hundred years, and how the local community saved it so that walkers could enjoy the park on both sides of the river so much better, but Ellie all but ignored it as she ran to the edge of the bridge and leaned against the railing to look over the side at the darkness below.

"Where was it?" she asked excitedly.

"Ellie," Jeff chastised. "It's not a game. A man died here, a man your mum loved. A man your mum still loves."

She appeared to be hurt by his words and shrank into herself a little, but she kept her eyes on the landscape below.

He stood beside her and placed his hands on her shoulders, then guided her across to the opposite side. He pointed at a pile of rocks that reached from the water's edge all the way up to the side of the walking trail that followed the course of the waterway, leading away at right angles from the bridge. "I think it was there," he mumbled. Then he gazed down the railing. "I don't know where he went through; they replaced it all when they made it a walkway, but it was probably about halfway along."

"Wow," she whispered, walking down the path and running her hand along the wooden barrier. She suddenly stopped and stared back at the rock. "I reckon it was here," she said quietly and stood there, staring at the crash site with an expression on her face that Jeff could not place, but which scared him more than he was willing to admit.

A rumbling sound reached their ears, and they looked up with a start.

It was coming from the opposite direction and growing louder and louder. Ellie ran back to her father, and he enveloped her with his arms, but neither of them made a move back towards their car. That sound was almost hypnotic in its powerful roaring as it grew closer and closer to them.

It was an unmistakable sound.

A motorbike, going at full throttle, its muffler modified to make it even louder than it otherwise would have been.

In the distance they saw the white beam of its single headlight cut through the night sky. The light grew brighter as the motorcycle neared them, the vehicle not slowing down.

Soon the engine noise became almost deafening as the bike headed straight for them at a stupid speed, the rider sitting upright so they could see a second pair of arms wrapped around their chest. It mounted the curb and roared along the

Causeway Bridge, as if aiming for the pair of them, standing in the light of its single headlight like two scared rabbits.

Then it seemed to skid on the surface of the bridge.

The bike slammed into the wooden guard-rail, crashing through it like it was made of paper.

"My God! Mum!" Ellie cried, but the woman holding onto the back of the rider was lost in her own world, eyes closed, a broad grin on her face.

The visor of the helmet shot up, and Jeff had a fleeting glimpse of the driver underneath it . . .

Of a grinning skull that appeared to be laughing all the way to the point of impact against the stone wall.

"Mum!" screamed Ellie, rushing to the side of the bridge as the fireball reached into the sky in a mushroom cloud of black and orange, the heat reaching her and her dad in a blast of rushing air. "Mum! Mum! No! No-o-o!!" she sobbed, and it took all of Jeff's strength to hold her back.

But he understood the truth.

Betty finally had the man she wanted, even if she had had to wait for twenty-five years to be with him.

Steven Streeter is from rural Australia and has been writing since childhood. He is a former professional wrestler, with two children, and has recently completed his third university degree. An unabashed fan of pulp fiction and escapist entertainment, he has had a number of short stories published in anthologies. He has also had a young adult horror novella published (*Under Ground*, Black Hare Press), and two adult horror novels (*Patch of Green*, Little Demon Books, *Invasive Species*, Am Ink).

LOLA

BY KAY HANIFEN

The third step from the top of the stairs always creaked, so Lola knew to skip it as she crept down. The TV droned below, her dad's snores drowning out the overly excited woman amazed by the latest infomercial gadget. Lola clung to her backpack and clunky combat boots, hardly daring to breathe as she slipped past him and to the door. Shutting it behind her, she relaxed for what felt like the first time in her life. She sat on the front steps to lace up her boots, and then stood up, straightened her thrifted skirt, and let a grin spread across her face. The concert plans had been months in the making. Months of saving up cash, buying components of her outfit to secret away in the darkest depths of her closet, and growing her hair out with the excuse that she wanted to look like Axl Rose. That night, after putting together her outfit and applying her makeup, she had stared in wonder at the mirror. For the first time in her life, she looked like herself. The contents of the backpack, though, was a reminder that she was only Cinderella. She could go out and dance as she was, but knew that she would return to her old rags at the end of the night.

Brian's ancient van pulled up and she got in, feeling lighter that she'd ever felt. Raven, Morrigan, and Brian were the only other goth kids at her school, so they had inevitably gravitated towards each other, finding solace in one another's weirdness and loneliness. Still, though, there was a part of herself she'd kept hidden until that night, something setting her apart from the rest of the group.

As the only one with a driver's license, Brian was in the driver's seat while Morrigan and Raven sat in the back, passing around a single beer and pretending to like the taste. With copious amounts of gel, Brian had shaped his hair into a spiky black mohawk. He had clearly borrowed his mom's mascara and eyeliner for his face, and wore his black jacket painted with an anarchy symbol.

Raven, a natural blonde, had been dying her hair a veritable rainbow of colors ever since she learned the Kool-Aid trick at a sleepover. The box dye color du jour was an electric blue stark against her black eyeshadow and lipstick. Her dress was frilly and artfully torn in several places. The last time Lola saw her wear it, the dress was intact and Raven was on her way to her grandmother's funeral. Raven looked her up and down, nodding in approval. "Looking good, Da —"

Lola cut her off, her heart pounding in her throat. "Actually, can you call me Lola? Just for tonight? I want to be myself for once."

"A girl?" Morrigan asked as she gave her a soft look. In the streetlight, the electric blue streaks in her hair gave her an almost ethereal glow. She shifted her layered black skirt so that Lola could sit beside her. God, sitting close to Morrigan was enough to make Lola's heart pound for completely different reasons.

Lola nodded, studying her shoelaces. "Yeah. I want to be a girl named Lola." Saying it out loud made her feel like Atlas after Hercules took his place holding up the sky.

"Lola, like the song?" Brian asked, earning a groan from Raven and Morrigan.

Well, he wasn't wrong. When she first heard the song about a man loving a woman with a man's body, the world shifted as though she'd spent her life with gravity pushing her a little bit sideways, and then, for the first time, she could walk upright. She bought the vinyl and listened to the record on repeat until her dad broke it in a fit of drunken rage. "Something like that, yeah."

He pumped his fist. "Rock on."

"You don't think that's weird?" she asked.

Raven threw an arm over her shoulder. "We're all weirdos. Since we're all coming out, I might as well say it—I think everyone's hot, guys, girls, and everyone in between."

"And I like girls," Morrigan replied, her dark brown eyes warm as she fiddled with her ankh necklace. Their eye contact lasted just a split second too long, and they turned away, their cheeks burning.

"Wait, does that make me the only normal one?" Brian asked.

Raven crumpled up an old McDonald's wrapper and tossed it at him. "You're the least normal out of all of us."

"I mean, something has to be wrong with you if you're actively choosing to hang out with us," Lola added.

He chewed his lip, thinking on her point. "Fair enough."

They spent the rest of the car ride laughing, joking, and jamming to the radio.

The venue was small, but the parking lot was packed. They had to park on the road and walk for five minutes just to get to the front door. They passed by men and women shouting Bible verses and that these gay satanic rockers were going to Hell. Lola anxiously pressed in closer to Morrigan while Raven flipped them off, yelling, "Awesome! I'll save you a seat right next to Satan's asshole."

Brian took her by the arm and pulled her away from them. "Okay, let's not antagonize the protestors."

"What are they gonna do? Exorcise me?" She turned back towards them, and cupping her hands around her mouth, shouted, "Your mother sucks cocks in hell!"

Morrigan hooked her arm around Raven's elbow as well, tugging more insistently. "For once, he's right. Don't let them ruin our fun."

"I'm having plenty of fun."

"It's the middle of the night. Don't they have anything better to do?" Lola muttered.

Morrigan shrugged. "I doubt it. It's either this or locking yourself up in the penance room to apologize for all your sins."

"And if they're feeling extra kinky, they'll whip themselves like they did during the plague," Raven added, earning a snort from Brian.

Reaching the door, they proffered their hands, the Sharpie X's marking them as minors. The inside was hot with a crush of human bodies packed so close that the four friends could hardly see the stage. The energy was electric, and Lola couldn't help but bounce on the balls of her feet to a tune all her own. Morrigan took her hand. "So, we don't lose each other," she shouted over the din.

The lights slowly went down as the band took the stage. The lead singer had a shaved head and broad shoulders that spoke to masculinity as well as a feminine shape and voice, making them somehow look like both and neither a man nor a woman. Seeing that filled Lola with an unexpected warmth.

"Are you ready to rock?" the singer shouted into the microphone to thunderous applause. "Then welcome one and all to Midnight Mass." The first notes of an electric guitar rang out, and the night had begun.

Swept away by the music, Lola drifted in a timeless void from the first set to the second, exhilarated by the crush of bodies and the feeling of Morrigan's hand in hers. Too soon, the concert was over, and they held onto each other, drunk on their own pleasure as they filed out of the venue.

Brian cheered and punched the air with a leap. "Whoo! That was awesome!"

"Can you say that a little louder?" Raven said, smiling good-naturedly. "I don't think they heard you in the next town over."

The backpack Lola carried felt heavier with each step. She wanted to wear her outfit as long as she could, dreading her return to the costume she wore every day just to survive. Morrigan pulled her close and whispered, "I don't think I told you, but you look amazing. The prettiest girl at the concert."

Despite the chill of the night, Lola suddenly felt warm all over. "You're just saying that. We all know you were the prettiest."

"Ugh, stop dancing around each other and get a room," Raven said. They'd reached Brian's van already, and she was half hanging out the door. The stragglers stepped inside, and she shut the door behind them.

"I'm cool with make-out sessions in the car," Brian said, "But no sex. I may have been conceived here, but I'm the only car baby allowed."

Faces burning like an inferno, Lola and Morrigan scooted apart. Raven rolled her eyes and threw another wrapper at him. "Way to go, Brian. Now they're even more repressed than before."

"And you made us think about your parents having sex," Morrigan added, throwing her own garbage.

Lola crumpled up a Taco Bell napkin and tossed it.

Brian winced. "Ow. *Et tu*, Lola?"

"Some sins cannot be forgiven," she replied.

"My friends are abusive," he muttered, putting the van into drive. Without the energy of the concert, the exhaustion from an all-nighter hit them in minutes. Morrigan's eyelids drooped as she sagged against Lola, while Raven snored against a window. "So . . ." Brian asked, breaking the silence, "how did you figure out that you were a girl?"

She struggled to find the words. "All my life, I've felt like something was different about me. I wanted to wear princess dresses and makeup and sparkly shoes as a kid, but I didn't know there were others like me until I heard the song on the radio."

"Wait, I was right? You named yourself after a Kinks song?"

Her face burned now for a completely different reason. "I—I guess."

"Awesome! You think you can convince Raven and Morrigan to start calling me Bruce Wayne?"

"You're making fun of me," she said flatly and watched his eyes widen in the rearview mirror.

"No, no, sorry. You know me. I've put my foot in my mouth so many times that my tongue tastes like gym socks. I think Lola's a great name."

"You don't think it's weird?" she asked softly.

He shrugged and turned onto an isolated road. "I think that you're my friend, and if being a girl named Lola makes you happy, then who am I to tell you not to be?"

Hearing that unraveled a portion of the Gordian knot binding the inside of her chest. She let out a slow breath. "Thank you for saying that. It means a lot. You're a good friend."

"Obviously," he said, winking into the mirror.

A shape in the middle of the road caught her eye. "Deer."

"I thought you wanted to be with Morrigan, but if you want to call me dear, I don't . . ."

"No—deer!" she exclaimed, pointing ahead of them.

With a shriek, he swerved to avoid the buck standing in the road. The wheels of the van screeched as it spun out of control. Lola clung to Morrigan and Raven as it tipped and rolled. For a moment, she was weightless, her seatbelt being the only thing tethering her to the seat. And then the world and the car righted itself. Thankfully, there was no encore performance. They all sat in stunned silence, catching their breath. Lola's heart pounded, and she could feel a growing soreness on her ribs from where the seatbelt had dug in. "Everyone okay?" she asked shakily.

"I'm fine," Raven said.

Morrigan stared down at herself, silent for so long that Lola almost repeated the question. "I'm okay, I think."

"Brian?"

"My mom's gonna kill me," he said, "and then my dad's gonna kill me when the insurance rate goes up. Bottom line is that I'm dead. You might as well start buying flowers for the funeral."

"He's fine." Raven undid her seatbelt. With some effort, she pulled open the van door and staggered out on shaky legs. Her eyes widened. "No fucking way . . ."

"What?" Lola undid her seatbelt, followed by Morrigan. The buck still stood in the middle of the street. It hadn't moved, standing completely still like a statue. She approached on shaky legs and realized it was so still because it was, in fact, a statue. "What the hell?"

"Is this some kind of joke?" Raven asked the air. "What kind of sick fuck would leave something like that in the middle of the road?"

Morrigan pointed to the headlights of an oncoming vehicle. "Someone who wants to set a trap."

Before they could run back, the car pulled up in front of them. An older man sat in the driver's seat, and a woman who was likely his wife sat beside him. He wore a sport coat and plaid shirt while his wife was in a floral dress, like a Norman Rockwell painting come to life.

"What on earth is that?" the man asked. "Don't they know how dangerous pranks like that are?"

"I hope you're all okay," the woman said. "I have no idea who would have done something like that. Harold, can you move that vile thing out of the way?"

"Of course, Mildred," he said. He exited the car and pushed the statue out of the street. Then he turned back to the girls and Brian, who had gotten out of the van, and said, "Do you all need a ride?"

"Excuse us." Raven pulled them aside. "So, this is obviously a trap, right? They're gonna take us back to their house and make us join the Stepford Wives."

"Oh, absolutely," Lola agreed.

"I mean, they just seem like a nice couple," Brian said.

"Just driving around in the middle of the night?" Morrigan hissed.

He thought for a moment before inclining his head with a half-shrug. "Good point."

"We're okay, thank you," Morrigan told the man and woman. "His mom's gonna pick us up. She knows the route we're taking, and if we're not back by sunrise, she'll come looking for us." Lola couldn't help but admire how quickly and smoothly she lied to their faces.

"Somehow, I doubt that. Let us at least drive you all to the nearest payphone."

"We're fine, really. Thank you for the offer, though."

Harold's hand went to his hip, revealing a gun. "I'm afraid we must insist."

Seeing a gun in real life wasn't anything like seeing a gun in a movie. It was much smaller than Lola would have expected but commanded the attention of everyone on that dark road all the same.

"Come along, children," Harold said.

They piled into the too-small car, clinging to one another with clammy hands.

"Told you they were fucking crazy," Raven whispered.

"Language!" Mildred chided. "I ought to wash your mouth out with soap."

"Clearly these kids lacked a good influence in their lives," Harold said. "What do you say, Mildred? Shall we take them in?"

She clucked like someone who had just caught their dog on the couch when it wasn't supposed to be. "I think we might have to. Rebellious children need a strong authority to keep them in line."

"You read my mind, darling," he said.

Lola's mouth was dry, her heart pounding the way it always did when she'd return home to the sound of the game on television and the smell of stale beer. Dread soured her stomach as she imagined the moment they'd figure out that she was not born a girl. Morrigan had tears in her eyes while Raven jutted her chin out defiantly. Brian was hardest to read. She knew his parents were strict at home, making him rebel even harder. Was this all familiar to him?

"What are your names, children?" Mildred asked.

"Raven." Her eyes glinted with barely suppressed rage.

"Morrigan," was the next response, with equal defiance despite the fear in her eyes.

"Come on now, it's not polite to lie. What are your *real* names?" Harold said, his voice low and dangerous.

"Christine," Raven gritted out.

"Emma," Morrigan said.

"Such lovely names," he replied, the threat seemingly forgotten.

"Just Brian," Brian replied, clearly relieved that he hadn't chosen to go by a different name.

"And you?" Mildred asked Lola.

Lola's heart sank. She looked to the rest of her friends for guidance, but they seemed just as unsure as she was. Right now, she looked enough like a girl that she could get away with telling them her name, but they'd find out eventually, and when they did, she had no idea what they'd do to her. Just as she opened her mouth to reply, Morrigan clutched at her head and groaned, falling over.

"Good lord," Mildred exclaimed, "what's wrong?"

"She—she must've hit her head in the crash," Brian said, propping her up and holding out two fingers, "How many fingers?"

Morrigan blinked at though she was trying to bring the world back into focus. "Which one of you?"

Mildred looked horrified. "Oh, poor dear!"

Morrigan buried her head in Lola's lap, turning just enough so she could see her wink. It was all an act, thank God.

"She needs a hospital," Raven said.

"I'm a doctor. I'll look her over," Harold replied, because of course they couldn't be that lucky.

Morrigan whimpered and Lola ran a hand through hair stiff with hairspray. "You'll be okay. We'll be okay."

Harold turned onto a gravel road. Every time he tried to start a conversation again, Morrigan whimpered and moaned, prompting Mildred to fuss over her. Lola was forgotten, and she couldn't be happier for it.

A fully lit house appeared nearby, seemingly from nowhere. It was a stately place, with gingerbread trimming on the front porch and an actual white picket fence. Harold pulled into the driveway, left the car, and opened the door for Mildred. "What are you waiting for?" he said to the kids. "Welcome to your new home."

Morrigan leaned on Lola as they filed out of the car and into the house. It looked like every grandmother's house, with ugly floral-print furniture, garishly colored rugs, crosses lining the walls, and family portraits of a smiling young Harold and Mildred along with a boy Lola assumed was their son covering most other surfaces. As Lola studied their smiling faces for any indication of what might be in store for them, she noticed that the son's photos only seemed to go up to his mid-teens while photos of Mildred and Harold aged all the way to the present. Judging by the bell bottoms and wide collars, all the oldest pictures of the son appeared to have been taken more than a decade ago.

"Sit her on the couch," Harold ordered. He grabbed a penlight and shone it in her eyes, ignoring her winces and whimpers as he felt her skull for any bumps. "Do you feel any dizziness or nausea?"

She nodded mutely, her eyes wet with unshed tears. "It hurts," she slurred.

Damn, she's good, Lola thought. *All those years in drama club finally paid off.*

Harold made Morrigan lie back. "Why don't you sleep it off?" he said. "We'll take care of the rest of the family while you relax. Mildred? Why don't you see our children to their rooms? Give them some proper pajamas and let them rest after tonight's ordeal. We can teach them the house rules tomorrow."

"Of course, dear," she replied. "Come along, children. Upstairs we go."

Not knowing what else to do, they followed her upstairs, and Lola prayed it wouldn't be her last night on earth.

Mildred took Brian to one room and handed him a set of over-sized flannel pajamas that clearly belonged to someone much older. "Get all that silly makeup off," she said. "It's inappropriate for a boy to wear something like that."

He gulped. "Y-yes, ma'am."

"Your room is this way, girls," Mildred said, pulling the two most frilly, grand-motherly nightgowns that Lola had ever seen from the hall closet. She let out a quiet sigh of relief that she was feminine-presenting enough that Mildred hadn't figured it out yet.

"I'm afraid you'll have to room together for now," Mildred continued. "The bathroom is right next door. I'll leave out towels for you to get all that gunk off your faces. Emma will be up once we're sure she isn't too badly hurt." The room she led them to looked as though it had belonged to a teenager at some point. The walls were covered in Elvis and Beatles posters and a massive stack of rock and roll records was piled in a corner. "I'm sorry for the state of the place. I haven't found it in me to clean it up yet."

"What happened to the person who lived here?" Raven asked.

Mildred shook her head, her lips tight as she gritted out. "He ... died. We couldn't save him." She blinked, returning once again to the picture of a sweet old lady. "But we won't let that happen to you. You're going to be perfect. The children I always wanted." She shut the door behind her. "Goodnight, darlings."

Raven held the frilly, moth-eaten nightgown between two fingers. "There's no way I'm wearing this."

Lola already had her back to her and her shirt off. "We should play along for now. They have to sleep sometime, and we can get away then."

"Or they'll just murder us. These people are crazy. Who knows what they'll do next?"

Raven had a point, and if they figured out Lola's sex, she'd probably be the first on the hangman's noose. But years of dealing with her dad had taught her that with some people it was better to play along and bide your time than it was to openly defy them.

"I don't think they'll kill us yet," Lola said. "They keep talking about wanting to save us, to be a good influence on us where our parents failed. If we do what they say, we might lull them into a false sense of security so that they won't see our escape attempt coming."

"Or they're crazy, and they'll just kill us," Raven said, but began the process of changing out of her funeral dress and into the nightgown. Some of the makeup smeared onto it when she pulled the nightgown over her head, her small way of rebelling against this situation wherever she could. After returning from the bathroom with a wet towel and still wiping off her face, she flopped onto the bed, staring up at the ceiling. "We'll do it your way, but if they kill me, I'm totally haunting you."

"Fair," Lola replied, taking a pillow off the bed and setting it out on the floor.

Raven picked up her head. "What are you doing?"

"I thought you might be uncomfortable sharing a bed with me," she replied, pulling a throw blanket off the end of the bed and laying it down.

Raven rolled her eyes. "How very chivalrous of you. But I don't care. You wouldn't be the first person I've shared a bed with." She mouthed, "Who has a dick."

"Thanks," Lola said, turning off the lights and laying down next to her. She stared up at the ceiling struggling to think of a plan. She wasn't sure how much time had passed—probably a few minutes but it could have been hours—when the room suddenly became a little lighter. She picked up her head.

At the end of the bed stood the glowing figure of a teenage boy in a leather jacket. His face was swollen as though he'd been punched repeatedly, and Lola covered her mouth to stop herself from screaming. Even with his face messed up, she recognized him as the son in the photographs.

"Told you they were serial killers," Raven whispered.

The ghostly figure brought a finger to his split lip and beckoned them to follow. With an exchanged look, they came to an agreement and slid cautiously out of bed. The halls were dark, and they could hear the rhythmic snores of Harold as he and Mildred slept. The boy paused by Brian's door and then passed through it. They heard a stifled yelp. Seconds later, the ghost reappeared, followed quickly by Brian opening the door.

The ghost led them downstairs, skipping the third step from the top. Lola noted this and copied him. When Brian stepped on it, the floor creaked and they all froze, listening for any signs of their captors awakening. When nothing happened, Raven smacked his arm and stepped down, skipping the third step.

Morrigan lay on the couch with her feet elevated. When she saw them she sat up, eyes wide as she took in the specter beside them.

"He's friendly," Lola whispered.

Morrigan tore her eyes from him to Lola and leapt to her feet, pulling her friends into a crushing bear hug. "I had no idea if I should keep up the act or try to find you. I didn't know where they took you."

"Outside of being forced wear to an ugly-ass nightgown, we're fine," Raven said.

"I happen to like my pajamas," Brian retorted. "I look good in plaid."

Raven gave him a funny look. "You keep telling yourself that, buddy."

"Let's save the bickering for after we grab the car keys and get outta here," Lola hissed.

Raven and Brian had the grace to look sheepish, and the ghost silently led them into the kitchen, where Harold and Mildred kept the car keys. Just as they were about to slip out the front door, Harold's voice interrupted them from the top of the stairs.

"Just where do you think you're going, kids?"

"As far away from you psychos as possible," Raven retorted, her eyes blazing. "We know what you monsters did to your own child."

"Hey, maybe don't tagonize-an the am-may with the un-gay," Brian said in a godawful attempt at pig Latin.

Harold gritted his teeth, his gun-hand shaking. "You have no idea what you're talking about."

"What did he do to deserve to get murdered?" she pressed. "Did he like rock and roll too much? Kiss the wrong girl? Or wait—it was the wrong boy, wasn't it?"

"I said be quiet."

The gun went off like a crack of thunder. For a single, breathless moment, they stared in abject horror at the red rose blooming on Raven's nightgown just above her knee. Then her legs collapsed under her, and they caught her as she fell. Morrigan bunched up her shirt and pressed it to Raven's outer thigh while Brian screamed.

And then all the commotion faded. Lola was still aware of it, but her eyes were intent on the specter. No, specters. A second ghost joined him, followed by a third and a fourth, their eyes wide and pleading. How many times had they done this? How many children had they "adopted" only to murder when they proved to be disappointments? One took the son's hand. Blood dripped down an open bullet wound in his chest.

"They didn't last nearly as long as I thought they would," Harold said, still pointing his gun at them.

Mildred sighed. "Well, you know what they say about one bad apple."

"Let's put this rotten bunch out of their misery."

"Wait!" Lola exclaimed, stepping between them with her hands up and no real plan. "You're right. My dad is a bad influence. All he does is drink and watch TV. I want to be good. Please, help me be good."

Harold and Mildred exchanged exasperated glances. Behind them, the ghosts glowed and grew more solid as Harold retorted, "That's what they all say, and I've yet to find a wayward child who really meant it. Our own son, God rest his soul, just couldn't help himself."

Lola's eyes met the ghost's and he nodded. With a slowly spreading grin, she said, "His soul isn't resting, because of what you did. In fact, he's right behind you."

Mildred looked over her shoulder and shrieked at the sight of the unquiet dead, prompting her husband to turn around. With a ghastly grin, their son pushed them, sending the couple tumbling down the stairs. They lay stunned at the bottom, gasping for breath while Lola kicked the gun away from Harold's hand and picked it up.

"Now, I've never handled one of these before," she said, "so I wouldn't make any sudden moves. That's how the worst accidents happen."

"I'll call an ambulance," Morrigan said. "Ask them the address."

"Well, you heard the lady," Lola said, her trigger finger twitching. Seeing that, Mildred caved and gave the address. While Morrigan ran to the kitchen for the phone and medical supplies, Lola turned her attention back to Harold and Mildred. "Now, where are the bodies?"

"Like I'd tell you," Harold spat. "Who are they going to believe? A helpless old man and woman, or four teenage punks?"

Lola pointed the gun away and fired. "Oops. Clumsy me."

The ghost approached, standing beside her with a pained look on his face. All the world seemed to melt away between them as his eyes met his mother's.

Mildred's eyes filled with tears, her lips wobbling like a toddler caught decorating the walls with Sharpies. "Oh, my boy, what did we do to you?" she whispered.

"Mildred . . ." Harold's voice was low, and the word carried with it an underlying threat of violence. "He couldn't be saved. We both knew his perversions were too strong."

"He was your son," Morrigan said from the doorway. She carried gauze, antiseptic, and tape to help keep pressure on the wound. With her bloodstained hands and the determined way she walked toward Raven, she reminded Lola of the Angel of Death. Or an angel of mercy. Was there a difference?

"Your job was to love him unconditionally and accept him for who he was," Lola said to Mildred. "It might not have changed him, but it's better to love someone as they are than to lose them."

Mildred looked away from the ruined face of her son. "They're in the back garden. I marked their graves with roses since we couldn't do headstones."

"Mildred!" Harold shouted, his face bright red in rage.

With the vein bulging in his forehead, Lola thought he might have an aneurysm. Wouldn't be a great loss if he did.

"Harold, it's time we finally do right by Evan."

"Doing right by him is what got us into this mess in the first place. If he had just listened when I told him to give up his lifestyle . . ."

"He'd still be gay, you fuckwad," Raven rasped. Her face had lost all color, and a sheen of sweat beaded across her brow. Blood pooled under her leg even with the pressure and the bandaging. Lola felt a pang of affection for her friend. Bleeding out and Raven still had the energy to rebel against authority. She flopped backwards, leaning against Brian. "People like you are the reason I am the way I am."

Her eyelashes fluttered and Brian shook her. "No, stay awake. You can't fall asleep just yet."

"The ambulance said they'd be here soon," Morrigan said as flashing blue and red cut through the early dawn light.

The next couple hours were a blur of police, EMTs, and endless questions about how all this happened. Lola could tell that at first the cops didn't believe them, but when Mildred confessed to burying bodies in the backyard, they began changing their tune.

Once all the questions were out of the way and the EMTs had checked the rest of them for serious injuries, Morrigan sat beside Lola outside the hospital waiting room. The doctors said Raven would be okay, but they still felt on edge. Lola's dad had seen her concert outfit and informed her that they'd talk later. But he couldn't be too mad. After all, she'd helped take down a couple of serial killers. They were all heroes. But she dreaded what would happen after the spotlight faded and the drinking came back.

Morrigan wordlessly took her hand and squeezed. If they could survive two serial killers, then they could survive anything.

Kay Hanifen was born on Friday the 13th and once lived for three months in a haunted castle. Her work has appeared in over 40 anthologies and magazines. When she's not consuming pop culture with the voraciousness of a vampire at a 24-hour blood bank, you can usually find her at kayhanifenauthor.wordpress.com.

BLACK CATS AND BONE DUST

BY CINDY O'QUINN

M oving day—October 13, 1978 —into the big yellow house at the end of Allen Street.

That's all I wrote in my journal after the long day of moving and unpacking boxes alongside my mom and stepdad. Most of my boxes were heavy with books. I loved to read, especially after Dad died. It was my escape. The darker the story, the better.

I was sore, deep beyond what my thirteen-year-old muscles were accustomed to. I stretched out across my antique twin bed with wrought-iron head and footboards. It was faded white from the last time Dad and I painted it. That was a little more than three years ago, shortly before he died. I couldn't bring myself to paint over it. I would paint my room without a second thought. It was the same hideous yellow as the big house, like someone tried to add sunshine where there was none. Must have been a helluva sale on piss-yellow paint.

Exhausted, my body gave in and I fell into a fitful sleep. Chased by nightmares for more than three years. That horrible day when Mom picked me up early from school. She cupped my face into the palms of her hands, and I looked into her red, tear-stained eyes. I knew before she spoke the words.

Those nightmares always ended with me standing beside a casket. I was barely tall enough to look down inside at what used to be my dad. The mortician had made a mockery of my dad, turned him into a poorly painted man-doll. What lay in the casket scared me.

The next day the stepdad started his new job. I was glad to see him go. If Dad had to be dead, I preferred it to be just Mom and me. She would have kept us in New Orleans, in the house we shared with Dad. But no, the stepdad couldn't seem to find his place in the work world. He told us he found the perfect job and the perfect community. Perfect, my ass! Maybe if you liked a Podunk town like Laurel, Mississippi. I for one did not.

I knew Mom loved me; we told each other every day. But when it came to the stepdad, she went along with whatever he wanted. At least that's what it felt like. My pleas for us to return to Louisiana fell on deaf ears. I broke Mom's heart when I screamed, "It only took you three years to replace my dad. That shows just how little you loved him!"

She looked away from me before any tears could spill over, walked out of my room, and closed the door gently behind her. That's how I knew I had broken her heart. She didn't yell or fight back. She just quietly slinked away. I stopped pouting over the move, turning instead to music, books, and writing. I shared my dad's love of rock music. Black Sabbath was our favorite. Their instrumental track "Rat Salad" led me to write words to go with it, which suited the stepdad to a tee. A rat!

Before Dad died, he had bought a large set of journals for me. I treasured them and was sad I was on the last one. I didn't want to run out of room, so I only wrote the important happenings.

I never trusted the stepdad. Mom assumed I would find something wrong with any man. It wasn't that at all, I mean yeah, no one was as good as Dad. The stepdad was just off. I believed he was mad, and madness had a way of changing the shape of one's thoughts. It didn't help matters he had an elongated Lurch-like face. He caught me watching him, and I nearly jumped out of my skin. I wondered if that would be his one good reason to kill me. The stepdad laughed and walked away.

Mom wasn't aware I knew about the life and auto insurances. The stepdad made my grieving mom fall for him. Marry him. And I worried he was after the money.

Dad taught me to read at age three. Reading gave me knowledge. Knowledge gave me power. Power made me a superhero, according to Dad. I would study this strange man, the stepdad, as though he was a science experiment.

I started by exploring the crappy house he put us in. The bedrooms, bathrooms, and kitchen were just what their titles stated, and they served their purpose. The basement, however, was a world of its own. The open-back stairs led me down to the creepy underbelly of the house. I held my breath until the lights proved there was no evidence of the stepdad's madness. I caught a glimpse of at least two rats. They scurried off into the shadows. The basement was home to rats and spiders. A furnace sat in the middle; it held a sinister grin as its opening. Against the far wall was a washer/dryer set, shelves of empty canning jars, and one of those old floor-model freezers with the big silver handle on the outside. The kind that trapped children inside. It wasn't plugged in, probably didn't work.

Note to self, never go to the basement alone with the stepdad. I learned all about stranger danger from my mom and dad. It was also taught in school. The way I looked at my current situation, the stepdad was Mom's husband, but to me, he was a stranger. I knew to trust my gut. The stepdad was bad like tainted meat, a poison which could kill.

Stepdad had beady eyes which glistened with malicious ideas. One day, when he and my mom were in the dating phase, he had clamped one of his ginormous hands down on my shoulder to put an end to my whining about staying with the babysitter and Mom leaving me. He left bruises on my shoulder. I carried his secret around on my skin, and it eventually faded. The bruising, but not the memory. The memory remained with me, and I ached to tell Mom. I couldn't be the reason to make her sadness return.

As soon as the "I-do's" were exchanged, I cried for Mom not to go on the honeymoon. That occasion made the stepdad grab my elbow, yanking me off my feet, while Mom's attention was on someone else. His beady eyes flamed as he told me to knock it off or I'd never see my mom again. I believed him. After they were on their way, I told my babysitter, the elderly neighbor, I had fallen and hurt my arm. She rushed me to the ER, and sure enough, he had yanked so hard he'd dislocated my shoulder. The earlier bruises were long gone, but the fresh ones on my elbow stood out as though under a spotlight. I told the doctor that someone had grabbed me, trying to prevent me from falling. She charted the conversation and assured me she was safe to talk to if I ever needed someone. I nodded understanding and held back my tears.

I continued my investigation. Since the stepdad wasn't home, I searched the den. He quickly claimed that room as his own by strewing his shit about. Whiskeys from Kentucky, Tennessee, and, of course, Mississippi. The bottles lined the top of the bookcase. Books about nothing important, and photos of him with supposedly important people. It was all just for show. I heard scuttling coming from behind the walls. I saw another rat, but it was in no hurry to hide. It turned and looked me in the eyes. I saw the same beady eyes as the stepdad.

I was disappointed how easily Mom fell for him. She was a smart person who I looked up to. What happened? Had her confidence died with Dad?

I discovered the paperwork for the big yellow rattrap. The stepdad had inherited the house from his grandfather. I found a recent receipt for twenty-five gallons of sunshine-yellow paint. It was marked fifty percent off. I laughed.

There was one last place to check out. The attic. The stairs creaked under the weight of my footsteps. I felt like I was in the midst of a B-horror flick. Spiderwebs everywhere. Once I reached the top, I didn't find a light switch. There was a small octagonal window at either end of the attic. Both were so dust covered, they allowed little light to make its way inside, leaving the center of the room in darkness. I knew that was where I would find a pull cord for a bare bulb. I lifted my right foot to move forward and stopped mid step. I heard a noise. It came from the far corner below the front window. I took three quick steps, and the noise came again. I felt something graze across my head. I reached up and found the cord and jerked. The light flickered before remaining on.

I walked to the corner where the noises originated and discovered a makeshift bed of scrap clothing. In the middle was a momma cat and three kittens. All had black and white spots except for one kitten that was solid black. I kept my find a secret from the elderly babysitter. The attic felt safe. I knew there'd be no rats with the big cat on guard. I would ask Mom if I could keep them when they returned from their honeymoon.

On Sunday morning, I got up with the first songbird. After cleaning my room, I bathed, put on my prettiest dress, allowed the sitter to braid my hair, and ate my breakfast on the front porch while waiting. Just non-messy fruit to avoid any stains. Finally, after an hour, they pulled into the drive.

Mom looked radiant. I hugged her tighter than ever, pulled her away from the car and away from the stepdad. She could see the excitement in my eyes and didn't hesitate to follow, even when her husband asked about help with the luggage. Up to the attic we went, and straight to the corner where the cat family waited. They were all meows and rubs against Mom's ankles. It was like they were putting on a show just for her.

"Can we keep them, Mom?"

"Oh, honey, there's four of them. I don't see how we could manage all of them. Maybe your stepdad would agree to one."

"You're my mother. It shouldn't be up to him. You should be able to say yes or no. It's you who has all the money in the family."

The sale of our house and Dad's insurance money. All the stepdad had was this big ugly house he slapped sunshine-yellow paint on, at a fifty percent discount, because no one else would dare buy such a shitty color.

Mom reached out and squeezed my hand. "And every bit of that money is in an account for *your* future. How in the world did you know all that information?"

"Dad wasn't raising a dumb ass! I put things together, Mom. Dad would be proud of me." I felt like shit for thinking Mom would do something so stupid. We hugged longer than we had since she'd started dating the man who became the stepdad.

"Honey, I'm proud of you, as well. Let's get this little family of yours downstairs."

"I'm sorry for being an ass. I love you, Mom."

"I love you, too. But please, enough with the curse words."

We took the cats down and put them in box lined with a fresh towel. Mom paid the sitter, who had quite the surprised look on her face when she saw the cats. She was leaving as the stepdad brought in the last of their luggage. He knew something was up when he got a look at our smiling faces.

The kittens started crawling out of the box one by one. Momma Cat meowed in protest. Stepdad's face changed into the elongated Lurch-face. It felt as though the house was suddenly colder. The sun hid behind dark clouds. There wasn't enough sunshine-yellow in the world to brighten the mood he wore like a mask.

One of the kittens sniffed at his shoe. He kicked, and the kitten went sliding across the kitchen floor. Momma cat hissed at him. The black kitten was nearby. I grabbed him up into my arms.

The stepdad made a sudden step towards Mom. She glared at him as though daring him to make another move. "What do you think you're doing?" she said. It was the first time I heard her use a harsh tone with her new husband. "We do not hurt animals in this home."

The stepdad said, "This is my home, and I'll damn well do as I see fit. There's not going to be a bunch of cats running around pissing and shitting in my house!"

He stormed into the den and slammed the door behind him. He would remain there until dinner like he did most evenings, drinking too many glasses of his fancy whiskeys. When he did come to dinner, his eyes would be bloodshot from drink, and he'd be unsteady on his feet.

Mom and I looked at one another. I could see the anger spread over her face. We were both furious. Momma Cat and I followed close behind as she carried the box to the basement and placed it behind the steps, where it was literally invisible. We gave them water and a bowl of milk. I told Momma Cat to keep her kittens in the box where they would be safe. We added a second box with shredded newspaper for them use as a litter box. Mom told me she would go to the grocery store after dropping her husband off at work. We still only had our station wagon. I couldn't understand why a grown, working man didn't have his own car.

After an uncomfortably quiet dinner, I excused myself, rinsed my plate, and snuck to the basement to retrieve my favorite kitten, the solid black one. He had kind eyes like my dad's. His fur shined like velvet and felt just as smooth. Momma Cat trusted me and didn't make a peep. I remained in my room all evening. Echoes of Mom and the stepdad talking loudly drifted up through the wall vent. It continued until Mom came in to kiss me goodnight. I hid the kitten under the covers.

I whispered to the kitten and told him all my secret thoughts and concerns, especially the ones about the stepdad. The way he had two completely opposite personalities. I felt bad for Mom but was glad she witnessed some of it firsthand. The kitten never looked away from my face the entire time I whispered to him, his eyes full of knowing, another trait of Dad's. Sounds weird, but it made me feel like Dad was watching over us.

I fought to stay awake but lost the battle around 2 a.m. My nightmares were infiltrated with screams, loud meows, and harsh words from an angry man. The smell of bacon frying woke me up. The kitten was sitting on my chest, waiting. I knew he was anxious to see his family, so I rushed to brush my teeth and throw some old clothes on.

Running by the kitchen, I saw Mom at the stove. Something wasn't right, and I skidded to a stop. "Mom, I thought you were taking your husband to work and going to the grocery store afterwards." I wondered when Mom would make me refer to him as something other than the stepdad or her husband. I could tell it bothered her.

"That was the plan, but he was gone with the station wagon when I got up. I did call the grocer and put in an order to be delivered first thing. It was quite the order with all the extras for the feline family. I imagine the cats will be kept busy with all the rats in the basement. I heard a ruckus down there last night. Your stepdad will eventually grow used to them. Hey, who's that in your arms?"

"I had to have at least this one in bed with me. We're headed downstairs. He's anxious to see the rest of his family. Be careful if you come down, Mom, there's a dead rat beside the steps."

"See, Momma Cat is already teaching the kittens to hunt," she said. "They're worth their weight in gold. You know how I dislike rats and mice. Your stepdad is actually afraid of them. The big strong man, pfft!"

I could hear the laughter in her voice, which quickly became hidden beneath screams. My screams. "Mom, they're gone! He did it! I know he did. I heard strange noises last night."

Mom ran down the steps and took in the entire scene. She saw the rat by the stairs. The cat bed was empty. She pointed out a few drops of blood that could be from the rat. And then she saw it. The side door was open and the screen door wasn't latched.

"Your stepdad knew I was taking him to work today," she said, as if thinking aloud. "Could he have snuck out this way to avoid the creaky front door? Surely, he wouldn't leave the door open on purpose. Would he?"

"Your car, Mom. And yes, I think he'd do it in a heartbeat. What's that hum? Did you plug in the freezer?"

"No, my plan was to have it hauled away. Our refrigerator-freezer combo upstairs is plenty big to meet our needs."

We walked up to the freezer side by side. She pulled the silver latch to open it. Frost vapors rolled out like smoke. After it cleared, we looked down inside. Two bags of peas and two bags of carrots, which neither of us had put in the freezer. I reached toward them, but Mom stopped me and moved the bags herself. There in a curled-up ball was Momma Cat. Frost tipped the edges of her fur.

My tears were immediate. "Mom, is she dead?"

Mom cursed the stepdad as she reached down and picked the cat up and held her to her chest. I yelled when I saw what was underneath her. The two kittens, so cold but still alive. Mom rubbed Momma cat with a towel until she let out a weak meow. We both cried tears of joy.

I confided to Mom about the two times the stepdad hurt me. The bruised shoulder before they were married and yanking my elbow so hard it pulled my shoulder out of joint on their wedding day. She was enraged at the images, but red fury in her eyes changed into the blue hot fires of anger mixed with a storm of shame as she recounted his violence on their honeymoon. He'd told her it was just too much alcohol and promised never do it again. Mom cried and held me close as she told me her concern should have been making sure I was safe.

She found the heating pad, put the setting on low, and placed Momma Cat and the two kittens on top. We watched as she fussed over her babies, even in her weakened state. She was a good mom. I hated to even consider how close they had been to running out of air.

The black kitten sat on my lap, listening intently. His eyes looked more intense than usual, and they shone. Almost glowed. They were filled with a fiery anger. And so were Mom's. Something I had never before seen in her.

I remembered the dead rat and thought of the words I'd made up to go along with the music to "Rat Salad." I asked Mom if I should get rid of it. She told me no, it was best to leave everything as we found it. There was a slight hint of a smile. I could tell her mind was working overtime, not unlike the black kitten's.

The stepdad pulled into the drive in an ugly, bright orange Corvette sports car. Not a family car. I looked him in the eyes as he walked by. His smirk told me I would be the next thing to go.

Mom walked up behind me. She saw the car and exploded. "What's this all about? Where's my station wagon? I hope you didn't trade it in on that ridiculous sports car. You would have had to forge my name if you did, and I won't stand for that. You'll just have to return it tomorrow and explain your mistake."

"I will do no such thing! I'm the man of this house, and what I say goes!" He headed for the den.

Mom's eyes held a wicked glint. "Well, could the man of the house please go get a bag of peas from the downstairs freezer before getting shit-faced?"

The stepdad was down in the basement for a good while. I could imagine his Lurch-face getting redder and redder. The evil man had to know he was busted.

Mom yelled downstairs, "You might as well bring all four bags of carrots and peas. I've arranged for someone to come pick up that old freezer. It's too big for our needs."

Before Mom closed the basement door, she allowed the black kitten through. He looked up at me with those knowing eyes, just like my dad's. I heard the stepdad yelling about the light going out. And then he screamed. I could have sworn he yelled out something about glowing eyes.

We heard a screech, a scream, a tumble, and a bone-cracking thud. We looked at each another in panic.

Mom opened the door and switched on the light that had mysteriously gone out. The rat lay on the top step. Her husband lay on the hard cement floor, blood pooling out around his head, one leg still on the bottom stair but twisted the wrong way, with a bone protruding through his slacks. The four bags of frozen veggies were on the floor by his side.

The black cat sat near the body, cleaning his paws. Stepdad must have tried to rush up the stairs, and came face to face with the dead rat or perhaps a vengeful cat. I guess we'll never know for sure, but we didn't need to.

Mom called 911, sounding calmer than perhaps she should have, and told the operator her husband had fallen down the basement stairs, and she feared he was dead. Paramedics arrived, along with the police. It was evidently just one of those horrible accidents. They all agreed and offered us their deepest condolences.

Mom said, "All for some frozen veggies. What a shame."

One of the police officers offered Mom a card for a counselor. She took it and thanked him for his kindness. When they were all gone, she tossed it in the trash. We sat at the counter and enjoyed delivery pizza and milk for supper. Conversation didn't come around about the stepdad until the next day.

Mom called her husband's work and told them of his passing. They informed her of an insurance policy that was paid for by the company. She was named the beneficiary. I thought that was a good thing—at least she would get her money back for the Corvette. But Mom didn't keep a penny of it. She donated it all to the Laurel, Mississippi, Animal Shelter.

The stepdad was cremated. Ironic in a way, because he ended up in an oven after he had tried to end the lives of a family of cats by putting them in a freezer. A couple weeks later his ashes were ready to be picked up. We had to wait for the custom-ordered urn with a black cat engraved on the front.

He was buried in the closest graveyard to the animal shelter. Mom and I were the only two in attendance, besides the black cat, who insisted on getting out of the car too. He circled the grave until we were ready to leave. The cat sat atop the small mound of dirt, his back towards the marker. It was peculiar, but I told Mom perhaps animals had their own traditions. My special black cat. Did he know what he was doing by tripping the stepdad, therefore putting an end to danger? I liked to think so.

We walked towards the car. The small U-Haul attached to it contained only our personal belongings. Mom and I were headed back to New Orleans, where a new home awaited our arrival. That included our family of happy cats. Mom sold the big yellow box, contents and all.

I glanced back just in time to witness the cat wiggle his raised tail, spray the grave, and paw at the dirt that covered the urn of bone dust. B.D. became his name then and there. Short for Bone Dust, of course.

Cindy O'Quinn is a four-time Bram Stoker Award-nominated writer. Author of "Lydia," from the Shirley Jackson Award winning anthology—*The Twisted Book of Shadows*, "The Thing I Found Along a Dirt Patch Road," "A Gathering on the Mountain," and "One and Done."

She is an Appalachian writer from West Virginia. Cindy now lives in Maine, on the old Tessier Homestead. It's the ideal backdrop for writing dark stories and poetry. Her work has been published or forthcoming in *The Bad Book*, *HWA Poetry Showcase Vol V*, *Northern Frights*, *Eerie Christmas*, *Under Her Skin*, *Were Tales: A Shapeshifter Anthology*, *Space & Time*, *Weirdbook*, *Chiral Mad 5*, and others.

Follow Cindy for updates: Facebook @CindyOQuinnWriter, Twitter @CO-QuinnWrites, and Instagram cindy.oquinn.

BORIS WAS HERE

BY E.F. SCHRAEDER

1950-2020

My mom told me the same thing at least a hundred times. "We never kill spiders in this house." She'd stare at me, her fiery eyes focused on me until I nodded. She provided me with two reasons. First, she said it'd bring bad luck, which I believed without asking for clarification. Second, she said that spiders were good luck in a house, which I doubted but went along with anyway.

Mom wasn't the kind of person who argued with people so much as at them, and sometimes it was just better to go along than to press a point. She never said spiders weren't scary, though. Because they were. Even if she didn't agree, she knew I thought so.

The first time she slammed the basement door behind me, I stood frozen on the top step. I don't remember how old I was because of some ongoing memory problems. But I was already in school and pretty lanky. What I do remember is how the dank air filled my nostrils, clammy moist air clung to my skin, sweat pricked my neck, and how fast the salty tears ran down my cheeks. Hot.

I flicked the switch a few times, but the bare bulb above me only crackled and popped. No light. My mom's laughter from the other side of the door.

Harsh.

"Mom, this isn't funny." I stopped myself from screaming because that would've only made her laughing come harder. I pounded on the door.

"Come on, hon. You've got to toughen up. Go get a light bulb."

I shivered. *Hating her.* The light bulbs were on a dingy rack of rusty metal shelves just under the basement staircase, the only part of the basement floor that wasn't guaranteed to be wet ninety-nine percent of the time. "Mom, open the door!" *She was my mortal enemy. This was unforgivable.*

Silence.

"Mom!" I didn't move. The possibility of webs tickled on my arms and neck. My imagination tangled with the images of a hundred stories of school children traveling into netherworlds through strange crevices in the dark.

This place wasn't going to take me to Narnia.

A clicking noise like a clock started in my head, timing how long until panic nested inside me. I counted the clicks, trying to calm down.

I knew what hung above me, long legs spreading on the cinder block wall. It was always there. *She,* my mother always corrected me. The half-dollar-sized spider lived in the corner of the stairwell and perched on the cool wall, nearly twenty-four hours a day. My mom always pointed the spider out like it was a big deal.

The first time she made a big production out of it. "Isn't she pretty?"

Was she joking? That fuzzy thing was big enough to have jointed legs . . .

"She's just like the one in *Charlotte's Web.* It's the spider's story after all, isn't it?"

I guessed so. We'd already stopped eating animals, so hindsight told me she was working to extend my circle of care to include all life, insects and spiders included. Even a creepy, large live-in spider in the basement fell into our circle of concern. Just because I wouldn't throw a shoe at the thing didn't mean I wanted to treat it like a sweet auntie in the attic.

"She's so much smaller than you," my mom said. "So delicate. Just think about that if you get scared. She's microscopic compared to you. Honestly, she's probably more scared of you than you are of her."

"You're right." I forced out a smile, but it couldn't have been very convincing.

"Should we name her?"

"Maybe Boris, like the song?"

"Oh, that's a good one." She smiled. "Besides, they're good luck. Remember that."

I smiled back at her. "Okay." I looked at Boris and then back at my mom. *Confession time.* "Some of the kids at school tried to set a spider on fire on the playground. They did it with a magnifying glass, but I told on them. The teacher made them stop." I ended the story there because I didn't want to tell her what they called me for the rest of the month. *Nature-girl. Spider-girl. Witch-girl.* The kinds of names that would follow a kid through middle school. Maybe even beyond.

"That's right. Good for you." She patted me on the head, a wide smile that warmed her entire face. "That's really sick, isn't it? I mean, we're all connected. Why would anyone want to torture a small creature like that?"

I said I didn't know.

"They have just as much right as anyone to be left alone. To live out their natural lives."

I agreed. Mom's eyes twinkled.

That was a nice moment between Mom and me. And the spider.

Not like now. Because now I was locked in the basement with a spider the size of my eye socket. The silence on the other side of the door infuriated me, but I knew crying wouldn't help. Maybe my mom was out there, listening. Maybe she'd gone on to something else. Bored or distracted by my repetitive whining. *I could be such a child.*

I took a slow breath. *I'm perfectly safe.* I repeated the words like a chant until I believed them.

She'd let me out, of course. There was never any risk of being locked down there forever. Not really. It wouldn't go on forever. Nothing did. That was another one of Mom's favorite lessons. I was a model student, and she was an excellent teacher.

This was just a dark room. Just because I didn't like it didn't mean anything. The moist air wasn't harmful. There was no real risk involved. Just a minor inconvenience, a slight interruption of the evening. Was I really going to let something so small ruin my day? A spider. That was a very tiny creature, after all.

I thought about every time we opened that door. How it was like a game to Mom. "Can you find her? Where is she?" She'd point to a corner thick with a swirl of webs. A thread-thin leg would jut out of some dusky spot.

Like it heard her.

"Uh huh," I'd stammer. It wasn't a very fun game.

Not to mention, I didn't want to find her. I didn't want to see her. Most of the time I just pretended to look.

"She's always been there and one like her always will be."

I nodded, not quite understanding. *Whatever.*

"The web of life. It's sacred, and that's what she represents."

Web of life my ass. I didn't want to be connected to that thing in the corner. Done recollecting, I noticed that my eyes had adjusted to the light within however long it takes for that kind of thing to happen. Minutes? Seconds? My heart palpitating, I was soaked with sweat and flooded with adrenaline, my brain smoldering with fight or flight.

Until it wasn't. Until I made it stop. Like I said, she was a very good teacher.

Also, kid-time doesn't work right. It was a moment or two. A flash of memory. A gag my mom pulled. My mind was all jumbled with fear, and what I know is that, however long it took, nothing happened. The spider didn't "get me" or whatever I was afraid of. I calmed myself down. Got the light bulbs. I called out calmly to say so, and when I did my mom opened the door.

"Thanks. I see you two are fine now." She pointed at the spider's post, grinning like someone in on the joke. "That wasn't so scary now, was it?"

Retrospective

Mom was young. She hadn't yet outgrown goofing around and teasing. Besides, our banged-up shack of a house sat on the edge of town, just outside the encroaching suburbia. Isolation lent itself to such antics. It looked tiny and old compared to the larger, newer houses nearby, and most people ignored it and us.

I knew by the time I was twelve that most of the neighborhood saw us as an undesirable little speck of blight, but I thought we were more like a spot of moonlight in a drab, colorless night. We had a thicket of thorny shrubs that hid our house, which sat deep on a wooded lot. A welcoming thatch of lavender graced the main door right beside a horseshoe cemented into the half-moon shaped steps, a little bell hung at the entrance on the right to warn of visitors, and a tiny crystal mounted in the kitchen window swung a rainbow of color into the house each day.

Our place was tucked into the forest, with shaggy tall meadow grass against the backdrop of trees. A painfully loud gathering of sleek, cawing crows always seemed to fill the branches and wires around us, and large, yellow-eyed cats peered out of every window. *Home.*

Not six months went by as far back as I could remember when someone didn't knock on the door with a random offer to buy the house, usually to tear it down and build three more in its place. But mom wouldn't sell. She wouldn't even let them in the hallway.

Listening from around the corner, I knew they were the kinds of people who'd kill Boris. They'd squash her without a second thought. They had crisp voices and used sentences full of big words and imaginary promises.

"I know you heard all that, so tell me. What'd you think of that one?" Mom asked after they left.

"He was a liar."

"You're right. How could you tell?"

"I heard him shifting on his feet, tap, tap, you know? He wouldn't answer you straight. Kept changing the subject when you were direct."

"You're a quick study."

Even if it was a little tricky and sometimes unreliable, human nature was straightforward.

"People want things, and they aren't good at hiding it. Once you know how to read that, you'll be able to get by just fine no matter what." That's what she always said. *She was right.*

At a certain age, I briefly wondered why she wouldn't sell because I think we lived on next to no money back then. But that was when I was wrong about what money could buy and what it couldn't. Pretty soon I realized what that place meant to us with every little ritual observance she made. How she kissed her palm and pressed it to the four walls of the living room any time she left, which wasn't often.

"Why'd you do that?"

"It's how I promise I'll be back, no matter what happens."

"Cool," I said. I meant it. I started doing it too, every day when I left for school. I had to cross two busy roads, and what the heck? It wouldn't hurt.

That's just one little example of her overall approach to parenting and how she was kind of magic. With or without dollars, Mom did everything she could to make everything fun. Even spiders.

Maybe my mom wanted me to learn how to handle myself when I got scared because I was scared a lot of the time. Practice makes perfect, right? So, watching a scary movie, reading from the old Grimm's collection or *Scary Stories*, or listening to that old recording of "The Tell-Tale Heart" was all rather medicinal. This kind of controlled terror was excellent practice for self-regulation. That's a generous set of assumptions about motivation, but I like to think there were some beneficial outcomes even if the methods were a little unusual.

On another level, I have no idea why she did the things she did. Maybe it was just for fun. The line between her process and purpose wasn't always clear. My boundaries were thin, and I wasn't always sure I was in on the joke. Still, it worked. I learned her rituals and ways like breathing. Kneading the dough of life, that was her specialty. Now it was my own.

Resurrection

I left the old house, really left it, only once. Many autumn moons passed.

Fortunes lost; futures sold. A thinning absence, as foretold.

Who knows how many spiders disappeared and never returned.

I returned after a spell away, just like I vowed with a kiss to the palm on the walls all those years ago.

Promises are sacred.

Nothing but ash remained of the person who inspired some direction in my own brief candle of a life. She becomes a box on the mantle, placed in an altar of remembrance: two shiny black feathers, a smooth pebble from the river in our woods, a clutch of sand. Small tokens for a life that persists in the crevices of my imagination, and maybe in some dark corner of the basement. The thought was disquieting, but it helped, since I didn't want to say goodbye.

We are all connected.

Who am I to say what's possible?

The longer I've lived here, the more I've come to think she knew something real about the spider in that hallway. She knew who Boris really was. One of our own.

E.F. Schraeder writes poetry and fiction, most often inspired by not-quite-real worlds. The author of *The Price of a Small Hot Fire* (Raw Dog Screaming Press, 2023), *What Happened Was Impossible* (Ghoulish Books, 2023), the Imadjinn Award finalist *Liar: Memoir of a Haunting* (Omnium Gatherum, 2021), and other works, Schraeder's work has also appeared in a number of journals and anthologies.

Wheels Against Wings

by Valerie B. Williams

Charlie rolled toward the racetrack, absorbing bumps from the uneven ground with his relaxed upper body. The sturdy cross-country wheels worked as designed and he remained upright. An extra blast of steam trailed behind him like a pennant as he powered toward the top of the steep hill. Traces of morning mist hovered in the crisp air.

Crowds lined either side of the track. A cacophony of cheers and clanging metal arose to greet him.

"Look! It's him. My money's on Old Charlie."

He waved to the crowd, shot a quick glance at one of two large tents, then rolled toward the other. A guard stood in front of the tightly closed flaps of his competitor's tent with arms crossed, the left arm under the right mechanical one. Brass and gears made up the length of the arm, which ended in a wicked-looking scimitar. The hybrid guard followed Charlie's movement with his glowing red left eye. The orb squeaked with each movement. *Hmm, she's not maintaining her staff*, he thought.

His assistant, Winston, waited in the tent.

"Ready to go, boss?" he asked, a wrench in his hand.

"Yep."

Charlie wheeled onto the lift and Winston cranked the handle.

"What are the oddsmakers saying?" Charlie asked. His weight shifted onto the lift when his wheels left the ground.

"Close, but you're still ahead." Winston removed the front set of cross-country wheels. There were some jobs where human limbs were still superior.

"Shouldn't even be close," grumbled Charlie. "Phil would be nowhere without me. The insolence!"

"Confidence, not insolence." Winston pulled off the other pair of wheels and reached for the front set of shiny rail wheels. "She's a chip off the old block."

Was that admiration in his voice? "Whose side are you on?" snapped Charlie. "She needs to be taught her place."

Charlie's youngest daughter and last surviving child, Philomena, had challenged him to today's race. The winner would earn the respect, and the position of Chief, of the Ros. The Ros was one of the larger tribes in what used to be New Mexico in what used to be the United States. *United.* Nothing was united anymore. Not since the people had divided into factions and torn each other apart in defense of their unyielding beliefs. A few cherished books remained that told of a time when people engaged in civilized debates rather than bloody battles.

Winston tightened the last of the bolts on the rear set of wheels. "It's too bad it's come to this. She was an excellent lieutenant." He sighed and wiped grease off his forehead with the back of his hand. "I miss her."

A pang of regret broke through Charlie's wall of anger. Phil had been the light of his life, blessed with her mother's beauty and her father's strength. And most importantly, unlike her brother and sister, she had survived the enhancement surgeries.

Winston dropped lumps of coal into the storage area above the firebox attached to Charlie's chair, ensuring plenty of fuel for the race ahead. One of the few benefits of the blasted landscape had been the creation of fossil fuels in mere decades instead of eons. The rapid and devastating loss of plant and animal (including human) life during the wars created extremely dense and long-burning coal.

Next, Winston topped off the water reservoir that fed the boiler. Finally, he rolled the lift to the twin rails that began at the corner of the tent. He cranked the lift down until Charlie's wheels settled on them with a soft clink.

Charlie moved back and forth, testing the smooth mechanism of his racing wheels. Engine pistons churned and warm steam floated up the stack running along his spine and out through his top hat. "Good," he grunted.

He was sure that Phil would be just as meticulous with her pre-race checks, despite the condition of her guard. She would put her resources where they counted—ensuring victory for herself and vengeance for her mother.

Charlie's lips tightened at the memory of his wife, splayed in abandon in Edgar's bed, his best friend's arm draped across her perfect breasts. Neither had expected his early return from battle. For a moment he'd frozen in the doorway, disbelief stealing his breath away as he stared at the sleeping pair. He remembered little after that until coming out of the nightmare covered in blood not his own. Lorene and Edgar would never betray him again.

He went before the Council of Elders and explained what he'd found. They had nodded and agreed that the punishment suited the crime. He suffered no consequences for his actions. At least none from the tribe. But the death of her mother launched Philomena on a quest to become strong enough to challenge him and take away his power, the only thing of consequence left in his life.

A flute trilled from outside the tent, summoning the racers. Charlie checked the gold buttons on his vest and secured his top hat. Winston lifted the tent flap and Charlie rolled toward the starting line, keeping his gaze fixed on the horizon. A whoosh of wings came from his right and a breeze ruffled his beard. He turned his head to meet his daughter's eyes, but she wasn't looking at him, instead smiling and waving at the gathered crowd. Large mechanical wings sprouted from her shoulders, covered with white feathers for the occasion. She wore a pure white tunic with silver trim. Mechanical silver talons at the ends of her muscular legs clutched a large wooden beam. She was magnificent!

Finally, she looked at him, her golden eyes a startling contrast to her jet-black hair. Hair like her mother's. But those golden eyes were as cold as a raptor's. A chill ran down his spine.

She nodded. "Charlie."

He returned the nod. "Philomena." She hadn't called him father since Lorene's death.

Stevenson, the head Elder, stood in front of the pair. "Are the racers ready?" he asked, addressing the seconds.

Winston spoke first. "Yes, sir. Mechanically sound and ready to go."

Hawkins, Phil's hybrid second, waved his mechanical arm toward his mistress. "Mechanically sound *and* beautiful. Is she not?" he said, playing to the crowd, which roared its agreement.

Steam shot from Charlie's hat. He shook his head. All that show would be for naught after the race. A pretty appearance may temporarily charm the people, but a strong victory would win their loyalty.

The flute sang again, soft and slow and gradually increasing in both volume and speed. Charlie reached for the goggles slung around his neck and secured them over his eyes, the boiler rumbling behind him as it built up steam. He stole a glance at his daughter. Her body canted forward in anticipation. With the sounding of the start note, Charlie shot down the hill, wheels sparking. Phil pushed into the air with her powerful legs, wings spread.

As in any race of wheels against wings, strict rules and conditions ensured a fair outcome. A net slung thirty feet above the entire length of the racetrack kept the flyer low, preventing the use of altitude to circumvent changes in elevation. Beginning on a downhill stretch allowed the wheeled racer to get a faster start, the challenge being to maintain that lead once the flyer gained momentum. The long straightaway was the final means of evening the race. Since the flyer used body strength and the wheeled racer used steam, the flyer would need to maintain speed despite tiring muscles.

Charlie lost sight of his daughter when she rose into the air. The chugging of the steam engine nearly drowned out the enthusiastic cheers of the crowd lining both sides of the racetrack. He caught a glimpse of a young, dark-haired boy waving a green and grey flag and his breath hitched. Alan? Not possible. Alan was ten years dead, killed by an infection caused by the surgery to attach an improved right leg. Lorene had argued against the enhancement. There had been nothing wrong with his son's leg, unlike Charlie's, which had been destroyed in the chemical wars. His enhancements were necessary, whereas Alan's were optional. But Charlie knew that the future belonged to the hybrids. His children would be strong.

The sounds of the crowd told him that Phil was gaining. He turned his face up and to the right. Strong wingbeats moved her along just under the net. She looked down and smiled, a cold triumphant smile that didn't reach her eyes. Then with an extra flap of her wings, she was past him.

He grasped the handle on his left and pushed it forward, increasing both the amount of fuel and the temperature of the firebox. A burst of steam powered him forward, and he began to close the distance. Charlie drew even with his daughter, sweat pouring off his face. A few drops slipped under the edge of his left goggle and blinded him. He shook his head to clear his vision and blinked rapidly. He moved the handle another couple of centimeters, praying that the engine still had something left. He caught up with his daughter and crept ahead.

The smell of the superheated steam brought back memories of Eliza, the daughter who'd adored him and wanted to be just like him. Charlie had basked in the attention and encouraged her ambitions, promising her the enhancements as soon as she was old enough. He'd been unprepared for her eagerness. She'd gone to an illegal enhancement clinic and survived the surgery, but perished when her steam engine malfunctioned, scalding her to death.

Eliza's death increased the distance between him and Lorene. Because Philomena was still young, Lorene stayed. But the marriage was effectively over. All he'd asked was that she not humiliate him. She couldn't even do that much.

The finish line was not yet in sight. If he could maintain this pace, Phil would soon begin to tire. But instead of tiring, she kept up, just a bit behind but well within reach. Then he lost sight of her. Had she dropped farther behind? A glance in the rear-view mirror showed her directly behind him. She'd moved into his slipstream and was drafting! A burst at the finish line would give her the win.

Charlie couldn't help the pride he felt at his daughter's strategy. During her time as his lieutenant, Phil had always come up with well-reasoned plans when other aides reacted emotionally. Only sixteen when she joined his staff, she'd listened and learned. Charlie had been considering stepping aside in her favor when Lorene had betrayed him. Now twenty-one, Phil had spent the two years since her mother's death training physically and mentally to topple him. Maybe after he won the race, he could also win back her service, if not her affection.

But first, the race. He thumbed the red button on the accelerator handle, waiting for the right moment. When her wings were fully raised in an upbeat, he pressed the button, releasing a jet of steam directly into her face. Phil shrieked and instinctively rose into the air. Her left wing hit the net and threw her off balance. She plummeted toward the ground, saving herself at the last minute by pushing off with her taloned feet and sweeping her powerful wings downward. Charlie watched her image shrink in his rear-view mirror and smiled. She was humiliated but unhurt. Well, her face might be blistered for a while, but she'd recover.

She was as formidable an opponent as she'd been valuable as an ally. She'd sacrificed her feet and the musculature of her back for increased strength and power. This was the one area she and her mother had disagreed upon. Lorene remained adamantly opposed to enhancements unless they were replacing non-functional parts.

He held the accelerator handle steady, stealing occasional glances in the mirror. The white shape began to grow larger. He'd underestimated her determination. And her strength. The needle of the engine's heat dial quivered in the red zone. If he pushed any harder, he risked an engine failure. Or an explosion. He spied the finish line on the horizon, but Phil was regaining lost ground. Careful not to get behind him again, she pulled alongside once more and turned her scalded face his way with a look of pure hatred.

A chill ran through Charlie's body, despite the heat from the steam engine. He pressed the handle forward. The engine screamed but responded. Somehow Phil kept up and the racers remained neck and neck, moving so fast it seemed the finish line was racing toward them rather than the other way.

With a mighty downbeat of her wings, Phil moved past him by a body length. Her talons trailed in the air just to his right, hazy sunlight reflecting off silver. The racers stayed in this arrangement for three beats of her wings before she screamed as a red stain spread across the left side of her back. Her left wing dropped to her side, useless. Her right wing continued its downward motion and pushed her body into a cartwheel. She tumbled across the rails in a flurry of white, her momentum sliding her forward in front of Charlie's wheels. He grabbed the brake handle and pulled with all his might, his instinct to protect his daughter overriding his lust for power.

Somehow, he slowed enough to allow Phil to roll off the tracks. He watched in the mirror as she lifted her head.

Relieved, he moved his gaze forward. A wall of flame obscured his vision. His top hat ignited and the smell of burning hair filled his nostrils as the fire spread. Charlie had become a rolling fireball, speeding toward the crowd gathered at the finish line. He yanked on the brake, hot metal searing his palm. The handle snapped off. If he reached the finish line, hundreds would die with him. He pressed the button and dumped all the remaining coal into the firebox.

Charlie exploded well shy of the finish line, saving his people and earning the grudging respect of his daughter, the new Chief.

Valerie B. Williams came to writing late in life but is making up for lost time. She has had several short stories published in anthologies and magazines. Her most recent publication, the short story "A Mischief in Gordonsville," appeared in September 2023 in the charity anthology *Dark Corners of the Old Dominion*. Her debut novel, *The Vanishing Twin*, will be released by Crossroad Press in 2024.

Valerie lives near Charlottesville, Virginia, with her husband and golden retriever. When not writing, she can be found reading and drinking either wine or tea, depending on the time of day. Visit her online at: Valerie B. Williams (valeriebwilliams.com), or Valerie B. Williams | Facebook.

SACRIFICE

AND SICK THINGS

T he penultimate collection is here for the devoted readers of *Vinyl Cuts*. Coming at you with seven twisted tales!

THE RED DUKE

BY JEREMIAH DYLAN COOK

I follow Jim and Sonya toward the football stadium turned rock venue. Security checkpoints and fencing encompass every entrance. A whiff of pot drifts over from the parking lot. I savor the scent of the smoke and the electricity of the crowd.

Ahead of me, Sonya walks through the metal detector into Hazel Park Stadium. Jim follows her. I set my wallet and keys in the provided plastic bin, pass through the detector, and rejoin my friends while collecting my items.

Sonya motions toward the stage. "So, ready to see the Red Duke in person?"

"From a distance." Jim holds his ticket up to align with our section number in the nosebleeds.

"As long as we can hear him, who cares?" I head toward the concession stand.

As I walk, I'm surprised I don't need to weave my way through people. Most of the audience must still be pre-gaming in the parking lot. I grab my overpriced beers in record time and head to the merchandise table, where Jim and Sonya await me.

"We should check out the performance setup before we go to our seats." I hand out the drinks and take a big sip of my hoppy beverage.

"Nick, you're the expert. Lead on." Sonya bows low, pantomiming a serf's gesture to a king.

I throw my free arm out as if commanding an army. "Onward."

Jim chuckles at our shenanigans and follows us down the aisle between the folding chairs. The lower seating area covers the faded football lines. A girl walks past us in a shirt with the words "Howard King and the Crawling Chaos" emblazoned in bloody lettering.

Jim's head turns to follow her. "Why'd King change the act's name again?"

"It's an homage to David Bowie's Thin White Duke persona." As I finish, I realize how pretentious I sound.

Sonya smiles. "Like I said, you're the expert."

We enter the shadow of the enormous speaker stacks, and our approach is halted by barricades keeping us from getting within arm's reach of the raised performance space. The microphone stand, guitar, bass, keyboard, and drums stare at us from across the small gulf. The chest-high stage floor is covered in chalk-drawn occult symbols with all the instruments encompassed in pentagrams connected to each other by straight lines.

"Reminds me of your necklace." Jim points to the collar of my plaid button-up.

I reach into my shirt and pull out the silver charm suspended by a leather cord. The talisman is a leaf shape, with five branches sprouting off a central limb, surrounded by an eye-like oval. I'd purchased it eight years ago for almost nothing at a dingy shop on Bleecker Street, during a folk music–inspired tour of Greenwich Village. "Carol almost broke up with me when I told her I was buying this."

Sonya nearly chokes on her beer. "That's rich. She's cheating on you with her coworker, and she threatens a breakup over your necklace choice?"

"Well, I didn't know she was cheating on me then. But now it's a totem to help me remember what a fool I was."

Sonya's expression changes to pity, and I feel my good vibes sliding away.

Jim shifts the subject back to the stage. "There's an ankh and the Eye of Horus."

"I see a few key shapes too," adds Sonya.

I point to one of the symbols nearest to us. It looks like a stick figure with a single angry eye. "That one is from the works of John Dee. He was an occultist who advised Queen Elizabeth the first. King became obsessed with it after recording his last record in England."

Jim chugs the rest of his beer. "So, what does the John Dee shape represent?"

I pull out my phone and take pictures of the stage. "Uh, the celestial elements, I think." I spin around and motion for Jim and Sonya to join me for a selfie.

We all smile as I stretch my arm out to capture us and the stage in frame. Once we're in position and smiling naturally, I take the picture. Jim and I start to turn back around.

Sonya doesn't move. "Hate it. I know I looked goofy. Let's do another."

Jim and I return to form as we snap a second group shot.

Sonya reviews the result. "Much better. We even got photo-bombed by someone."

They return to looking at the stage, leaning on the barricade for support. I zoom in on our picture. A guy stands in the shadows behind the drum kit, smiling maniacally. He's probably only a roadie, but the way the light catches his face makes his eyes look like inky pits. It causes me to shiver despite the summer heat. I check to see if I can spot the guy in person, but he's gone. When I post the image online, I edit him out.

Jim taps my shoulder. "Here come the fun police." He nods toward an approaching security guard.

"To the seats." Sonya mimics my commanding arm gesture from earlier.

We make our way back through the stadium and ascend the bleachers. My legs ache from climbing the aluminum stairs when Jim stops and points to our seats. Several settled attendees get up to let us pass to our designated spots on the bench. One portly fellow doesn't look happy as I squeeze past him and brush against his stomach. We make eye contact, and it becomes an awkward moment for both of us.

Jim reaches our assigned spaces and sits down, followed by Sonya. She sets her remaining beer on the ground between her legs. As my ass meets the firm metal, I immediately envy the people who brought plastic cushions.

Sonya pulls Jim and me into a hug. "So glad I get to be out with my two favorite guys."

Jim picks up Sonya's beer and polishes it off. "You see me every day."

"Yeah, but when we first started dating, Nick was with us all the time. We lived together for a year for god's sake. This feels like old times, and I love it."

"I had a ton of fun that year," I say, "but I'm glad I'm not sleeping on your floor anymore. The morning backaches from the air mattress were brutal."

Finished with the last of the alcohol, Jim is chattier. "Remember that night we listened to six hours of horror podcasts?"

"Yeah, we were all too scared to leave our apartment, even though we desperately needed toilet paper." I laugh at the memory.

Sonya stretches out her legs, and the light shimmers off her rainbow-colored boots. "As usual, it was left up to the woman to save the men."

"What about that time we came back to find Nick and Carol—" Jim abruptly cuts himself off. "Sorry. Didn't mean to bring her up again tonight. She's dead to us, dude."

"No worries. I'm over her." I certainly wasn't, but I didn't want to linger on the topic. "You can see the larger shape that all the stage symbols combine to form from up here."

Sonya plucks the plastic cup from my hand and claims the last gulp for herself. "Nick, you're the expert, what does it all mean?"

"I've seen some chatter online about the circles being," I pause to add air quotes, "magic stations." I look over the symbol formed by the interconnected chalk drawings. "And apparently each stop on the Red Duke's tour serves as another kind of station. One comment spammer was totally convinced that by moving from station to station the Red Duke planned to trigger mystical results."

A chilly gust of wind makes Sonya nestle into her boyfriend.

Jim clutches her tightly. "You think he'll play 'In the Mind of Madness'? I love that song."

I'm excited to play music aficionado again. "The last set-list I saw included it."

The sun dips behind the bleachers opposite us, and the first blast of bass booms out through the speakers. Everyone responds with a cheer as we stand to applaud the start of the show. The drummer crashes into the song as he hammers down on the cymbals before starting the backing beat. The stage remains dark until a spotlight flashes down on the guitarist, beginning the opening riff of "The Hermit in the Mirror."

The bassist, drummer, and keyboardist are given their own lights; each band member is dressed in black from head to toe. They're all jamming at the center of their own chalk pentagrams. Huge screens flanking the stage come to life to broadcast a better view of the performance to the cheap seats. Only the Red Duke himself remains to be seen.

Vocals screech out to announce Howard King's arrival: "The Hermit climbs to the top of the mountain, but if you put him in the mirror, he shows you the monster."

I don't have any idea how the stage crew accomplishes it, but Howard King, the Red Duke himself, appears out of thin air on stage. My eyes alternate between the live band and the screens. King wears a crimson vest and dress pants of the same color. Unlike at past concerts, his wild locks are slicked back into a 1950s-style pompadour. As he raises his arms to the crowd, the sleeves of his white dress shirt fall and reveal freshly carved cuts matching the occult symbols on the stage

Jim shouts over the song, "How much time do you think that paint took to apply?"

Sonya elbows him and shouts back, "Don't destroy the illusion."

I become consumed by the tune, and I'm grooving with everyone else as the band abruptly transitions into their next song, "Goat Headed God." As the music speeds up, I look over to see Sonya vanish. Before I can react, she's back and rocking out all the same, except the song is different now. We're on to "Baron's Tremble in the Lake of Langan," a slow melodic ballad. Something hits my hand, and I shake it, thinking a bug has landed on me.

Amber liquid spills out over the crowd in front of me. Everyone glares back in anger as they try to dry off. I look down to see a half-empty cup of beer in my hand. My mind struggles to make sense of this. I thought my drink had been empty, and I hadn't gotten a new one.

Sonya shakes her head. "Party foul."

I shout at my friends. "Where'd this come from? I didn't have this a second ago."

Jim leans over and takes the beer from me. "Calm down, man. Did you drink too much? I didn't think two beers would do you in."

"I never saw that thing glow before." Sonya points to my necklace.

I look down to see the leaf charm giving off a subtle blue hue.

The song ends, and King addresses the crowd. "You've been a great audience. We'll be back after a short break."

The color on the object hanging around my neck returns to normal. "What the fuck? What's going on? Did I miss the first set? Am I having a stroke? Are these stroke symptoms?" I sit down and take a deep breath.

Sonya sits next to me and rubs my back. "Calm down. Calm down. Jim, can you get him some water? Maybe he's having a bad reaction to something."

"Sure thing." Jim makes his way back down the aisle we'd come up.

People I'd spilled beer on venture off in search of something to dry themselves off with as they scowl at me.

"I didn't realize I had a beer in my hand," I say to the closest member of the departing group, a guy in designer sunglasses. "I'm sorry."

The guy shakes his head and follows Jim down the stairs. I notice the sun's gone now. Stadium lights illuminate the sky. Last I remembered, the sun was barely hidden behind the bleachers across from us. I can't catch my breath.

"Nick, relax. Did you smoke something we didn't see? Or take something?"

I shake my head in the negative.

"Well, maybe you just drank those beers too fast? Or maybe the heat's getting to you?"

As if in answer to her latest suggestion, an unseasonably cold gust makes us move closer together.

"Just take deep breaths. Squeeze my hand if you need to."

My fingers clutch hers tighter than I want to, and I try not to think about how she'd vanished a few moments ago. I need something else to think about. "Describe the first set to me. What'd they play?"

"They opened with 'The Hermit in the Mirror,' jumped into 'Goat Headed God,' and I snuck down to get us some more beer while King introduced the band. When I came back, they were halfway through 'Pan's Delight.'" Sonya stopped to catch her thoughts. "Then there was 'Graveyard Dreamscapes,' 'What About Birds,' 'The Golem,' and 'Night Prince,' and they just wrapped up 'Baron's Tremble.'"

"I don't remember hearing anything between the start of 'Goat Headed God' and 'Baron's Tremble.'" My breathing starts to return to normal, and despite the bizarre situation, I can't identify anything physically wrong with myself.

"You just got too into the tunes," proposes Jim as he returns with a cup in his hand. "This will help. Nothing like a little water."

I chug down the refreshing liquid.

Sonya squeezes my hand. "So, you don't remember hearing 'What About Birds'? You loved that one!"

Taking a deep breath, I shake my head. Drums start echoing through the stadium as the second set begins. People are retaking their seats around us.

"Do you want to head out? We can just bail if you're not feeling good." Jim remains standing over me.

"No way. We all love the Red Duke's music. I can't make us leave. I'll just take it easy through this part of the show. I must've pushed myself too hard earlier."

Jim and Sonya look as if they are debating whether to listen to me, but then the guitar kicks in, and they turn toward the stage. My view is blocked by everyone getting to their feet to jam to "In the Mind of Madness." Jim turns to look at me, and we share an excited nod.

I continue to focus on taking deep breaths as the crowd goes wild. Sweat pours out of me, and I wonder if I'm dehydrated. I'd put in two twelve-hour days this week to make sure I'd caught up on work to be here. Light draws my gaze, and I look down to see my charm glowing again. The brightness increases while "In the Mind of Madness" reaches its crescendo.

I grab Sonya's arm to get her attention, and I'm disgusted to feel slime instead of skin.

King's lyrics reverberate through the air as the audience stomps along to the bassline. "You're all trapped in the mind of madness, and your freedom lies with me."

I look up.

Sonya's arm is covered in blood. Realization dawns on me. It's not blood on her arm; it's her exposed muscles. The skin is missing.

A hideous plop draws my gaze down to the aluminum bench.

Her lost skin is collecting in a doughy puddle next to me. I look back to Sonya. She's fixed on the show as her neck flesh starts to slide the same way as her arms.

"Sonya?" I know I'm too quiet to hear over the raging guitar, but I'm terrified of what her reaction will be to what I'm seeing.

"One of you came with something special. You're in for the show of your life," King sings at the top of his lungs.

Despite the insanity of the moment, my brain recognizes that those aren't the usual lyrics to "In the Mind of Madness."

I look out at the crowd. Everyone else's skin is also sloughing off. I check myself and find that I'm the only one staying normal. The globs of flesh are oozing out and covering every trace of the bleachers. I lift my feet to avoid being touched by the spreading skin of the man whose stomach I'd grazed earlier. He looks at me and opens his mouth to say something when his face melts away.

I turn back toward Sonya to avoid the full horror of the man's new visage, but she's staring at me too. Her eyes roll back into her skull, and she collapses. Jim remains standing, focused on the show. He's not as far along in his deterioration as she is.

"No. No. Fuck no. Sonya." I dive forward to try to lift her up, but my hands sink into the liquifying remains of her body. "Jim, for god's sake. Help me. Your girlfriend is dying."

The keyboardist starts the intro to "Tremendum," and Jim's gaze never turns away from the stage. I think that might be a mercy as I withdraw my hands from Sonya. They're covered in a substance that feels like warm syrup mixed with Hamburger Helper. The white of Sonya's skull appears as the last of the flesh drips from her skeleton. I start to dry heave.

Jim chooses this moment to turn to me. "Why are they playing this song backward?"

I didn't notice it at first, but he's right. The keyboard solo is at the end of "Tremendum," not the beginning. As I stare at Jim, his body collapses in on itself. His head falls into his chest cavity, which crumples into his hips and causes his skeletal legs to topple.

I survey the stadium again, and I see nothing but bodily fluids and the crowd's remaining clothes. I retreat inward. I'm fading from my own consciousness, and I peer out of my eyes like windows. I know I'm going to pass out soon, but I manage to stand.

The Red Duke's band continues to produce music from their pentagram-encircled stations on stage.

They all stare up at me.

As I peer back, their forms grow pale and thin. Writhing feelers replace their limbs as they jam onward. The Red Duke's head explodes in a burst of ichor as something slithers out of his body to replace it.

I rip my gaze away from the morphing performers, but I'm confronted by a new horror.

Among the folding chairs on the field, a black void is birthed from the fifty-yard line. Tendrils reach out to consume the nearest bits of flesh. Inside the darkness, something bright flares to life, and I see spheres circling a flaming beacon. I realize I'm looking at a solar system like it's outside my bedroom window. Space itself starts to blot out the star, and I see inky fingers smothering the sun. Then the light is extinguished as the malevolent expanse swallows the celestial body in its maw. A geyser of black fluid explodes out of the void, and three eyes, the color of burning coal, form in the sky.

As if released from paralysis, I take my first step toward escape, and I slip on a crowd member's lost skin and tumble down the bleachers. I land hard in a glob of flesh that used to be a person. Midnight comes for my mind.

A sharp pain brings me out of unconsciousness. I open my eyes. The sun glares down at me from a cloudless sky.

"You have to get out of here, or I'm going to call the cops." A security guard pokes me with his baton. "I'd really prefer to avoid the headache of getting the cops involved. So, why don't you just save me some paperwork and head home?"

My mouth is devoid of moisture, and my skin pulses with pain from where the sun's cooked me. "I—"

"Had too much to drink and wandered in here or got high and climbed the fence. I've heard it all before. So long as you're not hurt and nothing was damaged, you can leave without us making this a thing."

I struggle to my feet as the security guard watches. "My friends? The concert?"

"No concert this week. We've got a football game scheduled tomorrow. Now get going." The security guard points his baton toward the stadium exit.

Nothing remains of the show I'd watched. There's no liquified human remains, no chairs set up on the field, no living void spewing death out of a black hole. It's like nothing ever happened.

I check my pocket and am relieved to find my keys in place. I pull out my cellphone to find the screen cracked in several places. When I try to use it, I'm unable to get it to respond.

The security guard slams his baton against the aluminum bleacher, causing it to clang.

"You're trying my patience." He gestures with his weapon toward the exit again. "Get out."

I start down the steps, and I continue looking for any signs of the Red Duke's concert. There's nothing. It's like it never happened.

When I reach the exit, the guard slams the gate loudly and locks it.

Before he can leave, I turn to face him. "What day is it? My phone's broke, I can't check."

The guard gives me a look of revulsion. "You need to clean your life up, kid. It's Saturday."

He walks away before I can ask another question. The concert was Friday, so Saturday means I was only out for the night if I didn't just imagine it all. Had I been on a drug bender? That would be like nothing I'd ever done before. I'd been afraid to try my roommate's low-grade acid in college.

I head toward my silver sedan, the only vehicle in the vast parking lot. Every step is worse than the last as I dry heave in my body's bid to expel any extra liquid to cool me down. My sweat is long gone. I must've been passed out beneath the sun for hours before the guard woke me.

When I reach the car, I open the door to vent the accumulated heat and immediately chug the warm bottle of water left in the center console. After sitting still with my eyes closed to recharge, I pull out my keys and start the vehicle. I crank the air conditioner to its top setting. As the air goes from hot to warm and finally to cold, the radio crackles to life.

"We've got the Red Duke himself in the studio today. He's dishing on his current tour, and we're dead excited to hear about his new song," the host announces. "So, what's this one called?"

"'The Sloughed Skin Show,'" the Red Duke says.

I picture my friends as liquified puddles of flesh on the stadium bleachers.

The host is ecstatic. "And what's it all about?"

"Oh, I never like to clearly state stuff like that. I like my listeners to make up their own minds, but I will say this one is inspired by the fans we've been enjoying on tour. Their sacrifices keep us producing."

I turn the radio off and put my foot on the gas.

When I barge into Jim and Sonya's apartment with the spare key they'd given me, nothing is out of place. Their orange cat, Lenny, charges forward and rubs against my legs. The couple is nowhere to be found.

"I'll be back," I say to the cat.

I leave the apartment and take the elevator to the lobby. The old woman at the front desk watches soap operas on an ancient portable television.

"Have you seen Sonya or Jim pass through here recently?" I ask.

She ignores me, and I knock the bell off her desk in anger. It clatters to the linoleum floor with a halfhearted jingle.

She looks up. "Can I help you?"

"Sonya and Jim? Have you seen them? Apartment 12-4!"

The receptionist goes back to her soaps. "No one lives in apartment 12-4. Please pick up the ringer on your way out."

"How do you explain the cat and all their stuff in there?"

The woman adjusts her glasses and stares up at me. "How would you know what's in there?"

I see her hand moving toward the panic button under the desk.

"Never mind. My mistake." I return the bell to the desk and head back to the elevator.

Fifteen minutes later, I slide the carrier containing Lenny into my backseat as a police car pulls into the parking lot. Part of me wants to run over and try to get the officers to listen to my story, but I know how it will sound. I'll end up committed.

When I get home to my apartment, I rush to the desk in my living room. I start my computer and locate hard evidence of Jim and Sonya's existence. All their social media pages are still up. Lenny's urgent meows break my attention from my monitor, and I open his carrier. He quickly meets my tabby cat, Helena. Neither feline seems happy with the other's presence.

I spend the next several hours trying to contact my lost friends, but I get no response. Their last posts are from before the concert. I reach out to Jim and Sonya's family members, but they all give me the same story. They've never heard of who I'm talking about. Even when I send direct links with pages clearly showing they're related, Jim and Sonya's parents deny knowing them.

Everything catches up to me at once, and I hit the floor and burst into tears. Sonya's melting body floods my mind as I try to visualize anything else. Jim's collapsing skeleton is there when I shut my eyes. The tide of blackness spewing out of the field swallows my consciousness.

I'm clutching my necklace tightly when my eyes open again. It's nearly midnight, and I'm sore from lying on the floor. I put out food and water for the cats before crawling into bed.

I'm back at the stadium. The keyboards in "Tremendum" play in reverse as Jim melts into goo next to Sonya. The inky patch opens before me, and the band mutates on stage. I look down at my neck, and I'm missing my glowing leaf charm. My stomach splits open, and my intestines fall onto the bleachers. I scream out as a slash appears in my forearm.

The bed is drenched in sweat, and my heart is pounding when I awaken, but I'm relieved to be at home instead of in the stadium. Helena is scratching at my wrist. I recoil in pain. She's clearly unhappy with the new visitor. My other hand confirms my necklace is still on. I get up for water and return to sleep, hoping not to dream again.

I wake to several missed calls from work, and I phone them with an excuse for not showing up. My track record is impeccable, so they don't argue with me. I vacate my bed, brew a cup of coffee, and get back on my computer.

I don't find much that helps, but I do find a few occult sites that list the leaf shape I'm wearing as a kind of protective ward. I try to recall the name of the store where I bought it, but I draw a blank. I even text Carol about it, and I'm surprised she gets back to me quickly and amicably, but she doesn't have the slightest idea about what the store's name was. Out of curiosity, I ask her if she remembers Jim and Sonya, but she only replies with question marks.

The enormity of the horror facing me is too great. Faced with no good options, the lone act of retaliation I can muster is destroying my collection of Red Duke merchandise. I shove my deluxe vinyl albums, my CDs, and my T-shirts into a trash bag and proceed to smash everything with a hammer. The contents of the bag crunch and shatter under my blows. Once the bag is tossed into my apartment complex's dumpster, I focus on the only thing I can. I make Jim and Sonya's cat as comfortable as possible in his new home.

Jeremiah Dylan Cook is a horror writer whose work has been published by The NoSleep Podcast, Castle Bridge Media, Tales to Terrify, Ghost Orchid Press, Cabbit Crossing Publishing, Timber Ghost Press, The Lovecraft eZine, Hippocampus Press, Necronomicon Press, and Eye Contact. He won Purple Wall Stories February 2021 Writing Competition, and the Ligonier Valley Writers 2018 Flash Fiction Contest. While pursuing his bachelor's degree at St. John's University, Jeremiah received the Mario Mezzacappa Memorial Award for Outstanding Achievement in Poetry and Prose. He completed his master of fine arts in writing popular fiction at Seton Hill University. Jeremiah is a member of the Horror Writers Association and the managing editor of *New Pulp Tales*. You can learn more about him at JeremiahDylanCook.com or follow him on X, @JeremiahCook1.

OH, BUT THEY'RE WEIRD AND THEY'RE WONDERFUL

BY KELL COWLEY

Rhonda follows Candy into the woods, her friend leading them through the trees towards the forest clearing where tonight's secret concert is supposedly taking place.

"It's a hoax," Rhonda mutters. "I keep telling you, it's a hoax."

Candy raises the torch from her map, shining it in Rhonda's face. "For the last time, Ronnie! The Jets are a real band. This show is really happening. And if you keep dragging your feet, we're going to be late. Come on!"

Rhonda hisses, shielding her eyes from the blinding beam. "Just listen! This whole thing could be Rocket pulling a prank."

Candy shakes her head, arm dropping down to her side. "If you'd listened to the tape, you'd know it wasn't a hoax."

Rhonda winces. Candy's been telling her to listen to the tape for weeks. The tape of the live sessions their friend Rocket recorded off the radio, before copying and sharing it around their school. In the weeks that'd followed this mysterious midnight airing of the Jets' eponymous debut album, the band had become a fast-spreading cult. Rocket and Candy have been encouraging new converts to sign up to the mailing list so they'll receive the first issue of the Jets' official fanzine. This mag is the only place where fans can see exclusive pictures of the reclusive band-members, albeit in the form of blurry black and white photos, their gaunt pale faces half masked by shadows. Images that are far too murky to convince Rhonda that the Jets and their enigmatic front woman, Bennie, really exist.

"You know, it could be something worse than a hoax," Rhonda goes on. "It could be they're . . . human traffickers or something. It could be they want to lure a bunch of teenagers into the forest to kidnap them and sell them into slavery."

Candy snorts, turning away and striding ahead. "Anyone who makes music like the Jets can't be anything other than wonderful."

Rhonda sighs, knowing there's nothing she can say to Candy that'll charm her ears more than the Jets' songs that she's been listening to on a loop for the last month. Rhonda couldn't make it past the strange synth-heavy intro of the opening track. She's a hard rock girl herself, preferring the sound of frenzied drums and overdrive guitars blasting from her boombox. Part of her is glad the Jets aren't to her taste, that she's not been brainwashed into seeing the singer Bennie as the second coming. But it hasn't stopped her being dragged along to the secret concert in the woods, having a ticket pressed into her palm and Rocket's frantic insistence that she can't miss it. That it'll be the greatest gig of all time.

Rhonda just wants to make sure Candy's okay. Earlier this evening, her friend had been straddling the sill of her bedroom window, readying to escape their pretend sleepover, vowing to go to the forest alone if Rhonda was lame enough to stay home. Their parents have no idea they're trekking through the trees after dark on a Wednesday night. Like their teachers who banned the Jets from the airwaves on the school radio, no adult seems to fall under the spell of the weird, otherworldly music like kids do. Kids besides Rhonda, that is.

"Hey, do you hear that?" Candy says, smiling, tipping her head towards the noise of distant voices. The voices that are already chanting Bennie's name at the empty stage in a forest clearing they can now dimly perceive beyond the treeline.

"Okay, *fine* . . . it's not a hoax," Rhonda muttersCandy nods. "This is going to be *so* real!"

Bernadine can hear the chants of the crowd through the walls of the trailer car that serves as the Jets' backstage area. Her band are tuning up their instruments, getting ready for their big entrance. She sits before the mirror, painting her face silver and dusting her lids with fuchsia pink eyeshadow, obscuring the inhumanly pale skin beneath. Her inky black hair hangs in heavy curtains around her cheeks, hiding their hollows.

"Hungry?" her bass player asks.

She glances down at the tray that's been placed at the sharp point of her elbow. The tray laden with the severed leg of the fox her band caught in the forest before nightfall. Its raw unskinned meat is still oozing blood, still warm to her touch.

She licks her lips, but pushes it aside. "I'll wait."

It's not that Bennie doesn't want to eat, *need* to eat, that her appetite isn't raging and ravenous. It's just that she has waited so long already. She would rather hold on for a meal that truly satisfies. The smell of the crowd drifts in through the trailer's windows, mingling with the voices still chanting her name: *BEN-NEE! BEN-NEE.*

She's never had a name before. Never been a he, nor a she. She's still getting used to the human form she's taken, the speech and manners that the species affect, how they shape their identities around things so trivial as their sex organs. When Bennie had shifted into one of their bodies, she had opted for the sort with internal genitals. It was preferable to having a vulnerable appendage dangling from the pelvic region. This made Bennie a *she*, according to most forms of human language. Though there are other female attributes she's not included in her fleshy disguise. She doesn't have any cumbersome breasts bulging from her narrow chest. Her six-foot frame is dressed in a fitted mohair suit, with a hulking set of silver boots for her size 11 feet. Her androgynous appearance may be the reason her fans shortened her chosen name of Bernadine into the simple boyish nickname of Bennie.

Humans, she's found, are very simple creatures.

It's a month now since Bennie and her crew have been in orbit of this little blue-green planet, floating in a lonely galaxy far from any other intelligent life. A month according to the way these earthlings choose to measure time by planetary spins, at least. Enough time to pick up their telecommunication signals and learn their words and cultures. The tongue they call English seems the best one to use as a rock star, and if Bennie has to take on a human trade as part of her disguise, then a rock star is clearly the thing to be.

Music is by far the best thing that Earth has to offer. Not only in the many forms and genres that its so-called dominant species has created. Bennie and her crew have enjoyed the singing of the birds and whales that their probes have picked up, too. But they all admit it is the rock music they like most. It'd taken them all a little over two earthling hours to master a selection of the planet's most popular instruments and use them to produce a ten-track album that they then delivered to the local radio station of a small town fringed by woodland. The animals inhabiting the woods know how to bait a trap for their prey. They've learned a lot from them. Bennie wishes her bandmates hadn't got so impatient and started eating them. She's promised that the real feast will be one worth hungering for.

Bennie turns away from her makeup mirror, crosses to the window, and stares out over the throng of Jets fans that have filled the clearing. These *lambs to the slaughter*, as the human idiom goes. Because yes, they're all very young. Humans only just growing into their bodies, as awkward and uncomfortable as Bennie feels in her own unfamiliar skin. She won't be wearing it for much longer. She and her crew have agreed they are only making a brief rest-stop at this planet. They've already collected specimens of the animals and plants that may be worthy of long-term study, humans not among them.

No, these humans are being gathered up for a different purpose. A purpose befitting the well-fed kids living on the western side of their global maps.

Something those in their food industries call *takeout*.

Towards the rear of the crowd, Rhonda has Candy on her shoulders, the smaller girl's thighs pressed to her neck, little feet dangling around her midriff. Rhonda's taller and broader, but still not burly enough to fight her way any closer to the stage. And besides, she doesn't want to draw attention to herself in case there are kids from school around. The same sort of kids who make fun of Rhonda's short hair and stocky build and spread rumours about her having lesbian crushes on Candy and every other pretty girl in town.

Rhonda's still figuring herself out, and until she's ready to decide how she identifies, she doesn't want to deal with rumours. Candy says if there's anyone she should have a crush on it's Bennie, the flamboyant singer in her sharp suits and electric boots. But Rhonda's not like other kids. She doesn't need any celebrity role model to tell her how to be or who to like, especially one whose songs don't speak to her. To her ears, this music is just a chaotic cosmic blast coming from the far side of the forest clearing. Above her head, Candy's screaming out every lyric, her voice off-key and her diction so slurry she might as well have been speaking Martian. But her friend's having fun and that's the important thing.

Rhonda still hasn't caught a glimpse of the band. She just grips Candy's bony knees, hoping this ordeal will be over soon. She still doesn't understand what it is about the Jets' music that has the crowd so enraptured. The singer's voice sounds weirdly artificial. It is all falsetto, nasally, and bubbly as if the frontwoman were singing underwater, every line her last drowning words. It must be something about Bennie's stage presence, her aura and persona, that has the crowd so transfixed. Rhonda finds she feels safer keeping her stare downcast. She feels like looking at the stage might be akin to staring at a solar eclipse, something that would scar her eyes and change her vision forever.

She catches her breath in the next break between songs.

"You ready to get down yet, Candy? You ready to go home?"

"Closer!" Candy whines, jiggling her feet. "Get closer!"

Rhonda just grits her teeth. "I can't. The crowd won't budge."

Her friend hushes a moment, then blurts out, "Turn around then! Turn and let me fall back. I'll crowd-surf my way to the stage. All the way to Bennie."

Rhonda snorts, already shaking her head. "Not a chance! If you don't get dropped on your head and trampled to death, then you'll be dragged away by security and I'll lose you. I won't get you home before your parents find our beds empty."

Candy places her wet palms on Rhonda's cheeks, then leans all the way forwards so her head and pigtail hang upside-down before Rhonda's gaze.

"Please, Ronnie," she implores, her breath hot. "I can't listen to this music without wanting to float off the ground. I want to fly. Please help me fly!"

"*God*. Have you heard yourself? You're so spaced."

Candy presses her lips to Rhonda's brow. Rhonda sighs, smelling the strawberry-flavoured kiss mark that's left behind. Her friend's real name is Claire, but lately, she's been insisting that everybody calls her Candy in tribute to both her sweet tooth and to Candy Darling, the beautiful transgender muse of Andy Warhol. Her parents don't object to her abandoning the name they've given her.

Their daughter smiled brightly, and they let her have her way. She always gets her way.

Rhonda reaches up, gently pushing her friend's face back.

"Don't blame me if you fall and break your neck."

Candy whips her head upright, letting out a little squeal of delight. Rhonda meanwhile struggles to find the elbow room to turn herself around. Soon as she's facing the treeline, she hears Candy holler *"SURF'S UP!"* before throwing herself back onto the uplifted hands of the people crowded ahead of them. Rhonda catches her friend's ankles, lifts them the rest of the way up and over her shoulders, before turning back around just in time to see Candy's little legs disappearing, swept away on a sea of strangers' palms.

Rhonda's stomach clenches like a fist. She wonders how she could've let her friend go so easily. In desperation, she turns to the man next to her, asking him to give her a boost so she can ride the wave of hands too, so that she can catch up with Candy and drag her back down to earth. But the man just looks over Rhonda's robust frame and then gives his head a decisive shake. She curses under her breath, eyes scanning the sweaty wall of bodies before her, searching for a break in the crowd she might slip through.

Suddenly there's a flash in the sky above. A quick flash of sheet lightning is her first thought. But the night around her is warm and dry with not even a hint of moisture in the air. Rhonda tips her head back, waiting for a roll of thunder to follow the lightning, waiting to feel rain on her cheeks. Neither comes, but she can feel a wind stirring around her. A wind that feels as though it is churning upwards, a strange suction wanting to pull the crowd off their feet and have them floating off the ground, just like Candy.

Nobody besides Rhonda seems to have noticed the change in weather. Their stares are still fixed on the stage ahead, their mouths chanting song lyrics as if they were incantations. Rhonda has the feeling this concert could lose gravity altogether, and they'd all just keep on singing as they levitated up into the darkness above them.

She squints, a realization hitting her. There's something about the darkness over this concert. Something impenetrable and oppressive. There are no clouds tonight, but the stars are missing as if there's something blocking them from view.

The lightning flashes again and that's when Rhonda sees it. For a moment, she feels certain her eyes must be playing tricks; that she's the one losing her mind, not the hordes of zealous Jets fans crammed around her. Because she's sure that in that split second of white light, she's seen what looks a lot like a ship hovering above the forest clearing. An actual flying saucer like the ones from her science fiction comics.

That lightning. Had it come from the sky or from this ship? Rhonda's unsure she can trust her own senses, but she knows in her gut that there's something wrong here. The temperature seems to be dropping rapidly and not just from the chill raised on her skin. The summer night is turning ice cold. And she needs to run. She needs to get Candy and go, flee fast as they can through the trees, back to the bedroom window they left open.

"Candy!" she cries at the top of her lungs. "*Candy!*"

Rhonda lowers her stare. In the narrow gap between heads, she sees her friend. She sees her under the spotlight, waving her hands in the air.

Candy has surfed all the way to the stage.

Bennie stops singing, the mic hanging limply in her palm. The music keeps playing behind her as she stares at the little human female that's invaded her terrain. The girl's scent fills her nasal passages—a sweet, succulent, and overpowering aroma.

The tubes of Bennie's temporary stomach gurgle.

And it's rather annoying. Bennie had been enjoying the experience of being a rock star. Strutting around the stage in her suit and silver boots. Carefully tuning every note that left her throat, so it blended with her crew's precise instrumentation. She'd be evacuating this human form shortly, but for the brief time that she's inhabited it, she's savoured the little rushes of dopamine flowing to her brain. The buzz she gets from a crowd of fans singing her song lyrics back at her, their puny arms thrust in the air.

And sure, she could still smell them. But the euphoria of their performance has been enough to distract her from her raging hunger until now. Until this girl was borne toward her by the crowd's hands, like their species had recognized Bennie and her crew as higher beings and were making an offering of this fatted calf to them.

The girl herself had laughed as she tumbled over the barrier and then scrambled onto the stage. And now she's here under the spotlight, the girl doesn't seem to know what to do. Bennie can see by her dazed expression there's been no forethought here, no purpose to her mission of getting closer to this sound she loves. She just bounces up and down, gesturing to the crowd and letting off piercing squeals. Their music has done the trick. Humans are the easiest damn species to hypnotise, especially if you get them young.

Bennie's lips split, baring her teeth. She's considering whether to seize the girl by her plaited hair, twirl her overhead like a slingshot before hurling her back into the crowd where she belongs. With the power she's hiding under her skin, Bennie could do it without breaking sweat. But such a stunt would send their crowd scattering into the woods, outside the range of their mothership's tractor beam. And they couldn't have that.

Bennie swallows, steeling herself to resist. But the girl turns and rushes towards her, her arms outspread. Arms that are then thrown about Bennie's waist, encircling her slender midsection and squeezing tight. The frontwoman tries to hold her breath as she tilts her head down to stare at the clinging earthling. And she wonders if she should feel any affection for this hapless little creature, the same way that humans themselves feel fondness towards the domesticated canines they keep as pets. Instead, Bennie salivates, and her stomach tightens, not just with an increase of appetite, but with a sudden contempt.

No, she can't bring herself to feel sympathy for the dominant species of this lonely little rock. She knows there's no point in sparing them. Her crew's studies have shown that humans are not far off extinction anyway. They have made their home-world overheat with their many and varied toxic emissions. They've shown themselves to be greedy self-serving parasites, hellbent on ravaging the natural miracles their planet has been blessed with, while making it uninhabitable for the hundreds of other lifeforms who have the misfortune to live alongside them. Their race seems to be incapable of mending their own genocidal bad habits or curbing their overbreeding. And yet humans will hypocritically cull or exterminate other animals they deem pests, detrimental to their food production.

Then there are the animals they kill just because they taste good.

Bennie lets go of the breath that she's holding. She takes in the scent of the girl still hugging her waist. A smell of warm flesh, salty perspiration, and sugared lips. And do these humans realize how good *they* will taste once they are skinned and stewed? A shiver passes through Bennie. Because now she's within biting distance of one of them, she is getting the sense that these earthlings will taste just as good if they're eaten raw.

That's when Bennie's own primal instincts take over. Suddenly, her feet are floating off the ground. She's forgetting to keep up her pretense that she is being held down by this planet's gravity. The girl clutching her waist lets out another shriek as she is lifted also, the two of them hovering several feet above the stage, bodies silhouetted by the spotlight's glare. The girl's wet palms slip from Bennie's hips, sliding down her legs. But before she can fall, Bennie bends in mid-air, catching the girl below her flailing arms.

The little human raises her flushing face to Bennie. Her eyes are wide with wonder and a burst of laughter is unleashed from her lips. Along with music, this is another human creation that tempts Bennie to feel endeared to the species. Their capacity to laugh, even in the face of such near and present danger. It's a powerful anaesthetic they have used to numb themselves through so many turbulent centuries of their existence.

Best to strike now, Bennie thinks, *while the girl is numb.*

With this thought, she lets her jawbone detach and her mouth stretch wide, so much wider than any human could ever open their mouth. The pale skin she's masked her face in begins to tear and the sharp teeth she has been hiding in her gums elongate to their true size. And the girl in her arms doesn't get a chance to scream. Her laughter freezes on her lips as Bennie pulls her close and sinks her teeth into her chest. The bones of her ribcage snap like twigs under Bennie's bite. She sucks out their contents in one single satisfying mouthful, the girl's heart still hot and beating as it slides onto her tongue. Bennie lets the little organ rest there for a tantalising moment, before sighing and swallowing it whole.

She lets the girl's body fall, her hands losing their grip now that her skin is peeling away. The human lands on the mellotron below, blood oozing from her open torso and trickling over its keys, so the instrument looks more like a sacrificial altar.

It's only then Bennie realizes the music has stopped.

Rhonda's fighting her way towards the rear of the throng when the screaming starts. She'd made the decision to flee after watching Candy floating off the stage in the frontwoman's arms. She could see what her friend was being lifted towards—the open base of that UFO hovering over the clearing, the ship nobody but she seems to have seen. Because nobody's looking up. The crowd is still watching the stage, spellbound.

As Bennie had levitated several feet into the air with an adoring Candy clinging to her sleeves and the music swelling behind them, it had been all gasps and whoops from those watching. Everyone besides Rhonda had reacted as though it must be part of the show, as if the frontwoman had been hoisted by invisible strings. They thought it was a bit of fun and nothing to fear. But the fear has set in now. Yes, there is fear erupting in the tight press of bodies all around her, and Rhonda can't bring herself to look back to see what's prompted it. She doesn't want to know what fate she's abandoned Candy to.

She just needs to get away. If it's too late to save her friend, she can at least save herself. It's not just the weather and the mood that's changing here. The ground under her feet really *is* losing its gravity. The Jets fans surrounding her are rising off the grass, being lifted towards the sky, like the faithful being summoned up to heaven by the Rapture. Only, Rhonda doubts there's any kind of salvation awaiting them in that ship overhead. And all too soon she finds herself being kicked about the head, panicked limbs striking at her from every side as the crowd are sucked skywards. Rhonda shields her face from the blows, then throws herself down on the ground, army-crawling towards the treeline.

She slithers on her belly over the trampled earth, dimly aware that somewhere beyond the screaming, the music has stopped. Yet there's still a buzzing in her ears. Not just the usual rock concert tinnitus. It feels like a force field of sound surrounding her, blocking her escape. Rhonda digs her fingers into the mud, clinging to blades of grass for dear life. And she knows she doesn't have the strength to resist its pull. She's already exhausted from an hour of Candy sitting on her shoulders. *Candy.* Beads of sweat trickle from Rhonda's brow, slipping into her eyes, mingling with her tears. She can still smell the strawberries.

Then suddenly a voice: "Didn't you like our music?"

Rhonda freezes. She knows who the voice belongs to, even though this is the first time that she's heard it speaking rather than singing. She really doesn't need to look over her shoulder to be sure. But she feels compelled to turn anyway.

Rhonda turns to see Bennie hovering over her.

She's about two feet taller now than she had been on stage. Bennie's sharp elbows have burst through her suit sleeves and are jutting from the sides of her body like fins. Her mouth hangs open—wide as the preying jaw of a basking shark—rows of long, bloodied teeth gleaming under the light from her ship. It's clear she's already fed, but Rhonda senses she's not yet had her fill. Her backing band lurks in the shadows behind her, seemingly waiting for her command before they pounce. They are alone in the clearing now. Some fifty feet above them, the last of the Jets fans are being drawn into the tractor beam's glow, their bodies limp and screams silenced as they are abducted by the alien vessel.

Rhonda keeps her eyes on Bennie while she scrambles backwards over the ground, her hands pawing desperately for something to throw, something to shield her, something to keep her tethered to the earth. To keep her from floating up into the ship, too. Her fingers close around a tree root. Rhonda is grateful for it. She can't help feeling like this little bit of nature is holding her hand, comforting her before she's—

"Leave this one," Bennie says abruptly, turning to her band and waving them off. "I said leave! We don't have to be greedy. We're not like them."

The Jets don't argue with their leader. They just turn their heads up to the ship, suck in a collective breath, and dematerialize, their human forms melting away and their clothes left as steaming heaps in the mud. Bennie lingers a moment longer, bringing her lips back together and wiping the blood from her chin. Then she too evacuates from the body she's disguised herself in, the shreds of her pale skin falling away like rags. The lights go out on both the stage and the ship, leaving Rhonda in darkness.

She pants for breath in the shadows, feeling seconds away from fainting. Her dazed eyes are struggling to see more than a few inches ahead of her, but Rhonda senses she's now completely alone in the clearing, the sole surviving witness to the Jets' debut performance, at least on this planet. She knows if she tries to tell anybody what she saw—if she talks of aliens and flying ships—they will call it a hoax. Call her out of her mind, even though she is the only one who kept her head when she heard their music. The only person here tonight who didn't fit in with the crowd, who wasn't singing along. And she's the one who gets left behind to tell the story of how Bennie and the Jets rocked her small town.

Their real fans aren't ever coming back down.

Kell Cowley wrote and illustrated her first book at age eight, telling the story of a runaway radish escaping from a salad bowl to explore the far reaches of the garden. She's been perplexing family and friends with her strange stories ever since. She holds a BA in performance writing from the wildly experimental Dartington College of Arts, she won a novelist's apprenticeship with the Adventures in Fiction development scheme and is the co-founder of Odd Voice Out Press, an indie lit label for diverse YA fiction. Her published works include the queer picaresque tale *The Vagabond Stage* and the cli-fi thriller *Shrinking Sinking Land*, both available to buy at the books page of www.oddvoiceout.com.

RED DOOR BLACK

BY JASON R. FREI

I was just eighteen when I saw the red door for the first time. Of course, it meant nothing then, but I know better now.

We booked a gig at a club in New York called Calamity Jane's. An ironic name, I suppose. It was our first real paying gig, and we were the headlining act. Kristina, my girlfriend, got it for us. I proposed to her that morning right after she got off the phone with the club. The guys were stoked, and we crammed into our old-ass RV with our name spray-painted on the side in large black letters—No Moss. Skatch, our driver and roadie, was a helluva nice guy—big beard, lots of muscle, even more tattoos—rumor had it he once rode with the Hell's Angels back in California. Why he came to Pennsylvania was anybody's guess, but we loved having him. He was a regular at the crappy little dive bar where we played on weekends for beer money. He told us that if we ever got big, he would drive us around in exchange for pizza and beer.

Kristina was our band manager and the love of my life. She had legs that went on for days and dark curly blond hair that was the stuff of every guy's wet dream. The bandmates used to rib me about dating out of my league, but they respected her. She put up with us and took no shit from anyone.

On the way to the show, we decided to celebrate our big night, both our first real gig and Kristina's and my engagement. We had a couple bottles of vodka and a few grams of blow. I had almost as much vodka on my leather jacket as I did inside me. Bobby never drank. He said it was bad for his vocal cords, but man, could he zigzag a line of coke.

By the time we got to the club, we were wasted. Not the pissing-on-your-self-stumbling-around-forget-your-name wasted, but the clarity kind, where you know your place in the universe all of a sudden and you know you're about to make it.

We got off the bus and came face to face with the brightest red fucking door I'd ever seen. It had a visceral look to it, like fresh blood on a white napkin. It reminded me of something—something bad, but I couldn't place it. It downright scared the shit out of me.

I felt myself pulled to the door. I was just about to reach out when Kresky ran up to it with his drumsticks in hand and beat a primal cadence on it. That broke the spell it had over me. Stan grabbed his bass, and me and Matt grabbed our guitars. Kresky swung the door open like he was announcing royalty and we walked right through like we owned the place. And that night, we fucking did.

Our set was tight. Every note was on point. Bobby's voice dripped golden and syrupy on the ballads and tore gritty and mean through the hard ones. We played rock and roll that went from blues to pop to hard rock without missing a beat. My solos shredded. Halfway through the second set, I was on fire. Literally.

I had finished an extended riff that ran into Kresky's drum solo, so I grabbed a smoke off my amp. I flicked my Zippo, and the vodka marinating on my jacket went up like a fireball. The crowd burst into applause as I calmly slid my guitar up and down and put out the flames. Epic!

We did so well that the owner asked us to stay for two more gigs. Every night before the show, Kresky ran up to that red door and tapped out a beat on it. He said it was lucky, and we believed him. Hell, by the third night, even Kristina walked up and kissed it. Her red lipstick blended perfectly with the door. That night was our big break.

After the show, a California-tan guy in a flashy suit and pearly white teeth introduced himself as a talent agent from Columbia Records. He wanted to sign us to a record deal. We quit our shitty day jobs and drove out the next morning.

We were on top of the world and nothing could bring us down. Or so we thought. Two days later, we were on the way to a studio for our first recording session when a truck ran a red light and T-boned us.

I woke up in the hospital with a broken collarbone and fourteen stitches in my forehead. I asked the nurses and doctors repeatedly about Kristina, but they lowered their eyes and said they didn't know. Fucking liars. It was Bobby who finally told me. She died from "severe trauma to the thoracic cavity." Turns out, in layman's terms, a piece of metal went through her chest and tore her heart out. She died instantly. It fucking tore my heart out too.

Kresky got it worse than Kristina. The truck crashed right into the seat he was sitting in. His right arm and leg got mashed together with the side of the RV and the grille of the truck. He never lost consciousness until they cut him out of the mess. He went through six hours of surgery and it didn't make a damn bit of good. He died on the table. Our record deal—hell, our careers—came to a screeching halt.

It took the rest of us a while to recover both physically and mentally, especially me. The band went on hiatus. I went on a fucking bender, ending up in rehab no less than three times in six months.

Columbia found us a new drummer. The rest of the guys started recording while I was on my third stint in the Motel California. They almost replaced me, but I came out sober the third time and meant to stay that way. I was going to make sure Kristina lived on in our music.

Two years after the accident, our self-titled album went to number one on the charts and we got our first chance at a real tour. We'd start in California, hit a few spots on the way to Texas, veer up north to Detroit, shoot down to Florida and end in our home state of Pennsylvania.

We kicked ass! By the time we rolled into PA, our name was known worldwide. We rocked our homecoming in a packed fucking stadium. I'd never seen that many people in one place before.

The stadium manager took us back to their green room, and that was the second time I saw it, the big red door. It looked like the exact same door from that club in New York. I swear, if you looked at just the right angle, you could still see Kristina's lipstick smeared on it. None of the other guys seemed to even notice the damn thing. The stage manager opened it up, and they walked right through. I slid past it as quick as possible, not daring to touch it. I was reminded again of something dangerous, something connected to my childhood.

From inside the green room, we heard the crowd chanting our name. I felt trapped. That door was between me and my screaming fans, but if I dared to touch it, I didn't know where it would lead me. I shook off my fear. I wasn't going to let some fucking door keep me from my destiny. I walked over to grab the handle and a big security guy yanked it open from the other side. He told us the show was delayed. The stage manager had just dropped over from a heart attack. The ambulance was on its way, but the guard said he thought they'd need a hearse instead.

When we finally went on, we were amazing and, to this day, it's one of the best shows I've ever played. It was the biggest stage we'd ever been on and I used every bit of it, except for the far left end. The first time I ran over there, I could see the red door out of the corner of my eye. It looked like it was pulsing, like a big red heart. I almost dropped my guitar, but it suddenly felt fused to my body and I couldn't have dropped it if I wanted. My fingers flashed over the frets and I truly believe that I could have died at that very moment and my fingers would have kept shredding.

After the show, we went back to the green room to unwind. Stan was so amped up he punched the red door with a big "Fuck yeah!" Now, I had stopped drinking and doing other drugs at this point, but I swear his fist went *into* the door, just a bit. As if the door was made out of flesh and muscle and it cradled Stan's fist. I shook it off as post-gig jitters, but that door gave me the fucking creeps.

A week later, Stan walked out of a record shop in Philly and got smashed flat by a falling piano, just like in a cartoon, but no one was laughing. One of the chains on the crane snapped, and it crashed down. The shattered sidewalk was a mess of black and white and red. A pattern started forming in my mind and it always came back to that red door.

Columbia came through in another dark moment for No Moss. They hooked us up with "Jolly" Jack Roger, an up-and-coming bassist who joined us in the studio with Kresky's replacement drummer, Bill "Paulie" Paulson. We cut another record, and it debuted on the charts in the number-one spot. *Out of Our Minds* was a critical and commercial success. The tour sold out, and they added six shows in Europe. We had dates in London, Paris, Toulouse, Madrid, Rome, and Berlin.

Before we played our last show in Berlin, the guys took me out to a huge underground restaurant. Gray and white brick walls curved up into a domed ceiling. Wrought-iron black lanterns hung down from wooden beams. Several large oak tables with sturdy chairs splayed out over the red-tiled floor. Panels of dark wood with intricate carvings of stags and wolves and lions adorned the walls.

We ate our fill of sausages, schnitzel, and warm potato salad. The guys downed mug after mug of dark German beer while I stuck to chugging water. Soon enough, we all had to take a leak.

We followed the signs for the pisser around a corner at the back of the place. I stopped dead in my tracks when the fucking red door to the bathroom came into view. Three small indents in the center, knuckle-sized, mocked me and the lipstick smear above them glared at me ominously. I pissed myself for the first time in my sober life. Jolly and Bobby laughed at me.

The door was a viscous red, like exposed muscle on an operating table. It made me think of Kresky; then a memory from my childhood flashed into my mind.

When I was six or seven, my grandpop suffered a massive heart attack. He climbed a ladder up to the roof to fix some broken shingles. When his heart gave out, he tumbled off. His leg shattered on impact with the rocky ground. I prayed day and night for him to pull through.

My grandpop was the only one in my life who really cared about me. My parents weren't around much, so I spent most of my time with him. He was a salty old man with a wicked sense of humor. He read me scary stories just before bed so I would hold him a little tighter in the night. Those stories—Poe, Faust, Dickens, Irving—all featured people selling their souls to the devil to get or keep the thing they wanted most. I always imagined the devil standing fiendishly behind a red door, just waiting for some poor sucker to knock.

When my prayers didn't seem to be working, I made a deal with the devil to trade my life for my grandpop's. He survived. I lived in fear for a while that the devil was going to show up and take me to hell through a red door. Two years later, another heart attack claimed my grandpop's life. I figured the deal was forfeit, but here I am, a goddamn rock star being chased by a hellspawn door sent by the devil himself to claim his due.

I stood gaping at the red monstrosity with piss running down my leg. I should have warned them, but fear paralyzed me. All I could do was point at the door, gibbering like some goddamn moron. Bobby and Jolly laughed so hard they fell back against the door, which swung inward. Matt just shook his head as he pushed through it. I heard a deep unearthly laughter mingling with the snickers from my mates. I turned and ran.

The Berlin show was surreal. At first, I was a bundle of nerves. My fingers twitched, my stomach roiled with acid, and my eyes insisted there was a pulsating red doorway to hell just at the periphery of my vision. I'd whip my head to the side, but there was nothing there.

By the time we hit the stage, my head was in a cloud, completely detached from my body. Sounds were muted. Colors were shaded. Sweat and shivers ran down my spine. I knew without a shadow of a doubt the goddamn door was after me.

Paulie tapped out a four count and my fingers, independent of my paralytic fear, leaped into action. The crowd roared deafeningly as I launched into a blistering intro while Bobby shouted out and revved up the crowd. Thirty seconds into the song, I couldn't stop even if I wanted to. At this point, the set became one long, blurred-together track.

We were almost to the first break when something shifted in the crowd. The screaming went from adulation to horror. The horde of people rushed forward, crushing those in the front row against the barriers. The back of the hall became hazy, smoky. Terror rippled through the mass as someone yelled, "FIRE!"

An orange glow flickered in the back. We dropped our gear and ran off the stage. Flames licked all around us. The air was thick with smoke and screams of anguish. I couldn't see my bandmates or get enough oxygen to breathe. I heard Jolly call out from my right. I dropped to the ground and crawled my way over to him. One of the light riggings crashed down and pinned him underneath it. A stack of speakers exploded outward just as Paulie ran in front of them. He was knocked through the air and landed in three pieces on the concert floor.

My eyes watered and my lungs burned. Flames were dangerously close. I couldn't save Jolly alone. I yelled hoarsely for Matt and somehow he found me. We strained to lift the rigging, but it was no use. I needed to find something to wedge under the rigging and lift it up. I'm ashamed to admit it, but I just wanted to get out of there before the whole damn place came down on me. I told Matt to stay with Jolly.

As I crawled my way backstage, someone suddenly gripped me from behind and threw me over their shoulder like a rag doll. I tried to yell, but my throat was clogged with smoke and soot. I was jostled along in pitch black. Whoever had a hold of me kicked open a door. The streetlights reflected off its blood-red paint. I wanted to scream, beg them to let me go. I'd rather die of smoke inhalation than whatever horror that damned door had in store for me. Instead, I blacked out.

Later, in the back of an ambulance, I found out that it was Skatch who manhandled me to safety. The paramedic said he dropped me on the sidewalk and ran back into the building through the red door. He never returned. Neither did Matt or Jolly. The whole damn place collapsed and was burnt up. Bobby survived but was taken to the nearest hospital with smoke damaged lungs and burns over most of his body.

From my gurney, I saw the paramedics wheel out a body bag from the charred remains of the building. The mangled face of the security guard poked out from the unzipped bag. The only thing of the club left standing was the red door—still as bright as if it had been painted yesterday.

No Moss was done. Columbia called us the most cursed band they'd ever dealt with. Bobby's looks and voice were shot. He never graced the stage again, but he made a decent living writing songs for other bands. Somehow, I survived with only minor injuries. I can still smell the sulfurous fumes everywhere I go. The doctors say it's psycho-something, that it's not real, but goddamn it, I can smell it all the time.

I'm a session player now in the studio for singers that want a backing band. It isn't stardom, but it pays the bills. People continue to talk about how great No Moss rocked. I think they're a little disappointed that I don't shred the way I used to.

I think a lot about my time in No Moss. The band gave me a family that I never had. My parents had called me worthless all the time and wished me dead. The only one that cared about me, my grandpop, was ripped from my life. No Moss picked up the pieces and became the family that I deserved. My whole life turned around because of them. Then they too were taken by that goddamn infernal door.

Whenever I walked through that door, it built up my hopes and dreams. It took control of me and released the potential I had inside. Without the door, I was good, but when I stepped through, I was great. It made me a fucking rock star. I loved the feeling, the high of being on the stage in front of thousands of adoring fans. It scared me too, but I didn't care as long as I continued to rise above. However, just like any other deal with the devil, the price eventually has to be paid.

It took away everything—my stardom, my band, my family. Everything but my life. My friends paid the price. Not once did I touch the door, the one thing that it wanted above all else. Instead, it compelled everyone connected to me to touch it, to complete the contract I made so long ago.

So now, here I am in a small recording studio in Nashville and this motherfucking door is standing right in front of me, daring me to touch it, to finish what I started when I was a child. I'm shaking so hard. My mouth feels like it's full of cotton balls. All I want to do is down a bottle of something strong.

The three little knuckle indents from Stan still mark the center of it. The smeared lipstick stain from Kristina sits above them. Just below is Skatch's massive boot print. I'm sure I'd see the prints from Matt, Jolly and Paulie if I only had a black-light to shine on the damnable thing.

The souls of my friends lie on the other side of that door. It whispers to me to touch it, just once. It promises to give them back if I just turn the handle and walk through.

Well, I have another idea. I'm going to paint it black. Then, with my guitar in hand, I'll open the door to hell, walk through like the fucking rock star that I am, and take my friends back.

Jason R. Frei lives in Eastern Pennsylvania, where he works as a therapist with children and adolescents. He writes speculative fiction culled from the experiences of his life and those he works with. He blends science fiction, fantasy, and horror into new creations. His fiction has appeared in anthologies by Pulse Publishing, Hellbound Books Publishing, Gravestone Press, Crimson Pinnacle Press, and the Horror Writer's Association. Besides writing, Jason enjoys all things geeky, from comics to D&D to video games. Visit him online: https://facebook.com/odinstones.

BALLROOM BLITZ

BY ALISON GARSHA

Andi could hear the baying of the hungry crowd through the closed curtains, even over the cacophony of Weintraub's band warming up. Amid trumpet squeaks and tuba farts, she checked her pocket mirror to confirm that the curve of her painted moustache was even, the powder white of her face still fresh.

"Are you ready yet, Stefan?" she said. "Without dancing, this place is just a brothel."

It wasn't an exaggeration—before midnight there would be a steady stream of couples following the narrow corridors on either side of the hall, from which dozens of doors opened onto private cells where untold pleasures waited.

"Every whore and every John knows the real fun is in the anticipation, Herr Andi." Stefan smoothed his thinning hair as he shot Andi a boyish wink, then turned back to his band. "Mick, you finished tightening that tom of yours or what?"

"Uh-huh," Mick said, not looking up.

"I don't speak American, darling."

"Yeah, okay. Let's go, fellas."

"*Wilkommen, meine Damen und Herren!*"

Andi's contralto rallying cry rang out through the packed ballroom, answered by the applause of the creatures of the night. Threadbare sequined gowns shimmered against sweat-covered flesh, while padded shoulders and billowing trousers obscured their wearers' true shapes. You could not tell who was a woman and who was a man. The faces flanking the stage looked up at her in a crazed frenzy, while those farther back offered up only world-weary, glassy stares.

"Now these are Berlin's true connoisseurs of culture, I can tell. No cheap thrills, just cheap dates!" At this, the crowd gave a whoop of approval.

"And what dates they are!" She raised a hand to shade her eyes from the stage lights and scanned the revellers. "Who needs girls on stage like at the Eldorado, when there are so many beauties in the crowd? You see—" she stepped towards them and raised a conspiratorial finger to her lips, "there are absolutely no ladies on the stage tonight." A laugh rippled through the audience.

"But here, there are some gentlemen I need to introduce to you. Stefan Weintraub!"

Stefan stood and waved, and when the crowd continued to applaud, gave a little jig and made a comic show of stretching his suspenders before taking a bow.

"And his Syncopators!"

At this cue, Mick tapped out four bars on his snare, and the rest of the band joined him on the cymbal crash for their first number: a frenetic, flamboyant piece that never failed to start the throng in motion.

Andi gripped the microphone provocatively and sang in a voice coloured by foreign cigarettes. "*Das Leben ist so schwer, wie du mich so schlecht behandelt . . .*"

The girl in the corner stood apart, sipping from the blood-red garnet cupped in her hand and sweeping her haughty gaze over the crowd of pleasure-seekers.

This was freedom and everything that came with it. Freedom to come home from work as Kristoff and leave for the evening as Christine, with warm blessings from the dotty landlady each way. Who knows if she thinks she has an extra border—at least the rent stays the same. Freedom to go where no one knows your story, and you don't want to know theirs. To give your body willingly to decadence and mystery—that is also free, but if a generous soul wants to sweeten the deal with a few marks, she isn't too proud to accept.

If you approached a woman, sometimes she would expect money. Men knew the score more often than not, but approaching them was out of the question. Best to stand back and let them come to you.

On entering the hall, she had removed the scarf designed to cover her Adam's apple during the walkover (another safety measure) and tied it around her hips. This added another dimension to her silhouette but also revealed what she thought to be her biggest tell—it was important that the illusion not be too perfect. Far better if everyone knew what to expect under the soft, reddish illumination of the back rooms.

A thick layer of smoke floated above the steaming dancehall. The women (or those who appeared to be so) looked like wicked faeries with their tiny, fragile bodies and kohl-rimmed eyes just beginning to run. The men, with their smooth features and slicked-back hair, moved like smears of paint on a busy canvas.

Andi downed the rest of her wine and headed over to the bar.

The back wall of the bar was plastered with an enormous advertisement for cigarettes, the kind you usually see in U-Bahn stations, featuring a blond-haired, cleft-chinned man. She leaned against the pock-marked walnut of the bar top, and her eyes met the same sort of healthy, rugged face as the advertisement, only this time it belonged to the flesh-and-blood man standing before her.

"Good evening. How can I help you?" His chilly voice matched his icy-blue eyes, which remained untouched by his otherwise perfect smile.

"Another red, please."

"Are you sure I can't interest you in this evening's special?" A slight twitch of recognition, of understanding, swiftly covered by the wolfish grin. "Schnapps, 25 pfennigs a glass. You'll never find a better bargain."

"No, thank you. Schnapps doesn't agree with me."

"Ah, but it's much healthier than your wine. Made from the land—potent bitter herbs grown in the Bavarian Alps, specially hand-picked to aid digestion and distilled for purity. Say—," again, that flash of understanding, "you sound like you're not from around here."

"No, I'm from France. I'll stick with my wine, thank you."

He smiled wider. "Tell you what, order the schnapps, and it's on the house."

"I—" Christine began.

Suddenly, a voice to her right, hoarse but feminine: "A red for her and lager for me."

It was Andi Wortmann, lifting her top hat to dab at her melting white forehead with a handkerchief. The band played an instrumental piece—she must have finished her song while Christine was distracted by the pushy bartender.

"And don't even think of offering me any of your horrid schnapps. I don't care how cheap it is. I never pay for drinks here anyway."

The bartender's smile fell as he uncorked a bottle of red, poured a glass, then filled a half-litre handled glass from the keg. He placed both glasses on the bar top without a word, then retreated to the back of the bar to watch the dancing congregants, his eyes flashing with the red of the tasseled lamps above his head.

Andi turned to Christine and raised her beer. "*À votre santé*," she said with a smile.

"*À la votre*." Christine returned the smile and clinked glasses, but felt her stomach sink. At least that response was clear, but surely she wouldn't . . .

Her worst fear was realised when a slur of soft speech bubbled from Andi's lips before spilling into a laugh. She looked at Christine expectantly.

She tried to copy Andi's laugh, but it must have been unconvincing because those painted eyebrows came together in suspicion. Christine took another swallow of wine and avoided eye contact.

"Ah, I see!" Andi shot her a knowing look. "A poseur. Don't worry; everyone here is pretending to be something else." She gestured to the dancefloor behind them with her free hand.

"I'm not—"

"It's okay, you don't have to explain anything to me. It'll be between us girls!"

But Christine wanted to explain, and she'd been trying to form the words when a woman's scream cut through the chaos, and they both whipped their heads around to look.

As the pack of dancers turned to do the same, a wave of shock traveled through the crowd, and more screams rang out. Those in the centre were repelled outwards, knocking over the people behind them. The music dropped out one instrument at a time until Mick's drumming alone remained, and then that, too, ceased. The hall filled with the sounds of trampling and shuffling, screams and choking, and somewhere in the centre of it all, a sound Christine had heard before—not in life, but somewhere she couldn't place. In her nightmares?

No, it was the sound her imagination had made to furnish the evil of Dr Caligari one evening at the cinema, something no orchestra could fill in for her. It was a wet, throaty laugh, too deep for any man alive, and echoing through the hall. As more and more patrons dropped to the floor and crawled to get away from whatever horror lay there, she finally caught a glimpse of its source.

A woman-child was kneeling over a slumped figure. At first, Christine and Andi could see only the top of her head, her hands and locks of curly hair concealing her face as her shoulders shook frantically. When she raised her face, they saw that it was streaked with red that dripped from her mouth down her neck and from her hands—*something in them, what was in them*—down her arms. She smiled wide, and a flood of crimson poured like wine from a bottle, and they saw that her eyes had become black marbles.

Another scream, this time from a man, and unmistakably of pain as well as fear. They watched as a suited figure dragged a shrieking banjo player from the stage. With one sharp yank of his leg, he slid from his chair onto the hard floor three feet below. It all happened so quickly that he couldn't grab hold of anything, and his bandmates could do nothing but look on in shocked horror. Now on the floor, he hit at the figure with his instrument, swinging wildly with twanging thuds, howling all the while. Then a wet crunch. You and his screams halted.

The band, seeing what Christine and Andi could not, all tried to stand, knocking over chairs in a frantic effort to disappear backstage. More screams as pockets of violence erupted through the pile of writhing bodies covering the dance-floor. People tried to stand, only to be brought down by others grasping at their ankles to try to hoist themselves up.

The few who remained on their feet stumbled through the crush, stepping over bodies before falling and joining the teeming mass themselves. Even fewer were those who hauled themselves onto the stage and followed the band's escape route, or else disappeared through the corridors on either side of the hall. And through it all—*how long can it have been only seconds since the first scream*—that laugh carried and shook the hall with the bass frequencies of another world.

Christine put her hands on the bar behind her and hoisted herself up to sit on the countertop. Andi did the same, and they swung their legs over in opposite arcs, knocking over glasses that shattered on the floor behind the bar as they brought down their feet. Christine, wearing only unprotected Mary Janes, winced as a shower of tiny shards embedded themselves in the tops of her feet.

The bartender still stood at the back, raising his hands to the ceiling and smiling a crazed smile. "Yes, you love chaos!" He was laughing. "Everyone attack! Have your flesh!"

He looked at Andi and Christine and spat. Then he turned and crashed through the swinging half-door of the bar and ran for the fire escape. He grabbed the handle and pushed, walking straight into unexpected resistance. He pulled instead. He tried again, pushing and pulling, then shook the door wildly, but it refused to budge. He turned on his heels and eyed the main entrance on the opposite end of the bar, where five people were already tugging at the handle and beating their fists against the unresponsive wood.

Then he looked back at the horde, at the chaos he had cheered for. Christine saw that it was now impossible to tell who was the attacker and who the helpless victim, moving erratically to try to get away. She saw only a blitz of fear and hectic violence, heard the screams and scrabbles and smelled the rich copper of blood and knew—*yes, I've been here before*—what it was. There it was, that old fear that meant the end of freedom, the end of control. There was only that blinding white panic. Nothing else, nothing... No, there was something beneath it, something lodged deep in the ice of her body, frozen for years but still there: instinct. She hoped it would be enough.

The blond man picked up a barstool and, swinging it through the air in desperate arcs, crept with his back against the wall towards the doorway to the right of the hall. Twice he had to stop to bring the stool down hard on a grasping hand, but he made his way there well enough. When he reached the doorway, he turned and disappeared into the narrow corridor.

As Andi began rifling through the drawers behind the bar, she muttered to herself. "That brownshirt son of a bitch, I knew there was something wrong with him." She slapped a small serrated knife onto the counter and continued searching. "Never seen him here before in my life!" She crouched down and grasped a bottle full of clear liquid, holding it up for Christine to see. There was no label, but it was obvious what it contained.

"Don't touch that," Christine said, crouching low beside her, her voice sounding all German now. "That's what's causing this. I can't explain it, but I know what gas can—"

"His comrades must have betrayed him. Aha, I knew Otto kept some spare firepower back here." Andi held a Luger between her thumb and forefinger. "I don't suppose you know how to use this?"

"I do."

"It's yours." She handed it to Christine. "Quick, let's get in the storeroom." With that, Andi hobbled to the doorway in the wall behind the bar, her feet crunching over broken glass, and Christine followed.

The room was pitch dark, and as both stood, it was the taller Christine who felt the tail of the light chain against her forehead and pulled. Both women screamed.

In the middle of the concrete floor lay a huge man, the handle of a knife in his curved belly pointing towards the ceiling, cascades of dried blood on his shirt and around his neck, still wet where it had settled around his body.

"Otto . . ." Andi swallowed.

"We need to build a barricade."

"Right. Those beer crates."

Together they began lifting the wooden boxes. They stacked one upon the other until the door was completely covered two layers deep, while the muffled screaming continued filtering through the door.

"Now that door," said Christine, pointing at the wall to the left of where they had come in.

"No need, it only opens one way. We can go out, but no one can come in. Just think if the whores could help themselves to as much beer as they wanted!" Andi forced a laugh, then winced. "Sorry."

Christine sat down with her back against the only wall of the small room that didn't have a door or shelves of glassware, setting the gun down beside her. "That the owner?" She pointed to the body in the middle of the room.

Andi nodded without looking over and sniffed. "I'd still be selling U-Bahn tickets out of a booth if it wasn't for Otto."

"There are worse ways to earn a living."

It hung in the air for several minutes as they sat in silence. A snick and a rattle as the doorknob turned behind their barricade, making the bottles tinkle inside the crates. Neither of them dared breathe until it subsided.

Christine swallowed. "You know, I'm not pretending. Not like you are, I mean."

Andi laughed. "I don't pretend, I *play*. I'm not fooling anyone, and I don't try to."

"I'm not trying to fool anyone either!" Christine seemed surprised at the volume of her own voice. Andi raised her eyebrows.

"Look, obviously, I pretended to be French." Christine stared at the floor as the words began to spill out. "There was a woman I knew in Lille. I met her when I was on leave. She was kind to me. I was kind to her—it was the others . . ." She broke down, sobbing into her knees. "I couldn't save her."

She raised her head and took a shaky breath, wiping her eyes. "So, I don't know. I like to feel like she's still with me."

Andi nodded. "Well, you nailed the accent."

"What I'm trying to say is that's the only thing I was pretending. The rest is real. The rest is me. The suit I put on every morning is the disguise."

"Darling," Andi sighed. "You don't need to explain this to me. This is *Berlin*, for god's sake. The best, shittiest city in the world."

"It's freedom," said Christine.

Andi nodded. "When you have nothing left to spend, everything must be free."

"We're safe here, in our foxhole. We could wait this out until morning."

"That we could."

"But we're not going to, are we?"

"No." And they both turned to look at the side door.

The door opened onto a world Christine had seen many times before, but never from this end of the telescope. She stayed low, with the pistol extended out in front of her. There was just enough light to avoid stepping on bodies, but mercifully not enough to see them in any great detail. Twelve closed doors lined the walls ahead of them like a row of playing cards.

"Any of these rooms have windows?" Andi whispered behind her.

"That would hardly be good for business, would it? The doors lock, but only from the inside. I bet he's trapped himself here."

"Or he might have gone back to the hall. You can't get backstage through here; one-way only."

Just then, one of the doors opened at the end of the hall and a woman, middle-aged and heavy, staggered out. One strap of her dress hung down in shreds, exposing the yellowed slip she wore underneath. She turned her away from them, trying the backstage door to no effect, then she turned and look right at Christine and Andi.

They froze, neither of them daring to breathe. They watched as the woman squared off to face them fully, feet planted wide. She took one step forward.

"Shoot her!" Andi whispered. Christine shook her head but trained the Luger on the woman's chest.

Another step. She wasn't looking down at the body-strewn floor as she walked, so she faltered and seemed nearly to fall but kept herself upright. One more step and then another, more quickly now, as her stumbling momentum carried her towards them.

"Now!" Andi said, more desperate than before.

"I need to be sure." Christine's voice was still and calm.

The woman was running at them now. She was just three paces away from them and Christine could see that smooth white face, the black shark's eyes, and that's when she pulled the trigger.

The shot cracked through the enclosed space, and Christine and Andi watched in deaf astonishment as she came to an abrupt halt, swayed for a moment in the air, then toppled sideways to come crashing into the wall, finally falling forward to lie still on the floor.

Andi, who had tried to cover her ears while cowering behind Christine, could hear the quick thudding of her heart somewhere beneath the ringing in the ears. No, on second thought, it wasn't her heartbeat; it was too sharp and too irregular for that. It was the sound of knocking coming from one of the doors.

She placed a hand on Christine's shoulder and stepped in front of her. She stretched out a hand to touch the first door she found. Still. Then the one across from that, and the next, until finally she found a door that thumped beneath her hand. It was then that she could just make out the voice behind it.

"*Kameraden*, I'm in here! There's no one else. Please, in here!"

Andi turned to look at Christine and waved her over. Christine stepped toward her with caution in the stillness of the corridor, not knowing what Andi was trying to tell her, but trusting her anyway. When she was standing beside her, directly in front of the door, she could hear it too.

"Please, help me. I'm alive and safe here!"

Christine closed her eyes and found the voice of Kristoff. Not the one she used during the day, when addressed by her supervisor at the printing press, but the one that had been hers ten years ago, in a time so different from her life now, and yet so like the current situation.

"*Kamerad*, we're here to rescue you. Let us in."

"Thank God you're here!" the voice replied.

Christine held the doorknob, and the moment she felt the click of it unlocking, she turned it and burst into the room, crashing into the man and knocking him and herself to the ground. Andi stepped in after, closed the door behind her, and blocked it with her body.

Christine grappled with the man, who was too stunned to fight back. She got in a quick jab at his unprotected face before rocking back on her knees. With the gun trained on him, she began patting him down with her left hand. Andi, seeing this, bent down to help her, and together they relieved him of a pistol and pocketknife.

Andi might not have known how to use a gun, but as a performer, she could at least hold it convincingly.

"Fucking degenerate scum bitches!" the man screamed, his face so livid the whites of his eyes turned pink. "You demons! Traitors!"

"They're only demons because you made them that way," said Andi.

"Urian and Urnell will claim their own if we only point the way. We are the true folk. Only we can summon them." His eyes were closed, and he shook his head violently. "Unnatural back-stabbing hags with your Jew music—"

He stopped short in surprise because Christine had started laughing. Laughing, first with an uncontrollable snort of derision, then a guffaw as her eyes turned for a moment towards the ceiling. Her arms convulsed, and she tried to make herself calm down, to at least hold the gun steady. Tears began to stream down her cheeks, and all she could see of his face was a rosy blur.

"You hear that, Andi? He thinks we were stabbed in the back." She used her left forefinger to try to catch the tears and clear each eye. "I pity you. I used to believe the same thing. But it's your officers who stabbed you. It's Willie who stabbed you. And to think you've spent the last decade getting stabbed over and over in your *Freikorps*..." She snorted again. "Free... corps! Free!" Once more, she dissolved into giggles.

Another minute passed, in which Andi and the man remained frozen before Christine brought herself under control once more. "Oh, look at his face! What's the matter? You didn't know girls could be soldiers, too?" She winked, said, "Close your eyes, Andi," and pulled the trigger.

The recoil knocked her onto her back, and the room filled with the smell of smoke. The man wasn't moving, but a puddle of blood was slowly spreading in a halo around his head.

Andi helped Christine to her feet, unlocked the door, and opened it without a word. They hobbled out into the corridor, and the first thing they noticed in the murky space was that the door that led to the hall was moving.

Someone was trying to open it, but the mass of bodies was stopping them, absorbing each push and shifting back each time it closed again.

Christine and Andi turned and stumbled the few steps to the backstage door and pounded on its surface with all four fists.

"Stefan! Mick! It's me, Andi! Let us in!"

The door opened towards them and, unable to step back, they toppled backwards onto the pile of corpses behind them.

"Andi, there you are!" It was Stefan, his face flushed, shirt drenched with sweat, and comb-over sticking up in the wrong direction, but he was ringed by a yellow light that looked and felt like freedom. He was clutching an axe, which he dropped to the floor behind him. He extended one arm to each woman, helped them haul themselves to their feet, and then shut the door tightly behind them.

"We saved everyone we could—we went through the stage door," he panted.

"We need to burn it down," said Andi.

"Are you crazy? These people are sick; they need our help."

"Trust me. You might not believe in hell, Stefan, but this is it. You must have seen their eyes. None of this can get out."

He rubbed his forehead and gave a single choked sob. "Yes. Yes, you're right."

"There are some old kerosene lamps in the dressing rooms . . ."

They were already moving, marching into the closet-sized rooms and plucking the delicate lamps from vanity tables before reconvening in the narrow space behind the stage, made even more crowded by the collections of disused painted backdrops. They set the half-dozen lamps on the wooden floor.

Andi pulled a box of matches out of her pocket, slid it open, and took out a match. She opened the hinged door of a lamp, scraped the match alight against the box that held its bedfellows, and lit the wick of the lamp. Her eyes fixed on the growing flame as she passed the matchbox to Christine and Stefan, who copied her moves like choreography.

They picked up the lamps, now incendiary missiles, and backed towards the stage door. Stefan heaved it open with one hip, letting in the cool night breeze. The sheer freshness of the air was astounding.

"Mick!" Stefan called into the night. "We need your Yankee baseball arm over here."

"You got it, chief," a sturdy voice spoke from the darkness. Mick stepped in, all shoulders and five-o'clock shadow. He raised his dark eyes and nodded at them in acknowledgment. "Hey, Andi, glad you're okay."

Stefan handed a lamp to him, then pointed to the dressing room at the far end of the hall.

Mick nodded again. "Right, better clear out, ladies."

They stepped behind him, keeping the door propped open. Mick raised his left knee and brought the lamp close to his chest before projecting it out in front of him at bullet speed. The next thing they knew, the lamp had exploded against the wall in a smash of glass and a roar of flames.

One, two, three, four, five smashes later, and it was done. Mick returned into the night, and they closed the door on the inferno.

"That oughta do it."

The four of them stepped into the centre of the road, joining the huddle of onlookers. Their faces were streaked with black and red, their clothes even worse for wear than they had been before, but they were still the same beautiful miscreants, and so they would continue because they were survivors.

Alison Garsha likes nothing more than to sit at an antique writing box with a pen and paper, thinking up new ways to make imaginary people suffer. She is obsessed with elephants, Ira Levin, and learning languages.

GOTTA GET OUT OF THIS PLACE

BY PAMELA K. KINNEY

Rissa Washington handed her friend Lynn a glass of fresh lemonade before she sat down in the blue Adirondack chair to sip her own. She stared out into the graying light of the early evening, while at the end of her backyard was just darkness.

That's because that's the Great Dismal Swamp, she thought. The park was closed for the season. No one was allowed to camp or be in the place after dark even during the rest of the year, except maybe for a park ranger.

No shadows or wispy things, she thought, like she'd seen for the past few days. She snickered in her head. *It's all that marijuana I've been smoking*. Before that, she believed that maybe the sleeping pills she'd been taking caused the hallucinations. Because lately the loneliness of the area had been getting to her. At least, that was the lie she told herself.

That gray twilight melted into black itself. The solar lighting Rissa had installed in the backyard lit up, surrounding the two women in a circle of warm white light.

Lynn said, "It's so dark and quiet here. Kinda creepy."

Rissa put down her half-full glass on the table beside her chair. "That's why I bought this house. I've gotten tired of all the noise living in Virginia Beach. I had to get out of there. My boss agreed to let me work out of my home during the pandemic. A year later, long as I finish my work on time and I come to the office once a week, I get to enjoy living here. So quiet and peaceful." Rissa turned her face to her friend. "Did you know a couple of my slave ancestors used to live in Dismal Swamp after they escaped from their plantation master? I guess I'm just coming back home, so to speak."

Lynn took a sip from her lemonade before she spoke. "I thought you said you came from New York."

"I did, but my many greats-grandmother and grandfather, Tildy and Joshua Sommers, are from Virginia. Tildy's parents escaped the plantation of a cruel master and hid in a shantytown in Dismal Swamp, as many maroons did. Tildy was born in the swamp. When the Civil War ended, and Lincoln freed all the slaves, Tildy left this area and traveled north, where she settled. She met Joshua along the way. He came from a plantation in Charles City." Rissa picked up her drink and drained what remained of the lemonade. She clenched the glass as she stared across the backyard again. "Mom said Tildy refused to talk about Dismal Swamp to her husband and her kids, except she'd lived there with her mother and father in the shantytown, so their former master would never find them. I assumed being free and not a slave was better. But she just clammed up whenever any of her kids wanted to know more about her time then. She was happy to 'git outta there,' was all she would tell them."

Lynn looked down at her smartphone before she leaped to her feet. "Oh God, my phone says it's six-thirty! I'd been here more than four hours." She looked at Rissa. "It was great spending time with you, but some of us have work tomorrow."

Rissa put down her empty glass on the metal table between the chairs and stood. "I'll see you to your car."

Rissa watched as her friend's car rolled away, the lights from the headlights finally vanishing in the dark. Unlike the city section of Suffolk, there were no streetlights along the road here, which was how Rissa liked it.

Except for tonight, when she talked about her ancestors and Dismal Swamp to somebody outside of her family when she never did it before—not here, anyway.

Besides, her ancestors wouldn't care about her talking about them. They were long dead and gone.

Damn, she needed to smoke some weed. That might make her mellow again, not all freaked out.

Rissa stepped inside her house, rolled a joint and grabbed a lighter, and went back outside. She sat down in her chair and, hitting Spotify on her phone, tapped "We Got to Get Out of This Place" by the Animals. A flick of her lighter, and after putting the flame to the rolled-up bud, she took a puff and blew out a cloud of smoke that filled the air around her head. Toward the end of the song, she never felt more mellow. Her uneasiness having vanished, she stared through the haze at the dark area that was Dismal Swamp. A snicker slipped out of her mouth.

"Hey, Great-Grandma Tildy, won't you and the others come join me to enjoy a good smoke or two and listen to some tunes? It will make you feel so good."

No one answered her, nor did she expect it—just a quiet night. Not even the hoot of an owl, or dogs howling from the neighbors nearby, marred the silence.

Come with us, Rissa.

She stiffened, almost dropping the joint. The solar lights nearest to her came on again. Had someone called to her?

Rissa drew in another hit and realized there wasn't much left. The roach fell from her fingers to the grass, burning itself out as the solar lights dimmed and went dark.

She saw a glowing mist close to the property line. It must obviously be smoke from the cannabis. Rissa stumbled to her feet and the solar lights flickered on as she waved her arms to dissipate the smoke. But it remained, and she realized it was not near her at all.

Her vision swam and her stomach roiled. She bent over, and lemonade and half-digested dinner spilled from her mouth.

Not even bothering to wipe at her lips, she straightened and saw that the mist no longer lingered by the end of her backyard. Instead, the light revealed a shadow standing before her.

It's all in my brain. Right? Maybe something in the weed. Can cannabis go bad? Like food gets food poisoning. Could it be beyond its expiration date?

But I just picked it the other day, before drying it.

Then what is all this weird shit going on? Because the supernatural doesn't exist.

The shadow drew closer, a spiral from it reaching out to touch her, burning cold as it wormed around her fingers and coalesced into a spectral hand.

Rissa caught her breath as she realized she could see her caramel-colored skin through it.

"Just the weed," she whispered. "It's not real."

Whatever it was, the vaporous being said, "Come with me. The others and I have something to show you." Rissa noticed other shadow things massing around her and the shadow that talked to her.

"Where?" asked Rissa, feeling strange as she felt her feet begin walking. "Where are we going?" Her mind railed against the movement of her legs, but her limbs kept going. If she had her way, she would have bolted inside her house, grabbed her purse and keys, and gotten in her car to drive away. Maybe never come back, either.

She sure as hell wouldn't follow this thing and the other hazy things toward the darkness at the end of her yard, right to Dismal Swamp.

You cannot leave. It is your fate.

Sure she can. It's her body to do what she wants with it. But her body didn't listen. She joined the surge of shadow people as they headed for the trees. Like a drug addict, she lost control. The only power belonged to the ghosts dragging her along. Whether from her mind or for real, the spirits were taking her with them.

Rissa looked closely at the one holding her hand and saw it become a glowing form of a black woman. She wore a white headwrap on her head and a gingham dress that flowed to the ground, and she had a nose and forehead just like those Rissa saw each morning in the bathroom mirror. Her mother told her it was the face of an African princess. Tildy was descended from a chieftain of a tribe from the west coast of Africa. Another tribe had captured him and his people and sold them to slave traders. The traders split up the tribe, and they sold the chieftain and his daughter to a cruel plantation owner in the Suffolk area. The old warrior had died for her by attacking their master so that she and her lover could escape. The couple ended up in the shantytown deep within Dismal Swamp, where the woman gave birth to Tildy. They lived there until the Civil War ended and all slaves were freed.

Rissa frowned, "Tildy, is that you? But you died in New York. Your grave is in a cemetery near Buffalo. Why would your spirit come back here?"

The phantoms stopped, and Tildy's turned to Rissa. "I was compelled to return here. I cannot leave, not until I sacrifice the descendant of the white slave owner who raped me and put a baby in my belly."

Confusion clouded Rissa's mind. "Excuse me, but you married a free black man, and he is the father of your children."

The spirit's eyes darkened. "Not my first child, Tom. The white master, Ben Brown, was his father. He found my parents and me at the end of the war and assaulted me. My father killed him."

Rissa shook her head as if unlodging the cobwebs. "No way. Tom had the same last name as your husband's. Sommers."

Tildy moaned, "Joshua knew in order to have me he needed to accept the white man's bastard as his. But when I died, I found I couldn't move on, not like Joshua and our children, our children's children, and so forth. I discovered I was cursed. Neither Heaven nor even Hell would let me in. No, I must walk the land of Dismal Swamp with the other spirits of the maroons who killed Ben Brown and their own masters." The ghost woman stared at Rissa, and the frightened living one saw swirling nothingness where her eyes had been. "Only a sacrifice of the blood of Ben Brown will free me. He begged Satan himself to curse them all and me, too. He believes he can always leave, but this is his Hell as a joke put on him by the dark angel himself. Part of that joke is he and the other murdered white men must always help us do the sacrificing."

"Oh God," cried out Rissa, backing up, "you mean to kill me so that you can leave?" Suddenly realizing she could move, she turned to run. "Why me? That white bastard did it. It's not my fault."

Something hit Rissa on the back of her head, and she fell to the ground. She turned onto her back and saw a tall shadow towering over her by the light of the moon.

Tildy's voice carried on the night air. "No, but he must sacrifice one from his bloodline for me to pass over." Tildy cupped Rissa's cheek. "Even if that same bloodline is also mine." Rissa heard the sadness in the ghost's voice. "I'm sorry, but the joke was put on the victims of the slave masters, too. And I am so tired of this swamp, even if my next destination is Hell."

The shadow dropped onto her. It shouldn't have felt solid, but it did. Rissa tried getting it off her, but it grew heavier. The moonlight revealed a white face of a man with green eyes and an aquiline nose. A lock of blond hair fell between his eyes as he flashed a cannibal-sharp grin of rotting teeth. He brought his face closer to hers, and his foul breath slammed up Rissa's nostrils.

"No darkie ever escapes me, never."

Rissa screamed and fought him. "I'm not Tildy. I'm a descendent of hers, and if she told the truth, you."

He laughed as he cocked his head. "It doesn't matter. I'm cursed—stuck for all eternity in this godforsaken swamp, forced to help all these haints so they can leave. Lucifer keeps me here to kill those of their bloodline and the blood of their slave masters. Setting them free. Of course, free of haunting Dismal Swamp, but having a spectral hand in the death of a member of their family just sends them to Hell." He placed his lips close to her ear.

Rissa recoiled. "You're my ancestor!"

"That will make this all the sweeter execution. A family affair."

Rissa spat in his face. "You Confederate monster!"

The ghost curled his hands around her throat and applied pressure. Rissa struggled, fighting him, and worked on sucking air into her lungs. Instead, it felt as if brackish water filled them, and darkness blinded her until she knew nothing more.

"What the hell is going on, Lyle?" asked a dark-skinned park ranger as he and another ranger dragged the body from the swamp water. "Why are these idiots coming to the park in the dead of night? They get lost, and most end up in the water, drowned."

Lyle shrugged after they laid the body on the dirt road nearby. "Who knows, John? A dare, alcohol, or drugs? It has happened over the years, but it appears to have grown worse during the pandemic. Maybe a sort of suicide?"

John stared down at the face. "This one was an African American woman. Like me. Just like the others."

Lyle shook his head. "Not sure why they keep coming here and killing themselves. Even those we thought was Caucasian or otherwise at first, the DNA tests found otherwise. Anyway, time to call the police." *Great, another one for the forensic specialists to find who this woman was and locate relatives to let them know.*

John frowned when he glanced at the water and saw a shadow hovering over it, right exactly where they found the body. He rubbed his eyes as if that would help. It didn't; the damn thing was still there, except now it looked like their drowning victim instead of a shadow. He turned away, feeling a need for a beer or something more robust. It would not help. He had been seeing bizarre things in the swamp for the past two years, ever since he transferred here. Maybe he needed to put in for a transfer to another national park. He had been ecstatic to get this job, as his slave ancestors came from this area, but lately he begun hating being here. He wrapped his arms around himself as he shivered.

The cursed dead shoved Rissa's shade closer to John. The other man never noticed, but then, most of the living never did. Only psychics and those who were connected to the bloodline of the cursed. And all the drugs and drink in the world wouldn't help. Never did. She knew what would happen to him because they told her he was a descendant of one of them and a white overseer. They told her what to say to him.

Her cold hands curling on his shoulders, she pressed against his back and whispered into his ear, "It's your turn next, and you're never going to get out of here."

Pamela K. Kinney gave up long ago trying not to listen to the voices in her head and has written bestselling horror, fantasy, science fiction, and nonfiction ghost and cryptid books ever since. Her horror short story "Bottled Spirits" was runner-up for the 2013 WSFA Small Press Award and considered one of the seven best genre short fiction for that year. She has had various short stories and poems published in fiction and nonfiction anthologies, magazines, and online zines, and has authored a science fiction novella, an urban fantasy novel, five nonfiction ghost books, and a nonfiction cryptid book. Her horror poem "Dementia" got her mentioned in *Best Horror of the Year, Volume Thirteen*.

Pamela is a member of the Horror Writers Association, James River Writers, and Virginia Writers Club. Learn more about her at http://www.PamelaKKinn ey.com.

WE WILL SURVIVE

BY EVE MORTON

"How long has it been?" said Jan.

I glanced at my watch, then at the clock on the idling car's dashboard. I wanted the times to be different, but they weren't. "At least a half hour."

"Shit. We're screwed. We're . . ."

I put a hand on Jan's shoulder, but Jan brushed me away, so I turned down the radio instead. As much as I wanted to keep listening to the sultry stylings of Gloria Gaynor, the song only reminded me of what Jan already knew and what I had refused to acknowledge for the past thirty-five minutes. We really were fucked.

Only three days before, we'd all been getting ready to perform our latest number in the Haven Bar, a place for queers, freaks, and all those in between. Jan was in the Miss Terri getup, transforming Jan's current buzz cut into something more dazzling with a blond wig and a dress that cascaded down slim and ever so delicate shoulders. Markus, or Miss Mary Quite Contrary, had been in her fur number, the one with the thick collar and long sleeves to disguise the big footballer's shoulders. Though Markus had not played the game in years, he often acted as the bouncer for Haven, so he had to cover up the muscles when he played his alter ego of Miss Mary. She was a stunning woman whenever she took the stage; a strong soprano with a show person's charm. Last year, when she'd sung

"Happy Birthday" to Haven's owner, she'd done the Marilyn Monroe version. Just stunning, just wonderful.

I felt a tear slide down my cheek now, just thinking about it. Markus had left to get us gas when we'd run out on the side of the road in Arkansas, and it was now clear he was not coming back.

"Why are we doing this?" Jan asked me, running a delicate hand through his short hair. "I mean, we hardly know this kid. We could just turn around right now. Go back."

"And do what?" I asked. "File a missing person's report for Markus, which will just be ignored because he's a big guy, or a faggy queen, and no one cares about us? Not to mention the other kid."

Jan looked down at his lap in shame. He'd looked the same when he'd called his father last Easter to wish him a happy holiday and a happy birthday, and his father pretended to not know who he was. *I have no son*, the stereotypical answer from all homophobic dads. Jan had been upset, but put on a stunning, cathartic performance of Miss Terri that night, as if to channel his father's pronouncement. He was not his son anymore. Damn right, Miss Terri was a vixen queen who helped the less fortunate.

I reminded Jan of that day now. "Your dad left you. My family left me. And we know Markus never really had a family to begin with. This kid . . ."

"Barry," he corrected me, and I knew he hadn't forgotten his heart.

"Right. Barry. He's just like us. He's come to watch us every single Saturday night for the past six months. Then he up and disappears. We know what's happened to him. It's what almost happened to all of us, what would have happened to us had there been such a thing as conversion therapy when we were his age."

"But there wasn't. We just ended up homeless."

"And fabulous." I tried to grin, but it was hard. The Arkansas woods around us, and the fact that Markus was still missing, got under my skin. The feeling seemed to have a life of its own. The moment we truly crossed into the Deep South, passed the freshness of Georgia's peach stands and into the swamps of Louisiana, I felt as if we were surrounded by ghosts. Civil War soldiers; slaves; and of course, the missing men and women who lay stranded like us, trying to channel Blanche Dubois and depend on the kindness of strangers, only to be taken off the earth.

I shook my head and tried to focus. Panicking was going to get us nowhere fast. "We have to keep going."

"But how?" Jan's eyes were deep blue and utterly desperate. "Markus was bigger than both of us. And if he's gone . . ."

"Then we need to rely on what we've always been good at." I looked into the backseat, where our bags had been tossed. Once we realized Barry was gone, and that his parents had sent him to one of those horrible rehabilitation camps that ran ads in the back of religious magazines, we had set off on our mission. There had been almost no discussion, just utter understanding between the three of us that we had to do this for the inner, abandoned child inside all of us. So we threw all of our clothing in a bag, plus some cash we had lying around and a map of the South that we found in the Haven's lost and found.

It'll be a fun road trip, Markus had said. *If nothing else.*

Oh, we'd been so naive. Three days ago, all that worried us was whether we'd be able to break a kid who was not related to us out of a camp his parents had probably paid good money for. We had some half-baked notion of walking in, claiming to be his cousins and that there was a family emergency he needed to attend to. Since Barry often worshipped us from afar at the bar and asked us for advice between sets—advice that mostly amounted to finding the right shoes in a man's size ten, not how to escape zealot family members—we were hoping that he'd recognize us out of makeup. If he didn't, we were planning on humming a few songs to prime his memory pump. And then he'd go with us, and we'd introduce him to being a newly independent queer kid, and everything would be hunky-dory.

Everything was not going hunky-dory. And without our strongest member, I had no idea what to do next.

Except to get dressed.

"I think we need a disguise," I said, and then shook my head. "No, no. I think we need to become who we really are. That's the only way we can fight this place. That's why Markus is missing—this would have never happened to Miss Mary. The land swallows you whole. You may as well be in a good skirt while it happens."

Jan looked at me as if I was crazy. Then as if I was a genius. He opened the passenger side door and, after a careful look around the woods where we were stuck, began looking through our travelling wardrobe in the backseat. "What are you waiting for, Miss Robin?"

Power pulsed through me at my stage name. Oh, I missed her. The badass girl who could leap over tall buildings, a better Dick Grayson than the real Robin. *And now we're crime fighters, too.* We looked through our clothing at the back, found the best outfits, and began to get dressed.

The entire time, I swore the woods were watching us. Be it ghosts or hicks or even Markus, lingering on the sidelines and waiting for us to emerge as our true selves, I could feel eyes on me.

And I thought, *we may as well give them a final show.*

Once we were dressed up, it was easier to find gas. We still had to walk from our broken-down car back towards the gas station we'd spotted off the interstate, but when we did it together it was less scary. We were also dressed in a toned-down version of our typical garb. We weren't performers right now; we were just women out for a walk because our car had broken down.

No one at the gas station looked too closely at either one of us. We were lucky, in a way. We could mix between the genders, an array of masculine and feminine, and no one would look too closely.

I asked softly for gas, holding a scarf over my Adam's apple, and then questioned the kid behind the counter. Did he remember a big burly man coming through here needing gas an hour earlier?

"That queer?" he said. He twisted his pockmarked face in disgust. "Yeah, I sold him gas."

"He's a little funny, but that's just because he's from New York," I said, and hoped that the explanation made sense. The kid just shrugged, reiterated that he'd sold him gas, but nothing else.

"So, he left here?" I asked.

"Yes'm."

The rest of the conversation was like talking to a brick wall, and I felt as if we were already risking so much. We walked back to the car, arm in arm, as the sun was setting.

"It's supposed to be summer," Miss Terri, Jan's alter ego, complained. "What happened to the sun staying out all night and beach parties and fun things?"

"We'll get them, my love," I told her, gripping her arm hard. "We just have to survive."

When Miss Terri began to hum the beginning bars of Miss Gloria Gaynor's hit, I thought it was the best idea we'd had so far. We hummed together, repeating the chorus like a call that would get us through this night. Because once there was gas in the car, and no other sign of Markus, we had to keep going forward.

Our plan at pretending to be Barry's cousins had now also changed. Our clothing made us feel powerful, and since we'd managed to get out of the Arkansas woods with them once, we didn't want to take any further chances.

"We have to go in as women," I said, once we were only a few miles from the camp. We'd been passing billboards as we turned deeper in Arkansas, each one proclaiming a line from the Bible about damnation and salvation or broadcasting an alert about another missing kid with a black-and-white photo. None of them were Barry, but so many looked the same: wispy hair, a genuine smile, and a fae presence that left me with a faint stirring of recognition. Oh, these boys. These were my boys and they were in trouble.

Miss Terri had been quiet, but when I met her gaze, she nodded. She reached down into her purse and grabbed more makeup and started to put it on, using the car's mirrors for guidance.

"What are you doing?" I asked.

"We're going in as ladies of the night," she said, as if it was obvious. "We're someone's dates now. Someone in the camp, or someone working at the camp. Doesn't matter. But they've called for us, so we gotta get in somehow."

I debated the merits of this. Either they'd see through the thin disguises we had on now, call us the faggots and queers and sinners we were to them, or they'd see us tarted up like Jezebels and try to get us. Or maybe we'd dazzle them. Maybe there would be just enough ambiguity that we could slip in while the confusion was still fresh, and pluck Barry to go home with us.

Along with any other boy who wanted to come along.

"You think there are lesbians there, too?" I asked.

"Of course. These people make no distinction. Probably make 'em play house together, too. Like some sick Norman Bates nonsense."

We both shuddered. I hated *Psycho*. Just gave dressing up a bad rap. As Jan continued to put on more makeup, fully becoming the elegant Miss Terri in the flesh, I continued to drive. The road changed from paved to dirt. She was done with her eyes by then, so the shaking didn't rattle her around too much. But the lights that I had once relied on for the road, and the lingering sun, were now almost completely blotted out. The trees surrounding the dirt road became thicker and thicker. I slowed down on impulse, feeling as if I was going into a jungle.

And that feeling of being watched came back. Ghosts or goblins or hicks, but definitely not the eager eyes of the audience I was used to. "Miss Terri," I whispered. "I need to put on makeup."

She handed me her purse, her makeup, without caring. She could feel the eyes, the strange gazes from the woods, too.

"Maybe we should . . ."

"We're not turning back," I said.

"No. But I think that's the camp. And we can't drive up like this. We need to keep our car as a getaway vehicle." She gestured into the distance. I was convinced she was crazy, that her vision was going, but the orb that I thought had been the moon rising on the horizon wasn't that at all. There was no moon in the sky that night. I would later look up. Just blackness, just stars—and this single lamp outside the camp.

We pulled the car into thick brush between two trees. I finished a quick slather of my makeup, hands shaking as I did, and then we walked towards the light. We held hands, arms and elbows, interlocking with each step forward. Each crunch of the dirt and rocks under our feet made us jump. Each snap of the trees in the woods filled my stomach with dread. I wanted to go back. Desperately so. But each time I remembered that look on Barry's young face when we performed, longing and despair mixed into one, and I crept forward. I wished someone had done this for me. I wished someone had done this for all the missing boys I'd seen on those billboards as we came in.

"Hello?" called a man's voice from our left.

We turned to see a shadowy figure wearing thick army coveralls and a camouflage jacket. He was clean-cut, and something gold glimmered around his neck. A cross, maybe. He was part of the camp.

"Can I help you ladies?" he asked.

"Yes. We're a present for one of your guests." Miss Terri smiled and leaned close to him. She was acting brilliantly; only I saw that her hands shook as she made up our cover story. "Is Bobby inside?"

"Yes, ma'am." The man seemed baffled by our presence, but he was also polite. And when asked a direct question by a lady, or someone who seemed like a lady, you answered. "I didn't know it was his birthday."

"It's a bit early, yes. But we've been called in as special entertainment."

The man looked from Miss Terri to me and then back again. "I don't think that's a good idea."

"No?"

"No." He reached for something in the side of his pants, and in that split second, Miss Terri jumped on him. She wrestled his hand away from whatever was in his holster, and then used her much more massive body weight to pin him to the ground. When he struggled, she reached behind herself, grabbed a high heel, and gouged it deep into his stomach. He cried out in pain and released his hand from his pocket.

"It's a fucking walkie-talkie!" Miss Terri threw the device away with her free hand and huffed. He struggled underneath her as she tried to feel him up and down for weapons. There were none. "What do I do now?"

I grabbed the walkie-talkie instead of answering. I pressed the button to listen and heard murmurs of conversations, then I let it go and addressed the man we had pinned. "How many of you are touring the base?"

"What?"

"How many of you?" I got close to his face. "You have this walkie-talkie to talk to someone. So, how many someones?"

He struggled under Terri. He spat at us. Miss Terri held his head against a rock, threatening him in muffled gasps, until he finally mumbled, "Three."

"Three?" Miss Terri repeated, but he was silent. She threatened him with the rock again, but he said nothing else.

So she knocked him out.

"Okay," she said, looking to me. "Don't worry, he's not dead. But let's take care of these brutes before we go inside."

We did the smart thing and stuck together, walking clockwise around the perimeter until we stumbled on two more men, just like the one we'd found earlier. Miss Terri distracted the closest man while I approached the other one from behind. On a silent count of three, we knocked them out, but didn't kill either one, because we did not want to be murderers. It was tough work, though, and both of our knees were bloody, and parts of our dresses were torn by the end of it.

"We have three now." Miss Terri gestured with her head, her hair only slightly out of place, towards the front gate of the camp. We could see three main cabins now, and the one with the light on was the largest. "Let's subdue whoever's there, then move on to free all the troops. I sort of like the idea of the woods being filled with free gays and lesbians."

I chuckled, feeling the adrenaline pumping through me. But I also looked over my shoulder. I still felt like we were being watched. The men we'd knocked out, we'd also tied up with zip ties we'd found on their persons, but there was something else. Something more.

"Hey, wait," I said to Miss Terri, hurrying to catch up as she took the lead. "Did that guy mean three, including him, or three . . ."

I didn't get a chance to finish my question. Only paces in front of me, Miss Terri stepped into the light of the main cabin, and a different shadowy figure ran out of the dark and tackled her from the waist and into a thatch of trees. I froze and saw nothing, only heard grunts and screams of a struggle. My bladder seized with fear as I heard the piteous cries of someone losing a fight.

I backed away from the cabin's light and ran towards the woods. I was all fear, all animal instincts. I ran and ran, twigs and branches scraping against my dress and my face. My heels broke off, nearly tripping me, so I was running in flats and then in bare feet. I was almost shirtless, shoeless, and bleeding from both knees and one cheek by the time I reached our car. I got behind the wheel, only to realize that Miss Terri had the keys. Her dress was the only one with pockets. And it had seemed like a good idea at the time for her to carry them, like this whole thing seemed like a good idea only three days ago.

"Oh no, no, no." I sobbed onto the wheel, shuddering and shaking with fear. I kicked the floor, the dashboard, and then the radio. Something blinked in the car's engine, and for a brief second, the car came to life. A snippet of the Gloria Gaynor song came on the air. It left just as quickly, and no matter how many times I kicked the car again, it did not return. Only her voice in my head lingered, the memories I had of performing it with my two other darling ladies.

Markus was gone. Jan was gone.

It was only me now.

And I was determined to survive.

I dressed all in black, the outfit I usually wore to weddings and funerals. And baptisms, had I ever been invited. I thought of it as my "birth and death" dress, the little black number that all girls needed, whether they were bio-girls or something else. I'd packed it on a whim, as if this new adventure would have ended in Barry's eventual christening into a new life. I shimmied my way into it under the starlight of the Arkansas woods. I trembled as I slipped on new shoes, sneakers that did not go with the dress, but would help me as I went back into the woods and took back the only thing I could: Barry.

And hopefully some dignity, too.

When I returned to the camp, I made sure to take a different pathway. I walked through the woods with careful footfalls and over fallen logs; I waited and listened and hunted like my father tried to teach me when I was younger. I was almost grateful for my violent, alcoholic father in that moment, though hunting anything still left me feeling weak. But the one thing he had given me before he kicked me out was the patience to wait for whatever you wanted, be it doe or buck or to save the queer kid from a life of horrible repression.

I soon saw the men with walkie-talkies. Four of them. Damn. Each one we'd tied was now untied. I verified their numbers at least six times before I followed them with the grace that I still had from years of performing.

"What should we do with the prisoners?" one of them said.

"Didn't one get away?" another spoke up.

"Damn. We'll need to canvass the woods."

"With who? We need to watch the freak we still have. How are we supposed to find the other?"

"That girly man is gone. Scared."

"Right. But the other one, the big one that got away. How do we get that back?"

"Hmm. Maybe if we use the campers?"

The four of them looked at one another and let out a laugh. "Of course," one of them said. "Make them do the dirty work. I'll wake them."

I waited on the edge of the forest, not moving from my position, as the four guards scattered into the base camp again. Lights flicked on in each one of the cabins that had once been shrouded in darkness. A whistle sounded, followed by a bell. And then masses and masses of boys and girls, none no more than seventeen years old and some seeming as young as twelve or thirteen, spilled out of the cabins. They all gathered in pajamas—drab and grey—in front of the base camp. The four men—boys, really, they had been so young—in army jackets with walkie-talkies took a secondary position while a man, tall and bone-thin, stepped out of the main cabin to address all of them. He wore a preacher's outfit, sleek and dark and accented with a golden crucifix. When he spoke, he swayed from side to side as if this was a congregation.

"Ladies and gentlemen, we have intruders on the base," he proclaimed with high theatrics and in a Southern drawl. "We have caught some of the miscreants, but I am afraid their power of sin is no match for us. We need your help to scatter the evil that has laid waste to this camp and tried to turn it into a den of iniquity. You know your missions here."

The crowd tittered. Everyone seemed too tired and yet utterly afraid to move. The preacher man leaned towards the crowd, cupping a hand by his ear. "What do you say?"

"We are here to live clear and righteous," the crowd said in a dull, flat voice. "We will fight for the light of the Lord."

"Very good. Now go!"

The four boys walked through the crowd and gave them large sticks to use as weapons. At first, I thought they were merely walking sticks, or the type of poles you'd give teams in Capture the Flag, but one teenager slammed it into the ground. It stuck up out of the dirt like a butter knife.

"I'm not using this," the boy said. "I won't kill anyone."

Barry. I knew that voice. That was Barry. I wanted to run to him, put my arms around him, but my joy was cut from me by a powerful slap. One of the guards had hit him, and then lectured him on the use of force. "You will protect the camp. You will protect your right to live a just life. Say it now."

"I will protect the right to live a just life," Barry said, though the words were clouded by tears.

I wanted to vomit and cry along with him. But I forced myself to slink closer to the tree I was watching from, trying to blend into the night. The rest of the cabin's inhabitants scattered into the woods. The movement sounded like a harsh echo, a wave of violence and sighs from the mouths of babes who did not want to do this, but only wanted, like we all wanted, to survive.

Barry moved slowly with his weapon. He was half-hearted in all his actions until the guard disappeared into the base camp with the preacher. They truly were letting the young ones do their dirty work. Maybe they were calling in reinforcements or doing something sinister behind closed doors—but it was here, as the main antagonist ostensibly went to bed, that I thought I had a chance.

I tiptoed to Barry. He was skimming close to the edge of the forest, looking more at the flora and fauna around him than truly in search of intruders. I had to be careful to not scare him, so instead of calling his name, I hummed.

He froze, holding his back rigid, utterly afraid. When he recognized the song with a shoulder sway, I braved to say his name. "Barry."

He turned towards the sound but made no other movement. I emerged from the forest and hoped I didn't look too beat up. He needed to recognize me for this to work. He needed—

Barry ran into my arms, tossing his stick on the ground as he did. I embraced him easily, and when I thought of all I had lost to get here, I held him even tighter. "Come on," I said, though my voice trembled. "We do not have a lot of time to waste."

Before we ran deeper and deeper into the woods, he grabbed his stick. *Good boy*, I thought. *Thank you for that.* I had no idea how we were going to escape beyond the woods. All I knew was that we had to run. Whenever we couldn't run anymore, we were going to have to fight. As I repeated the words to "I Will Survive" in my head, I used it like a chant to spur myself forward. Like these small soldiers and the young men who trained them probably used Bible verses to convince themselves that what they were doing was right and just and true.

Only I was right. *I may not survive this,* I thought as we reached the edge of the woods and the world became darker all around me, *but I know we are right.* I regretted nothing of this strange errand. Except maybe that I definitely tore my dress.

"What do we do?" said Barry as we burst out of the woods. He was out of breath, like me, and I had stopped us where the car was parked.

But the car wasn't there.

"No, no, no," I moaned. Damn. We were so close. We were … I got on my knees, my wounds stinging as I did because there were tire tracks. The car had been here. I wasn't lost.

"I don't understand." Barry stabbed his stick in the dirt, frustrated. "What do we do?"

I wanted to scream at him that I was out of fucking ideas. This was it. I had nothing else other than to embrace our death with dignity. And as I saw bright headlights come towards us, I knew that was the next step.

I was ready, world, to be taken into the arms of whoever was on the other side. Maybe I'd see Marilyn and Judy and the other queens I'd loved. I remained on the dirt road, my arms open in supplication.

"Oh, Mary," I cried. "I'm ready to come home."

The car stopped in front of me. And Markus stuck his head out of the driver's side window. "I'm not Mary right now, but it would definitely please me if you got in this car right fucking now."

I gasped, touching the headlights in front of me as if they truly were a heavenly vision. The car was back. The car was running. Miss Terri was in the passenger seat—looking a little worse for wear, as did Markus—but they were there. My Miss Mary and my Miss Terri, back in my life. Alive!

A door slammed. Barry had already gotten in the backseat while I was still on my knees. Oh, that was ironic. I rose quickly and got into the other side. We'd left the stick behind, an abandoned flag for an unconquered land, but it didn't matter. Not even as swarms and swarms of other kids came out of the woods with their sticks, along with the preacher and his minions, and surrounded the car with a violent, aggressive swarm. We had gas. We had a vehicle.

And we had Miss Gloria Gaynor on the stereo.

"You ready?" Markus asked though he was already driving. "Better put on your seatbelts. We're gonna need to go fast and rough."

"My middle name. All of them," I said, just as Markus floored it. I hit my head on the back window, seeing stars, but I didn't care. Hours later, with the camp behind us, we would figure out what to do next, where to go next, and who to perform as next since our drag names were now discoverable. We'd bandage ourselves and sleep the restful sleep of the free.

Until then, though, I was going to enjoy the music.

Eve Morton lives in Waterloo, Ontario, Canada, with her partner and two sons. She spends the days running after those boys and the nights brainstorming her next creative project. At some point, she writes things down, usually while drinking copious amounts of coffee. Find updates at authormorton.wordpress. com.

PRINCE CHARMLESS

BY VIRGINIA NELSON

C lara Martin didn't usually manage to get her wing precise when she bothered to do her makeup. One eye inevitably ended up with a thicker or curved or otherwise flawed line, but she'd managed to nail it on that drizzly October day, a feat she wished she could tell someone about. Actually, all of her makeup ended up perfect, a nice partner to the floor-length ballgown she'd donned for her special night.

Instead of trying to reach out to someone to tell them about her makeup or even snapping a selfie, she unloaded the dishwasher, carefully putting her bright blue ceramic dishes back in the cupboard like any other Tuesday. They stacked neatly next to the matching bowl and mug set, and she let out a little sigh of satisfaction at how nice it looked.

Once she finished that, she headed to the laundry room, swapped the load from the washer into the dryer, and glanced at the laundry basket. Empty for once—she'd managed the impossible, finishing the laundry. With a pleased smile, she hummed along to the music playing from her playlist. Sure, not many Millennials were into rock from the '50s, but it reminded her of this video game she used to play—back before life got too busy—so she swayed a little, dancing with an invisible partner as the Five Satins sang about the still of the night.

Her ballgown swished as she headed back to the kitchen to clean the stovetop. Random crumbs and grease splatters marred the shiny black surface, and she used a combo of spray and a rough sponge to scrub them away. Why didn't she clean it more often? Sure, life got hectic, especially near the holidays because she worked in retail, but shouldn't her pride in ownership make her enjoy the menial tasks more rather than less? After all, owning a home in her thirties was a massive accomplishment these days, and she'd saved and worked hard to pull it off. Moving forward...

Best not to think about that, Clara reminded herself, and scrubbed a bit harder.

Once the stovetop gleamed under the dim under-cupboard lights, she practically danced to her living room. Hers. All of it wonderfully hers, from the colorful abstract area rug to the stylish teal couch she'd found online in a social media group for a steal of a price. Above them, she'd hung framed prints of black and white photos of the last family reunion. For a moment, she stopped to look at them—sure, she'd hung them to appear urbane, chic, cool, but did she normally take the time to appreciate how Grandpa laughed at the lopsided cake her aunt brought him for his birthday? Look at her mother...

Tears threatened, but she blinked fast to keep them from falling. Wouldn't want to ruin the perfect wing, after all.

The heavy guitar riffs from "Spirit in the Sky" took over when the Five Satins finished, so she closed her eyes and raised her arms to dance. The ballgown swished against the hardwood floor, a nice soothing sound.

Another noise interrupted her dancing, so she simply turned up the volume on the speakers with her phone app. Opening the phone was a mistake—messages all pinged, headlines from news sources, but she ignored them and returned to dancing. "Never been a sinner, never sinned," she sang loudly, eyes still closed as she put her arms around the imaginary dance partner and rocked out.

Another thud, more scratching noises, so she turned the volume to max and continued dancing. Maybe she wouldn't open her eyes anymore, just vibe with the music and enjoy.

The whine of the guitar faded out, and the noises seemed louder in the absence of sound. Her heart thudded hard, and her palms slicked with sweat, but she breathed through her anxiety, trying to dissociate from the noises. She tried to ignore how her hand shook while she pulled up the playlist, quickly clicking on another song so she could go back to dancing and ignore it all.

There! CCR, some "Fortunate Son." Good loud music, an epic classic rock ballad she could get lost in. For a moment, she met her own eyes in the mirror above the fireplace. Her hair, curled carefully and pulled into an updo, with loose tendrils escaping in a way that reminded her of when she had it done for her sister's wedding. Hadn't they danced together to this song at the reception afterward, two sisters happy and just enjoying the day? Of course, the ugly-ass dress her sister insisted she wear that day didn't hold a candle to the woven silver threads of the heavy ballgown she currently wore. Still, the basic image matched—the wedding took place six months ago, after all, before...

Best not to think about that.

The song wasn't working, but that was okay. She had a whole playlist of songs she liked, after all, and rarely had the time to actually listen to them. Why was life like that? She worked so hard, spent so many hours working, attending events—but how often did she really just take a few hours to travel, make art, read and relax...

That was her theme of the day, wasn't it? She'd done exactly what she wanted all day. Slept in late, rolled out of bed, and, instead of her usual rushed shower, filled herself up a lovely, hot bath. Went all out, too, lighting candles, using the good bath bomb—the one that had a ring, which she currently wore on the finger where an engagement ring should be.

After the bath, she'd watered the plants, vacuumed, and mopped the whole house. Not once did she turn to the internet or flip on the television—instead, sticking with her playlist and enjoying peace and her space.

It had been the perfect day.

The scratching ended, replaced with thuds. Pinching her eyes closed, Clara again fought off tears. They would be wasted, wouldn't they? Why cry about it when she could enjoy her music, her ballgown, and her beautiful home?

She'd always meant to get a dog, funnily enough. Not a puppy—with her work schedule, it wasn't like she'd have time to train the animal—but a rescue dog. An older fellow who just needed a friend to curl up by when the evenings were long and chilly.

Of course, if she went down the road of things she meant to do, the list got long and rather terrifying. She planned to see so many things—Paris, castles in Ireland, palm trees swaying by some white-sanded beach... She meant to get married, to start a family in this home, do things right. Wasn't that why she'd saved for so long? To have a home for her family to come to escape all of the scary things.

Glass broke in the distance, and her head twisted with a painful jerk toward the noise. Well, at least she knew the window was clean before it got broken. She laughed, imagining explaining how clean the window was to the insurance adjuster.

What insurance adjuster? she thought, and the darkness threatened again. Her heart beat so hard that it hurt her chest, so she put her palm against it as if to give comfort to the overworking organ.

The mirror still showed her reflection—a beautiful woman in her prime, all dressed up to go to a ball. She tried out a smile, just to see the reflection change. For a moment, she imagined her Prince Charming spotting her across the room and seeing just this—the image of her with the perfect wings, great hair, fabulous dress, and a soft, welcoming smile.

Yeah, he wouldn't know what hit him. She grinned, her panic dissipating a bit in the illusion. She didn't want a Prince Charming, though. No, she always liked a bad boy. Something about the dangerous look of them...

Her fingers flew across the screen on the phone. Where was that song? The one that made her think of a man in jeans and a white T-shirt, sleeve folded to hold a pack of smokes—she'd seen a picture like that once, an old black and white one, so she just imagined him as her prince dance partner for the night.

Yeah, some Fleetwood Mac, "Rhiannon." Closing her eyes again, she swayed into his imaginary arms. A crash in the back part of her house might have made her trip a little on the skirt of the ballgown, but her prince caught her—or she caught her own balance, but did the details matter?

He wouldn't be able to resist her, that mysterious stranger. He'd capture her hand—

The smell hit her first. Once, when she was a kid, she'd decided the leftover ham that went bad in the fridge would still feed bugs and animals, so she threw it over the bank in the yard and into the ditch. Unable to resist checking on it, she'd gone daily to watch the pink meat turn a distinctly sea blue-green color. Sickening sweetness soon overtook their whole yard, all because of one slab of rotting ham.

This smell was worse—like the ham times a thousand. She gagged a little, realizing it had undertones of cheese. Different notes made themselves obvious with each inhale—the stale scent of urine, the pungent bite of fecal matter, and a weird slimy scent like spoiled potatoes. She had to swallow three times to keep from vomiting outright but then managed to breathe through her mouth.

Maybe keeping her eyes closed would be the best course of action moving forward, but that was fine. The view behind her eyelids was even better than the sight of her lovely home. She could picture her sister, back when they were kids playing in the backyard with an old boombox pumping out the music. In those days, her biggest worry was when would her mosquito bite stop itching, or her sunburn turn to a golden tan. Could she ride her bike faster than her older sister? Would the neighbor girl finally let her play with her Malibu Barbie?

Something caught her wrist, and she grinned a little madly. Oh, her prince wanted to dance in real life? She caught the hand, ignoring how the nails scratched at her hand greedily. Blindly, she caught his waist and spun him to dance with her.

The playlist automatically started another song when the last one ended—CCR returned to tell her about the grapevine. When they were kids, they had these raisin toys, which had been her first and only introduction to the song. Her dance partner didn't exactly cooperate, but she managed to spin him a couple of times before he caught her close.

A whiff of the smell hit her again, and she did gag, chest heaving as her stomach tried to revolt, but it didn't matter.

Not anymore. He held her now. Teeth chomped at the big poofy sleeve of the dress at her shoulder, and she laughed despite the situation. Who knew? Ballgowns were somewhat zombie proof.

But then another caught her from behind, knocking her off her feet. How many times had she imagined being swept off her feet on the dance floor? Of course, her imaginings didn't compare to her current situation. Her eyes flew open as she fell, and the phone in her hand slipped out of her grip.

Not before her touch clicked on something besides her playlist, though. Screams filled the apartment—apparently, she'd clicked on a video of the news, when newscasters still tried to cover the situation and warn everyone.

The warnings hadn't lasted long. People didn't believe it—a zombie virus taking over the world? *Yeah, right.*

Eventually, the government response ended. Whatever control they'd tried to push into the populace abandoned in an attempt to find someplace safe, someplace to hide from the virus.

There wasn't a safe place, at least not for people like Clara. She saw talks of martial law, of staying inside to stay safe, but she ignored it as she still had to go to work. Maybe some people could afford to just sit at home and wait the thing out, but she had a mortgage.

Yesterday, everything had collapsed. Social media exploded with videos of people filming what ended up being their last moments before they got chomped...

She'd watched all of it from bed, and cried most of the day, but today she'd woken with such a sense of acceptance. If it was her time, fine.

But with the zombie only a scant few inches away and his scent strong in her nostrils, Clara couldn't pretend to be calm anymore. Some survival instinct kicked in, and she scrabbled to her feet and lunged for the front door.

Two of them inside, at least so far. She couldn't take down two grown men, even if they were zombies, and most especially not in a ballgown. Why did she put on the stupid dress, anyway? Sure, she'd never gotten to wear it, but how was she supposed to *move* in the thing? Maybe, if she just made it to the porch...

Throwing open the door, she didn't expect three more of them to fall in on her. They'd surrounded the house, apparently, and she didn't even have the sense to be drunk for this.

If ever there was a time in her life when she wished she'd done drugs or drank too much, this was that time.

But she hadn't, and so as they fell on her, she felt each bite, each tear, each rip. She gagged and screamed and clawed, but it didn't matter.

One of them grabbed her head as if to bite her face, but another of the zombies grabbed his wrist, causing him to slam her head into the floor. Pain shot up from the back of her head, greying her vision even as she choked on something. Something bad. Something cold and gooey. Was one of them bleeding into her mouth, or was it some other ungodly bodily fluid?

Another slam of her head into the floor, and the pain receded. Darkness threatened, and she tried to remain sane. Tried to remember it was a good life, after all, even if it ended like this.

The playlist came back on—one of them must have bumped the phone—and "Born on the Bayou" began to play. If she could laugh past the pain, past the reek, past it all, she might.

Would she awaken again like them? A creature born in Louisiana, in the actual bayou, in a lovely little house with clean laundry and neatly stacked blue ceramic dishes? She didn't know. And then the darkness won, and she was gone, not born at all. Instead, gone, vanished, and her last thought was, "Well, at least I don't have to worry about the mortgage this month."

Virginia Nelson is best known for her contemporary and paranormal romances—*The Penthouse Prince* hit the *USA Today* bestseller's list at #50, went on to be localized to other languages, then became a bestselling interactive video game, not to mention the rest of her impressive backlist. After moving to Oregon and getting engaged, she decided to fulfill her dreams of leaving characters in *un*happy ever afters in horror. Virginia holds a bachelor's in English and an associate of science from Kent State University, and a master of fine arts in writing popular fiction from Seton Hill University. You can find her on all of the social medias as well as on her website virg-nelson.com.

B SIDES

THREE FINAL TERRORS!

We couldn't just leave you without a few B-side tracks. Three final stories to terrify you are up next!

SEVENTIES WEREWOLF DETECTIVE

BY CHRISTIAN PATCHELL

Los Angeles, 1977

Mulholland Drive

That kicking and screaming you hear is the girl in my trunk. It's just before dawn and I'm speeding down Mulholland trying to beat the sun. I have to admit that this case got away from me a little. The name's Lorne, folks call me Lor for short, and I'm a Werewolf Detective. Used to be on the force, but that's kind of a long story. Got bit on a call for a domestic situation. Turns out what we thought was a dog was a kid. My partner, an old-timer, shot the little shaver. I left the force just after. It was too much for the department to explain and way too much for me to process. Guess that's not a long story after all. My partner knew something that I had to learn the hard way—

L.A. is filled with meat puppets and monsters.

Now I'm a private dick for Ghouls, Ghosts, and whatever else wants to pay my bills. L.A. ain't cheap and I likes to eat. Not human flesh or nothing. I'm partial to my eggs runny and my bacon crisp. That's where this case all started. Me enjoying a tasty breakfast at my favorite greasy spoon slash office, Nick's on West Pico. You ever heard of it?

24 Hours Earlier

Nick's Coffee Shop

Normally, not many souls at Nick's at four in the morning, just me and Maggie, my waitress. I call her Maggie May, and she hates it. I'm sitting at my usual locale tucked way in the back, just being handsome and human and enjoying the funny pages. That's when I hear the tinkle of the door and he walks in. I know two things as soon as I see this Riff Raff–looking mother-humper. One, he's a Ghoul, and two, he's there to see me.

I call over to Maggie, who's dozing at the counter. "Wake up, Maggie. I got something to say . . . "

"Fuck off," Maggie snorts, without opening her eyes.

"More coffee, please, sweetness," I say.

"Comin' up, Dick," she says, touching upon my profession and what she really thinks of me.

"And a cup for my friend here, Corpse Face McGillicutty," I say, nodding to the walking death in a three-piece suit that's shuffling my way.

"Are you Mr. Lorne Callahan? The detective?" he asks through candy corn teeth.

"My friends call me Lor. You can keep calling me Mr. Callahan. What can I do ya for, pally?"

Gruesome sits down, and Maggie comes over with a fresh pot and an empty mug. The Ghoul smells like he's wearing formaldehyde aftershave. His long white hair sticks to his shoulders like cobwebs. Maggie fills his cup, and he warms his fingerless gloved hands on it.

"Get you anything?" she asks. Gotta love her, ever the jaded Angeleno; she doesn't even bat an eye at the Ghoul.

"This is fine. Thank you, madam," says Gruesome.

"How about you, Dick?" she asks me as she takes my empty plate.

"It's pie-time, Maggie May. I'm thinking apple."

"No apple, just cherry. We always have cherry. Why do you insist on ordering apple when you know all we have is cherry?"

"I know I amuse you, but maybe not like I used to. Oh, Maggie, why don't you have apple pie anymore?" I say as I rubbed my belly. Maggie gives me the middle finger and goes to get my pie. I turned my attention back to Lurch. "Like I said, pally, what can I do for you?"

"My name is Calcifcer Von Holstrom."

"Of course it is."

"I am in the employ of a woman that finds herself in a predicament. She would rather remain nameless." Calcifcer reaches into his suit jacket, and I tense—once a cop, always a cop. He produces a Polaroid and slides it across the table. I take a peep. It's what appears to be a floating Wednesday Addams–looking dress, no face or hands. There's a newspaper with yesterday's date hovering in front of the scene. The hand holding the paper is big and covered with Egyptian tattoos.

"Vampire kidnapping? Member of your boss's coven? Looks like it could be worshippers of Sekhmet, by the tattoos." I hand the picture back.

"Very good, Mr. Callahan. You should keep the picture. It might help with the case."

"Not interested. Just pay whoever they are and get the kid back."

"You misunderstand. We don't intend to pay a ransom. It's not our style." The way he says the word "style," is like a momma bird regurgitating breakfast for her kiddos. The Crypt Keeper continues, "We want you to find Lisa Ann and bring her home. The coven is quite . . . concerned."

"I'm sure they are. Listen here, Kemosabe, this ain't gonna work. Vamps and Lyks are like oil and water these days. This town has been a powder keg with a short fuse since the Rebellion of '65. You remember that, dontcha? When your kind tried to erase mine. I think it'd be best if you guys took care of this internally."

"The child does not know what she is."

"How'd you pull that off?"

"It's rather complicated. You can understand that, considering how you came about your *gifts*? Can you not?"

"Listen, Calcified Von Nom Nom, or whatever your name is, you best stay outta my business. You don't know me, and I don't know you. And I certainly don't know your employer, and that's rule numero uno in the Private Dicks's Handbook—don't work for mysterious strangers."

The Polaroid slides back my way as the door jingles entry one more time. In glides a woman in black. I don't think her feet even touch the ground as she approaches our booth; her face hidden by her overly large black umbrella. The umbrella closes to reveal a jet-black bob, arched eyebrows, and full red lips. I knew those lips hid fangs, but I just couldn't take my eyes off of them. They were the only color in this black-and-white portrait. I was afraid I just might wolf out as the hair stood up on the back of my arms. Her cinched waist looked smaller than it used to on the boob tube, if you can believe that.

She looks me square in the eyes, and tilts her head to one side just like she did on her television show. Then the dark dames eyebrows rise just a little, and she parts those red lips, and asks, "Mr. Callahan, would you please find my Lisa Ann?" She follows up with those four words that call every true detective worth his salt to his diligent duty: "We can pay you."

"Maggie May, I'll take that pie to go. I'm on a case."

Just Before Dusk

The La Brea Tar Pits

So, I do a little digging and see what I can find out. But really, I am just killing time till dusk. If you wanna know what monsters are up to, you gotta ask a monster. I go see Yo-Yo. His real name is Yosef, but he doesn't mind the nickname as long as I bring a six-pack of Coors.

Yosef's a Golem and the best informant in the biz. I hooked him up with lodging, and he gives me the dirt on whatever mess I'm cleaning up. You see, I found him the sweetest spot in all of the Gold Coast—the La Brea Tar Pits. Well, perfect for a Golem. Yo-Yo fricken' loves it.

Turns out the night security guard at the pits deals a little weed on the side and would prefer that I not let his bosses (or the authorities) in on our itty-bitty secret. In exchange for me looking the other way on his dime-bag business, Yo-Yo gets to dwell in the heat of the sweet, dark muck. He says it's like a schvitz and is great for his lower back. It's gotta be murder being made outta clay. That's a heavy load to carry.

Just as the sun is taking a nosedive behind the hills, I roll up with a cooler and a lawn chair. All that I have to do is pull the first tab, and Yo-Yo shows up like a stray cat hearing the opening of a can of tuna. A large, dark, dripping hand emerges from the depths of the black sludge and reaches for my beer.

"Get yer own!" I yell and slap his hand away. I can hear him laugh under the muck. There are bubbles and a sucking sound when Yo-Yo rises from the tar.

Like clockwork, I ask, "Did you just lay a gasser?"

Yo-Yo chuckles back, "Shaddap! Don't be a putz."

Whenever I see this gargantuan of mud and clay, I'm always taken aback a bit. But I keep it to myself. Don't want to make the guy self-conscious or nothing. He reaches into the cooler and grabs an ice cold one for himself and hands it to me.

"You know I can't open them. Not with these." Yo-Yo shows me a pair of mitts that could palm a Volkswagen. I pull the tab and hand him back his beverage.

"What? No chair for me?" he says as he saddles up on a small boulder.

"No dice, big man. You crushed the last one. I'm not made of lawn chairs. Now what do ya hear?"

This is kind of a loaded question because Yosef hears everything. It has something to do with a combination of the magic that created him and how sound resonates within his hollowed form? Yada, yada, yada. To be honest, he's explained it to me a bunch of times, but damn if I remember. We're usually a six-pack or two into the explanation, it's all pretty fuzzy. I don't even want to know where all his beer goes.

"All kinds of stuff. Looking for anything in particular?" he asks.

He drains the can in one gulp. I open him another.

"I need the skinny on a missing Vamp kid. A girl. She can't be more than about nine or ten in human form. Went missing a day or so ago."

That's all Yo-Yo needs. He gets that faraway look in his hollowed-out eyes. It's like he's listening to a song that no one else can hear. I'm betting even if we heard it we wouldn't understand half of it. The way Yo-Yo describes the noise in his noggin, "It's like someone playin' all the radio stations at once. So, you gotta turn your head and tune 'em in."

I set him up with another beer as he finishes his second and listens.

"I'm getting like eight or nine perps. One with a lady's voice. Real sweet-like. They got the girl held up in a room. Doesn't sound too good. She's okay, but I hear crying. You gotta help dis kid, Lor."

"You got an address, or do I have to drive all over La-La Land looking for a little girl with waterworks?"

"I'm hearing a lot of wind. Oh, that's weird. It's like I'm in the clouds—or looking over a canyon." Yo-Yo stops for a hot minute and moves his head just a hair. "Got it, Mulholland Drive. One of dem places on stilts, real swanky joint. Can't miss it, only one on the block."

Like I said, best informant in the biz. "All right then, Starsky, I gotta Hutch," I say and thank him, open the last few beers, and give him mine, untouched. I'm on the clock. Then I reach into the cooler and gave Yo-Yo a healthy helping of pie compliments of Nick's.

The last thing Yo-Yo says is, "Ooh, is it apple?"

I laugh and hit the road.

After Midnight

Stilt House on Mulholland

I drive up and down the block twice to scope the joint out before I pull in. Swanky, just like Yo-Yo said. Wasn't too hard to find, either.

Not many places up on stilts overlooking the canyon. As the Olds makes its way up the gravel driveway, I see a lummox of a human being waiting at the far end. The tattoos all along his arms tell me I'm at the right address. He's got a large container of McDonald's french fries in one hand and a sawed-off in the other. If he's not careful, he just might blow his face off, but I'm never that lucky.

"Outta the car, chief," he says, pointing a fry at me. Guess I should be glad it's not the gun he's pointing with.

"Sure thing, Grimace. I'm here to see Mayor McCheese." I turn off the car and hope he's not gonna frisk me.

"Huh? What do ya mean, 'Grimace'?"

Clearly this gentleman's family tree never forked.

"Oh yeah, I forgot, I'm out by the canyon. I'll speak slower. I'm here to see the head honcho. The big cheese. The boss. *Comprende?*"

"Up against the hood." Grimace handles me with all the delicacy of a professional wrestler. He frisks me and finds the gun that I lovingly refer to as Felix in my shoulder holster. Luckily, he's more interested in his meal than me, and he misses Oscar tucked away in my boot.

"What's this 'bout?" he says, barely audible with a mouth filled with deep-fried taters.

"I'm here for the girl." I wipe away bits of expelled french fry from the lapel of my leather. "And watch it, jackass. This is my favorite jacket."

"Is that right. Well, this way, Mr. Fonzarelli. The boss lady is awaiting."

Inside is pretty posh. Nice furniture, what there is of it. The center of what should be the living room has a large marble desk. The walls are decked out with all kinds of Egyptian doodads and knickknacks. Gold ankhs, scarabs, and such—stone reliefs, a few framed pieces of hieroglyphic-ridden papyrus that could say "Eat at Joe's" for all I know.

I take off my leather jacket and lay it on the back of the chair opposite the desk to make Grimace nervous and to protect it from what lies ahead. I wasn't kidding about it being my favorite coat. As I'm making myself at home in the chair, that's when I see the huge stone relief behind the desk is of Sekhmet, the warrior goddess. I get to thinking, as the sculpture of a giant cat stares me down, how much I hate being right all the time. There are two doors on either side of the idol; the boss lady enters through the one on the left.

When I tell you who she looks like, you're not going to believe me. So, I'll just come right out and say it—she looks like Elizabeth Taylor. Exactly like she did when she was in *Cleopatra*. I'm not talking ceremonial headdresses and broad gold collars or nothing. There was something about her eyes, the green dress with a gorgeous gold brooch, even the way she wore her hair. Everything about her had the whiff of Liz.

"Does he have the money?" she asks the Happy Meal as if I'm not sitting across from her.

"Not carrying nothing but this." Mongo the Fry-Eater puts my gun on the desk in front of her as she sits down.

"I suppose you want proof of life?" she smiles as she finally addresses me.

"Kinda funny way of saying hello you have there," I retort. "Plus the fact that she's undead, it would sorta defeat the purpose." I hear Grimace snicker a little behind me, and the boss lady gives him the ol' stink eye.

"Fine then, where's the money?" she says.

I clap my hands together and say, "Well, that's a funny story, lady. Change of plan. You give me the girl, and you live to snatch another child." I lean back in the chair and let that nugget settle in.

"I don't think you know the gravity of your situation, my dear." Her lips roll around the words like a serpent's kiss. "If the answer to my next question is not a resounding yes, I am going to have my associate, Heqet here, snap your neck. Listen to me closely: Do you have the ransom?"

"Yes! Wait—what were you saying? I just got a piece of lettuce out from between my teeth that was driving me crazy."

"Kill him."

I feel the big guy's gun on my shoulder and figure it's time to make with the change-o-rama. Little something they get wrong in all those flicks—you don't need a full moon, and it doesn't take long to turn into a Werewolf. It's like a sneeze. An extremely painful sneeze. And you gotta pick your zone. If you go full wolf, a hell of a lot of good that'll do you in fisticuffs.

In a situation like this, you wanna go Arnold Palmer, half and half. That way you can scare the shit outta them but you don't wake up naked in Encino. I do the deed, and I feel the gun move off of me, but the reception is way less than expected. People in this town have seen it all, I guess.

"Assholes sent a Werewolf," says boss lady. "By Sekhmet's whiskers, Heqet, I said kill him."

Since fangs didn't faze them, I figure I'll just fill them full of lead. I grab Oscar, the gun in my boot, and fire. Another little-known fact—it's extremely difficult to shoot straight with claws. To be honest, I was lucky I could pull the trigger. The bullet goes wide, missing Miss Manners, and hits the stone relief of their cat goddess behind her. This sculpture falls off the wall and breaks apart when it hits the floor.

"Aw man, fucking Mummies!" I say or growl rather. You would have, too, if you saw the loveliness that is Liz Taylor turn into a grey prune wrapped in old tissue paper right before your peepers. The statue on the wall must have been their magical totem or some such nonsense. That would explain how the chick looked like Liz and the fact that no one was bugging out about a Werewolf in the living room. Either way, I'm never going to be able to wash that withered image of her out of my eyeballs.

I stand, turn around, and behold! Heqet is now a dust bag as well. I ever so gently removed his arms from his torso and beat him over the head with them. The only way to kill a Mummy is to tear them limb from limb. Or at least that's the hypothesis I'm working under until proven incorrect. All that's left of Grimace when I'm done is the empty fry box atop a pile of dust. That's when I feel two shots in my back. She frickin' shot me in the back. Regular bullets don't kill me, but they hurt like a bitch. I then turn my attention back to Pruneface Liz.

"All right, lady, where's the kid?"

She shoots me one more time. The bullet lands in my chest, and I wince as I push the lead out. It leaves my body with a pop.

"You think I'd put silver bullets in my own gun?"

Then she spits on me, throws the gun at my noggin, and starts to utter something. While she's making with the magical mumbo-jumbo, I grab a nice big gold ankh off the wall and just as she's about to scream the last of her spell I stab her with it. The force of my staking her in the ol' bullseye pins her scrawny butt to the wood paneling. She throttles about like an epileptic marionette, and I tell her politely, "Stick around. I'll be right back." I love a good pun. I know that's not one, but I love a good one, and you're never gonna find it without looking.

I now have a choice to make, and I can hear Monty Hall in my head as I pick the door on the left, the one Liz came through. On the other side are another half a dozen beef jerky–looking waste-walkers. They're quite confused and kinda pissed that I disturbed their dinner of Big Macs and a rather loud episode of *Charlie's Angels*. Lucky me. I turn to them just before they pounce and tell them a story.

"Every morning I get up and I take my Flintstone vitamins. Two of 'em, just like the bottle says." They're more confused than seconds ago when a Werewolf complicated their McMeal, which is just how I want them. I continue, "You can tell if you're gonna have a good day when you get a Fred or a Wilma—or, dare I say, the Holy Grail: a Betty. This morning I got two fucking Barneys. I knew I should've stayed in bed!"

At that, they attack. I ramp up my wolfin' to about a seven. Bigger and badder, a lot less human, way more tail. More fur lines my back as my snout grows longer, and the fangs of my underbite drip with saliva. I'll save you the gory details, since you probably deduce—I mean, I am telling you the story—that I pulverize them.

The real reason I hate Mummies has nothing to do with fighting them. Old corpses tend to fall to bits when mauled, clawed, and fanged; it's just that I'm not a fan of dead-people dust all over me. I am gonna be blowing grey snot for weeks.

That room being a bust, I head out to try door number two. Liz is still making with the dance of the dead, held fast to the wall, when I grab my jacket. Before opening the door, I change back to my human form. The kid's been through enough already. I don't want to frighten her. Any more than a guy covered in the dirt of a dozen pharaohs and looking like Bruce Banner on a bender might scare you.

My heart drops when I enter.

The small room is empty except for a mattress and the girl huddled in the corner, sporting the same Wednesday Addams getup as in the Polaroid. The windows are covered in newspaper, but there are holes cut like Swiss cheese. To let in rays of sunlight.

These dickhead Mummies tormented the little shaver. I fight the urge to wolf-out and tear the place down to its foundations. She has a few burns on her arms. She knows what she is now. Vamped-out and hungry. I flash to a memory of me, clothes shredded, covered in blood, and huddled in a hollowed-out log in the middle of the woods. She takes one look at me and tries to push herself further into the corner.

"Are y-you one of them?" she squeaks.

"No, Lisa Ann. Your family sent me. I'm here to take you home."

"Th-then you're like me?"

"Not quite." I sneeze loudly and turn half-wolf for the kid. Makes my nephews lose their shit. "Ahhhhcchhhhoooowl!" The little girl giggles for the first time in what musta felt like a lifetime.

I wrap her up in my jacket, take her in my arms, and make for the door. As we enter the main room, Mummy boss lady is still trying to wiggle free. Lisa Ann whispers in my ear, and we walk over to her.

When we get close enough, the kid hisses with her fangs bared, flips her the bird, and socks her in the face. A withered grey jaw flies clean across the room. If I'm not careful, I could find myself really liking this kiddo.

Outside, it's a little too close to dawn for my liking, so I pop the trunk.

"Listen, darling. We gotta get you home pretty quick. Just to play it safe, how do you feel about riding in the trunk?"

"Can I wear the jacket? Be sure to blast the radio and blow the red lights," she says.

Yep, kinda love this kid.

As I'm placing her in the trunk, we're joined by what had to have been the last of the Mummies. I'm thinking he was in the shitter or something? With a face like a dehydrated avocado, he runs out the front door, firing at me wildly and screaming. I smile—he's got my gun, Felix. I grab it along with a bit of his wrapping and punch him in his stupid throat. I return to the open trunk, and Lisa Ann, still holding the chump's gauze in my hand.

"Let's play a game, shall we? Here, hold this." I hand her the end of the Mummy's bandage, tuck her head down with my paw, and gently close the trunk.

I think we drug that sonuvabitch for a quarter mile before we lost him at the first sharp turn on Mulholland. The slippery bastard.

Just Before Dawn

Heading Back to L.A.

That about catches you up. As requested, we're blasting tunes down Mulholland. The kicking and screaming you hear is the kid. She's singing at the top of her lungs and thumping her legs to the beat of "We Will Rock You." Any *poquita chiquita* that digs on Mr. Mercury is okay in my book. Vamp or not. The address they gave me in Burbank is about twenty minutes away and sunrise is in about fifteen. I make it there in ten.

We pull up to a modest two-story. Burbank ain't what she used to be. Lady Vamp and Baron Von Creepy-Crawly are waiting at the doorstep looking relieved as all get out. I pop the trunk and the kid jumps right at me, fangs out and giggling. I get the bearhugs of all bearhugs and then she runs over to the awaiting guardian-types. After the howya do's and hugs the lady of the house saunters on over, gliding again with the big black umbrella.

"I want to thank you, Mr. Callahan. Lisa Ann speaks very highly of you. You have a new fan. She believes you're some kind of Werewolf superhero."

"Call me Lor, ma'am."

"Call me Maila."

"Not Vampi . . ."

"Most certainly not," she smiles with those red lips. "Merely a stage name. Hiding in plain sight, so to speak."

We both look over at Lisa Ann. She's reenacting her duke-out with Prune Face for Calcifcer the Ghoul. He's clapping, and they hi-five when she's done.

"The kid packs a great right hook. What's her story, anyway?"

"We found her, left for dead, down on Skid Row. She was so very sick. We had to go against the laws of the coven in order to save her. We were hoping to tell her what she was, over time. But as you see, Lisa Ann has a fire. I believe she'll make it past this." Maila closes the umbrella. "About your money..."

I don't know if it's meeting this celebrity bombshell or hearing the kid's story but I find myself saying two words I've never uttered in my life.

"Pro bono," I say, and my gums keep flapping. "Let's call it one small step towards an accord between Lyks and Vamps."

A lotta times my mouth gets me into heaps of trouble. It's nice every now and then when it does the opposite. Maila leans in and lays one on my cheek. Couldn't keep my cool and I wolfed out just a bit. You would have too.

"Definitely an accord between this Vamp and Lyk. Make that—two new fans."

Lisa Ann joins us and returns my jacket.

"Thanks, kid."

She looks up at me with these big dark eyes and says what every private di—er, private eye, worth his salt wants to hear after saving the day.

"Fucking Mummies." Then she giggles wildly as the two of them walk back to the house holding hands. I can't help but crack a smile myself.

I put on my jacket. My clothes are still a mess and I got dead-guy grit in all my no-no places. But today was a good day and I want some breakfast. I hop in the front seat of the Olds and turn the key. Bowie comes on the radio singing about heroes and I chuckle to myself. That's when I feel something hard in my jacket pocket. I reach into my leather and pull out a gold brooch. The one that Mummy boss lady was wearing. The kid musta palmed it just before she socked her in the jaw. It's official, I love that little vamp.

Next stop, Matteo's Pawn Shop, followed by some crispy bacon and runny eggs. I wonder what kind of pie Nick's has today.

Christian Patchell is an author, educator, and artist, from Philadelphia, Pa. Patch, his lovely wife, and their family of plants live in a tree house on the top of the highest hill where they spend much of their time making pictures and telling stories.

Patch is the creator of "The Brothers Brimm" an award-winning animated short and comic series as well as the writer of "Patriot Tales" a time-hopping comic for the Valley Forge National Parks. He is also the author of the book *I Put the Can in Cancer: A Journey Through Pictures,* which catalogues his life-changing battle with cancer. Patch's art and design have appeared on everything from greeting cards to comic books. His theory on both art and storytelling: Monsters and Robots make everything better.

You can see more of Patch's work at @monster_comics on Instagram and at artbypatch.com

AETHER SANCTIFIED

BY SABA RAZVI

Bella watched the flicker of shadows tumbling from corner to corner—a black and white kaleidoscope, projected by so many candles in competition. The high walls of the loft apartment resonated Siouxsie Sioux's banshee wail, the screeches leaving her hair standing on end against the aural embodiment of voodoo-queen dreams, aptly titled *Juju*. Drapes of tattered white lace and chiffon lingered in the doorways like the cobwebs of ghosts. And pinwheels of silver and blue lined the windowsill so that any gust of air sent the room trembling like startled moths. Sheltered in the eerie canopy of transparent, gauzed senses, she sketched. At the edges of her daydreams, soft layers of smoke whispered to her, taunting her sleepless eyelids. Long face, chin pointed like anime, long hair like willow strands, the figure slowly gathered shape. Frowning as she placed him beside her feet, she thought, "How very like him, paper and ink and nothing more real than skin, and solemnly, resolutely incomplete." Even now, so many months later, she could not admit to missing something still there, especially not something so mercurial.

Bella put down her inks reluctantly and smeared the dust of unfinished out-lines onto her face, trying to pretend that the phone's ringing was no more than part of the song. But she knew that it had been days since she'd answered a call or message, and that continuing to ignore them would only press her further into the painful parts of her head, the parts she wanted most to occupy but knew better than to stay in for much longer.

"Hello?" Trying not to sound so morose always had the opposite effect. Her solemnity bled through the cracks at every given opportunity.

"Bella, is that you?" Bathory replied. "And if it is, where *have* you been? Hiding again, I suppose. But then, you always are these days, aren't you?"

Bella smiled at how her friend always had so much energy, words sometimes almost incomprehensible in their own graffitied echoes and backdrops.

"How many lines tonight, Bathory? I've been a little busy, I guess."

"Oh, you little wench! Not even going to tell me his name? Or have you come to your senses and joined the other side, finally? I wouldn't mind showing you a thing or two. You know, purely as a friendly gesture, of course. Heh. And since when did lines matter? None yet, but thanks for the idea."

"I don't think so," Bella said, "but I'm flattered, love. It's not like that. I've really been working. You know, this series of panels I started is starting to look . . . well, like I just started. Hell, I dunno, maybe it was just conceptual work, but I had to sort of hibernate for a bit."

"Whatever you wanna call it, it's still moping to me, gloomy-chick. You *are* coming tonight." Half questioning, mostly dictating, Bathory was always so very sure of things.

"I don't know . . ."

"*Oh, just pull on your hair,*" Bathory sang, "and let's hit the Styxx tonight. Murky Darkling's playing with DJ Morbid, and *he's* gonna notice if you aren't there again."

"I think I don't feel like going. Not much in the mood, you know?"

"Bella, you haven't gone in weeks. And if you're not in the mood, then at least you don't have to paint on too much attitude—you'll have just the right shade of apathetic angst."

Bathory always knew just how to make Bella laugh. In fact, she knew how to make most anyone laugh, once she got the idea in her mind. And that gravelly voice had taken on so many different pitches in the past few minutes that Bella figured she deserved to be humored for a little while. Besides, a few hours couldn't hurt enough anyway.

"Yeah, that's it," Bella said. "I want to look just like a well-rehearsed six-teen-year-old."

"Come on, I have just the thing for you to wear. I've been making something new that you absolutely *must* wear tonight."

"Hmm, let's see . . . are you trying to convince me not to go? 'Cause I already don't want to."

"Oh, bah! You *have* to. Besides, I made it about you."

"Don't you mean *for* me?"

"Dammit, don't you ever listen to your fucking messages? It's the one about the dream."

"Bathory, I haven't checked the phone in a week. What dream?"

"Okay, I'll tell you . . . it was about you. And you were so vivid, and you just have to wear this thing 'cause the damn dream inspired me to make it."

"Please tell me you didn't just ask me out to model your new line of clothing."

"I didn't! Sheesh. Well, not solely, anyway."

Arms like twisted rope, draped in fishnet and velvet, waved gently, and Bella watched the door through a cobweb of tinted appendages. She pretended not to and pretended that she wasn't jittery, that it was just the music getting in her veins. The walls throbbed with lamentations and declarations of aches, and the serpentine-shifting bodies each imagined themselves to be the only ones that understood the cries. Each weaved in and out of dramatic poses as if only they heard the sounds, seemingly oblivious to the others that they made a point of joining each week; no matter that they didn't know all of the others— the other voices, so many different names— just that they were subversive brethren in some way.

Cradled by funerary wallflowers of PVC and ragged lace, Bathory swooned and bowed with the others. Bella had decided to accept that she was only here for two reasons and sat down to her sour, honey-sweetened red tea, remembering. This sour taste was one of the few senses she could safely think of in connection with Blake, one taste less ferric than not.

"Care for some warm *blood*?" he had asked, teasingly. This was how he had introduced his thick Egyptian tea, and she had taken a liking to it. She had enjoyed laughing at his jokes; his esoteric references seemed somehow intimate. They had been discussing the younger spooky-kids and the unfortunately delusional adults who went even a few steps above implanted fangs, introducing themselves as *vahm*-pyres. They were almost as bad as the Ren-fest kids who actually wore their faerie wands and undeniably fake accents out on a daily basis. Almost.

This was back at the beginning, before the misunderstandings and the guilt trips. Much before the resentment began, when they had things to talk about, things that didn't bleed out of insults or rust under scrutiny. And before the long, empty silences could have been imagined. Things did not seem so brittle, then, or as melodramatic as the plush red carpet at her feet.

And in contrast to the subtle memory, the club looked suddenly like a massive mouth, bleeding tongue and painful dark cavities, resonating something ugly and real and wanting not to be said. And silently screaming.

Cursing Bathory under her breath for bringing her out tonight, cursing herself for being talked into coming out here tonight, she pulled out a half-empty pack of Djarum Blacks, lighting one carefully.

Her hair hung dangerously close to the neon orange of the flame; waving rhythmically in the black light, it reminded her of the dream. She exhaled a significant puff of sweet clove smoke which settled around her form, and glowed, too, under the black lights, leaving the impression of a severely warped halo.

Bathory had dressed her as a frozen shadow, stuck somewhere between the underworld and winter, the way she'd dreamt her.

Appearing as some kind of water-nymph, with droplets of water fanning out like wings and gliding in such a way that the waves left her a swirling, watery tail, Bella had emerged all shimmering and white.

She walked up onto a shore sanded with mirror dust, shards of slivered glass. A shivering array of movements under each foot, she seemed to drift above the ground, while swiftly freezing to transparent dark from the feet up.

Bella had been some kind of frozen shadow then, face and arms and neck all silvery-white frost, and the rest gauzy black.

Loose black chiffon clung distractingly to her form, while her legs and body were covered in tight black fabric.

At least the boots, steel-toed and laced to the knees, were comfortable enough to make up for the arms heavily caked with glitter, the stiff face-makeup, and the hair that Medusa might flaunt after spending a week in Antarctica.

And Bathory was right about the ennui—it added to the effect. People were stopping to look, even here at the club.

The rest of the dream was weird, to say the least. An ice maiden who looked like Bella had fallen in love with some sort of fire spirit, a shape-shifting and brazen thing who looked like a genie on fire.

Confusing glass with ice, she went away with him. They had become absolute transparencies of one another, she dissolving and he fizzling out, leaving nothing but slick, warm darkness.

Bathory likened it to bundling up in down comforters on a snowy evening. And, of course, the thought of beds inevitably made her say that the dream had to mean she was going to meet someone new to go home with and maybe more.

She believed that all her dreams were omens, except maybe the one in which she was forced at gunpoint to eat an endless string of ramen noodles while chasing a train into a gorilla's mouth; *that*, she decided, was too much vodka and bad acid.

And she seemed to always find a way to fit her dreams into that week's plans.

Bathory squeaked over in head-to-toe PVC complete with gaping spaces of flesh, settling down, legs criss-crossed on the chair across from Bella with her rum and Coke.

She twirled one braid of her long maroon hair with the idle hand and shifted the drink onto the small, square table with the other. As self-assured as only a person with four-inch magenta nails could be, she grinned.

"I told you you'd look great. Everyone's talking about you. So, aren't you glad now that you came out?"

"I guess." Bella glanced suspiciously at the door.

Bathory turned to check the same direction. "You aren't waiting for him to show up, are you? I mean, it's been ages. Even so, I'm sure it won't seem remotely familiar to you. Everything's changed. And besides, we *do* have to find you a sweet little submissive to take home tonight."

Rolling her eyes, Bella managed to smile. "You're impossible, you know."

"Thanks, I do try. Anyway, see those two lovelies in the corner in velvet and fishnet? We're taking off for a bit. You wouldn't mind finding a way home, would ya? I mean, hey, would you pass up a chance this inviting?"

"Go on ahead, Bathory. I don't mind. Besides, I suppose I could find Oliver. He said he'd be here tonight."

"Yeah, that's a good idea. Or maybe you could find this guy I dreamt. I'll call you tomorrow." Too caught up in some kind of excitement, Bathory didn't notice that Bella's lying skills hadn't improved in just a few hours, and disappeared into the next song, leaving Bella to contemplate dreams.

There was something sacred about a dream that wouldn't be remembered in waking, leaving only an impression of a mood to linger through the day. But dreams that were remembered, Bella thought, often held a message, and though not sacred, they held something of the same source.

Bella didn't quite find Bathory's nearly literal interpretations of dreams as accurate, and they certainly would not have held true for her own enigmatic fragments of image. Sometimes these small moments stuck so deeply in her mind like dream-sand that they consumed her attention each time her eyes closed.

But she did not proclaim her illusions, she painted them. She left them to haunt her canvas, exorcising them from sleepless eyelids, to live out shadow lives in solid dimension: omens caught in transit . . .

A wraith-girl at the riverbank, gathering dripping red petals into the upturned hem of her somber dress, listens distractedly. Her head cocked to one side, bird-like and inquisitive, her expression is lost in puzzled eyebrows. She is hazy, seen through gauze as if wrapped in the beginnings of a cocoon.

Bursting through her pale skin are deep blue wings, weaving through her silver hair. She looks up at the bridge at her solid self, who is chanting a prayer for the lost souls.

A pale girlchild hung in a hammock between aching trees, surrounded by six watchful figures, at moments protective guardians, at moments hungry and intense. They are tall, ten feet or more, lean with taut skin and definitive bones. Their eyes are deep, angled slits like slashes in leather stretched slightly open.

They have giant wings folded up and held close to their backs, towering several feet above stern heads that are bald and slick, gentle heads that are covered with soft down, laughing heads that spill inky, mercurial locks. Smooth, bat-like wings, each bone visible like crinoline through a sheath of silk.

Two figures, silhouetted in silver against a blue setting sun. The sky is violet-black with painfully red cuts. There are no stars, and the land is barren except for windswept currents of dry earth. One carries the other, lays the other down and kneels beside the figure, prostrate and shaking.

A chipped stone bench, carved like an altar stolen from the Telesterion creeping with ivy so lifelike that it looked fossilized and with orchids in marble that once may have been the Tryian Blue of velvet wings.

There was some kind of barren sadness in this capturing of life in stony, icy cold sculptures. On this altar, a woman is sitting, holding a box of dead butterflies on her lap.

She unfolds their wings, sheer like organza or chiffon but velveteen, exposing them to probing eyes. She examines the worth of these creatures whose lives were cut in half to decorate the gardens of the new court. She had black eyes and a red mouth like strawberries, and then she flashed momentarily in a blue, blue dress, Atlas beetles at her painted toenails.

She laid out the ones with broken wings, leaving them to soak in the sun—she would crush them later for bird fodder—and singled out the perfect ones for private collection. There were black velvet cattle hearts with scarlet streaks, like bleeding hearts lining the jagged lower wings.

There were blue morphos like luminescent sorrow, Tyrian Blue with black highlights; speckled brown on the outside to hide the secret colors, resembling blue eyes batting coyly open. All dead or decaying.

On her bed lay a quilt, a huddle of Atlas beetles on scarlet, a flash of white in the center on which lay a perfect blue morpho, open and bare, its edges fragmented like crushed wings. In her hair as she sank down were offerings of red anemones.

Bella frowned, snapping back into the smoky Styxx, noticing that her clove cigarette was singeing her fingertips and had dripped ash in a straight column beside the ashtray.

Too many thoughts of perfect wings had wasted this perfectly decent clove, like too many other abstractions of purity had wasted . . . other chances.

And then, in a blur of violet-blue–lit smoke and red and black flashes of fabric, Blake walked through the same door she had been distractedly watching all evening. His head was still shaved, clean and soft. And remembering how she had shaved off that lovely black hair, waist-length, and hypnotic, she sighed.

Why did he still keep it that way? She wasn't there anymore. She didn't remark that he was too angelic with those inky locks, too hypnotic.

And still, he was painfully beautiful, more painfully so with the knowledge that he had asked her to do this to please her own obsessions, that he had kept this continual sacrifice, even after she had gone.

"Who left you in a freezer?" Blake mumbled.

She was frowning, deeply, thinking of those too-blue eyes, the straight nose and soft lips. She was thinking of the times she had taught him to ink his own eyes and lips in makeup, grays and blacks, how his eyes had stayed Atlantic. She hadn't noticed him cross the room, sit down in the chair Bathory had left some time ago. She didn't notice the silence.

"Hey, it was just a joke. You look really good."

"Blake. I wasn't paying attention . . . where did you come from?" She stammered a too-vague greeting, as always.

His eyes, kohl-rimmed, looked a little vacant, a little relieved. His black poet's shirt had been quite modified, the ruffles removed, and the arms opened out to bells with red triangles of velvet fabric showing through.

The black vinyl pants had similarly been altered so that the red fabric trickled up to his knees. Both arms and legs were bound with black electrical tape and barbed wire.

He looked like he'd been set on some kind of slow, animated fire, appendages up, and the allusion to Bathory's dream disturbed her. If Bathory hadn't been trying to make her forget him, Bella would have thought she had done this intentionally.

"You're always off in some other world," he said. "Thinking of another painting?"

As if on cue, she imagined the canvas with his face from earlier in the evening, his arms and feet pointing downwards, bound with thorns and flame, poised like an ancient arrowhead. Wings stretched out behind his charring figure, devoured save a few burning bones like a decaying Japanese fan. And still bright, his eyes and hair.

"Yeah, I think so . . . I mean, it isn't really fully developed, just an impression," she stammered, thinking that if she didn't at least act calm, he'd know how much this was affecting her.

"It's been a long time . . . how are you?"

"I've been keeping busy. Working, painting . . . you know."

"Too busy to get out at all? I haven't seen you anywhere. I tried calling, but . . . never made it past two rings before I hung up." He sighed. "I miss you, Bella."

She winced, not having counted on his saying her name like that, so intimately, sincerely.

"I'm sorry," she said.

"Not as much as I am."

They sat in heavy silence, against the hollow backdrop of Black Tape for a Blue Girl's "Remnants of a Deeper Purity" and then London After Midnight's "Psychomagnet" and then The Cure's "Charlotte Sometimes," the songs badly spliced together in ragged patches of sound, none stealing more than a glance of the others. Months of words would not speak; they had starved and died and then littered the air like ashes of the dead, like desiccated butterfly wings. And when a new song broke the solemnity, he spoke first.

"What is he singing? Do you know this band?"

"I don't know . . . " she murmured, thinking of another time he had asked that.

"Listen to this; it's my favorite song on the album." She stretches out, eyes closed, letting the song play out under her eyelids.

"What's he singing? Be sure I'm *naked*? Hah."

She rolls her eyes at him. "He is singing, 'Be sure I'm *aching* . . . Be sure I'm *aching*. My heart is *aching* for your safe return. We don't have the power to break these chains.'"

"It still sounds like naked."

She turns over to her side, settling into her pillow and ignoring him for the remainder of the song. "Is nothing sacred?"

"No," he says; whether he is mocking the question or speaking in dead earnest is nearly indiscernible.

"That's the saddest thing I have ever heard. Really. I mean that."

A pause, set to wailing music. He's rethinking his answer. "There are sacred things," he says, tentatively, "Change. Chaos. Laughter—at the most inappropriate times."

She doesn't doubt now that the raven is his totem animal spirit. Suddenly, he is too much like Loki, too unlike the helpless scarecrow she once saw.

"Oh, well," Blake said. "I guess it doesn't matter. They'll post the set-list tomorrow anyway."

She plunged back into the gaping mouth that was the Styxx, the present moment, with his words. "Yeah, that's true."

"Do you think of me? At all, Isabella?"

Silence. She blinked back the trepidation, the desire to forgive and resume things again. She knew he was serious, because only when things really mattered did he use her whole name.

"Fuck," he said. "I know it's not cool to bring this up, not right now and right away. But I have to know, Bella. Please, don't just push me away . . ."

"What do you want me to say?"

"*Yes*. I want you to say yes, you think of me. I want you to miss me, too. I'm sorry."

"You're sorry? After what you did, after what happened, you're going to use that pathetic apology?"

He frowned, and those brilliant eyes dulled, sank a little. She knew he meant it, that this was harsh. After all, it had been partly her own fault, too. If she hadn't kept promising . . .

"Yes, Bella. I *am*. I didn't mean to hurt you, at least not in an unpleasant way." He attempted a mischievous half-grin. "I know it sounds cheesy and overdone, but it's sincere. It's the truth. And don't you always say that without truth, there isn't any purity? It's hard for me to do this, but I know I have to. Please say you don't hate me. I . . . don't know what I'd do if . . ." His voice trailed off, broken.

Bella drew in her knees and sighed. She never liked confrontation, and she certainly hadn't expected to deal with this. This was more than just reacting to him across a throbbing room. And she couldn't help letting go, naively and wishfully. "I don't hate you, Blake."

He breathed slowly, heavily, managed a sort of relieved half-laugh. "I guess that's a start, eh?"

Bella couldn't help but think of how Bathory would combust if she watched this now. Weakly laughing, she half wished the girl hadn't left, half thanked whatever omens had pulled her away.

The music began to die down, the lights sifting back on, and Blake asked suddenly, "Who'd you come with? I didn't see your car."

"Oh, damn! Bathory already left. I was supposed to look for Oliver . . ."

"Hey, I can give you a ride back . . ."

Bella looked over at Blake, mistrusting the bandaged gap of space that bled for so many days. She didn't think she had been up to talking but managed. She didn't know if that extended to talking without the myriad androgynes around them.

"If you want," he added. "I mean, it's okay. I understand if you'd rather not . . ."

"No, it's okay," she found herself saying. "I'd appreciate that."

In the car, surprised at how little awkwardness she felt after her initial reaction, Bella noticed how like any other ride home this felt. Another hour and a half of stiff, dark freeway. They had always gone back home tired, slightly intoxicated with each other. And already, she had begun to forget why she had become so wary of Blake.

He talked about the poem he had been working on, something he had just begun, something inspired by her, something to try and win her forgiveness. Which she knew he'd never finish. And then he flipped on his Dead Can Dance tape, probably wondering whether to mention any more.

She watched the shifting landscape, unsure how to respond. The trees looked so anguishingly human, like trapped bohemian spirits, bound by a soil that would always be the same. Padlocked dryads. And the wailing from the speakers lamented, a cry that perfectly matched pleading branches like arms and gnarled, struggling bodies, sinewy from suffering.

A pale girl, arms raised up in anguish, and also a tree with wispy leaves for hair, too many arms, branching a dozen longings. In the middle of another painting in her head, she fell asleep, becoming the girl whose icicle hair grew bark and lichen, whose feet stood firmly pulling down towards her own prison.

Blake stopped in the small driveway in front of her building and watched her. He hoped that whatever dream was anguishing her was sacred, that she wouldn't remember it in the morning, that she would forget, too, all that had shattered in the previous months. He whispered, "Isa-bel-la," and then picked her up carefully and brought her inside the apartment building. Gently pulling the keys from her sleep-laden fist, he opened the familiar door and brought her in, deposited her on the unmade bed.

He tried not to drag his feet, not to look back at the frail figure lying there, as he walked away, focusing instead on the floorboards. He hoped that somehow she would think fondly of this encounter in the morning. He hoped that she really didn't hate him, that she wasn't so angry anymore; with Bella, he could never tell. The things that hurt her most she locked inside, and then pooled them again through her dreams and painted them out of her head, distanced and yet so much more intimately telling.

Shaking the thought out of his head, he noticed that part of a sheet on the bed had caught on the barbed wire on his leg. Surprised that his wrists hadn't pinched Bella out of her sleep, he moved the sheet away, noticing his own face emerging from some kind of cloudy canvas. So, she *had* thought of him, too. In the deepening frown was the faint impression of dissipating fire.

Saba Razvi is the author of: "In the Crocodile Gardens" (Elgin Award—nominee), "heliophobia" (on the preliminary ballot for the Bram Stoker Award ® for Superior Achievement in Poetry), "Limerence & Lux," "Of the Divining and the Dead," and "Beside the Muezzin's Call & Beyond the Harem's Veil," as well as other poetry, fiction, and essays. She's an associate professor of English and creative writing at the University of Houston in Victoria, TX. Her website is www.sabarazvi.com.

DAWN OF A NEW ERA

BY CATRIN SIAN RUTLAND

W ell, he wasn't quite the son of a preacher man, but he was called Billy, and all our parents liked church. Nearly half the village, including our families, were in the church, that fourteenth-century foreboding stone fortress, the night it all happened. Not me and my Billy, though; we were hiding out in the woods. I would like to say we were up to no good, but really, we were just chatting away about our impending exams and eating the chocolates we had managed to smuggle out of our homes. The holidays were always a good time for pinching those extra goodies—sweets, bonbons, toffee apples-—it was a free-for-all in December.

We were trying to sneak a look at the castle illuminations. The lasers shining on the buttresses, disco balls spinning in the trees, flames arising from metal vessels in the river, a million lights twinkling along the trail, and forest-animal carvings glowing between the bushes. The light show was too expensive for us to actually pay good money for, but the castle was surrounded by fields and woods.

A bit of a climb up the steep hill, through some barbed wire, around the frozen lake via a fair bit of mud, and we could get a good view of those gardens and woodland decorations. With the cold snapping at our noses and the fog of our breath seeping into the air, we might even slip into the castle itself, warm ourselves by the vast open fires, and see the great rooms "dressed for a Victorian Christmas," as the adverts had said. If we summoned up the courage, we might even try to break into the dungeons or creep up into the attic.

It was a bit lucky, really, given the events of that night, that we were near the castle and our folks were in the church. As the snow gently floated down and the mist started rising, it all seemed so romantic. My Billy turned and kissed me, and I felt as light as the snowflakes settling on my coat. We ventured on despite the snow and mud, waiting to see where security were, and working out whether we could slip past them with ease. We spotted the security lady in her conveniently coloured neon-yellow jacket, and as she turned her back we hopped to our feet and tagged onto a group who had just arrived by minibus.

Our efforts were rewarded by our eventually being able to enjoy the wonders of the garden trail like everyone else. Practically paying customers. A random voice made us jump until we realised it was a projection onto a tree of an elf, blaring out a recorded message telling us to avoid the water feature and to mind our step along the slippery path.

As Billy and I walked along the route, holding hands, we marveled at the mechanical butterflies gently spreading their wings and the beauty of the moon shining down into the field of shimmering LED poppies. Although the night was dark and misty, the snow, illuminations, flames, and moonlight combined made for an inspiring sight against the backlit castle.

After a couple of hours, we were half frozen. Some cute little chalets near the castle walls were selling delicious-smelling mulled wine and whiskey-laden hot chocolate. Not much chance of us getting one of those, given our age, but we did decide to share a drink. I can still taste that mint-flavoured dark chocolate now.

My Billy would steal a kiss, just like in that old song I loved so much, but then he wasn't really stealing much. I always wanted to hold his hand and to look into his eyes as we kissed; it's not stealing if you give something away willingly. When I think about it, it was the last thing we did before the night turned on us.

We gazed into the Japanese garden and into the fields beyond as the snow fell with more urgency. I could see the corn waving in the gentle breeze. It made quite mesmerizing patterns as if small whirlwinds were forming in different parts of the field.

The odd cracking sound faintly in the distance, combined with the strange dancelike ripples in the field, felt so eerie. As the odd star made an effort to shine through the mist, the field almost looked alive, the sad crops swaying then falling, each grass slumping against its neighbour until it hit the ground. As we stared at the field, the pace picked up, and whole clumps began to drop.

Other people started gathering near us to watch the spectacle. Perhaps it was part of the show, but something didn't feel quite right. I noticed people were also now at the castle windows, gawping at the land beyond the hill.

The woman next to us was muttering on about how the farmer should have harvested before the snow, despite the bad summer weather that had hindered growth. I had no idea snow would kill the crop so quickly, yet I could see the proof right in front of my eyes. In minutes, half the field had fallen and death was spreading to the fields farther away. All around us, crops were falling like dominoes.

Hypnotic as it was, I just wanted to get away from that strange vision, so Billy and I headed for the castle to warm up. Apart from anything, I didn't fancy the trip home walking in the deceased fields just yet. Our parents wouldn't miss us for a bit, and I was freezing. As the snow crunched under our feet, Billy and I debated about how stems could snap so quickly, and why that didn't happen normally to other plants in the winter months.

By the time we got into the castle, folks were starting to talk about the emerging wildlife—rabbits, foxes, mice, voles, even a sturdy badger. All the animals were venturing into the shining lights of the illuminated gardens below. Slowly at first, but then in greater numbers, seemingly ignoring each other. Too late for the usual dusk feed for the cute little herbivores and way too dangerous with the foxes around. Yet even the younger kittens were out with their mothers, and not a fox kill in sight despite the many individuals gathering.

Although the decorations and fireplaces looked warm and festive inside the castle, I could not help but look at the bits of animals festooned everywhere. The tiger rug on the floor, the deer antlers on the walls, and stuffed peacocks on the sideboard.

Just as we were pondering the lack of rabbit kills on the lawn, the people outside the castle grounds started shouting and running. Birds were dive-bombing them from every direction. The plump little robins through to the blackbirds, all swooping in on their victims.

Kids screamed as they were dragged away by their fathers, babies in prams being pushed along the cobble paths by anxious mothers, everyone trying to reach the castle. We watched as one man tried to protect his family with an umbrella, stunned as the black material was torn to shreds.

Doors and windows slammed as the people outside darted in, and those already safe tried to protect themselves. Some birds made it in, which caused people to throw Christmas decorations, ancient tapestries, and even books at the intruders. Others ran around looking for first aid kits to patch up the bleeding tears in their faces and hands.

Billy and I stood there in a daze, not sure what to do, trying to block out the screams that had turned into desperate squeals amidst the squawks and screeches of the angry avians. Then thuds as people hit the now firmly closed doors. Billy and I turned to beg the adults to let those people in but by now they were firmly agreed that no more birds would get in.

Others were running around, barricading the great paneled doors with ancient oak desks and mahogany bookcases. The birds smashed into the glass panes but dropped dead upon impact with the decorative lead strips. As quickly as they had started, the birds ceased their attack and flew off towards the village, the murderous flock looking for more victims.

We called our parents. Mine didn't answer, but after several attempts, Billy got through to his father. The same was happening with them; they told us to stay in the castle until it was safe. The security guard told everyone the news stations were talking of aberrant events throughout the country and possibly abroad, possibly as a result of a strange weather system, but even the quickly assembled experts really had no idea.

As we looked outside, the rabbits were gnawing at the crops and electric wires. The man next to us pointed out the foxes chewing something on the cars. He told us it was probably the brake cables, but we weren't sure why a fox would even want to do such a thing.

The earth in the gardens writhed with insects as they rose up and pushed garden walls over, so many species, thousands of individuals working together to create small craters, overturning the foundations laid so many centuries ago. Soon the cattle from the barn and the horses from the stables were running free, tearing down sheds, smashing car windows and knocking down the fences and buildings that had previously held them in.

The sheep were jumping over the enclosures and snacking on the bodies lying near the castle entrance. Dead birds, deceased humans, they didn't seem to differentiate. The birds were joining in on the feast. I never even knew they ate meat; this weather system was something else!

Watching the animals eating the few unlucky people who had not made it into the safety of the castle walls was grotesque. I was trying to hold back the tears, frightened I would vomit and devastated to see those around me sobbing for their loved ones. Billy and I moved into one of the quiet corners and started blanking out the mayhem around us.

The noise was too much. Not just the sound of people crying but the sudden bangs as the walls fell, electricity pylons dropped, and wires snapped, accompanied by great sparks flying as the badgers and squirrels worked tirelessly to bring down the world around us. Our mobile signals went dead; Wi-Fi, electricity, and 4G ceased functioning. We were stranded with no information. No way to communicate with the outside world.

As people tried to help the injured or bemoaned the fact they had left people outside to die, Billy sang our song to me. For the first time since I met him, I knew that everything was not all right and we might never get away again tonight. We were trapped in the castle, with no idea why the animals had turned against us and whether our families were okay.

My innocence was shattered. Seeing the castle cat ripping the tongue out of my next-door neighbour lying lifeless in the snow, seeing the young backpacker tourist hiding against the bushes, clinging onto his bag as the rest of him bled onto the snow, seeing my world dissipating in front of my eyes; nothing would be right again.

As the dawn broke, the birds refused to sing. A peaceful lull surrounded our castle as the mist started to lift and the snow began to melt. Small puddles of blood and disturbed soil ran along the side of the road and into the gutter. The final autumnal reddened leaves fell from the trees, yet not a bird or squirrel was busy on their branches. The sheep and cows were dotted around, grazing as normal as the sun rose red against the hazy sky.

Red sky at night, shepherd's delight, red sky in the morning, shepherd's warning, I thought, the Biblical advice bringing a sudden wave of fear over me.

Was it over, or was there more to come? The old proverb talking about the righteous man having regard for the life of his animal—did we ever show regard for their lives? The insects had stripped the crops, mammals had killed their top predator, the wild birds had brought down our structures, and for all we knew the beasts had ended our civilisation.

Despite the peace outside, nobody moved. Not a single soul braved the outside world. Billy and I only left once we saw our parents breathlessly running up the hill towards our stronghold. With tears streaming down our faces, we went back with them to hide in the church, one of the few buildings still standing, until the police arrived with their sirens blazing.

Things never went back to normal. The animals resumed their normal day-to-day lives, sitting in hutches, playing in fields, sitting in sheds, or being loyal pets. Fewer people wanted pets, and even fewer people were left to farm the bigger animals, given the loss of lives due to stampedes.

People were nervous. Funerals were held for the dead, and the dying and injured filled hospitals and town halls. Buildings were slowly rebuilt, crops were replanted for the now considerably smaller population, and people tried to return to their old lives.

As communication networks were restored, we learned that much of the world had been hit. Some very rural places, with simple villages, and smaller island communities and countries remained completely intact, whereas bigger cities were completely ravaged.

Billy and I listened to the adults around us in the following years, full of their theories on the wild, unrestrained nature of animals or the stories of Earth's electrical charges going astray that night. They hypothesised about how the moon's orbit or maybe pollution had changed the animals, or how some government had secretly poisoned the water, or that aliens had landed to take over our planet and hypnotized the creatures.

Nothing seemed right to us. We had seen the animals turn, watched them join forces. The only prey that night was humans, and every single animal had become our predator.

They had tired of being slaves to humans, having their land taken away by us for growing crops where forests once stood or putting up shopping malls where meadows once lay. They had been housed in cages or used as labourers. The animals did bring down civilisation that night, where necessary, and I am not sure anyone will ever know how they collaborated or why they mounted their attack that evening.

Billy and me, we have our own theory. Once humankind has fully rebuilt society, cultivated all the land again, and polluted the rivers even more, the animals will rise again. This time was a warning; next time, we will be slaughtered.

Catrin Sian Rutland is an associate professor. She teaches, lives, and researches science, writing both nonfiction and fiction books and publications. Her fiction explores the world beyond what is (presently) possible, known, proven, or in existence. Writing allows Catrin to explore these ideas and to understand society and the world around us. Her stories tend towards Dark Fiction in several genres, including horror, sci-fi and fantasy, dystopian and apocalyptic. Her work has been published in many languages throughout the world. Catrin has previously worked with Scary Dairy Press, with stories included in *Terror Politico: A Screaming World in Chaos* and *Mother's Revenge: A Dark and Bizarre Anthology of Global Proportions*.

When she is not researching, teaching, or writing, Catrin enjoys exploring new cities and countries with her fiancé, Andrew or reading a good book alongside their cat, Button.

VINYL CUTS PLAYLIST

TUNES THAT INSPIRED THE TALES

1. D.O.A.—Bloodrock (1970)

2. Magic—Olivia Newton John (1980)

3. You're the Devil in Disguise—Elvis Presley (1968)

4. Werewolves of London—Warren Zevon (1978)

5. Crystal Ship—The Doors (1967)

6. Tonight You Belong to Me—Patience and Prudence (1956)

7. Only Women Bleed—Alice Cooper (1975)

8. I Put a Spell on You—Jalacy "Screamin' Jay" Hawkins (1956)

9. White Rabbit—Jefferson Airplane (1967)

10. Gold Dust Woman—Fleetwood Mac (1977)

11. Sympathy for the Devil—The Rolling Stones (1968)

12. Rock and Roll Never Forgets—Bob Seger (1976)

13. Cherry Lips—The Robins (1956)

14. Welcome to My Nightmare—Alice Cooper (1975)

15. Splish Splash—Bobby Darin (1958)

16. The Leader of the Pack—The Shangri-Las (1965)

17. Lola—The Kinks (1970)

18. Honky Cat—Elton John (1972)

19. Boris the Spider—The Who (1966)

20. Locomotive Breath—Jethro Tull (1971)

21. Station to Station—David Bowie (1976)

22. Bennie & the Jets—Elton John (1974)

23. Paint It Black—Rolling Stones (1966)

24. Ballroom Blitz—The Sweet (1973)

25. We Gotta Get Outta This Place—The Animals (1965)

26. I Will Survive—Gloria Gaynor (1978)

27. Rhiannon—Fleetwood Mac (1975)

28. We Will Rock You—Queen (1977)

29. Bela Lugosi's Dead—Bauhaus (1979)

30. Son of a Preacher Man—Dusty Springfield (1969)

AFFIRMATION OF COPYRIGHTS

T he following authors have copyright to their stories listed and contained in this anthology:

"Lola" @2024 Kay Hanifen
"Black Cats and Bone Dust" @2024 Cindy O'Quinn
"Boris Was Here" @2024 E.F. Schraeder
"Wheels Against Wings" @2024 Valerie Williams
"The Red Duke" @2024 Jeremiah Dylan Cook
"Oh, But They're Weird and They're Wonderful" @2024 Kell Cowley
"Red Door Black" @2024 Jason R. Frei
"Ballroom Blitz" @2024 Alison Garsha
"Gotta Get Out of This Place" @2024 Pamela Kinney
"We Will Survive" @2024 Eve Morton
"Prince Charmless" @2024 Virginia Nelson
"Seventies Werewolf Detective" @2024 Christian Patchell
"Aether Sanctified" @2024 Saba Syed Razvi, PhD
"Dawn of a New Era" @2024 @ Catrin Rutland

BOOK REVIEWS

G ratitude and joy! That's what we feel every time we know someone has read our anthology—particularly if the reader enjoyed it. This project was a true labor of love with our editors, cover designer, authors, and preliminary readers.

Our team and our authors would love to hear your thoughts about *Vinyl Cuts*, so if you will, head on over to Amazon, or Goodreads, or wherever you purchased this book and give us a rating and a review. We would really appreciate it. Thank you so much for reading, and may the music forever stay in your soul!

The Scary Dairy Press Team

www.ingramcontent.com/pod-product-compliance
Lightning Source LLC
Chambersburg PA
CBHW072124250626
47159CB00007B/2553